A Season for Love

Two Novels in One

A Wallflower Christmas

AND

Mine Till Midnight

LISA KLEYPAS

St. Martin's Paperbacks

This is a work of fiction. All of the characters, organizations, and events portrayed in this book are either products of the author's imagination or are used fictitiously.

Published in the United States by St. Martin's Paperbacks, an imprint of St. Martin's Publishing Group

A SEASON FOR LOVE: A WALLFLOWER CHRISTMAS copyright © 2008 by Lisa Kleypas and MINE TILL MIDNIGHT copyright © 2007 by Lisa Kleypas.

For information, address St. Martin's Publishing Group, 120 Broadway, New York, NY 10271.

www.stmartins.com

ISBN: 978-1-250-81681-8

Our books may be purchased in bulk for promotional, educational, or business use. Please contact your local bookseller or the Macmillan Corporate and Premium Sales Department at 1-800-221-7945, ext. 5442, or by email at MacmillanSpecialMarkets@macmillan.com.

Printed in the United States of America

St. Martin's Paperbacks edition 2021

10 9 8 7 6 5 4 3 2 1

A Wallflower
Christmas

To Jennifer Enderlin,
who has so many personal graces;
wisdom, talent, beauty, and generosity of spirit.
Thank you for bringing so much joy
to my life and my work.
Love always,
LK

Prologue

Once there were four young ladies who sat at the side of every ball, soiree, and party during the London season. Waiting night after night in a row of chairs, the wallflowers eventually struck up a conversation. They realized that although they were in competition for the same group of gentlemen, there was more to be gained from being friends rather than adversaries. And even more than that, they liked one another. They decided to band together to find husbands, starting with the oldest, Annabelle, and working down to the youngest, Daisy.

Annabelle was unquestionably the most beautiful wallflower, but she was virtually penniless, which put her at the greatest disadvantage. Although most London bachelors hoped for a wife with a pretty face, they usually settled for one with a handsome dowry.

Evie was unconventionally attractive, with flaming hair and abundant freckles. It was well-known that someday she would inherit a fortune from her father. However, her father was a common-born ex-boxer who owned a gambling club, and such a disreputable background was a difficult obstacle for a young lady to surmount. Even worse, Evie was cripplingly shy and had a stammer. Any man who tried to talk to her would later describe the encounter as an act of torture.

Lillian and Daisy were sisters from New York. Their family, the Bowmans, were astonishingly, vulgarly, almost unimaginably wealthy, having made their fortune with a soap manufacturing business. They had no good blood, no manners, and no social patrons. Lillian was a fiercely loving friend, but also strong-willed and bossy. And Daisy was a dreamer who often fretted that real life was never quite as interesting as the novels she read so voraciously.

As the wallflowers helped one another navigate the perils of London society, and consoled and supported one another through very real dangers, sorrows, and joys, they each found a husband, and no one referred to them as wallflowers anymore.

In every social season, however, there was no shortage of new wallflowers. (Then, as now, there were always girls who were overlooked and ignored by gentlemen who really should have known better.)

But then there was the Christmas when Rafe Bowman, Lillian and Daisy's oldest brother, came to England. After that, life for one London wallflower would never be the same. . . .

Chapter One

It's official," Lillian, Lady Westcliff, said with satisfaction, setting aside the letter from her brother. "Rafe will reach London in precisely a fortnight. And the clipper's name is the *Whirlwind,* which I think is quite apt in light of his impending betrothal."

She glanced down at Annabelle and Evie, who were both on the parlor floor working on a massive circle of red velvet. They had gathered at Lillian's London house, Marsden Terrace, for an afternoon of tea and conversation.

At the moment Annabelle and Evie were making a tree skirt, or rather trying to salvage the fabric from Lillian's previous efforts. Evie was snipping at a piece of brocade ribbon that had been stitched unevenly on one side, while Annabelle was busy cutting a new edge of fabric and pinning it.

The only one missing was Lillian's younger sister Daisy, who lived in Bristol with her new husband. Annabelle longed to see Daisy and find out how marriage suited her. Thankfully they would all be together soon for the Christmas holiday in Hampshire.

"Do you think your brother will have any difficulty convincing Lady Natalie to marry him?" Annabelle asked, frowning as she encountered a large, dark stain on the fabric.

"Oh, not at all," Lillian said breezily. "He's handsome, charming, and very rich. What could Lady Natalie possibly object to, aside from the fact that he's an American?"

"Well, Daisy said he's a rake. And some young women might not—"

"Nonsense!" Lillian exclaimed. "Rafe is not at all a rake. Oh, he's sown a few oats, but what red-blooded man hasn't?"

Annabelle regarded her doubtfully. Although Lillian's younger sister Daisy was generally regarded as a dreamer and a romantic, she had a streak of clear-eyed pragmatism that made her judgments quite reliable. If Daisy had said their oldest brother was a rake, there was undoubtedly strong evidence to support the assertion.

"Does he drink and gamble?" Annabelle asked Lillian.

A wary frown. "On occasion."

"Does he behave in rude or improper ways?"

"He's a Bowman. We don't know any better."

"Does he pursue women?"

"Of course."

"Has he ever been faithful to one woman? Has he ever fallen in love?"

Lillian frowned at her. "Not that I'm aware of."

Annabelle glanced at Evie with raised brows. "What do you think, Evie?"

"Rake," came the succinct reply.

"Oh, all right," Lillian grumbled. "I suppose he is a rake. But that may not be an impediment to his courtship of Lady Natalie. Some women like rakes. Look at Evie."

Evie continued to snip doggedly through the brocade ribbon, while a smile curved her lips. "I don't l-like *all* rakes," she said, her gaze on her work. "Just one."

Evie, the gentlest and most soft-spoken of them all, had been the one least likely to capture the heart of the notorious Lord St. Vincent, who had been the *definitive* rake. Although Evie, with her round blue eyes and blazing red hair, possessed a rare and unconventional beauty, she was unbearably shy. And there was the stammer. But Evie also had a reserve of quiet strength and a gallant spirit that seemed to have seduced her husband utterly.

"And that former rake obviously adores you beyond reason," Annabelle said. She paused, studying Evie intently before asking softly, "Is St. Vincent pleased about the baby, dear?"

"Oh, yes, he's—" Evie broke off and gave Annabelle a wide-eyed glance of surprise. "How did you know?"

Annabelle grinned. "I've noticed your new gowns all have front and back pleats that can be let out as your figure expands. It's an instant giveaway, dear."

"You're expecting?" Lillian asked, letting out a tomboyish whoop of delight. She launched off the settee and dropped beside Evie, throwing her long arms around her. "That is *capital* news! How are you feeling? Are you queasy yet?"

"Only when I saw what you had done to the tree skirt," Evie said, laughing at her friend's exuberance. It was often difficult to remember that Lillian was a countess. Her spontaneous nature had not been subdued one whit by her new social prominence.

"Oh, you should *not* be on the floor," Lillian exclaimed. "Here, give me the scissors, and I'll work on this dratted thing—"

"*No,*" Evie and Annabelle said at the same time.

"Lillian, dear," Annabelle continued firmly, "you are not to come anywhere near this tree skirt. What you do with a needle and thread should be considered a criminal act."

"I do try," Lillian protested with a lopsided grin, settling back on her heels. "I start out with such good intentions, but then I get tired of making all those tiny stitches, and I start to hurry through it. But we *must* have a tree skirt, a very large one. Otherwise there will be nothing to catch the drips of wax when the tree candles are lit."

"Would you mind telling me what this stain is from?" Annabelle pointed to a dark ugly splotch on the velvet.

Lillian's grin turned sheepish. "I thought perhaps we could arrange that part in the back. I spilled a glass of wine on it."

"You were drinking while sewing?" Annabelle asked, thinking that explained quite a lot.

"I hoped it would help me to relax. Sewing makes me nervous."

Annabelle gave her a quizzical smile. "Why?"

"It reminds me of all the times my mother would stand over me while I worked on my sampler. And whenever I made a mistake, she rapped my knuckles with a ruler." Lillian gave a self-deprecating grin, but for once the amusement didn't reach her lively brown eyes. "I was a terrible child."

"You were a dear child, I'm sure," Annabelle said gently. She had never been quite certain how Lillian and Daisy Bowman had turned out so well, given their upbringing. Thomas and Mercedes Bowman somehow managed to be demanding, critical, *and* neglectful, which was quite a feat.

Three years earlier the Bowmans had brought their two daughters to London after discovering that even their great fortune could not induce anyone from the New York upper circles to marry the girls.

Through a combination of hard work, luck, and a necessary ruthlessness, Thomas Bowman had established one of the largest and fastest-growing soap companies in the world. Now that soap was becoming affordable for the masses, the

Bowmans' manufactories in New York and Bristol could scarcely keep up with the demand.

It took more than money, however, to achieve a place in New York society. Heiresses of undistinguished bloodlines, such as Lillian and Daisy, were not at all desirable to their male counterparts, who also wanted to marry up. Therefore London, with its ever-growing pool of impoverished aristocrats, was fertile hunting ground for American *nouveaux riches*.

With Lillian, ironically, the Bowmans had reached their highest pinnacle in having married her to Marcus, Lord Westcliff. No one could have believed that the reserved and powerful earl would have wed a headstrong girl like Lillian. But Westcliff had seen beneath Lillian's brash façade to the vulnerability and fiercely loving heart she tried so hard to conceal.

"I was a hellion," Lillian said frankly, "and so was Rafe. Our other brothers, Ransom and Rhys, were always a bit better behaved, although that's not saying much. And Daisy would take part in my troublemaking, but most of the time she daydreamed and lived in her books."

"Lillian," Annabelle asked, carefully rolling a length of ribbon, "why has your brother agreed to meet with Lady Natalie and the Blandfords? Is he truly ready to marry? Has he need of the money, or is he seeking to please your father?"

"I'm not certain," Lillian said. "I don't think it's the money. Rafe has made a fortune in Wall Street speculations, some of them a bit unscrupulous. I suspect he may finally have tired of being at loggerheads with Father. Or perhaps . . ." She hesitated, a shadow crossing her face.

"Perhaps?" Evie prompted softly.

"Well, Rafe affects a carefree façade, but he has never

been a terribly happy person. Mother and Father were abominable to him. To all of us, really. They would never let us play with anyone they thought was beneath us. And they thought *everyone* was beneath us. The twins had each other, and of course Daisy and I were always together. But Rafe was always alone. Father wanted him to be a serious-minded boy, so Rafe was kept isolated from other children. Rafe was never allowed to do anything that Father considered frivolous."

"So he eventually rebelled," Annabelle said.

Lillian grinned briefly. "Oh, yes." Her amusement faded. "But now I wonder . . . what happens when a young man is tired of being serious, and also tired of rebelling? What's left after that?"

"Apparently we'll find out."

"I want him to be happy," Lillian said. "To find someone he could care about."

Evie regarded them both thoughtfully. "Has anyone actually *met* Lady Natalie? Do we know anyth-thing about her character?"

"I haven't met her," Lillian admitted, "but she has a wonderful reputation. She's a sheltered girl who came out in society last year and was quite sought after. I've heard she is lovely and exceedingly well bred." She paused and made a face. "Rafe will frighten her to death. God knows why the Blandfords are advocating the marriage. It must be that they need the money. Father would pay anything to pump more blue blood into the family."

"I wish we could speak with s-someone who is acquainted with her," Evie mused. "Someone who might advise your brother, give him little hints about things she likes, her f-favorite flowers, that sort of thing."

"She has a companion," Lillian volunteered. "A poor

cousin named Hannah-something. I wonder if we could invite her to tea before Rafe meets Lady Natalie?"

"I think that's a splendid idea," Annabelle exclaimed. "If she's even a little forthcoming about Lady Natalie, it could help Rafe's case immensely."

"YES, YOU MUST GO," LORD BLANDFORD SAID DECISIVELY.

Hannah stood before him in the parlor of the Blandford home in Mayfair. It was one of the smaller, older houses in the fashionable residential district, tucked in a little enclave near Hyde Park on the west.

Comprised of handsome squares and broad thoroughfares, Mayfair was home to many privileged aristocratic families. But in the past decade there had been new development in the area, oversized mansions and towering Gothic-style houses cropping up in the north, where the recently moneyed class was establishing itself.

"Do anything you can," Blandford continued, "to help facilitate an attachment between my daughter and Mr. Bowman."

Hannah stared at him in disbelief. Lord Blandford had always been a man of discernment and taste. She could scarcely believe that he would want Natalie, his only child, to be married off to a crass American manufacturer's son. Natalie was beautiful, polished, and mature beyond her twenty years. She could have any man she chose.

"Uncle," Hannah said carefully, "I would never dream of questioning your judgment, but—"

"But you want to know if I've taken leave of my senses?" he asked, and chuckled as she nodded. He gestured to the upholstered armchair on the other side of the hearth. "Have a seat, my dear."

They did not often have the opportunity to speak privately.

But Lady Blandford and Natalie were visiting a cousin who had taken ill, and it had been decided that Hannah would remain in London to prepare Natalie's clothes and personal items for the upcoming holiday in Hampshire.

Staring into the wise, kind face of the man who had been so generous to her, Hannah asked, "May I speak frankly, Uncle?"

His eyes twinkled at that. "I have never known you to speak otherwise, Hannah."

"Yes, well . . . I showed you Lady Westcliff's invitation to tea as a courtesy, but I had not intended to accept it."

"Why not?"

"Because the only reason they would want to invite me is to ferret out information about Natalie, and also to impress me with all the supposed virtues of Mr. Bowman. And Uncle, it is obvious that Lady Westcliff's brother is not nearly good enough for Natalie!"

"It appears he has been tried and convicted already," Lord Blandford said mildly. "Are you so severe upon Americans, Hannah?"

"It's not that he's American," Hannah protested. "Or at least, that's not his fault. But his culture, his values, his appetites are entirely foreign to someone like Natalie. She could never be happy with him."

"Appetites?" Blandford asked, raising his brows.

"Yes, for money and power. And although he is a person of consequence in New York, he has no rank here. Natalie isn't used to that. It's an awkward match."

"You're right, of course," Blandford surprised her by saying. He settled back in his chair, weaving his fingers together. Blandford was a pleasant, placid-faced man, his head large and well shaped, the bald skin hugging his skull tightly and then draping in more relaxed folds around his eyes, cheeks, and jowls. The substantial framework of his body was lank and bony, as if nature had forgotten to weave the necessary amount of muscle to support his skeleton.

"It is an awkward match in some regards," Blandford continued. "But it may be the saving of future generations of the family. My dear, you are very nearly a daughter to me, so I will speak bluntly. There is no son to inherit the title after me, and I will not leave Natalie and Lady Blandford to the questionable generosity of the next Lord Blandford. They must be provided for. To my profound regret, I will not be able to leave a satisfactory income for them, as most of the Blandford monies and lands are entailed."

"But there are Englishmen of means who would dearly love to marry Natalie. Lord Travers, for example. He and Natalie share a great affinity, and he has generous means at his disposal—"

"*Acceptable* means," Blandford corrected quietly. "Not generous. And nothing close to what Bowman has now, not to mention his future inheritance."

Hannah was bewildered. In all the years she had known Lord Blandford, he had never displayed an outward concern for wealth. It was not done among men of his station, who disdained conversations about finance as bourgeois and far beneath them. What had prompted this worry over money?

Reading her expression, Blandford smiled morosely. "Ah, Hannah. How can I explain adequately? The world is moving altogether too fast for men like me. Too many new ways of doing things. Before I can adjust to the way something changes, it changes yet again. They say before long the railway will cover every green acre of England. The masses will all have soap and tinned food and ready-made clothing, and the distance between us and them will grow quite narrow."

Hannah listened intently, aware that she, with her lack of fortune and undistinguished birth, straddled the line between Blandford's own class and "the masses."

"Is that a bad thing, Uncle?"

"Not entirely," Blandford said after a long hesitation. "Though I do regret that blood and gentility are coming to mean so little. The future is upon us, and it belongs to climbers like the Bowmans. And to men like Lord Westcliff, who are willing to sacrifice what they must to keep pace with it."

The earl of Westcliff was Raphael Bowman's brother-in-law. He had arguably the most distinguished lineage in England, with blood more blue than the Queen's. And yet he was known as a progressive, both politically and financially. Among his many investments, Westcliff had garnered a fortune from the development of the locomotive industry, and he was said to take a keen interest in mercantile matters. All this while most of the peerage was still content to garner its profits from the centuries-old tradition of maintaining tenants on its private lands.

"Then you desire the connection to Lord Westcliff, as well as the Bowmans," Hannah said.

"Of course. It will put my daughter in a unique position, marrying a wealthy American *and* having a brother-in-law such as Westcliff. As the wife of a Bowman, she will be seated at the lower end of the table . . . but it will be Westcliff's table, and that is no small consideration."

"I see," she said pensively.

"But you don't agree?"

No. Hannah was far from persuaded that her beloved Natalie should have to make do with an ill-mannered boor as a husband, merely to have Lord Westcliff as a brother-in-law. However, she was certainly not going to impugn Lord Blandford's judgment. At least not aloud.

"I defer to your wisdom, Uncle. However, I do hope that the advantages—or disadvantages—of this match will reveal themselves quickly."

A quiet laugh escaped him. "What a diplomat you are. You have a shrewd mind, my dear. Probably more than a young woman has need of. Better to be pretty and empty-headed like my daughter, than plain and clever."

Hannah did not take offense, although she could have argued both points. For one thing, her cousin Natalie was anything but empty-headed. However, Natalie knew better than to flaunt her intelligence, as that was not a quality that attracted suitors.

And Hannah did not consider herself plain. She was brown-haired and green-eyed, and she had a nice smile and a decent figure. If Hannah had the benefit of lovely clothes and adornments, she thought she might be considered very appealing. It was all in the eye of the beholder.

"Go to tea at Marsden Terrace," Lord Blandford told her, smiling. "Sow the seeds of romance. A match must be made. And as the Bard so aptly put it, 'The world must be peopled.'" He glanced at her significantly. "After we manage to marry off Natalie, you will no doubt find your own suitor. I have my suspicions about you and Mr. Clark, you see."

Hannah felt color rising in her face. For the past year she had undertaken some minor secretarial duties for Samuel Clark, a close friend and distant relation of Lord Blandford's. And Hannah entertained some private hopes regarding the attractive bachelor, who was fair haired and slim and not much older than she. But perhaps her hopes were not as private as she had thought. "I'm sure I don't know what you mean, Uncle."

"I'm sure you do," he said, and chuckled. "All in good time, my dear. First let us secure a satisfactory future for Natalie. And then it will be your turn."

Hannah smiled at him, keeping her thoughts private. But inwardly she knew that her definition of a "satisfactory future" for Natalie was not quite the same as his. Natalie deserved a man who would be a loving, responsible, trustworthy husband.

And if Rafe Bowman were that man, he would have to prove it.

Chapter Two

At the risk of sounding arrogant," Rafe said, "I don't think I need advice about how to court a woman."

Rafe had arrived in London the day before. Today, while Westcliff was off visiting the locomotive works in which he had a share, Rafe gathered he was supposed to have tea with Lillian and her friends.

Rafe would have preferred to tour the locomotive works. He was a manufacturer's son, and the lure of new machines and gadgetry held an unending fascination for him. On the other hand, Lillian had asked him to stay, and he had never been able to refuse her anything. He adored his sisters, who in his opinion were the best things his parents had ever accomplished.

"Miss Appleton is not going to give you advice," Lillian retorted, ruffling his hair fondly. "We've invited her to tea so that she can tell us more about Lady Natalie. I should think you'd like to find out as much as you can about your future bride."

"That's still in question," Rafe reminded her wryly. "Even if I want to marry her, it's still left to Lady Natalie to consider whether she'll have me."

"Which is why you're going to be *so* charming that Miss Appleton will run back home to deliver a glowing report about you to Lady Natalie." Lillian paused and gave him a mock-threatening glance. "Aren't you?"

Rafe smiled at his sister while he dandled her eight-month-old infant Merritt on his knee. The baby was dark haired and brown eyed like both her parents, with rosy cheeks and grasping little hands. After tugging off one of his waistcoat buttons with a determined yank, the baby attempted to put it in her mouth. "No, darling," Rafe said, prying the button out of the wet clenched fist, and Merritt began to howl in protest. "I'm sorry," he said contritely. "I'd scream too if someone took away something I fancied. But you might choke on that, love, and then your mother would have me shanghaied to China."

"That's only if Westcliff didn't reach you first," Lillian said, taking the squalling baby from him. "There, darling. Mommy won't let mean old Uncle Rafe bother you any longer." She grinned and wrinkled her nose impishly at him as she soothed her daughter.

Marriage and motherhood became Lillian, Rafe thought. His sister had always been a headstrong creature, but now she seemed calmer and happier than he had ever seen her before. He could only credit Westcliff for that, although how such a proper and autocratic man could accomplish such a change in Lillian was a mystery. One would have thought the pair would have killed each other within the first month of marriage.

After the baby had quieted and Lillian had given her to a nurserymaid to take upstairs, Annabelle and Evie arrived.

Rising to his feet, Rafe bowed to the ladies as introductions were made.

Mrs. Annabelle Hunt, wife to the railroad entrepreneur Simon Hunt, was said to be one of the great beauties of England.

It was difficult to imagine that any woman could eclipse her. She was the perfect English Rose, with honey-blond hair and blue eyes, and a pure, fair complexion. Not only would her figure have driven a saint to sin but her expression was so lively and beguiling that it instantly put him at ease.

Evie, Lady St. Vincent, was not nearly so approachable. However, Lillian had already warned Rafe that Evie's shyness was often mistaken for reserve. She was unconventionally lovely, her skin lightly freckled, her hair rampantly red. Her blue eyes contained a cautious friendliness and vulnerability that touched Rafe.

"My dear Mr. Bowman," Annabelle said with an engaging laugh, "I should have known you anywhere, even without an introduction. You and Lillian share a distinct resemblance. Are all the Bowmans so tall and dark haired?"

"All except Daisy," Rafe replied. "I'm afraid the first four of us took up so much height, there was nothing left for her when she arrived."

"What Daisy lacks in height," Lillian said, "she makes up for in personality."

Rafe laughed. "True. I want to see the little scamp, and hear from her own lips that she married Matthew Swift willingly, and not because Father bludgeoned her into it."

"Daisy truly l-loves Mr. Swift," Evie said earnestly.

At the sound of her stammer, which was something else Lillian had warned him about, Rafe gave her a reassuring smile. "I'm glad to hear it," he said gently. "I've always thought Swift was a decent fellow."

"It never bothered you, the way Father adopted him as a *de facto* son?" Lillian asked acerbically, seating herself and gesturing for the others to do the same.

"Just the opposite," Rafe said. "I was glad of anyone or anything that took Father's attention away from me. I've had enough of the old man's damned short fuse for a lifetime. The only reason I'm willing to put up with it now is because I want joint proprietorship of the company's European expansion."

Annabelle looked bemused at their frankness. "It appears we're not bothering with discretion today."

Rafe grinned. "I doubt there is much about the Bowmans that Lillian hasn't already told you. So by all means, let's dispense with discretion and move on to the interesting subjects."

"Are the ladies of London a subject of interest?" Lillian asked.

"Definitely. Tell me about them."

"They're different here than in New York," Lillian warned him. "Especially the younger ones. When you are introduced to a proper English girl, she will keep her gaze fixed on the ground, and she won't chatter and gush on as we Americans do. English girls are far more sheltered, and not at all used to the company of men. So don't even think about discussing business or political affairs, or anything of the sort."

"What am I allowed to talk about?" Rafe asked apprehensively.

"Music, art, and horses," Annabelle said. "And remember that English girls seldom offer their views on anything, but instead prefer to repeat their parents' opinions."

"But after they are m-married," Evie said, "they will be far more inclined to reveal their true selves."

Rafe gave her a wry glance. "How difficult would it be to find out about a girl's true self *before* I marry her?"

"Almost imp-possible," Evie said gravely, and Rafe began to smile until he realized she wasn't joking.

Now he was beginning to understand why Lillian and her friends were trying to find out more about Lady Natalie and her character. Apparently it wasn't going to come from Lady Natalie herself.

Looking from Lillian's face to those of Annabelle and Evie, Rafe said slowly, "I appreciate your help, ladies. It occurs to me that I may need it more than I thought."

"The person who will be most helpful," Lillian said, "is Miss Appleton. One hopes." She parted the lace curtains at the window to glance at the street. "And if I'm not mistaken, she has just arrived."

Rafe stood in a perfunctory manner while Miss Appleton came into the entrance hall. Lillian went to greet her while a servant collected her coat and bonnet. Rafe supposed he should be grateful to the old biddy for coming to visit, but all he could think of was how quickly they might be able to obtain the necessary information and be rid of her.

He watched without interest as she came into the parlor. She wore a dull blue gown of the practical and well-made sort seen on retainers and the higher caliber of servants.

His gaze traveled up to the neat shape of her waist, the gentle curves of her breasts, and then to her face. He felt a little stab of surprise as he saw that she was young, no more than Daisy's age. From her expression, one could deduce that she wasn't any happier to be there than Rafe. But there was a suggestion of tenderness and humor in the soft shape of her mouth, and delicate strength in the lines of her nose and chin.

Her beauty was not cool and pristine, but warm and slightly disheveled. Her brown hair, shiny as ribbons, seemed to have been pinned up in a hurry. As she removed her gloves with a neat tug at each fingertip, she glanced at Rafe with ocean-green eyes.

That look left no doubt that Miss Appleton neither liked nor trusted him. Nor should she, Rafe thought with a flash of amusement. He was not exactly known for his honorable intentions where women were concerned.

She approached him in a composed manner that annoyed Rafe for some reason. She made him want to . . . well, he wasn't certain what, but it would begin with scooping her up and tossing her onto the nearby settee.

"Miss Appleton," Lillian said, "I should like to introduce my brother, Mr. Bowman."

"Miss Appleton," Rafe murmured, extending his hand.

The young woman hesitated, her pale fingers making a slight flutter beside her skirts.

"Oh, Rafe," Lillian said hastily, "that's not done here."

"My apologies." Rafe withdrew his hand, staring into those translucent green eyes. "The handshake is common in American parlors."

Miss Appleton gave him a speculative glance. "In London, a simple bow is best," she said in a light, clear voice that sent a ripple of heat down the back of his neck. "Although at times a married lady might shake hands, an unmarried one rarely does. It is usually regarded here as a lower-class practice, and a rather personal matter, especially when done without gloves." She studied him for a moment, the hint of a smile curving her lips. "However, I have no objection to beginning in the American fashion." She extended a slender hand. "How is it done?"

The unaccountable heat lingered on the back of Rafe's neck and crept across his shoulders. He took her slim hand in his much larger one, surprised by the needling sensation in his abdomen, the shot of acute awareness. "A firm grip," he began, "is usually considered—" He broke off, unable to speak at all as she cautiously returned the pressure of his fingers.

"Like this?" she asked, glancing up into his face. Her cheeks had turned pink.

"Yes." Dazedly Rafe wondered what the matter with him was. The pressure of that small, confiding hand was affecting him more than his last mistress's most lascivious caress.

Letting go of her, he dragged his gaze away and struggled to moderate his breathing.

Lillian and Annabelle exchanged a perplexed glance in the charged silence.

"Well," Lillian said brightly as the tea trays were brought in, "let's become better acquainted. Shall I pour?"

Annabelle lowered herself to the settee beside Lillian, while Rafe and Miss Appleton took chairs on the other side of the low table. For the next few minutes the rituals of tea were observed. Plates of toast and crumpets were passed around.

Rafe couldn't seem to stop staring at Miss Appleton, who sat straight-backed in her chair, sipping carefully at her tea. He wanted to pull the pins from her hair and wrap it around his fingers. He wanted to tumble her to the floor. She looked so proper, so good, sitting there with her skirts precisely arranged.

She made him want to be very, very bad.

Chapter Three

Hannah had never been so uncomfortable in her life. The man sitting next to her was a beast. He stared at her as if she were some carnival curiosity. And he had already confirmed much of what she had heard about American men. Everything about him advertised a brand of excessive masculinity that she found distasteful. The slouchy, informal way he occupied his chair made her want to kick his shins.

His New York accent, the flattened vowels and lax consonants, was foreign and annoying. However, she had to admit that the voice itself . . . a deep, polished-leather baritone, was mesmerizing. And his eyes were extraordinary, dark as pitch yet gleaming with audacious fire.

He had the sun-browned complexion of a man who spent a great deal of time out of doors, and his close-shaven jaw showed the grain of a heavy beard. He was an excessively, uncompromisingly masculine creature. Not at all a match for Natalie in any regard. He was not appropriate for the drawing room, or the parlor, or any other civilized surroundings.

Mr. Bowman addressed her with a directness that seemed nothing short of subversive. "Tell me, Miss Appleton . . . what does a lady's companion do? And do you receive wages for it?"

Oh, he was horrid to ask such a thing! Swallowing back her indignation, Hannah replied, "It is a paid position. I do not receive wages, but rather an allowance."

He tilted his head and regarded her intently. "What's the difference?"

"'Wages' would imply that I am a servant."

"I see. And what is it you do in return for your allowance?"

His persistence was galling. "I provide companionship and conversation," she said, "and on occasion I act as chaperone to Lady Natalie. I also do light sewing, and I do small things that make Lady Natalie's life more comfortable, such as bring her tea or go on errands."

Mockery flickered in those heathen eyes. "But you're not a servant."

Hannah gave him a cool glance. "No." She decided to turn the tables on him. "What exactly does a financial speculator do?"

"I make investments. I also watch for people who are being idiotic with their investments. And then I encourage them to go at it full-tilt, until I'm left with a profit while they're standing in a pile of smoking rubble."

"How do you sleep at night?" she asked, appalled.

Bowman flashed an insolent grin. "Very well, thank you."

"I didn't mean—"

"I know what you meant, Miss Appleton. I rest easy in the knowledge that I'm doing my victims a service."

"How?"

"I teach them a valuable lesson."

Before Hannah could reply, Annabelle broke in hastily. "Dear me, we mustn't allow the conversation to drift into business talk. I hear far too much of that at home. Miss Appleton, I have heard such lovely things about Lady Natalie. How long have you been her companion?"

"For three years," Hannah answered readily. She was slightly older than her cousin, two years to be exact, and she had watched as Natalie had blossomed into the poised and dazzling girl that she was now. "Lady Natalie is a delight. Her disposition is amiable and affectionate, and she has every grace of character one could wish for. A more intelligent and charming girl could not be found."

Bowman gave a low laugh edged with disbelief. "A paragon," he said. "Unfortunately I've heard other young women advertised in equally rapturous terms. But when you meet them, there's always a flaw."

"Some people," Hannah replied, "will insist on finding flaws in others even when there are none."

"Everyone has flaws, Miss Appleton."

He was too provoking to be endured. She met his keen, dark gaze and asked, "What are yours, Mr. Bowman?"

"Oh, I'm a scoundrel," he said cheerfully. "I take advantage of others, I care nothing for propriety, and I have an unfortunate habit of saying exactly what I think. What are yours?" He smiled at her wide-eyed silence. "Or are you by chance as perfect as Lady Natalie?"

Hannah was struck speechless by his boldness. No man had ever spoken to her in such a manner. Another woman might have withered at the derision in his voice. But something in her would not be cowed.

"Rafe," she heard Lillian say in a warning undertone, "I'm sure *our guest* doesn't wish to be subjected to an inquisition before we've even brought out the scones."

"No, my lady," Hannah managed to say, "it's quite all right." She stared directly at Bowman. "I am far too opinionated," she told him. "I believe that is my worst flaw. I am often impulsive. And I'm dreadful at small talk. I tend to become carried away in conversation, and I go on for far too long." She paused strategically before adding, "I also have little patience with insolent people."

A brief, tumultuous silence followed as their gazes locked. Hannah could not seem to look away from him. She felt her palms turning moist and hot, and she knew her color was high.

"Well done," he said softly. "My apologies, Miss Appleton. I did not mean to give any impression of insolence."

But he had. He had been testing her, needling her deliberately to see what she would do. Like a cat playing with a mouse. Hannah felt a warm sensation bristling down her spine as she stared into the heathen depths of his eyes.

"Rafe," she heard Lillian exclaim with exasperation, "if this is an example of your parlor manners, there is much work to be done before I will allow you to meet Lady Natalie."

"Lady Natalie is quite sheltered," Hannah said. "I fear you will not get very far with her, Mr. Bowman, if you are anything less than gentlemanly."

"Point taken." Bowman gave Hannah an innocent glance. "I can behave better than this."

I doubt that, she longed to say, but bit the words back. And Bowman smiled as if he could read her thoughts.

The conversation returned to the topic of Natalie, and Hannah provided answers to such questions as her preferred flowers, her favorite books and music, her likes and dislikes. It had crossed Hannah's mind to be untruthful, to put Mr. Bowman at a disadvantage with Natalie. But it was not in her nature to lie, nor was she very good at it. And then there was Lord Blandford's request. If he truly believed it would be to

Natalie's advantage to marry into the Bowman family, it was not Hannah's right to stand in the way. The Blandfords had been kind to her, and they did not deserve an ill turn.

She found it a bit peculiar that Bowman asked very little about Natalie. Instead he seemed content to let the other women question her, while he drank his tea and stared at her with a coolly assessing gaze.

Of the three women, Hannah liked Annabelle the most. She had a knack for keeping the conversation entertaining, and she was amusing and well versed in many subjects. In fact, Annabelle was an example of what Natalie might become in a few years.

Were it not for Mr. Bowman's disturbing presence, Hannah would have been sorry for teatime to end. But it was with relief that she received the news that Lord Blandford's carriage had arrived to convey her back home. She didn't think she could abide much more of Bowman's unsettling stare.

"Thank you for the lovely tea," Hannah said to Lillian, standing and smoothing her skirts. "It has been a delight to make your acquaintance."

Lillian grinned with the same flash of mischief that Bowman had displayed before. With their spicy brown eyes and gleaming sable hair, there was no doubting their family resemblance. Except that Lillian was far nicer. "You are very kind to tolerate us, Miss Appleton. I do hope we haven't behaved too badly."

"Not at all," Hannah replied. "I look forward to seeing you in Hampshire soon."

In a matter of days, Hannah would be leaving for Lillian and Lord Westcliff's country estate with Natalie and the Blandfords for an extended visit over Christmas. It would last more than a fortnight, during which time Mr. Bowman and

Natalie would have ample opportunity to discover whether they suited. Or not.

"Yes, it will be a grand, glorious Christmas," Lillian exclaimed, her eyes glowing. "Music, feasting, dancing, and all kinds of fun. And Lord Westcliff has promised that we will have an absolutely *towering* Christmas tree."

Hannah smiled, caught up in her enthusiasm. "I've never seen one before."

"Haven't you? Oh, it's magical when all the candles are lit. Christmas trees are quite the fashion in New York, where I was brought up. It started as a German tradition, and it's catching on rapidly in America, though it's not common in England. Yet."

"The royal family has had Christmas trees for some time," Annabelle said. "Queen Charlotte always put one up at Windsor. And I've heard that Prince Albert has continued the tradition after the manner of his German heritage."

"I look forward to viewing the Christmas tree," Hannah said, "and spending the holiday with all of you." She bowed to the women, and paused uncertainly as she glanced up at Bowman. He was very tall, his presence so forceful and vital that she felt a shock of awareness as he moved closer to her. As she glanced up at Bowman's handsome, arrogant face, all she could think of was how much she disliked him. And yet dislike had never made her mouth go dry like this. Dislike had never sent her pulse into a swift, tripping beat, nor had it knotted in the pit of her stomach.

Hannah nodded to him in the approximation of a bow.

Bowman smiled, his teeth very white in his sun-browned face. "You shook my hand before," he reminded her, and extended his palm.

Such audacity. She didn't want to touch him again, and he knew it. Her chest felt very tight, compressing until she was forced to take an extra breath. But at the same time she felt a wry, irrepressible smile curve her lips. He was a scoundrel indeed. Natalie would discover that soon enough.

"So I did," Hannah said, and reached out for his hand. A quiver went through her frame as she felt his fingers close around hers. It was a powerful hand, capable of crushing her delicate bones with ease, but his hold was gentle. And hot. Hannah sent him a bewildered glance and tugged free, while her heart pounded heavily. She wished he would stop staring at her—she could actually feel his gaze on her downbent head. "The carriage is waiting," she said unsteadily.

"I'll take you to the entrance hall," she heard Lillian say, "and we'll ring for your cloak and—" She broke off as she heard the sound of a crying baby. "Oh, dear."

A nurserymaid came into the parlor, holding a dark-haired infant bundled in a pink blanket. "Beg pardon, milady, but she won't stop crying."

"My daughter Merritt," Lillian explained to Hannah. Reaching out for the infant, she cuddled and soothed her. "Poor darling, you've been fretful today. Miss Appleton, if you'll wait a moment—"

"I'll see myself out," Hannah said, smiling. "Stay here with your daughter, my lady."

"I'll go with you," Bowman offered easily.

"Thank you, Rafe," came Lillian's grateful reply, before Hannah could object.

Feeling a pang of nerves in her stomach, Hannah left the parlor with Rafe Bowman. Before he reached for the bell pull, she murmured, "If you have no objection, I would like to speak with you privately for a moment."

"Of course." His gaze swept over her, his eyes containing the devilish glint of a man who was well accustomed to having private moments with women he barely knew. His fingers slid around her elbow as he drew her with him to the shadow beneath the stairs.

"Mr. Bowman," Hannah whispered with desperate earnestness, "I have neither the right nor the desire to correct your manners, but . . . this matter of the handshake . . ."

His head bent over hers. "Yes?"

"Please, you *must* not extend your hand to an older person, or to a man of greater prestige, or most of all to a lady, unless any of these people offer their hands to you first. It's simply not done here. And as vexing and annoying as you are, I still don't wish you to be slighted."

To her surprise, Bowman appeared to listen closely. When he replied, his tone was infused with quiet gravity. "That is kind of you, Miss Appleton."

She looked away from him, her gaze chasing round the floor, the walls, the underside of the stairs. Her breath came in anxious little gusts. "I'm not being kind. I just said you were vexing and annoying. You've made no effort to be polite."

"You're right," he said gently. "But believe me, I'm even more annoying when I'm trying to be polite."

They were standing too close, the crisp scents of his wool coat and starched linen shirt drifting to her nostrils. And the deeper underlying fragrance of male skin, fresh and spiced with bergamot shaving soap. Bowman watched her with the same intensity, very nearly fascination, that he had shown in the parlor. It made her nervous, being stared at in such a way.

Hannah squared her shoulders. "I must be frank, Mr. Bowman. I do not believe that you and Lady Natalie will suit in any way. There is not one atom of likeness between you. No common ground. I think it would be a disaster. And it is my duty to share this opinion with Lady Natalie. In fact, I will do whatever is necessary to stand in the way of your betrothal. And though you may not believe this, it is for your own good as well as Lady Natalie's."

Bowman didn't seem at all concerned by her opinion, or her warning. "There's nothing I can do to change your opinion of me?"

"No, I'm quite stubborn in my opinions."

"Then I'll have to show you what happens to women who stand in my way."

His hands slipped around her with an easy stealth that caught her completely unaware. Before she comprehended what was happening, one powerful arm had brought her against the animal heat of his hard masculine body. With his other hand, he grasped the nape of her neck, and tilted her head backward. And his mouth took hers.

Hannah went rigid in his arms, straining backward, but he followed and secured her more firmly against him. He let her feel how much bigger he was, how much stronger, and as she gasped and tried to speak, he took swift advantage of her parted lips.

A wild jolt went through her, and she reached up to push his head away. His mouth was experienced and unexpectedly soft, possessing hers with seductive skill. She had never thought a kiss could have a taste, an intimate flavor. She had never dreamed that her body would welcome something her mind utterly rejected.

But as Bowman forced her to accept the deep, drugging kiss, she felt herself going limp, her senses overrun. Her traitorous fingers curled into the thick raven locks of his hair, the strands as heavy as raw silk. And instead of rebuffing him, she found herself holding him closer. Her mouth trembled and opened beneath his expert persuasion as liquid fire raced through her veins.

Slowly Bowman took his lips from hers and guided her

head to his chest, which moved beneath her cheek with strong, uneven breaths. A mischievous whisper tickled her ear. "This is how we court girls in America. We grab them and kiss them. And if they don't like it, we do it again, harder and longer, until they surrender. It saves us hours of witty repartee."

Looking up at him sharply, Hannah saw a dance of laughter in his wicked dark eyes, and she drew in a breath of outrage. "I'm going to tell—"

"Tell anyone you like. I'll deny it."

Her brows pulled together in a scowl. "You are worse than a scoundrel. You're a *cad*."

"If you didn't like it," he murmured, "you shouldn't have kissed me back."

"I did *not*—"

His mouth crushed over hers again. She made a choked sound, hitting his chest with her fist. But he was impervious to the blow, his hand coming up and engulfing her entire fist. And he consumed her with a deeply voluptuous kiss, stroking inside her, doing things she had never suspected people did while kissing. She was shocked by the searing invasion, and even more by the pleasure it gave her, all her senses opening to receive more. She wanted him to stop, but more than that, she wanted him to go on forever.

Hannah felt his breath rush fast and hot against her cheek, his chest rising and falling with unsteady force. He let go of her hand, and she leaned weakly against him, gripping his shoulders for balance. The urgent pressure of his mouth forced her head back. She surrendered with a soft moan, needing something she had no name for, some way to soothe the anxious rhythm of her pulse. It seemed that if she could just pull him closer, tighter, it might ease the sensual agitation that filled every part of her.

Drawing back reluctantly, Bowman finished the kiss with

a teasing nudge of his lips, and cradled the side of her face in his hand. The amusement had faded from his eyes, replaced by a dangerous smolder.

"What is your first name?" His whisper fanned like a waft of steam across her lips. At her silence, he dragged his mouth lightly over hers. "Tell me, or I'll kiss you again."

"Hannah," she said faintly, knowing she could not bear any more.

His thumb caressed the scarlet surface of her cheek. "From now on, Hannah, no matter what you say or do, I'm going to look at your mouth and remember how sweet you taste." A self-mocking smile curved his lips as he added quietly, "Damn it."

Releasing her with care, he went to the bell pull and rang for a housemaid. When Hannah's cloak and hat were brought, he took them from the maid. "Come, Miss Appleton."

Hannah couldn't bring herself to look at him. She knew her face was terribly red. Without doubt, she had never been so mortified and confused in her life. She waited in dazed silence as he deftly draped the cloak around her and fastened it at her throat.

"Until we meet again in Hampshire," she heard him say. The tip of his forefinger touched her chin. "Look up, sweetheart."

Hannah obeyed jerkily. He placed the hat on her head, carefully adjusting the brim. "Did I frighten you?" he whispered.

Glaring at him, she lifted her chin another notch. Her voice shook only a little. "I am sorry to disappoint you, Mr. Bowman. But I am neither frightened *nor* intimidated."

A gleam of humor flickered in those obsidian eyes. "I should warn you, Hannah: when we meet at Stony Cross Park, take care to avoid the mistletoe. For both our sakes."

* * *

AFTER THE DELECTABLE MISS APPLETON HAD DEPARTED, Rafe remained in the entrance hall, lowering himself to a heavy oak bench. Aroused and bemused, he pondered his unexpected loss of control. He had only meant to give the young woman a peck, just enough to fluster and disconcert her. But the kiss had flared into something so urgent, so fiercely pleasurable, that he hadn't been able to stop himself from taking far more than he should have.

He would have liked to kiss that innocent mouth for hours. He wanted to demolish every one of her inhibitions until she was wrapped around him, naked and crying for him to take her. Thinking of how difficult it would be to seduce her, and how much damned fun it would be to get under her skirts, he felt himself turning uncomfortably hard. A slow, wry smile crossed his face as he reflected that if *this* was what he could expect from Englishwomen, he was going to take up permanent residence in London.

Hearing footsteps, Rafe lifted his gaze. Lillian had come into the entrance hall. She regarded him with fond exasperation.

"How's the baby?" Rafe asked.

"Annabelle's holding her. Why are you still out here?"

"I needed a moment to cool my . . . temper."

Folding her slender arms across her chest, Lillian shook her head slowly. She was beautiful in a bold, clean-featured way, as spirited and raffish as a female pirate. She and Rafe had always understood each other, perhaps because neither of them had been able to tolerate the stringent rules set by their parents.

"Only you," Lillian said without heat, "could turn a respectable teatime visit into a sparring match."

Rafe grinned without remorse and glanced at the front

door reflectively. "Something about her brings out the devil in me."

"Well, you had better contain it, dear. Because if you wish to win Lady Natalie, you'll have to display far more courtesy and polish than you did in that parlor. What do you think Miss Appleton is going to tell her employers about you?"

"That I'm an unprincipled, ill-mannered villain?" Rafe shrugged and said in a reasonable manner, "But they already know I'm from Wall Street."

Lillian's gingerbread-colored eyes narrowed as she regarded him speculatively. "Since you don't seem at all concerned, I'll have to assume that you know what you're doing. But let me remind you that Lady Natalie wants to marry a gentleman."

"In my experience," Rafe said lazily, "nothing makes women complain nearly so much as getting what they want."

Lillian chuckled. "Oh, this should be an interesting holiday. Will you come back to the parlor?"

"In a moment. Still cooling."

She gave him a quizzical glance. "Your temper takes a long time to subside, doesn't it?"

"You have no idea," he told her gravely.

Going back into the parlor, Lillian stood in the doorway and regarded her friends. Annabelle sat with Merritt resting placidly in her arms, while Evie was pouring a last cup of tea.

"What did he say?" Annabelle asked.

Lillian rolled her eyes. "My idiot brother doesn't seem the least bit worried that Miss Appleton is sure to deliver a scathing report about him to the Blandfords and Lady Natalie." She sighed. "That didn't go at all well, did it? Have you *ever* seen such instant animosity between two people for no apparent reason?"

"Yes," Evie replied.

"I believe so," Annabelle said.

Lillian frowned. "When? Who?" she demanded, and was mystified when they smiled at each other.

Chapter Four

To Hannah's astonishment, Natalie was not only *not* shocked by her account of the visit with Rafe Bowman, she was highly entertained. By the time Hannah had finished the account of the kiss beneath the stairs, Natalie had collapsed on the bed in a fit of giggles.

"Natalie," Hannah said, frowning, "clearly I haven't managed to convey how dreadful that man was. *Is.* He's a barbarian. A brute. A *clod.*"

"Apparently so." Still chortling, Natalie sat up. "I look forward to meeting him."

"What?"

"He's quite manipulative, our Mr. Bowman. He knew you would tell me what he had done, and that I would be intrigued. And when I see him in Hampshire, he'll act the perfect gentleman in the hopes of setting me off balance."

"You shouldn't be intrigued, you should be appalled!"

Natalie smiled and patted her hand. "Oh, Hannah, you don't know how to manage men. You mustn't take everything so seriously."

"But courtship is a serious matter," Hannah protested. It

was at moments like this that she understood the differences between herself and her younger cousin. Natalie seemed to have a more thorough understanding of social maneuvering, of the process of pursuit and capture, than Hannah ever would.

"Oh, heavens, the moment a girl approaches courtship as a serious matter is the moment she's lost the game. We must guard our hearts and hide our feelings carefully, Hannah. It's the only way to win."

"I thought courtship was a process of revealing one's heart," Hannah said. "Not winning a game."

Natalie smiled. "I don't know where you get such ideas. If you want to bring a man up to scratch, never reveal your heart to him. At least not early on. Men only value something when they have to put some effort into getting it." She tapped her forefinger on her chin. "Hmm . . . I shall have to come up with a good counterstrategy."

Climbing off the bed, Hannah went to retrieve some gloves and stockings and other items that had been dropped carelessly to the floor. She had never minded tidying up after Natalie. Hannah had met other lady's companions whose charges had made their lives a misery, treating them with contempt and subjecting them to all kinds of small cruelties. Natalie, on the other hand, was kind and affectionate, and although she could be a trifle self-absorbed on occasion, it was nothing that time and maturity wouldn't cure.

Placing the personal articles in a dresser drawer, Hannah turned to face Natalie, who was still ruminating.

Natalie was a pretty sight, tumbled on the white ruffled bed, her hair falling in golden curls. Her blue-eyed sunny appeal had stolen many a gentleman's heart during her first season. And her delicately regretful rejections of her suitors had done nothing to dampen their ardor. Long after the season had ended, towering arrangements of flowers were delivered to the Blandford mansion, and calling cards piled up on the silver tray in the entrance hall.

Absently Natalie wound a lock of shimmering hair around her finger. "Mr. Bowman is betting on the fact that since I went through an entire season without settling on someone, I must have tired of all these bland, respectable lords of leisure. And since it's been months since the season ended, he also assumes that I am bored and eager for a challenge." She gave an abbreviated laugh. "He is correct on all counts."

"The proper way for him to get your attention is not to ravish your companion," Hannah muttered.

"You weren't ravished, you were kissed." Natalie's eyes twinkled mischievously as she asked, "Now confess, Hannah—does he kiss nicely?"

Remembering the warm erotic sensation of Bowman's mouth, Hannah felt the damnable color sweep over her again. "I don't know," she said shortly. "I have no basis for comparison."

Natalie's eyes widened. "You mean you've never been kissed before?"

Hannah shook her head.

"But surely Mr. Clark—"

"No." Hannah raised her fingers to her hot cheeks.

"He must have tried," Natalie insisted. "You've spent so much time in his company."

"I've been working for him," Hannah protested. "Helping with his manuscript and papers."

"You mean you've actually been taking dictation from him?"

Hannah gave her a bewildered glance. "What else would I have been doing?"

"I always assumed when you said you'd been 'taking dictation' from him that you were letting him kiss you."

Hannah's mouth fell open. "When I said I'd been 'taking dictation,' I meant that I had been taking dictation!"

Natalie was clearly disappointed. "My goodness. If you have spent *that* much time with him, and he has never once kissed you, I'd say that is proof of the fact that his passion for his work will eclipse all else. Even a wife. We must find someone else for you."

"I wouldn't mind taking second place to Mr. Clark's work," Hannah said earnestly. "He will be a great man someday. He will do so much good for others—"

"Great men don't necessarily make good husbands. And you're too dear and lovely to be wasted on him." Natalie shook her head in disgust. "Why, any of my leftovers from last season would be better for you than silly old Mr. Clark."

A troubling thought occurred to Hannah, but she was almost afraid to voice her suspicion. "Natalie, did you ever let one of your suitors kiss you?"

"No," Natalie said reassuringly.

Hannah let out a sigh of relief.

"I let nearly all of them kiss me," Natalie continued cheerfully. "On separate occasions, of course."

Aghast, Hannah leaned hard against the dresser. "But . . . but I was watching over you . . ."

"You're a terrible chaperone, Hannah. You often become so absorbed in conversation that you forget to keep an eye on me. It's one of the reasons I adore you so."

Hannah had never dreamed that her pretty, high-spirited cousin would have let any young man presume so far. Much less *several.* "You know you should never allow such liberties," she said weakly. "It will cause rumors, and you might be labeled as fast, and then . . ."

"No one will enter an engagement with me?" Natalie smiled wryly. "Last season I received four proposals of marriage, and had I cared to encourage any more, I could have gotten another half dozen. Believe me, Hannah, I know how to manage men. Bring my hairbrush, please."

Obeying, Hannah had to acknowledge that there was good reason for Natalie to be so self-assured. She was, or would be, the ideal bride for any man. She gave the silver-backed brush to Natalie and watched her draw it through a flurry of rich blond curls. "Natalie, why didn't you accept any of those offers last season?"

"I'm waiting for someone special," came the thoughtful reply. "I should hate to settle for anyone ordinary." Natalie smiled as she added flippantly, "When I kiss a man, I want to hear the angels sing."

"What about Lord Travers?" Of all the gentlemen who had shown an interest in Natalie, the one Hannah had the highest regard for was Edward, Lord Travers. He was a sober, quiet gentleman, careful in appearance and bearing. Although his countenance did not lend itself to outright handsomeness, his features were strong and regular. He did not seem dazzled by Natalie, and yet he paid a close and respectful attention to her whenever she was present. And he was rich and titled, which, along with his other qualities, made him an excellent catch.

The mention of Travers drew a frown from Natalie. "He is the only man of my acquaintance who will not make an advance to me, even when handed a perfectly good opportunity. I chalk it up to his age."

Hannah couldn't help laughing. "His age?"

"He is on the wrong side of thirty, after all."

"He is mature," Hannah allowed. "But he is also confident, intelligent, and from all appearances, in full vigor."

"Then why hasn't he kissed me?"

"Because he respects you?" Hannah suggested.

"I would rather be regarded with passion than respect."

"Well, then," Hannah said wryly, "I would say that Mr. Bowman is your man."

The mention of Bowman restored Natalie's good spirits. "Possibly so. Now, Hannah, tell Mama and Papa that Mr. Bowman was exquisitely well behaved. No, they won't believe that, he's American. Tell them he was quite presentable. And not one mention of the kiss under the stairs."

Chapter Five

Hannah had never expected to have the opportunity to see Stony Cross Park. Invitations to Lord Westcliff's famed country estate were not easy to obtain. Located in the southern county of Hampshire, Stony Cross Park was reputed to have some of the finest acreage in England. The variety of flowering fields, fertile wet meadows, bogs and ancient forests made it a beautiful and sought-after place to visit. Generations of the same families had been invited to the same annual events and parties. To be excluded from the guest list would have resulted in the most inconsolable outrage.

"And just think," Natalie had mused on the long carriage ride from London. "If I marry Lord Westcliff's brother-in-law, I will be able to visit Stony Cross Park any time I wish!"

"All for the price of having Mr. Bowman as your husband," Hannah said dryly. Although she had not told Lord and Lady Blandford about the stolen kiss, she had made it clear that she did not believe Bowman would be a suitable partner for Natalie. The Blandfords, however, had counseled her to reserve judgment until they all became better acquainted with him.

Lady Blandford, as blond and lovely and ebullient as her

daughter, caught her breath as Stony Cross Manor loomed in the distance. The house was European in design, built of honey-colored stone with four graceful towers so tall they seemed about to pierce holes in the early evening sky, which was washed with an orange and lavender sunset.

Set on a bluff by the Itchen River, Stony Cross Manor was fantastically landscaped with gardens and orchards, riding courses, and magnificent walking paths that led through massive tracts of forest and parkland. Owing to Hampshire's felicitous southern location, the climate was milder than the rest of England.

"Oh, Natalie," Lady Blandford exclaimed, "to think of being affiliated with such a family! And as a Bowman, you could have your own country manor, and a London house, and a villa on the Continent, not to mention your own carriage and team of four, and the most beautiful gowns and jewels . . ."

"Heavens, are the Bowmans *that* rich?" Natalie asked with a touch of surprise. "And will Mr. Bowman inherit the majority of the family business?"

"A handsome portion of it, to be sure," Lord Blandford replied, smiling at his daughter's bright-eyed interest. "He has his own wealth, and the promise of much more to come. Mr. Bowman the elder has indicated that upon your betrothal to his son, there will be rich rewards for both of you."

"I should think so," Natalie said pragmatically, "since it would be a comedown for me to marry a commoner when I could just as easily have a peer." There was no disparagement or arrogance intended in her statement. It was a fact that some doors would be open to a peer's wife that would never be open to the wife of an American manufacturer.

As the carriage stopped before the manor entrance, Hannah noticed that the estate was laid out in the French manner, with the stables located at the front of the house instead of being concealed to the side or behind it. The stables were housed in a building with huge arched doorways, forming one side of a stone-flagged entrance courtyard.

Footmen helped them from the carriage, and Westcliff's stablemen came to help with the horses. More servants hurried to collect the trunks and valises. An elderly butler admitted them into the massive entrance hall, where regiments were going back and forth: housemaids with baskets of linens, footmen with crates and boxes, and others engaged in cleaning, polishing, and sweeping.

"Lord and Lady Blandford!" Lillian came to them, looking radiant in a dark red gown, her sable hair neatly confined in a snood made of jeweled netting. With her brilliant smile and relaxed friendliness, she was so engaging that Hannah understood why the famously dignified earl of Westcliff had married her. Lillian bowed to them, and they responded in kind.

"Welcome to Stony Cross Park," Lillian said. "I hope your journey was comfortable? Please excuse the clamor and bustle, we're desperately trying to prepare for the hordes of guests who will pour in tomorrow. After you refresh yourselves, you must come to the main parlor. My parents are there, and of course my brother, and—" She broke off as she saw Natalie. "My dear Lady Natalie." Her voice softened. "I have so looked forward to meeting you. We will do everything possible to make certain you have a lovely holiday."

"Thank you, my lady," Natalie replied demurely. "I have no doubt it will be splendid." She smiled at Lillian. "My companion told me there will be a Christmas tree."

"Fourteen feet high," Lillian said enthusiastically. "We're having a devil of a . . . that is, a most difficult time decorating it, as the top branches are impossible to reach. But we have extending ladders and many tall footmen, so we will prevail." She turned to Hannah. "Miss Appleton. A pleasure to see you again."

"Thank you, my—" Hannah paused as she realized that

Lillian had extended her hand. Bemusedly Hannah reached out to take it, and gave her a quizzical glance.

The countess winked at her, and Hannah realized she was being teased. She burst out laughing at the private joke, and returned the warm pressure of Lillian's fingers.

"In light of your remarkable tolerance for the Bowmans," Lillian told her, "you must come to the parlor too."

"Yes, my lady."

The housekeeper came to show them to their rooms, leading them across what seemed to be miles of flooring.

"Hannah, why did Lady Westcliff shake your hand?" Natalie whispered. "And why did you both seem to find it so amusing?"

NATALIE AND HANNAH WERE TO SHARE A ROOM, WITH Natalie occupying the main bed and Hannah sleeping in a cozy antechamber. The room was beautifully appointed with flowered paper on the walls and mahogany furniture, and a bed with a lace canopy.

While Natalie washed her hands and face, Hannah found a clean day dress for her and shook it out. The dress was a becoming shade of blue, with a dropped shoulder line filled in with lace, and long slim-fitting sleeves. Smiling in anticipation of meeting the Bowmans, Natalie sat before the vanity mirror while Hannah brushed and repinned her coiffure. After making certain that Natalie's appearance was perfect, her nose lightly dusted with powder, her lips smoothed with rosewater salve, Hannah went to her own valise and began to rummage through it.

Lady Blandford appeared in the doorway, looking refreshed and poised. "Come, girls," she said serenely. "It is time for us to join the company downstairs."

"A few more minutes, Mama," Natalie said. "Hannah hasn't yet changed her dress or tidied her hair."

"We mustn't keep everyone waiting," Lady Blandford insisted. "Come as you are, Hannah. No one will notice."

"Yes, ma'am," Hannah said obediently, concealing a pang of dismay. Her traveling clothes were dusty, and her hair was threatening to fall from its pins. She did not want to face the Bowmans and the Westcliffs in this condition. "I would prefer to stay up here and help the maids to unpack the trunks—"

"No," Lady Blandford said with an impatient sigh. "Ordinarily I would agree, but the countess requested your presence. You must come as you are, Hannah, and try to be unassuming."

"Yes, ma'am." Hannah pushed the straggles of loose hair back from her face and dashed to the washstand to splash her face. Water spots made little dark patches on her traveling gown. Groaning inwardly, she followed Natalie and Lady Blandford from the room.

"I'm sorry," Natalie whispered to her, frowning. "We shouldn't have taken so much time getting *me* ready."

"Nonsense," Hannah murmured, reaching out to pat her arm. "You're the one everyone wants to see. Lady Blandford is right—no one will notice me."

The house was beautifully ornamented, the windows swathed in gold silk edged with dangling gold tinsel balls, the doorways surmounted by swags of beribboned evergreens and holly and ivy. Tables were loaded with candles and arrangements of everlasting flowers such as chrysanthemums and Christmas roses and camellias. And someone, slyly, had adorned several doorways with kissing balls hung with evergreen ropes.

Glancing at the bunches of mistletoe, Hannah felt a stab of nervousness as she thought of Rafe Bowman. *Calm yourself,* she thought with a self-deprecating grin, glancing down at her disheveled dress. *He certainly won't try to kiss you now, not even beneath a cartload of mistletoe.*

They entered the main parlor, a large and comfortably furnished room with a game table, and piles of books and periodicals, a pianoforte, a standing sewing hoop, and a small secretary desk.

The first person Hannah noticed was Marcus, Lord Westcliff, a man with an imposing and powerful presence that was unusual for a man still only in his thirties. As he stood to meet them, Hannah saw that the earl was only of medium height, but he was superbly fit and self-assured. Westcliff carried himself with the ease of a man who was entirely comfortable with his own authority.

While Lillian made the introductions, Hannah shrank back into the corner of the room, observing the scene. She stared discreetly at the Bowmans as they met the Blandfords.

Thomas Bowman was stout, short, and ruddy, his mouth overhung with a large walruslike mustache. And his shining head was adorned with a toupee that seemed ready to jump off his scalp and flee the room.

His wife Mercedes, on the other hand, was whippet-thin and brittle, with hard eyes and a smile that fractured her face like cracks in a frozen pond. The only thing the pair seemed to have in common was a sense of dissatisfaction with life and each other, as if it were a blanket they both huddled under.

The Bowman children resembled each other far more than either parent, both of them tall and irreverent and relaxed. It seemed they had been formed by some magical combination of just the right features from both parents.

Hannah watched covertly as Lillian introduced Rafe Bowman to Natalie. She could not see Natalie's expression, but she had an excellent view of Bowman. His strapping form was clad in a perfectly fitted dark coat, and gray trousers, and a crisp white shirt with a neatly knotted black cravat. He bowed to Natalie and murmured something that elicited a breathless laugh. There was no denying it—with his unvarnished masculinity and bold dark eyes, Rafe Bowman was, to put it in a popular slang term, a stunner.

Hannah wondered what he thought of her cousin. Bowman's face was unreadable, but she was certain that he could find no fault with Natalie.

As everyone in the room made small talk, Hannah inched toward the door. If at all possible, she was going to slip from the room unnoticed. The open threshold beckoned invitingly, promising freedom. Oh, it would be lovely to escape to her room, and change into clean clothes and brush out her hair in privacy. But just as she reached the doorway, she heard Rafe Bowman's deep voice.

"Miss Appleton. Surely you won't deprive us of your charming company."

Hannah stopped abruptly and turned to find the collective gaze on her, just at the moment she least wanted attention. She longed to glare at Bowman. No, she longed to *kill* him. Instead, she adopted a neutral expression and murmured, "Good afternoon, Mr. Bowman."

Lillian called to her immediately. "Miss Appleton, do come forward. I want to introduce you to my husband."

Repressing a heavy sigh, Hannah pushed back the locks that dangled over her face and came forward.

"Westcliff," Lillian said to her husband. "This is Lady Natalie's companion, Miss Hannah Appleton."

Hannah bowed and glanced apprehensively at the earl. His features were dark and austere, perhaps a bit forbidding. But as his gaze rested on her face, she saw that his eyes were kind. He spoke in a gravel-in-velvet voice that fell pleasantly on her ears. "Welcome, Miss Appleton."

"Thank you, my lord," she said. "And many thanks for allowing me to spend the holiday here."

"The countess enjoyed your company at tea last week," Westcliff replied, smiling briefly at Lillian. "Anyone who pleases her also pleases me." The smile transformed him, warming his face.

Lillian spoke to her husband with breezy casualness, as if he were a mere mortal man instead of England's most distinguished peer. "Westcliff, I think you will want to talk to Miss Appleton about her work with Mr. Samuel Clark." She glanced at Hannah as she added, "The earl has read some of his writings, and quite enjoyed them."

"Oh, I do not work *with* Mr. Clark," Hannah said hastily, "but rather *for* him, in a secretarial capacity." She gave the earl a cautious smile. "I am a bit surprised that you would have read anything by Mr. Clark, my lord."

"I am acquainted with many progressive theorists of London," Westcliff said. "What is Mr. Clark working on now?"

"Currently he is writing a speculative book on what natural laws might govern the development of the human mind."

"I would like to hear more about that during supper."

"Yes, my lord."

Lillian proceeded to introduce Hannah to her parents, who responded with pleasant nods. It was clear, however, that they had already dismissed Hannah as a person of no consequence.

"Rafe," the countess suggested to her brother, "perhaps you might take Lady Blandford and Lady Natalie on a walk round the house before supper."

"Oh, yes," Natalie said at once. "May we, Mama?"

"That sounds lovely," Lady Blandford said.

Bowman smiled at them both. "It would be my pleasure." He turned to Hannah. "Will you come also, Miss Appleton?"

"No," she said quickly, and then realized her refusal had

been a shade too forceful. She softened her tone. "I will tour the manor later, thank you."

His gaze swept over her and returned to her face. "My services may not be available then."

She stiffened at the feather-soft jeer in his voice, but she couldn't seem to break their shared gaze. In the warm parlor light, his eyes held glints of gold and cinnamon-brown. "Then somehow I will have to make do without you, Mr. Bowman," she replied tartly, and he grinned.

"You didn't tell me that Mr. Bowman was so handsome," Natalie said after supper. The hour was late, and the long journey from London, followed by a lengthy repast, had left both girls exhausted. They had retired to their room while the company downstairs lingered over tea and port.

Although the menu had been exquisite, featuring dishes such as roasted capon stuffed with truffles, and herb-crusted standing ribs of beef, supper had been an uncomfortable affair for Hannah. She was well aware of her own disheveled appearance, having found barely enough time to wash and change into a fresh gown before she'd had to dash to the dining hall. To her dismay, Lord Westcliff had persisted in asking her questions about Samuel Clark's work, which had drawn more unwanted attention to her. And all the while Rafe Bowman had kept glancing at her with a kind of audacious, unsettling interest that she could only interpret as mockery.

Forcing her thoughts back to the present, Hannah watched as Natalie sat before the vanity and pulled the combs and pins from her hair. "I suppose Mr. Bowman could be considered attractive," Hannah said reluctantly. "If one likes that sort of man."

"You mean the tall, dark-haired, dazzling sort?"

"He's not *dazzling,*" Hannah protested.

Natalie laughed. "Mr. Bowman is one of the most splendidly formed men I have ever encountered. What flaw could you possibly find in his appearance?"

"His posture," Hannah muttered.

"What about it?"

"He slouches."

"He's an American. They all slouch. The weight of their wallets drags them over."

Hannah couldn't prevent a laugh. "Natalie, are you more attracted by the man himself or the size of his wallet?"

"He has many personal attractions, to be sure. A full head of hair . . . those lovely dark eyes . . . not to mention the impressive physique." Natalie picked up a brush and drew it slowly through her hair. "But I wouldn't want him if he was poor."

"Is there any man you would want if he was poor?" Hannah asked.

"Well, if I *had* to be poor, I'd rather be married to a peer. That's far better than being a nobody."

"I doubt Mr. Bowman will ever be poor," Hannah said. "He seems to have acquitted himself quite well in his financial dealings. He is a successful man, though I fear not an honorable one."

"Oh, he's a rascal, to be sure," Natalie agreed with a light laugh.

Tensing, Hannah met her cousin's gaze in the mirror. "Why do you say that? Has he said or done anything inappropriate?"

"No, and I don't expect him to, with the betrothal still on the table. But he has a sort of perpetual irreverence . . . one wonders if he could ever be sincere about anything at all."

"Perhaps it's a façade," Hannah suggested without conviction. "Perhaps he's a different man inside."

"Most people don't have façades," Natalie said dryly. "Oh,

everyone thinks they do, but when you dig past the façade, there's only more façade."

"Some people are genuine."

"And *those* people are the dullest ones of all."

"*I'm* genuine," Hannah protested.

"Yes. You'll have to work on that, dear. When you're genuine, there's no mystery. And above all men like mystery in a woman."

Hannah smiled and shook her head. "Duly noted. I'm off to bed now." After changing into a white ruffled nightgown, she went into the little antechamber and crawled into the clean soft bed. After a moment, she heard Natalie murmur, "Good night, dear," and the lamp was extinguished.

Tucking one arm beneath her pillow, Hannah lay on her side and pondered Natalie's words.

There was no doubt that Natalie was right—Hannah had nothing close to an air of mystery.

She also had no noble blood, no dowry, no great beauty, no skill or abilities that might distinguish her. And aside from the Blandfords, she had no notable connections. But she had a warm heart and a good mind, and decent looks. And she had dreams, attainable ones, of having a home and family of her own someday.

It had not escaped Hannah that in Natalie's privileged world, people expected to find happiness and love outside of marriage. But her fondest wish for Natalie was that she would end up with a husband with whom she could share some likeness of mind and heart.

And at this point, it was still highly questionable as to whether Rafe Bowman even had a heart.

Chapter Six

While Westcliff shared cigars with Lord Blandford, Rafe went with his father to have a private conversation. They proceeded to the library, a large and handsome room that was two stories high, with mahogany bookshelves housing over ten thousand volumes. A sideboard had been built into a niche to make it flush with the bookshelves.

Rafe was thankful to see that a collection of bottles and decanters had been arranged on the sideboard's marble top. Feeling the need for something stronger than port, he found the whisky decanter. "A double?" he suggested to his father, who nodded and grunted in assent.

Rafe had always hated talking with his father. Thomas Bowman was the kind of man who determined other people's minds for them, believing that he knew them better than they knew themselves. Since early childhood Rafe had endured being told what his thoughts and motivations were, and then being punished for them. It hardly seemed to matter whether he had done something good or bad. It had only mattered what light his father had decided to cast his actions in.

And always, Thomas had held the threat of disinheritance

over his head. Finally Rafe had told him to cut him off entirely and be damned. And he had gone out to make his own fortune, starting with practically nothing.

Now when he met with his father, it was on his own terms. Oh, Rafe wanted the European proprietorship of Bowman's, but he wasn't going to sell his soul for it.

He handed a whisky to his father and took a swallow, letting the creamy, sweet flavor of ester roll over his tongue.

Thomas went to sit in a leather chair before the fire. Frowning, he reached up to check the position of the toupee on his head. It had been slipping all evening.

"You might tie a chin strap on it," Rafe suggested innocently, earning a ferocious scowl.

"Your mother finds it attractive."

"Father, I find it difficult to believe that hairpiece would attract anything other than an amorous squirrel." Rafe plucked the toupee off and dropped it onto a nearby table. "Leave it off and be comfortable, for God's sake."

Thomas grumbled but didn't argue, relaxing in his chair.

Leaning an arm against the mantel, Rafe regarded his father with a faint smile.

"Well?" Thomas demanded, his heavy brows lifting expectantly. "What is your reaction to Lady Natalie?"

Rafe hitched up his shoulders in a lazy shrug. "She'll do."

The brows rushed downward. "'She'll do'? That's all you can say?"

"Lady Natalie is no more and no less than what I expected." After taking another swallow of whisky, Rafe said flatly, "I suppose I wouldn't mind marrying her. Although she doesn't interest me in the least."

"A wife is not supposed to be interesting."

Ruefully Rafe wondered if there wasn't some hidden wisdom in that. With a wife like Lady Natalie, there would be no surprises. It would be a calm, frictionless marriage, leaving him ample time for his work and his personal pursuits. All he would have to do would be to supply her with generous bank drafts, and she would manage the household and produce children.

Lady Natalie was pleasant and beautiful, her hair blond and sleek, her manner remarkably self-assured. If Rafe ever took her to New York, she would acquit herself splendidly with the Knickerbocker crowd. Her poise, breeding, and confidence would make her much admired.

An hour in her company, and one knew virtually everything there was to know about her.

Whereas Hannah Appleton was fresh and fascinating, and at supper he hadn't been able to take his gaze off her. She did not possess Natalie's meticulously manicured beauty. Instead, there was a haphazard, cheerful bloom about her, like a fistful of wildflowers. Her hair, springing in little locks around her face, drove him mad with the urge to reach out and play with the shiny loose strands. She had a kind of delicious vitality he had never run up against before, and he instinctively wanted to be inside it, inside her.

The feeling had intensified as Rafe had witnessed Hannah conversing earnestly with Westcliff. She had been animated and adorable as she had described Samuel Clark's work concerning the development of the human mind. In fact, she had become so absorbed in the subject that she had forgotten to eat, and then she'd glanced wistfully at her still-full soup bowl while a footman had removed it.

"You will offer for her, won't you?" his father demanded, steering his thoughts back to Lady Natalie.

Rafe stared at him without expression. "Eventually. Am I supposed to get a ring, or have you already picked one out?"

"As a matter of fact, your mother purchased one she thought would be appropriate—"

"Oh, for God's sake. Would you like to propose to her for me, and come fetch me when she's given her answer?"

"I daresay I'd do it with a damned sight more enthusiasm than you," Thomas retorted.

"I'll tell you what I would do with some enthusiasm, Father: establish a large-scale soap manufacturing industry all over the Continent. And I shouldn't have to marry Lady Natalie to do it."

"Why not? Why should you be exempt from paying a price? Why shouldn't you try to please me?"

"Why indeed?" Rafe gave him a hard look. "Maybe because I knocked my head against that particular wall for years and never made a dent."

Thomas's complexion, always prone to easy color, turned a dull plum hue as his temper ignited. "You have been a trial to me at every stage of your life. Things always came too easily to you and your siblings—spoiled, lazy creatures all of you, who never wanted to do anything."

"Lazy?" Rafe struggled for self-control, but the word set his own temper off like a match held to a tinderbox. "Only you, Father, could have five offspring do everything short of standing on their heads to impress you, and say they weren't trying hard enough. Do you know what happens when you call a clever person stupid, or a hardworking man lazy? It makes him realize there's no damn point in trying to get your approval."

"You've always thought I owed you my approval merely because you were born a Bowman."

"I don't want it any longer," Rafe said through gritted teeth, vaguely surprised to discover that the velocity of his own temper wasn't far behind his father's. "I want—" He checked himself and tossed back the rest of his whisky, swallowing hard against the velvety burn. When the glow had faded from his throat, he gave his father a cool, steady look. "I'll marry Lady Natalie, since it doesn't matter in any case. I was always going to end up with someone like her. But you can keep your damned approval. All I want is a share of Bowman's."

IN THE MORNING THE GUESTS BEGAN TO ARRIVE, AN ELEGANT clamor of well-heeled families and their servants. Trunks, valises, and parcels were brought into the manor in an un-ending parade. Other families would stay at neighboring estates or at the tavern in the village, coming and going to the various events that would take place at the manor.

Once Hannah was awakened by the muffled, busy sounds beyond the room, she couldn't go back to sleep. Taking care not to wake Natalie, she rose and took care of her morning ablutions, finishing by braiding her hair and pinning it in a knot at the base of her neck. She dressed in a gray-green wool gown trimmed with kilt pleating and closed in front with gleaming black buttons. Intending to go for a walk out of doors, she donned a pair of low-heeled boots and picked up a heavy plaid shawl.

Stony Cross Manor was a labyrinth of hallways and clustered rooms. Carefully Hannah made her way through the bustling house, pausing now and again to ask directions from one of the passing servants. She eventually found the morning room, which was stuffy and crowded with people she didn't know. A large breakfast buffet had been set out, featuring fish, a flitch of fried bacon, breads, poached eggs, salads, muffins, and several varieties of cheese. She poured a cup of tea, folded a bit of bacon in some bread, and slipped past a set of French doors that led to an outside terrace. The weather was bright and dry, the chilled air fomenting her breath into white mist.

Gardens and orchards spread before her, all delicately frosted and clean. Children played across the terrace, giggling as they raced back and forth. Hannah chuckled, watching them stream across the flagstones like a gaggle of goslings. They were playing a game of blow-the-feather, which involved two teams trying to keep a feather aloft by turns.

Standing to the side, Hannah consumed her bread and tea. The children's antics grew ever wilder as they hopped and blew at the feather in noisy gusts and puffs. The feather drifted to her, descending lazily.

The little girls screamed in encouragement. "Blow, miss, blow! It's girls against boys!"

After that, there was no choice. Fighting a smile, Hannah pursed her lips and exhaled sharply, sending the feather upward in a fluttering eddy. She did her part whenever the feather drifted to her, running a few steps here and there, heeding the delighted cries of her teammates.

The feather sailed over her head, and she backed up swiftly, her face upturned. But she was startled to feel herself crashing against something behind her, not a stone wall but something hard and pliant. A man's hands closed around her arms, securing her balance.

From over her head, the man blew a puff that sent the feather halfway across the terrace.

Hooting and squealing, the children raced after it.

Hannah remained still, stunned by the collision, but even more so by the realization that she recognized the feel of Rafe Bowman. The grip of his hands, the tough-muscled length of him along her back. The clean, pungent spice of his shaving soap.

Her mouth had gone dry—probably the effects of the feather game—and she tried to moisten her inner cheeks with her tongue. "What a remarkable amount of air you are able to produce, Mr. Bowman."

Smiling, he turned her carefully to face him. He was large and dashing, standing with that relaxed looseness that bothered her so. "Good morning to you, too." He looked her over with an insolently thorough glance. "Why aren't you still abed?"

"I'm an early riser." Hannah decided to throw the audacious inquiry right back at him. "Why aren't you?"

A playful glint shone in his eyes. "There's no point in lingering in bed when I'm alone."

She glanced at their surroundings to make certain none of the children could overhear. The imps had tired of their game and were filing inside the house through doors that led to the main hall. "I suspect that is a rare occurrence, Mr. Bowman."

His bland tone disguised all sincerity. "Rare, yes. Most of the time my bed is busier than a sheepfold at spring shearing."

Hannah viewed him with patent distaste. "That doesn't speak well of the women you associate with. Or of you for being so indiscriminate."

"I'm not indiscriminate. It just so happens that I'm good at finding women who meet my high standards. And I'm even better at persuading them to come to my bed."

"And then you fleece them."

A rueful smile crossed his lips. "If you don't mind, Miss Appleton, I want to retract my sheep analogy. It's becoming disagreeable even to me. Would you like to take a morning stroll?"

She shook her head in puzzlement. "With you? . . . Why?"

"You're wearing a walking dress and boots. And I assume you want to find out what my opinion of Lady Natalie is. Keep your enemy close, and so forth."

"I already know what your opinion of Lady Natalie is."

His brows lifted. "Do you? Now I insist that we walk together. I'm always fascinated to hear my opinions."

Hannah considered him sternly. "Very well," she said. "First I'll take the teacup in, and—"

"Leave it."

"On an outside table? No, someone will have to tidy up."

"Yes. That someone is called a servant. Who, unlike you, will get a salary for it."

"That doesn't mean I should make more work for someone else."

Before she could retrieve the cup, Bowman had taken it up. "I'll take care of it."

Hannah's eyes widened as she saw him stroll nonchalantly to the stone balustrade. And she gasped as he held the teacup over the side and dropped it. A splintering crash sounded from below.

"There," he said casually. "Problem solved."

It required three attempts until Hannah could finally speak. "Why did you do that? I could easily have carried it inside!"

He seemed amused by her astonishment. "I would have thought my lack of concern for material possessions would please you."

Hannah stared at him as if he had just sprouted horns. "I wouldn't call that a lack of concern for material possessions, but rather a lack of respect for them. And that's every bit as bad as overvaluing them."

Bowman's smile faded as he comprehended the extent of her ire. "Miss Appleton, Stony Cross Manor has at least ten different sets of china, each one with enough teacups to help caffeinate all of Hampshire. They're not lacking for cups here."

"That makes no difference. You shouldn't have broken it."

Bowman gave a sardonic snort. "Have you always had such a passion for porcelain, Miss Appleton?"

Without a doubt, he was the most insufferable man she had ever encountered. "I'm sure you'll consider it a failing that I'm not amused by wanton destruction."

"And I'm sure," he returned smoothly, "that you'll use this as an excuse to avoid walking with me."

Hannah contemplated him for a moment. She knew that he was annoyed with her for placing such importance on the loss of a small item of china that would make no difference in the scheme of things. But it had been the boorish gesture of a rich man, deliberately destroying something for no reason.

Bowman was right—Hannah was indeed strongly tempted to cancel the proposed walk. On the other hand, the cool defiance in his eyes actually touched her. He had looked, for just a moment, like a recalcitrant schoolboy who'd been caught in an act of mischief and was now awaiting punishment.

"Not at all," she told him. "I am still willing to walk with you. But I wish you would refrain from smashing anything else along the way."

She had the satisfaction of seeing that she had surprised him. Something softened in his face, and he looked at her with a kindling interest that caused a mysterious quickening inside her.

"No more smashing things," he promised.

"Well, then." She pulled up the hood of her short cloak and headed to the stairs that led to the terraced gardens.

In a few long strides Bowman had caught up with her. "Take my arm," he advised. "The steps might be slippery."

Hannah hesitated before complying, her bare hand slipping over his sleeve and coming to rest lightly on the bed of muscle beneath. In her efforts to keep from waking Natalie earlier, she had forgotten to fetch her gloves.

"Would Lady Natalie have been upset?" Bowman asked.

"About the broken teacup?" Hannah considered that for a moment. "I don't think so. She probably would have laughed, to flatter you."

He sent her a sideways smile. "There's nothing wrong with flattering me, Miss Appleton. It makes me quite happy and manageable."

"I have no desire to manage you, Mr. Bowman. I'm not at all certain you're worth the effort."

His smile vanished and his jaw tautened, as if she had touched an unpleasant nerve. "We'll leave it to Lady Natalie, then."

They crossed an opening in an ancient yew hedge and began along a graveled path. The carefully trimmed bushes and mounded vegetation resembled giant iced cakes. High-pitched calls of nuthatches floated from the nearby woodland. A hen harrier skimmed close to the ground, its wings tensed in a wide V as it searched for prey.

Although it was rather pleasant to hold on to Bowman's strong, steady arm, Hannah reluctantly withdrew her hand.

"Now," Bowman said quietly, "tell me what you assume my opinion of Lady Natalie is."

"I've no doubt you like her. I think you're willing to marry her because she suits your needs. It is obvious that she will smooth your path in society and bear you fair-haired children, and she'll be sufficiently well bred to look the other way when you stray from her."

"Why are you so certain I'll stray?" Bowman asked, sounding curious rather than indignant.

"Everything I've seen of you so far confirms that you are not capable of fidelity."

"I might be, if I found the right woman."

"No you wouldn't," she said with crisp certainty. "Whether or not you're faithful has nothing to do with the woman. It depends entirely upon your own character."

"My God, you're opinionated. You must terrify nearly every man you meet."

"I don't meet many men."

"That explains it, then."

"Explains what?"

"Why you've never been kissed before."

Hannah stopped in her tracks and whirled to face him. "Why do you . . . how did you . . ."

"The more experience a man has," he said, "the more easily he can detect the lack of it in someone else."

They had reached a little clearing. In the center of it stood a mermaid fountain, surrounded by a circle of low stone benches. Hannah climbed onto one of the benches and walked its length slowly, and hopped over the little space to the next bench.

Bowman followed at once, walking beside the benches as she made a circle around them. "So your Mr. Clark has never made an advance to you?"

Hannah shook her head, hoping he would ascribe her rising color to the cold temperature. "He's not my Mr. Clark. As for making an advance . . . I'm not altogether certain. One time he . . ." Realizing what she had been about to confess, she closed her mouth with a snap.

"Oh, no. You can't leave *that* dangling out there. Tell me what you were going to say." Bowman's fingers slipped beneath the fabric belt of her dress and he tugged firmly, forcing her to stop.

"Don't," she said breathlessly, scowling from her superior vantage on the bench.

Bowman put his hands at her waist and swung her to the ground. He kept her standing before him, his hands lightly gripping her sides. "What did he do? Say something lewd? Try to look down your bodice?"

"Mr. Bowman," she protested with a helpless scowl. "Approximately a month ago, Mr. Clark was studying a book of phrenology, and he asked if he could feel my . . ."

Bowman had gone still, the spice-colored eyes widening ever so slightly. "Your what?"

"My cranium." Seeing his blank expression, Hannah went on to explain. "Phrenology is the science of analyzing the shape of someone's skull and—"

"Yes, I know. Every measurement and indentation is supposed to mean something."

"Yes. So I allowed him to evaluate my head and make a chart of any shapings that would reveal my character traits."

Bowman seemed vastly entertained. "And what did Clark discover?"

"It seems I have a large brain, an affectionate and constant nature, a tendency to leap to judgment, and a capacity for strong attachment. Unfortunately there is also a slight narrowing at the back of my skull that indicates criminal propensities."

He laughed in delight. "I should have guessed. It's always the innocent-looking ones who are capable of the worst. Here, let me feel it. I want to know how a criminal mind is shaped."

Hannah ducked away quickly as he reached for her. "Don't touch me!"

"You've already let one man fondle your cranium," he said, following as she backed away. "Now it makes no difference if you let someone else do it."

He was playing with her, Hannah realized. Although it was altogether improper, she felt a giggle work up through the layers of caution and anxiety. "Examine your own head," she cried, fleeing to the other side of the fountain. "I'm sure there are any number of criminal lumps on it."

"The results would be skewed," he told her. "I received too many raps on the head during my childhood. My father told my tutors it was good for me."

Though the words were spoken lightly, Hannah stopped and regarded him with a flicker of compassion. "Poor boy."

Bowman came to a stop in front of her again. "Not at all. I deserved it. I've been wicked since birth."

"No child is wicked without a reason."

"Oh, I had a reason. Since I had no hope of ever becoming the paragon my parents expected, I decided to go the other way. I'm sure it was only my mother's intervention that kept my father from tying me to a tree beside the road with a note reading 'Take to orphanage.'"

Hannah smiled slightly. "Is there any offspring your father *is* pleased with?"

"Not especially. But he sets store by my brother-in-law Matthew Swift. Even before he married Daisy, Swift had become like a son to my father. He worked for him in New York. An unusually patient man, our Mr. Swift. Otherwise he couldn't have survived this long."

"Your father has a temper?"

"My father is the kind of man who would lure a dog with a bone, and when the dog is in reach, beat him with it. And then throw a tantrum if the dog doesn't hurry back to him the next time."

He offered Hannah his arm again, and she took it as they headed back toward the manor.

"Did your father arrange the marriage between your sister and Mr. Swift?" she asked.

"Yes. But somehow it seems to have turned into a love match."

"That happens sometimes," she said wisely.

"Only because some people, when faced with the inevitable, convince themselves they like it merely to make the situation palatable."

Hannah made a soft *tsk tsk* with her tongue. "You're a cynic, Mr. Bowman."

"A realist."

She gave him a curious glance. "Do you think you might ever fall in love with Natalie?"

"I could probably come to care for her," he said casually.

"I mean real love, the kind that makes you feel wildness, joy, and despair all at once. Love that would inspire you to make any kind of sacrifice for someone else's sake."

A sardonic smile curved his lips. "Why would I want to feel that way about my wife? It would ruin a perfectly good marriage."

They walked through the winter garden in silence, while Hannah struggled with the certainty that he was even more dangerous, more wrong for Natalie, than she had originally believed. Natalie would eventually be hurt and disillusioned by a husband she could never trust.

"You are not suitable for Natalie," she heard herself say wretchedly. "The more I learn about you, the more certain I am of that fact. I wish you would leave her alone. I wish you would find some other nobleman's daughter to prey upon."

Bowman stopped with her beside the hedge. "You arrogant little baggage," he said quietly. "The prey was not of my choosing. I'm merely trying to make the best of my circumstances. And if Lady Natalie will have me, it's not your place to object."

"My affection for her gives me the right to say something—"

"Maybe it's not affection. Are you certain you're not speaking out of jealousy?"

"Jealousy? Of Natalie? You're mad to suggest such a thing—"

"Oh, I don't know," he said with ruthless softness. "It's possible you're tired of standing in her shadow. Watching your cousin in all her finery, being admired and sought after while you stay at the side of the room with the dowagers and wallflowers."

Hannah sputtered in outrage, one of her fists clenching and rising as if to strike him.

Bowman caught her wrist easily, running a finger lightly over her whitened knuckles. His soft, mocking laugh scalded her ears. "Here," he said, forcibly crooking her thumb and tucking it across her fingers. "Don't ever try to hit someone with your thumb extended—you'll break it that way."

"Let go," she cried, yanking hard at her imprisoned wrist.

"You wouldn't be so angry if I hadn't struck a nerve," he taunted. "Poor Hannah, always standing in the corner, waiting for your turn. I'll tell you something—you're more than Natalie's equal, blue blood or no. You were meant for something far better than this—"

"Stop it!"

"A wife for convenience and a mistress for pleasure. Isn't that how the peerage does it?"

Hannah stiffened all over, gasping, as Bowman brought her against his large, powerful form. She stopped struggling, recognizing that such efforts were useless against his strength. Her face turned from him, and she jerked as she felt his warm mouth brush the curve of her ear.

"I should make you my mistress," Bowman whispered. "Beautiful Hannah. If you were mine, I'd lay you on silk sheets and wrap you up in ropes of pearls, and feed you honey from a silver spoon. Of course, you wouldn't be able to make all your high-minded judgments if you were a fallen woman . . . but you wouldn't care. Because I would pleasure you, Hannah, every night, all night, until you forgot your own name. Until you were willing to do things that would shock you in the light of day. I would debauch you from your head down to your innocent little toes—"

"Oh, I despise you," she cried, twisting helplessly against him. She had begun to feel real fear, not only from his hard grip and taunting words, but also from the shocks of heat running through her.

After this, she would never be able to face him again. Which was probably what he intended. A pleading sound came from her throat as she felt a delicately inquiring kiss in the hollow beneath her ear.

"You want me," he murmured. In a bewildering shift of mood he turned tender, letting his lips wander slowly along the side of her throat. "Admit it, Hannah—I appeal to your criminal tendencies. And you definitely bring out the worst in me." He drew his mouth over her neck, seeming to savor the swift, unsteady surges of her breathing. "Kiss me," he whispered. "Just once, and I'll let you go."

"You are a despicable lecher, and—"

"I know. I'm ashamed of myself." But he didn't sound at all ashamed. And his hold didn't loosen. "One kiss, Hannah."

She could feel her pulse reverberating everywhere, the blood rhythm settling hard and low in her throat and in all the deepest places of her body. And even in her lips, the delicate surface so sensitive that the touch of her own breath was excruciating.

It was cold everywhere they pressed, and in the space between their mouths where the smoke of their exhalations mingled. Hannah looked up into his shadowed face and thought dizzily, *Don't do it, Hannah, don't,* and then she ended up doing it anyway, rising on her toes to bring her trembling lips to his.

He closed around her, holding her with his arms and mouth, taking a long hungering taste. He pulled her even closer, until one of his feet came between hers, under her skirts, and her breasts urged tight and full against his chest. It was more than one kiss . . . it was a sentence of unbroken kisses, the hot sweet syllables of lips and tongue making her drunk on sensation. One of his hands moved up to her face, caressing with a softness that sent a fine-spun shiver across her shoulders and back. His fingertips explored the line of her jaw, the lobe of her ear, the color-scalded crest of her cheek.

The other hand came up, and her face was caught in the gentle bracket of his fingers, while his lips drifted over her face . . . a soft skim over her eyelids, a stroke over her nose, a last lingering bite of her mouth. She breathed in a gulp of sharp winter air, welcoming the snap of it in her lungs.

When she finally brought herself to look up at him, she expected him to look smug or arrogant. But to her surprise, his face was taut, and there was a brooding disquiet in his eyes.

"Do you want me to apologize?" he asked.

Hannah pulled back from him, rubbing her prickling arms through her sleeves. She was mortified by the intensity of her own urge to huddle against the warm, inviting hardness of him.

"I don't see the purpose in that," she said in a low voice. "It's not as if you would mean it." Turning from him, she walked back to the manor in hurried strides, praying silently that he wouldn't follow her.

And knowing that any woman foolish enough to become involved with him would fare no better than the shattered tea-cup on the terrace.

Chapter Seven

As Hannah went into the entrance hall, the warm air caused her cold cheeks to prickle. She kept to the back of the entrance hall, trying to avoid the crowd of newly arrived guests and servants. It was a prosperous, richly dressed group, the ladies glittering with finery and dressed in fur-trimmed cloaks and capes.

Natalie would be awake soon, and she usually began each day with a cup of tea in bed. With so much activity, Hannah was skeptical that they would be able to summon a housemaid. She considered going to the breakfast room to fetch a cup of tea for Natalie and bring it upstairs herself. And perhaps one for Lady Blandford—

"Miss Appleton." A vaguely familiar voice came from the crowd, and a gentleman came forward to greet her.

It was Edward, Lord Travers. Hannah had not expected him to come to Stony Cross Park for the holidays. She smiled warmly at him, the agitated pressure in her chest easing. Travers was a comfortably buttoned-up man, secure in himself and his place in the world, polite in every atom. He was so conservative in manner and appearance that it was almost surprising to see up close that his face was yet unlined and there was no gray in his close-trimmed brown hair. Travers was a strong man, an honorable one, and Hannah had always liked him tremendously.

"My lord, how pleasant it is to see you here."

He smiled. "And to find you all in a glow, as usual. I hope you are in good health? And the Blandfords and Lady Natalie?"

"Yes, we're all quite well. I don't believe Lady Natalie knew of your imminent arrival, or she would have mentioned it to me."

"No," Travers admitted, "I had not planned to come here. My relations in Shropshire were expecting me. But I'm afraid I prevailed on Lord Westcliff for an invitation to Hampshire." He paused, turning sober. "You see, I learned of Lord Blandford's plans concerning his daughter and . . . the American."

"Yes. Mr. Bowman."

"My desire is to see Lady Natalie happy and well situated," Travers said quietly. "I cannot conceive how Blandford could think this arrangement would be best for her."

Since she could not agree without criticizing her uncle, Hannah murmured carefully, "I also have concerns, my lord."

"Surely Lady Natalie has confided in you. What has she said on the matter? Does she like this American?"

"She is disposed to consider the match, to please Lord Blandford," Hannah admitted. "And also . . . Mr. Bowman is not without appeal." She paused and blinked as she saw Rafe Bowman at the far side of the entrance hall, talking with his father. "In fact, Mr. Bowman is standing over there."

"Is he the short, stout one?" Travers asked hopefully.

"No, my lord. That is Mr. Bowman the elder. His son, the tall one, is the gentleman to whom Lord Blandford wishes to betroth Lady Natalie."

In one glance, Travers saw everything he needed to know. Rafe Bowman was unreasonably good-looking, the power of his lean, striking form no less evident for his relaxed posture. His sable hair was thick and wind ruffled, his complexion infused with healthy color from the outside air. Those coal-dark eyes glanced around the room in cool appraisal, while a faint, ruthless smile curved his lips. He looked so predatory that it made the memory of his elusive gentleness all the more startling to Hannah.

For someone like Lord Travers, a rival such as Bowman was his worst nightmare.

"Oh, dear," Hannah heard him murmur softly.

"Yes."

EVIE CAME INTO THE BALLROOM CARRYING A HEAVY TWO-handled basket. "Here are the l-last of them," she said, having just come from the kitchen, where she and two scullery maids had been filling small paper cones with nuts and dried fruit, and tying them closed with red ribbons. "I hope this will be enough, considering it's such a l-large t—" She stopped and gave Annabelle a perplexed glance. "Where is Lillian?"

"Here," came Lillian's muffled voice from beneath the tree. "I'm arranging the tree skirt. Not that it matters, since one can hardly see it."

Annabelle smiled, standing on her toes to tie a little cloth doll on the highest branch she could reach. Dressed in winter white, with her honey-colored hair drawn up in curls and her cheeks pink from exertion, she looked like a Christmas angel. "Do you think we should have chosen such a tall tree, dear? I'm afraid it will take from now until Twelfth Night for us to finish decorating it."

"It had to be tall," Lillian replied, crawling out from beneath the tree. With a few pine needles stuck in her sable hair and shreds of cotton batting clinging to her dress, she didn't look at all like a countess. And from the wide grin on her face, one could tell that she didn't give a fig. "The room is so cavernous, it would look silly to have a short one."

Over the next fortnight several events would take place in the ballroom, including a dance, some games and amateur entertainments, and a grand Christmas Eve ball. Lillian was determined that the tree would be as splendid as possible, to add to the festive atmosphere. However, decorating it was turning out to be more difficult than Lillian had anticipated. The servants were so busy with the household work that none of them could be spared for extra duties. And since Westcliff had forbidden Lillian and her friends from climbing on ladders or high stools, the top half of the tree was, so far, completely bare.

To make matters worse, the new fashion in gowns featured a slim-fitting, dropped-shoulder sleeve that prevented a lady from reaching for anything higher than shoulder level. As Lillian emerged from beneath the tree, they all heard the sound of splitting fabric.

"Oh, bloody hell," Lillian exclaimed, twisting to view the gaping hole beneath her right sleeve. "That's the third dress I've torn this week."

"I don't like this new style of sleeve," Annabelle commented ruefully, flexing her own graceful arms in their limited range of motion. "It's quite vexing not to be able to reach upward. And it's uncomfortable to hold Isabella when the cloth pulls over my shoulder so."

"I'll find a n-needle and thread," Evie said, going to hunt in a box of supplies on the floor.

"No, bring the scissors," Lillian said decisively.

Smiling quizzically, Evie complied. "What shall I do with them?"

Lillian raised her arm as much as she was able. "Cut this side to match the other."

Without batting an eye, Evie carefully snipped a gap beneath the sleeve and a few inches along the seam, exposing a white flash of skin.

"Freedom at last!" Lillian raised both arms to the ceiling like some primitive sun worshipper, the fabric gaping at her armpits. "I wonder if I could start a new fashion?"

"Dresses with holes in them?" Annabelle asked. "I doubt it, dear."

"It's so lovely to be able to reach for things." Lillian took the scissors. "Do you want me to fix your dress too, Annabelle?"

"Don't come near me with those," Annabelle said firmly. She shook her head with a grin, watching as Evie solemnly held up her own arms for Lillian to cut holes beneath her sleeves. This was one of the things she most adored about Evie, who was shy and proper, but often willing to join in some wildly impractical plan or adventure. "Have you both lost your minds?" Annabelle asked, laughing. "Oh, what a bad influence she is on you, Evie."

"She's married to St. Vincent, who is the worst possible influence," Lillian protested. "How much damage could I do after that?" After flexing and swinging her arms, she rubbed her hands together. "Now, back to work. Where's the box of candles? . . . I'll wire more of them on this side."

"Shall we sing to pass the time?" Annabelle suggested, tying a little angel made of cotton batting and a lace handkerchief onto the tip of a branch.

The three of them moved around the tree like industrious bees, singing the "Twelve Days of Christmas." The song and the work progressed quite well until they came to the ninth day.

"I'm sure it's ladies dancing," Annabelle said.

"No, no, it's lords a-leaping," Lillian assured her.

"It's *ladies,* dear. Evie, don't you agree?"

Ever the peacemaker, Evie murmured, "It doesn't m-matter, surely. Let's just choose one and—"

"The lords are supposed to go between the ladies and the maids," Lillian insisted.

They began to argue, while Evie tried to suggest, in vain, that they should abandon that particular song and start on "God Rest Ye Merry Gentlemen" or "The First Noel."

They were so intent on the debate, in fact, that none of them were aware of anyone entering the room until they heard a laughing female voice.

"Lillian, you dunderhead, you always get that wrong. It's *ten* leaping lords."

"Daisy!" Lillian cried, and went in a mad rush to her younger sister. They were uncommonly close, having been constant companions since earliest memory. Whenever anything amusing, frightening, wonderful, or awful happened, Daisy had always been the first one Lillian had wanted to tell.

Daisy loved to read, having fueled her imagination with so many books that, were they laid end to end, would probably extend from one side of England to the other. She was charming, whimsical, fun-loving, but—and here was the odd thing about Daisy—she was also a solidly rational person, coming up with insights that were nearly always correct.

Not three months earlier Daisy had married Matthew Swift, who was undoubtedly Thomas Bowman's favorite person in the world. At first Lillian had been solidly against the match, knowing it had been conceived by their domineering father. She had feared that Daisy would be forced into a loveless marriage with an ambitious young man who would not value her. However, it had eventually become clear that Matthew truly loved Daisy. That had gone a long way toward softening Lillian's feelings about him. They had come to a truce, she and Matthew, in their shared affection for Daisy.

Throwing her arms around Daisy's slim, small form, Lillian hugged her tightly and drew back to view her. Daisy had never looked so well, her dark brown hair pinned up in intricate braids, her gingerbread-colored eyes glowing with happiness. "Now the holiday can finally begin," Lillian said with satisfaction, and looked up at Matthew Swift, who had come to stand beside them after greeting Annabelle and Evie. "Merry Christmas, Matthew."

"Merry Christmas, my lady," he replied, bending readily to kiss her proffered cheek. He was a tall, well-formed young man, his Irish heritage apparent in his coloring, fair skinned with black hair and sky-blue eyes. Matthew had the perfect nature for dealing with hot-tempered Bowmans, diplomatic and dependable with a ready sense of humor.

"Is it *really* ten ladies dancing?" Lillian asked him, and Swift grinned.

"My lady, I've never been able to remember any part of that song."

"You know," Annabelle said contemplatively, "I've always understood why the swans are swimming and the geese are a-laying. But why in heaven's name are the lords a-leaping?"

"They're chasing after the ladies," Swift said reasonably.

"Actually I believe the song was referring to Morris dancers, who used to entertain between courses at long medieval feasts," Daisy informed them.

"And it was a leaping sort of dance?" Lillian asked, intrigued.

"Yes, with longswords, after the manner of primitive fertility rites."

"A well-read woman is a dangerous creature," Swift commented with a grin, leaning down to press his lips against Daisy's dark hair.

Pleased by his obvious affection toward her sister, Lillian said feelingly, "Thank heaven you're here, Matthew. Father's been an absolute tyrant, and you're the only one who can calm him down. He and Rafe are at loggerheads, as usual. And from the way they glare at each other, I'm surprised they don't both burst into flames."

Swift frowned. "I'm going to talk to your father about this ridiculous matchmaking business."

"It does seem to be turning into an annual event," Daisy said. "After putting the two of us together last year, now he wants to force Rafe to marry someone. What does Mother say about it?"

"Very little," Lillian replied. "It's difficult to speak when one is salivating excessively. Mother would love above all else to have an aristocratic daughter-in-law to show off."

"What do we think of Lady Natalie?" Daisy asked.

"She's a very nice girl," Lillian said. "You'll like her, Daisy. But I could cheerfully murder Father for making marriage a condition of Rafe's involvement in Bowman's."

"He shouldn't have to marry anyone," Swift commented, a frown working across his brow. "We need someone to establish the new manufactories—and I don't know of anyone other than your brother who understands the business well enough to accomplish it. The devil knows I can't do it—I've got my hands full with Bristol."

"Yes, well, Father's made marrying Lady Natalie a nonnegotiable requirement," Lillian said with a scowl. "Mostly because Father lives for the chance to make any of his children do something they don't want to do, the interfering old—"

"If he'll listen to anyone," Daisy interrupted, "it's Matthew."

"I'll go look for him now," Matthew said. "I haven't yet seen him." He smiled at the group of former wallflowers and added only half in jest, "I worry about leaving the four of you together. You're not planning any mad schemes, are you?"

"Of course not!" Daisy gave him a little push toward the ballroom entrance. "I promise we'll be perfectly sedate. Go and find Father, and if he has burst into flames, please put him out quickly."

"Of course." But before he left, Matthew drew his wife aside and whispered, "Why do they have holes in their dresses?"

"I'm sure there's a perfectly reasonable explanation," she whispered back, and pressed a fleeting kiss on his jaw.

Returning to the others, Daisy hugged Evie and Annabelle. "I've brought loads of gifts for everyone," she said. "Bristol is a marvelous place for shopping. But it was rather difficult to find presents for the husbands. They all seem to have everything a man could want."

"Including wonderful wives," Annabelle said, smiling.

"Does Mr. Hunt have a toothpick case?" Daisy asked her. "I bought an engraved silver one for him. But if he already happens to own one, I do have alternate presents."

"I don't think he does," Annabelle said. "I'll ask him when he arrives."

"He didn't come down with you?"

Annabelle's smile turned wistful. "No, and I hate being parted from him. But the demand for locomotive production has become so great, Mr. Hunt is always buried in work. He is interviewing people to help carry the load, but in the meantime . . ." She sighed and shrugged helplessly. "I expect he'll come after the week's end, if he can free himself."

"What of St. Vincent?" Daisy asked Evie. "Is he here yet?"

Evie shook her head, the light sliding over her red hair and striking ruby glints. "His father is ill, and St. Vincent thought it necessary to visit him. Although the duke's doctors said his condition wasn't serious, at his age one never knows. St. Vincent plans to stay with him at least three or four days, and then come directly to Hampshire." Although she tried to sound matter-of-fact, there was a shadow of melancholy in her voice. Of all the former wallflowers and their mates, Evie's connection with St. Vincent had been the least likely, and the most difficult to fathom. They were not publicly demonstrative, but one had the sense that their private life was intimate beyond ordinary measures.

"Oh, who needs husbands?" Annabelle said brightly, sliding an arm around Evie's shoulders. "Clearly we have more than enough to keep us *very* busy until they arrive."

Chapter Eight

It was Hannah's particular torture to have been cast as chaperone, and therefore be forced to sit beside Natalie during the musical soirée that evening, while Rafe Bowman took Natalie's other side. The entwined harmonies of two sopranos, a baritone, and a tenor were accompanied by piano, flute, and violins. Many of the older children had been allowed to sit in rows at the back of the room. Dressed in their best clothes, the children sat straight and did their best not to fidget, whisper, or wiggle.

Hannah thought wryly that the children were behaving far better than their parents. There was a great deal of gossiping going on among the adults, especially in the lulls between each musical presentation.

She observed that Rafe Bowman was treating Natalie with impeccable courtesy. They seemed charmed by each other. They discussed the differences between New York and London, discovered they had similar tastes in books and music, and they both passionately loved riding. Bowman's manner with Natalie was so engaging that if Hannah had never encountered him before, she would have said he was the perfect gentleman.

But she knew better.

And Hannah perceived that she was one of many in the room who took an interest in the interactions between Bowman and Natalie. There were the Blandfords, of course, and the Bowman parents, and even Lord Westcliff occasionally glanced at the pair with subtle speculation, a slight smile on his lips. But the person who paid the most attention was Lord Travers, his expression stoic and his blue eyes troubled. It made Hannah's heart ache a little to realize that here was a man who cared very much about Natalie, and with very little encouragement would love her passionately. And yet all indications pointed to the fact that she would probably choose Bowman instead.

Natalie, you're not nearly as wise as you think you are, she thought wistfully. *Take the man who would make sacrifices for you, who would love you for who you are and not for what he would gain by marrying you.*

The worst part of Hannah's evening came after the entertainment had concluded, when the large crowd was dispersing and various groups were arranging to meet in one location or another. Natalie pulled Hannah to the side, her blue eyes gleaming with excitement. "In a few minutes, I'm going to sneak away with Mr. Bowman," she whispered. "We're going to meet privately on the lower terrace. So make yourself scarce, and if anyone asks where I am, give them some excuse and—"

"No," Hannah said softly, her eyes turning round. "If you're seen with him, it will cause a scandal."

Natalie laughed. "What does it matter? I'm probably going to marry him anyway."

Hannah gave a stubborn shake of her head. Her experiences with Bowman had left no doubt in her mind that he would take full advantage of Natalie. And it would be Hannah's fault for allowing it to happen. "You may meet him on the lower terrace, but I'm going with you."

Natalie's grin faded. "*Now* you've decided to be a vigilant chaperone? No. I'm putting my foot down, Hannah. I've always been kind to you, and you know you're in my debt. So go off somewhere and do *not* make a fuss."

"I'm going to protect you from him," Hannah said grimly. "Because if Mr. Bowman compromises you, you will no longer have any choice. You'll have to marry him."

"Well, I'm certainly not going to consider a betrothal without finding out how he kisses." Natalie's eyes narrowed. "Don't cross me, Hannah. Leave us alone."

But Hannah persevered. Eventually she found herself standing unhappily at the side of the lower terrace while Natalie and Rafe Bowman conversed. Bowman seemed unperturbed by Hannah's presence. But Natalie was furious, her voice lightly caustic as she observed aloud that "One can never talk about anything interesting when a chaperone is present," or "*Some* people can never be gotten rid of."

Having never been the focus of such brattiness from Natalie before, Hannah was bewildered and hurt. If Hannah was in Natalie's debt because the girl had always been kind to her, the reverse was also true: Hannah could have made Natalie's life far less pleasant as well.

"Don't you find it irksome, Mr. Bowman," Natalie said pointedly, "when people insist on going where they're not wanted?"

Hannah stiffened. Enough was enough. Although she had been charged with the responsibility of looking after Natalie and chaperoning her, she was not going to allow herself to be subjected to abuse.

Before Bowman could say anything, Hannah spoke coolly. "I will leave you with the privacy you so clearly desire,

Natalie. I have no doubt Mr. Bowman will make the most of it. Good night."

She left the lower terrace, flushed with outrage and chagrin. Since she could not join any of the gatherings upstairs without raising questions concerning Natalie's whereabouts, her only options were to go to bed, or find some place to sit alone. But she was not in the least sleepy, not with the anger simmering in her veins. Perhaps she could find a book to keep her occupied.

She went to the library, peeking discreetly around the doorjamb to see who might be inside. A group of children had gathered in there, most of them sitting on the floor while an elderly bewhiskered man sat in an upholstered chair. He held a small gold-stamped book in his hands, squinting at it through a pair of spectacles.

"Read it, Grandfather," cried one child, while another entreated, "Do go on! You can't leave us there."

The old man heaved a sigh. "When did they start making the words so small? And why is the light in here so poor?"

Hannah smiled sympathetically and entered the room. "May I be of help, sir?"

"Ah, yes." With a grateful glance, he rose from the chair and extended the book to her. It was a work by Mr. Charles Dickens, titled *A Christmas Carol*. Published two years earlier, the story of redemption had been an instant sensation, and had been said to rekindle the cynical public's joy in Christmas and all its traditions. "Would you mind reading for a bit?" the old man asked. "It tires my eyes so. And I should like to sit beside the fire and finish my toddy."

"I would love to, sir." Taking the book, Hannah looked askance at the children. "Shall I?"

They all cried out at once. "Oh, yes!"

"Don't lose the page, miss!"

"The first of the three spirits has come," one of the boys told her.

Settling into the chair, Hannah found the correct page, and began.

"Are you the Spirit, sir, whose coming was foretold to me?" asked Scrooge.

"I am."

The voice was soft and gentle. Singularly low, as if instead of being so close beside him, it were at a distance.

"Who, and what are you?" Scrooge demanded.

"I am the Ghost of Christmas Past."

Glancing around, Hannah bit back a grin as she saw the children's mesmerized faces, and the delighted shivers that ran through them at her rendition of a ghostly voice.

As she continued to read, the magic of Mr. Dickens's words wrought a spell over them all and eased the doubt and anger from Hannah's heart. And she remembered something she had forgotten: Christmas wasn't merely a single day. Christmas was a feeling.

IT CERTAINLY WOULD HAVE BEEN NO HARDSHIP TO KISS Lady Natalie. But Rafe had refrained from taking any such liberty, mainly because she seemed so determined to entice him into it.

After Hannah had left the lower terrace, Natalie had been defensive and sheepish, telling him that men were fortunate not to require chaperones everywhere they went, because at times it could be maddening. And Rafe had agreed gravely that it must indeed be quite inconvenient, but at the same time Miss Appleton struck him as tolerable company.

"Oh, most of the time Hannah is a dear," Natalie said.

"She can be rather bourgeois, but that is only to be expected. She comes from the poor side of the family, and she's one of four unmarried sisters, no brothers at all. And her mother is deceased. I don't mean to sound self-congratulatory, but had I not told Father I wanted Hannah as my companion, she would have suffered *years* of drudgery looking after her sisters. And since she never spends a shilling on herself—she sends her allowance to her father—I give her my cast-offs to wear, and I share nearly everything that's mine."

"That is very generous of you."

"No, not at all," she said airily. "I like to see her happy. Perhaps I was a bit harsh on her a few moments ago, but she was being unreasonable."

"I'm afraid I have to disagree," Rafe told her. "Miss Appleton is a good judge of character."

Natalie smiled quizzically. "Are you saying that she was correct in her assessment of you?" She drew closer, her lips soft and inviting. "That you're going to make the most of our privacy?"

"I hate to be predictable," he told her regretfully, amused by her frowning pout. "Therefore . . . no. We should probably take you upstairs before we cause gossip."

"I have no fear of gossip," she said, laying her hand on his arm.

"Then you clearly haven't yet done anything worthy of being gossiped about."

"Perhaps it's only that I haven't been caught," Natalie said demurely, making him laugh.

It was easy to like Lady Natalie, who was clever and pretty. And it would be no hardship to bed her. Marrying her would hardly be a difficult price to pay, to get the business deal he wanted with his father. Oh, she was a bit spoiled and pettish, to be sure, but no more than most young women of her position. Moreover, her beauty and connections and breeding would make her a wife whom other men would envy him for.

As he walked with her toward the main entrance hall, they passed by the open door of the library, where he had conversed recently with his father. A very different scene greeted his gaze now.

Warm light from the hearth pushed flickering shadows to the corners, spreading a quiet glow through the room. Hannah Appleton sat in a large chair, reading aloud, surrounded by a group of avidly listening children.

An elderly man had nodded off by the hearth, his chin resting on the ample berth of his chest. He snuffled now and then as a mischievous boy reached up to tickle his chin with a feather. But the boy soon left off, drawn into the story of Ebenezer Scrooge and his visitation by a Christmas spirit.

Rafe had not yet read the wildly popular book, but he recognized the story after hearing a few lines. *A Christmas Carol* had been so quoted and discussed that its ever-growing fame had become rather off-putting to Rafe. He had dismissed it as a bit of sentimental candy floss, not worthy of wasting his time with.

But as he watched Hannah, her face soft and animated, and heard the lively inflections of her voice, he couldn't help being drawn in.

Accompanied by the Spirit of Christmas Past, Scrooge was viewing himself as he had been as a schoolboy, lonely and isolated during the holidays until his younger sister had come to collect him.

"Yes!" said the child, brimful of glee. "Home, for good and all . . . Father is so much kinder than he used to be, that home's like Heaven! He spoke so gently to me one dear night when I was going to bed, that I was not afraid to ask him

once more if you might come home; and he said Yes, you
should; and sent me in a coach to bring you . . ."

Becoming aware of their presence in the doorway, Hannah
glanced up briefly. She flashed a quick smile at Natalie. But
her expression was more guarded as she looked at Rafe. Returning her attention to the book, she continued to read.

Rafe was aware of that same warm, curious pull he felt
every time he was near Hannah. She looked adorably rumpled, sitting in the large chair with one slippered foot drawn
up beneath her. He wanted to play with her, kiss her, pull that
shiny hair down and comb his fingers through it.

"Let's leave," Natalie whispered beside him.

Rafe felt a mild sting of annoyance. Natalie wanted to go
somewhere else and continue their earlier conversation, and
flirt, and perhaps have a taste of the adult pleasures that were
so new to her, and so damnably familiar to him.

"Let's listen for a moment," he murmured, guiding her into
the room.

Natalie was too clever to show her impatience. "Of course,"
she returned, and went to arrange herself gracefully in the
unoccupied chair by the hearth. Rafe stood at the mantel,
leaned a shoulder against it, and glued his gaze to Hannah
as the story continued.

Scrooge witnessed more from his past, including the merry
Fezziwig ball. A mournful scene followed, in which he was
confronted by a young woman who had loved him but was
now accepting that his desire for riches had surpassed all else.

". . . if you were free to-day, to-morrow, yesterday, can even
I believe that you would choose a dowerless girl . . . choosing
her, if for a moment you were false enough to your one guid-
ing principle to do so, do I not know that your repentance and

regret would surely follow? I do; and I release you. With a
full heart, for the love of him you once were . . ."

"Spirit!" said Scrooge in a broken voice, "remove me from
this place."

Rafe disliked sentiment. He had seen and experienced enough
of the world to resist the pull of maudlin stories. But as he
stood listening to Hannah, he felt unaccountable heat spreading through him, and it had nothing to do with the crackling
fire in the hearth. Hannah read the Christmas story with an
innocent conviction and pleasure that was too genuine for
him to resist. He wanted to be alone with her and listen to her
low, charming voice for hours. He wanted to lay his head in
her lap until he could feel the curve of her thigh against his
cheek.

As Rafe stared at her, he felt the quickening of arousal,
the rising warmth of tenderness, and an ache of yearning. A
terrible thought had sprung to his mind, the wish that *she*
were Blandford's daughter instead of Natalie. Sweet God,
he would have married her on the spot. But that was impossible, not to mention unfair to Natalie. And thinking it made
him feel every bit the cad that Hannah had accused him of
being.

As Hannah finished the second chapter, and laughingly
promised the clamoring children that she would read more
the following night, Rafe made an unselfish wish for someone else for the first time in his life . . . that Hannah would
someday find a man who would love her.

AFTER PRAISING THE SINGERS AND MUSICIANS FOR THEIR
fine performance, and leading a group of ladies into the parlor for tea, Lillian returned to the drawing room. Some of the
guests were still congregated there, including her husband,

who stood in the corner speaking privately with Eleanor, Lady Kittridge.

Trying to ignore the cold needling in her stomach, Lillian went to Daisy, who had just finished talking with some of the children. "Hello, dear," Lillian said, forcing a smile. "Did you enjoy the music?"

"Yes, very much." Staring into her face, Daisy asked bluntly, "What's the matter?"

"Nothing's the matter. Nothing at all. Why do you ask?"

"Whenever you smile like that, you're either worried about something, or you've just stepped in something."

"I haven't stepped in anything."

Daisy regarded her with concern. "What is it, then?"

"Do you see that woman Westcliff is talking to?"

"The beautiful blond one with the smashing figure?"

"Yes," came Lillian's sour reply.

Daisy waited patiently.

"I suspect . . ." Lillian began, and was startled to feel her throat closing and a hot pressure accumulate behind her eyes. Her suspicion was too awful to voice.

Her husband was interested in another woman.

Not that anything would come of it, because Westcliff was a man of absolute honor. It was simply not in him ever to betray his wife, no matter how acute the temptation. Lillian knew that he would always be faithful to her, at least physically. But she wanted his heart, all of it, and to see the signs of his attraction to someone else made Lillian want to die.

Everyone had said from the beginning that the earl of Westcliff and a brash American heiress were the most improbable pairing imaginable. But before long Lillian had discovered that beneath Marcus's outward reserve, there was a man of passion, tenderness, and humor. And for his part, Marcus had seemed to enjoy her irreverence and high-spirited nature. The past two years of marriage had been more wonderful than Lillian could have ever dreamed.

But lately Westcliff had started paying marked attention to Lady Kittridge, a gorgeous young widow who had everything in common with him. She was elegant, aristocratic, intelligent, and to top it all off, she was a remarkable horsewoman who was known for carrying on her late husband's passion for horse breeding. The horses from the Kittridge stables were the most beautiful descendants of the world's finest Arabians, with an amiable sweetness of character and spectacular conformation. Lady Kittridge was the perfect woman for Westcliff.

At first Lillian had not worried about the interactions between Lady Kittridge and her husband. Women were always throwing themselves at Westcliff, who was one of the most powerful men in England. But then a correspondence had begun. And soon afterward he had gone to visit her, ostensibly to advise her on some financial matters. Finally Lillian had begun to experience the pangs of jealousy and insecurity.

"I . . . I've never been able to quite make myself believe that Marcus is truly mine," she admitted humbly to Daisy. "He is the only person, aside from you, who's ever truly loved me. It still seems a miracle that he should have wanted me enough to marry me. But now I think . . . I fear . . . he might be tiring of me."

Daisy's eyes turned huge. "Are you saying you think that he . . . and Lady Kittridge . . ."

Lillian's eyes turned hot and blurry. "They seem to have an affinity," she said.

"Lillian, that is *madness*," Daisy whispered. "Westcliff adores you. You're the mother of his child."

"I'm not saying that I think he's unfaithful," Lillian whispered back. "He's too honorable for that. But I don't want him to *want* to."

"Has the frequency of his . . . well, husbandly atten-
tions . . . lessened?"

Lillian colored a little as she considered the question. "No,
not at all."

"Well, that's good. In some of the novels I've read, the unfaithful spouse pays less attention to his wife after he begins
an affair."

"What else do the novels say?"

"Well, sometimes a cheating husband may wear a new
scent, or start tying his cravat in a different way."

A worried frown gathered on Lillian's forehead. "I never
notice his cravat. I'll have to start looking at it more closely."

"And he develops an untoward interest in his wife's
schedule."

"Well, that doesn't help—Westcliff has an untoward interest in *everyone's* schedule."

"What about new tricks?"

"What kind of tricks?"

Daisy kept her voice low. "In the bedroom."

"Oh, God. Is that a sign of infidelity?" Lillian gave her a
stricken glance. "How do the bloody novelists know these
things?"

"Talk to him," Daisy urged softly. "Tell him your fears.
I'm sure Westcliff would never do anything to hurt you, dear."

"No, never deliberately," Lillian agreed, her smile turning brittle. She glanced at a nearby window, out at the cool
black night. "It's getting colder. I hope we'll have snow for
Christmas, don't you?"

Chapter Nine

Although Hannah and Natalie had tacitly decided to put their tiff of the previous evening behind them, the relations between them were still cool the next day. Therefore, Hannah was relieved not to be included when Natalie and Lady Blandford went with a group of ladies on a festive carriage ride through the countryside. Other women had elected to stay at Stony Cross Park, conversing over tea and handiwork, while a sizable contingent of gentlemen had left for the day to attend an ale festival in Alton.

Left to her own devices, Hannah explored the manor at her leisure, lingering in the art gallery to view scores of priceless paintings. She also visited the orangery, relishing the air spiced with citrus and bay. It was a wonderfully warm room, with iron grillwork vents admitting heat from stoves on a lower floor. She was on her way to the ballroom when she was approached by a small boy whom she recognized as one of the children she had read to.

The boy appeared apprehensive and uncertain, hurrying through the hallway in an erratic line. He was clutching some kind of wooden toy in his hand.

"Hello. Are you lost?" Hannah asked, squatting to bring herself to face level with him.

"No, miss."

"What is your name?"

"Arthur, miss."

"You don't seem very happy, Arthur. Is there anything the matter?"

He nodded. "I was playing with something I shouldn't, and now it's stuck and I'll get thrashed for it."

"What is it?" she asked sympathetically. "Where were you playing?"

"I'll show you." Eagerly he seized her hand and pulled her along with him.

Hannah went willingly. "Where are we going?"

"The Christmas tree."

"Oh, good. I was just heading there."

Arthur led her to the ballroom, which, fortunately for both their sakes, was empty. The Christmas tree was quite large, glittering with decorations and treats on the bottom half, but still unadorned on the upper half.

"Something has stuck in the tree?" Hannah asked, perplexed.

"Yes, miss, right there." He pointed to a branch well over their heads.

"I don't see any . . . Oh, good Lord, what *is* that?"

Something dark and furry hung from the branch, something that resembled a nest. Or a dead rodent.

"It's Mr. Bowman's hair."

Hannah's eyes widened. "His toupee? But why . . . how . . ."

"Well," Arthur explained reasonably, "I saw him taking a nap on the settee in the library, and his hair was dangling off him, and I thought it might be fun to play with. So I've been shooting it with my toy catapult, but then it went too high, up into the Christmas tree, and I can't reach it. I was going to put it back on Mr. Bowman before he woke, I truly was!" He looked at her hopefully. "Can you get it down?"

By this time Hannah had turned away and covered her face in her hands, and she was laughing too hard to breathe. "I shouldn't laugh," she gasped, "oh, I shouldn't . . ."

But the more she tried to stifle her amusement the worse it got, until she was forced to blot her eyes on her sleeve. When she had calmed herself a bit, she glanced at Arthur, who was frowning at her, and that nearly set her off again. With a potential thrashing in store, he didn't find the situation nearly as amusing as she did. "I'm sorry," she managed to say. "Poor Arthur. Poor Mr. Bowman! Yes, I'll fetch it down, no matter what I have to do."

The hairpiece had to be retrieved, not only for Arthur's sake, but also to save Mr. Bowman from embarrassment.

"I already tried the ladder," Arthur said. "But even when I got to the top, I still couldn't reach it."

Hannah viewed the nearby ladder appraisingly. It was an extending ladder, an A-frame made of two sets of steps with a third, extendable ladder braced between them. One would slide the middle ladder up or down to adjust the overall elevation. It had already been raised to full height.

"You're not very big," Arthur said doubtfully. "I don't think you can reach it, either."

Hannah smiled at him. "At least I can give it a try."

Together they repositioned the ladder close to one of the seating niches in the wall. Hannah took off her shoes. Taking care not to step on the hem of her own skirts, she gamely climbed the ladder in her stocking feet, hesitating only briefly before continuing up the extension. Higher and higher, until she had reached the top of the ladder. She reached for the toupee, only to discover with chagrin that it was approximately six inches out of her reach.

"Blast," she muttered. "It's almost within my grasp."

"Don't fall, miss," Arthur called up to her. "Maybe you should come down now."

"I can't give up yet." Hannah looked from the ladder to the overhanging ledge that surmounted the wall niche. It was about a foot higher than the top rung of the ladder. "You know," she said thoughtfully, "if I were standing on that ledge, I think I could reach Mr. Bowman's hairpiece." Carefully she levered herself up and crawled onto the ledge, pulling the mass of her skirts along with her.

"I didn't know ladies as old as you could climb," Arthur commented, looking impressed.

Hannah gave him a rueful grin. Minding her footing, she stood and reached for the drooping locks of the unfortunate toupee. To her disappointment, it was still too high. "Well, Arthur, the bad news is that I still can't reach it. The good news is, you have a *very* effective catapult."

The boy heaved a sigh. "I'm going to get a thrashing."

"Not necessarily. I'll think of some way to retrieve it. In the meantime—"

"Arthur!" Another boy appeared at the ballroom entrance. "Everyone's looking for you," he said breathlessly. "Your tutor says you're late for your lessons, and he's getting crosser and crosser by the second!"

"Oh, thunderbolts," Arthur muttered. "I have to go, miss. Can you get down from there?"

"Yes, I'll be fine," Hannah called down to him. "Go on, Arthur. Don't be late for your lessons."

"Thank you," he cried, and hurried from the room. His companion's voice floated in from the hallway. "Why is she up there . . . ?"

Hannah inched toward the ladder slowly. Before she climbed back onto it, however, the middle extension collapsed, a loud *clack-clack-clack* echoing through the ballroom.

Dumbfounded, Hannah stared at the A-frame stepladder, which was now far, *far* below her.

"Arthur?" she called, but there was no response.

It dawned on Hannah that she was in a fix.

How had her peaceful morning come to this, that she was stuck halfway up the side of the ballroom with no way to get down, and the manor mostly empty? In trying to save Mr. Bowman from embarrassment, she had brought no end of it on herself. Because whoever found her was certainly not going to be quiet about it, and the story would be repeated endlessly until she was the laughingstock of the entire holiday gathering.

Hannah heaved a sigh. "Hello?" she called hopefully. "Can anyone hear me?"

No response.

"Bollocks," she said vehemently. It was the absolute worst word she knew.

Since it appeared she might be in for a long wait before someone came to rescue her, she considered lowering herself to sit on the ledge. But it was rather narrow. If she lost her balance, she was undoubtedly going to break something.

Bored and mortified and anxious, she waited, and waited, until she was certain that at least a quarter hour had passed. Every few minutes she called for help, but the manor was deadly silent.

Just as she felt the gnawing of acute self-pity and frustration, someone came to the doorway. She thought it was a servant at first. He was dressed with shocking informality in black trousers and his shirtsleeves rolled up to reveal powerful forearms. But as he entered the room with a relaxed saunter, she recognized the way he moved, and she closed her eyes sickly.

"It *would* be you," she muttered.

She heard her name spoken in a quizzical tone, and opened her eyes to view Rafe Bowman standing below her. There was an odd expression on his face, a mixture of amusement and bafflement and something that looked like concern.

"Hannah, what the devil are you doing up there?"

She was too distressed to reprove him for using her first name. "I was fetching something," she said shortly. "The ladder collapsed. What are you doing here?"

"I was recruited by the wallflowers to help decorate the tree. Since the footmen are all occupied, they had need of tall people who could climb ladders." A deft pause. "You don't seem to qualify on either account, sweetheart."

"I climbed up perfectly well." Hannah was red everywhere, from her hairline to her toes. "It's merely coming down that poses a problem. And don't call me 'sweetheart,' and . . . what do you mean, wallflowers?"

Bowman had gone to the ladder and had begun to ratchet up the middle extension. "A silly name my sisters and their friends call their little group. What were you fetching?"

"Nothing of importance."

He grinned. "I'm afraid I can't help you down until you tell me."

Hannah longed to tell him to go away, she would prefer to wait for *days* before accepting his help. But she was getting tired of standing on the blasted ledge.

Seeing her indecision, Bowman said casually, "The others will be coming in here momentarily. And I should probably mention that I have an excellent view up your skirts."

Drawing in a sharp breath, Hannah tried to gather her dress more closely around her, and her balance wobbled.

Bowman cursed, his amusement vanishing. "Hannah, *stop*. I'm not looking. Be still, damn it. I'm coming up there to get you."

"I can do it by myself. Just set the ladder close to me."

"Like hell. I'm not going to risk you breaking your neck." Having extended the ladder to full length, Bowman ascended it with astonishing swiftness.

"It might collapse again," Hannah said nervously.

"No, it won't. There's an iron locking bracket on either side of the middle ladder. They probably weren't snapped into place before you climbed up. You should always make certain both brackets are locked before using one of these things."

"I don't plan to climb anything ever again," she said with vehement sincerity.

Bowman smiled. He was at the top of the ladder now, one hand extended. "Slowly, now. Take my hand and move carefully. You're going to put your foot on that rung and turn and face the wall. I'll help you."

As Hannah complied, it occurred to her that the logistics of getting down were a bit more difficult than going up had been. She felt a rush of gratitude toward him, especially since he was being far nicer than she would have expected.

His hand was very strong as it closed around hers, and his voice was deep and reassuring. "It's all right. I have you. Now step toward me and put your foot—no, not there, higher—yes. There we are."

Hannah went fully onto the ladder, and he guided her down until his arms closed on either side of her, his body a hard, warm cage. She was facing away from him, staring through the rungs of the ladder, while he was pressed all along her from behind. As he spoke, his breath was warm against her cheek. "You're safe. Rest a moment." He must have felt the shiver that went through her. "Easy. I won't let you fall."

She wanted to tell him that she wasn't at all afraid of heights. It was just the strange sensation of being suspended and yet held, and the delicious scent of him, so clean and male, and the brace of muscles she could feel through the thin linen of his shirt. A curious heat began to unfold inside her, spreading slowly.

"Will the ladder hold both of us?" she managed to ask.

"Yes, it could easily hold a half-dozen people." His voice was quietly comforting, the words a soft caress against her ear. "We'll go down one step at a time."

"I smell peppermint," she said wonderingly, twisting enough to look at him more fully.

A mistake.

His face was level with hers, those eyes so hot and dark, his lashes like black silk. Such a strong-featured face, perhaps the slightest bit too angular, like an artist's line sketch that had not yet been softened and blurred. She couldn't help wondering what lay beneath the tough, invulnerable façade, what he might be like in a tender moment.

"They're making candy ribbons in the kitchen." His breath was a warm, sweet rush of mint against her lips. "I ate a few of the broken pieces."

"You like sweets?" she asked unsteadily.

"Not usually. But I'm fond of peppermint." He stepped to a lower rung, and coaxed her to follow.

"The hairpiece," Hannah protested, even as she descended with him.

"The what?" Rafe followed her gaze, saw his father's toupee dangling from a branch, and made a choked sound. Pausing in his descent, he lowered his head to Hannah's shoulder and fought to suppress a burst of laughter that threatened to topple them both from the ladder. "Is that what you were trying to reach? Good God." He steadied her with one of his hands as she searched for her footing. "Putting aside the question of how it got there in the first place, why were you risking your pretty neck for a wad of dead hair?"

"I wanted to save your father from embarrassment."

"What a sweet little soul you are," he said softly.

Fearing he was mocking her, Hannah stopped and twisted around. But he was smiling at her, his gaze caressing, and his expression set off a series of hot flutters in her midriff. "Hannah, the only way to spare my father embarrassment is to keep him from finding that damned toupee again."

"It's not very flattering," she admitted. "Has anyone told him?"

"Yes, but he refuses to accept the fact that there are two things money can't buy. Happiness, and real hair."

"It is real hair," she said. "He just didn't happen to grow it himself."

Bowman chuckled and guided her down another rung.

"Why isn't he happy?" Hannah dared to ask.

Bowman considered the question for so long that they had reached the floor by the time he answered. "That's the universal question. My father has spent his entire life pursuing success. And now that he's richer than Croesus, he's still not satisfied. He owns strings of horses, stables filled with carriages, entire streets lined with buildings . . . and more female companionship than any one man should have. All of which leads me to believe that no one thing or person will ever be enough for him. And he'll never be happy."

Once they were on the ground, Hannah turned to face him fully, standing in her stocking feet. "Is that your fate as well, Mr. Bowman?" she asked. "Never to be happy?"

He stared down at her, his expression difficult to interpret. "Probably."

"I'm sorry," she said gently.

For the first time since she had met Bowman, he seemed robbed of speech. His gaze was deep and dark and volatile, and she felt her toes curl against the bare floor. She experienced the feeling she sometimes had when she'd been out in the cold and damp, and came inside for a cup of sugared tea . . . when the tea was so hot that it almost hurt to drink it, and yet the combination of sweetness and searing heat was too exquisite to resist.

"My grandfather once told me," she volunteered, "that the secret to happiness is merely to stop trying."

Bowman continued to stare at her, as if he were intent on memorizing something, absorbing something. She felt an exquisite constriction between them, as if the air itself were pushing them together.

"Does that work for you?" he asked huskily. "The not trying?"

"Yes, I think so."

"I don't think I can stop." His tone was reflective. "It's a popular belief among Americans, you know. The pursuit of happiness. It's in our Declaration, as a matter of fact."

"Then I suppose you have to obey it. Although I think it's a silly law."

A swift grin crossed his face. "It's not a law, it's a right."

"Well, whatever it is, you can't go looking for happiness as if it were a shoe you lost under the bed. You already have it, you see? You just have to let yourself *be*." She paused and frowned. "Why are you shaking your head at me like that?"

"Because talking with you reminds me of those embroidered quotes they're always putting on parlor pillows."

He was mocking her again. If she'd been wearing a pair of sturdy boots, she would probably have kicked him in the shins. After giving him a scowl, she turned to look for her discarded shoes.

Realizing what she wanted, Bowman bent to pick up her slippers. In a lithe movement he knelt on the floor, his thighs spread. "Let me help you."

Hannah extended her foot, and he placed the slipper on her with care. She felt the light brush of his fingers on her ankle, the smooth fire racing from nerve to nerve until it seemed her entire body was alight. Her mouth went dry. She looked down at the broad span of his shoulders, the way the heavy locks of his hair lay, the shape of his head.

He lowered her foot to the floor and reached for the other. It surprised her to feel the softness of his touch. She had not thought a large man could be so gentle. He fitted the shoe onto her foot, discovered that the top edge of the leather upper had folded under in the back, and ran his thumb inside the heel to adjust it.

At that moment, a few people entered the room. The sound of female chatter stopped abruptly.

It was Lady Westcliff, Hannah saw in consternation. How must the scene have appeared to them?

"Pardon us," the countess said cheerfully, giving a look askance at her brother. "Are we interrupting something?"

"No," Bowman replied, rising to his feet. "We were just playing Cinderella. Have you brought the rest of the decorations?"

"Loads of them," came another voice, and Lord Westcliff and Mr. Swift entered the room, carrying large baskets.

Hannah realized she was in the middle of a private gathering . . . there was the other Bowman sister, Mrs. Swift, and Lady St. Vincent, and Annabelle.

"I've enlisted them all to help finish the decorating," Lillian said with a grin. "It's too bad Mr. Hunt hasn't arrived yet . . . he would hardly need a ladder."

"I'm nearly as tall as he is," Bowman protested.

"Yes, but you don't take orders nearly so well."

"That depends on who gives the orders," he countered.

Hannah broke in uncomfortably, "I should go. Excuse me—"

But in her haste to leave, she forgot all about the A-frame ladder directly behind her. And as she turned, her foot caught on it.

In a lightning-fast reflex, Bowman grabbed her before she

could fall, and pulled her against his solid chest. She felt the flex of powerful muscle beneath his shirt. "If you wanted me to hold you," he murmured in a teasing undertone, "you should have just asked."

"Rafe Bowman," Daisy Swift admonished playfully, "are you resorting to tripping women to gain their attention?"

"When my more subtle efforts fail, yes." He released Hannah carefully. "You don't have to leave, Miss Appleton. In fact, we could use another pair of hands."

"I shouldn't—"

"Oh, do stay!" Lillian said with enthusiasm, and then Annabelle joined in, and then it would have been churlish for Hannah to refuse.

"Thank you, I will," she said with a sheepish smile. "And unlike Mr. Bowman, I take orders quite well."

"Perfect," Daisy exclaimed, handing Hannah a basket of handkerchief angels. "Because with the exception of the two of us, everyone else here loves to give them."

It was the best afternoon Rafe had spent in a long time. Perhaps ever. Two more ladders were brought in. The men wired candles onto the branches and hung ornaments where directed, while the women passed decorations up to them. Friendly insults flew back and forth, not to mention flurries of laughter as they exchanged reminiscences of past holidays.

Climbing the tallest ladder, Rafe managed to snatch the dangling toupee before anyone else saw it. He glanced at Hannah, who was standing below. Surreptitiously he dropped it to her. She caught it and shoved it deep into a basket.

"What was that thing?" Lillian demanded.

"Bird's nest," Rafe replied insouciantly, and he heard Hannah smother a laugh.

Westcliff poured an excellent red wine and passed glasses

around, even pressing one on Hannah when she tried to refuse.

"Perhaps I should water it," she told the earl.

Westcliff looked scandalized. "Dilute a Cossart Gordon '28? A sacrilege!" He grinned at her. "First try it just as it is, Miss Appleton. And tell me if you can't detect flavors of maple, fruit, and bonfire. As the Roman poet Horace once said, 'Wine brings to light the hidden secrets of the soul.'"

Hannah smiled back at him and took a sip of the wine. Its rich, exquisite flavor brought an expression of bliss to her face. "Delicious," she conceded. "But rather strong. And I may have secrets of the soul that should remain hidden."

Rafe murmured to Hannah, "One glass won't overthrow all your virtues, much to my regret. Go ahead and have some."

He smiled as she colored a little. It was a good thing, he thought, that Hannah had no idea how badly he wanted to taste the wine on her lips. And it was also fortunate that Hannah seemed to have no idea of how much he desired her.

What puzzled him was that she wasn't using any of the usual tricks women employed . . . no flirtatious glances, no discreet strokes or caresses, no suggestive comments. She dressed like a nun on holiday, and so far she hadn't once pretended to be impressed by him.

So the devil knew what had inspired all this lust. And it wasn't the ordinary sort of lust, it was . . . spiced with something. It was a steady, ruthless warmth, like strong sunlight, and it filled every part of him. It almost made him dizzy.

It was rather like an illness, come to think of it.

As the wine was consumed and the decorating continued, the large room echoed with laughter, especially when Lillian and Daisy tried to harmonize a few lines of a popular Christmas carol.

"If that sound were produced by a pair of songbirds," Rafe

told his sisters, "I would shoot them at once to put them out of their misery."

"Well, *you* sing like a wounded elephant," Daisy retorted.

"She's lying," Rafe told Hannah, who was stringing tinsel below him.

"You don't sing badly?" she asked.

"I don't sing at all."

"Why not?"

"If one doesn't do something well, it shouldn't be done."

"I don't agree," she protested. "Sometimes the effort should be made even if the results aren't perfect."

Smiling, Rafe descended the ladder for more candles, and stopped to look directly into her ocean-green eyes. "Do you really believe that?"

"Yes."

"I dare you, then."

"You dare me to what?"

"Sing something."

"This moment?" Hannah gave a disconcerted laugh. "By myself?"

Aware that the others were observing the interaction with interest, Rafe nodded. He wondered if she would take the dare and sing in front of a group of people she barely knew. He didn't think so.

Flushing, Hannah protested, "I can't do it while you're looking at me."

Rafe laughed. He took the bundle of wires and candles she handed to him, and obediently went up the ladder. He twisted a wire around a candle and began to fasten it to a branch.

His hands stilled as he heard a sweet, soft voice. Not at all distinguished or operatic. Just a pleasant, lovely feminine voice, perfect for lullabies or Christmas carols or nursery songs.

A voice one could listen to for a lifetime.

Here we come a-wassailing
Among the leaves so green,
Here we come a-wand'ring
So fair to be seen.
Love and joy come to you,
And to you your wassail, too,
And God bless you, and send you
A Happy New Year,
And God send you a Happy New Year.

Rafe listened to her, barely aware of the two or three candles snapping in his grip. This was getting bloody ridiculous, he thought savagely. If she became any more adorable, endearing, or delectable, something was going to get broken.

Most likely his heart.

He kept his face calm even as he struggled with two irreconcilable truths—he couldn't have her, and he couldn't *not* have her. He focused on marshaling his breathing, stacking his thoughts into order, pushing away the mass of unwanted feeling that kept flooding over him like ocean waves.

Finishing the verse, Hannah looked up at Rafe with a self-satisfied grin, while the others clapped and praised her. "There, I took your dare, Mr. Bowman. Now you owe me a forfeit."

What a smile she had. It set off sparks of warmth all through him. And it took all his self-control to keep from staring at her like a lovestruck goat. "Would you like me to sing something?" he offered politely.

"*Please,* no," Lillian cried, and Daisy added, "I *beg* you, don't ask him that!"

Descending the ladder, Rafe came to stand beside Hannah. "Name your forfeit," he said. "I always pay my debts."

"Make him pose like a Grecian statue," Annabelle suggested.

"Demand that he give you a l-lovely compliment," Evie said.

"Hmm . . ." Hannah eyed him thoughtfully, and named a popular parlor-game forfeit. "I'll take a possession of yours. Anything you happen to be carrying right now. A handkerchief, or a coin, perhaps."

"His wallet," Daisy suggested with glee.

Rafe reached into his trouser pocket, where a small penknife and a few coins jingled. And one other object, a tiny metal figure not two inches in height. Casually he dropped it into Hannah's palm.

She regarded the offering closely. "A toy soldier?" Most of the paint had worn off, leaving only a few flecks of color to indicate its original hues. The tiny infantryman held a sword tucked at his side. Hannah's gaze lifted to his, her eyes clear and green. Somehow she seemed to understand that there was some secret meaning to the little soldier. Her fingers curved as if to protect it. "Is he for luck?" she asked.

Rafe shook his head slightly, hardly able to breathe as he felt himself suspended between an oddly pleasurable sense of surrender, and an ache of regret. He wanted to take it back. And he wanted to leave it there forever, safe in her possession.

"Rafe," he heard Lillian say with an odd note in her voice. "Do you still carry that? After all these years?"

"It's just an old habit. Means nothing." Stepping away from Hannah, Rafe said curtly, "Enough of this nonsense. Let's finish the blasted tree."

In another quarter hour, the decorations were all up, and the tree was glittering and magnificent.

"Imagine when all the candles are lit," Annabelle exclaimed, standing back to view it. "It will be a glorious sight."

"Yes," Westcliff rejoined dryly. "Not to mention the greatest fire hazard in Hampshire."

"You were absolutely right to choose such a large tree," Annabelle told Lillian.

"Yes, I think—" Lillian paused only briefly as she saw someone come into the room. A very tall and piratical-looking someone who could only be Simon Hunt, Annabelle's husband. Although Hunt had begun his career working in his father's butcher shop, he had eventually become one of the wealthiest men in England, owning locomotive foundries and a large portion of the railway business. He was Lord Westcliff's closest friend, a man's man who appreciated good liquor and fine horses and demanding sports. But it was no secret that what Simon Hunt loved most in the world was Annabelle.

"I think," Lillian continued as Hunt walked quietly up behind Annabelle, "the tree is perfect. And I think *someone* had very good timing in arriving so late that he didn't have to decorate even one bloody branch of it."

"Who?" Annabelle asked, and started a little as Simon Hunt put his hands lightly over her eyes. Smiling, he bent to murmur something private into her ear.

Color swept over the portion of Annabelle's face that was still exposed. Realizing who was behind her, she reached up to pull his hands down to her lips, and she kissed each of his palms in turn. Wordlessly she turned in his arms, laying her head against his chest.

Hunt gathered her close. "I'm still covered in travel dust," he said gruffly. "But I couldn't wait another damned second to see you."

Annabelle nodded, her arms clutching around his neck. The moment was so spontaneously tender and passionate that it cast a vaguely embarrassed silence through the room.

After kissing the top of his wife's head, Hunt looked up with a smile and extended his hand to Westcliff. "It's good to be here at last," he said. "Too much to be done in London—I left with a mountain of things unfinished."

"Your presence has been sorely missed," the earl said, shaking his hand firmly.

Still holding Annabelle with one arm, Hunt greeted the rest of them cordially.

"St. Vincent is still away?" Hunt asked Evie, and she nodded. "Any word on the duke's health?"

"I'm af-fraid not."

Hunt looked sympathetic. "I'm sure St. Vincent will be here soon."

"And you're among friends who love you," Lillian added, putting her arm around Evie's shoulders.

"And there is v-very good wine," Evie said with a smile.

"Will you have a glass, Hunt?" Westcliff asked, indicating the tray on a nearby table.

"Thank you, but no," Hunt said affably, pulling Annabelle's arm through his. "If you'll pardon us, I have a few things to discuss with my wife." And without waiting for an answer, he dragged Annabelle from the ballroom with a haste that left no doubt as to what would happen next.

"Yes, I'm sure they'll be chatting up a storm," Rafe remarked, and winced as Lillian drove her elbow hard into his side.

Chapter Ten

Every common room of the manor was busy after supper. Some guests played cards, others gathered around the piano in the music room and sang, but by far the largest group had gathered in the drawing room for a game of charades. Their shouting and laughter echoed far along the hallways.

Hannah watched the charades for a while, enjoying the antics of competing teams that acted out words or phrases, while others shouted out guesses. She noticed that Rafe Bowman and Natalie were sitting together, smiling and exchanging private quips. They were an extraordinarily well-matched pair, one so dark, one so fair, both young and attractive. Glancing at them made Hannah feel positively morose.

She was relieved when the case clock in the corner showed that it was a quarter to eight. Leaving the room unobtrusively, she went into the hallway. It was such a relief to be out of the crowded drawing room, and not to have to smile when she didn't feel like it, that she heaved a tremendous sigh and leaned against the wall with her eyes closed.

"Miss Appleton?"

Hannah's eyes flew open. It was Lillian, Lady Westcliff, who had followed her out of the room.

"It is a bit of a crush in there, isn't it?" the countess asked with friendly sympathy.

Hannah nodded. "I'm not fond of large gatherings."

"Neither am I," Lillian confided. "My greatest pleasure is to relax in a small group with my friends, or better yet, to be alone with my husband and daughter. You're going to the library to read to the children, aren't you?"

"Yes, my lady."

"That's very nice of you. I heard they all enjoyed it tremendously last evening. May I walk with you to the library?"

"Yes, my lady, I would enjoy that."

Lillian surprised her by linking arms with her, as if they were sisters or close friends. They went along the hallway at a slow pace. "Miss Appleton, I . . . oh, hang it, I hate these formalities. May we use first names?"

"I would be honored for you to call me by my given name, my lady. But I can't do the same. It wouldn't be proper."

Lillian gave her a rueful glance. "All right, then. Hannah. I've wanted to talk with you all evening—there is something highly private I want to discuss with you, but it must go no further. And I probably shouldn't say anything, but I must. I won't be able to get any sleep tonight otherwise."

Hannah was dumbfounded. Not to mention rabidly curious. "My lady?"

"That forfeit you asked of my brother today . . ."

Hannah paled a little. "Was that wrong of me? I'm so sorry. I would never have—"

"No. No, it's not that. You did nothing wrong at all. It's what my brother gave to you that I found so . . . well, surprising."

"The toy solider?" Hannah whispered. "Why was that surprising?" She had not thought it all that unusual. Many men carried little tokens with them, such as locks of hair from loved ones, or luck charms or touch pieces such as a coin or medal.

"That soldier came from a set that Rafe had when he was a little boy. Having met my father, you won't be surprised to learn that he was quite strict with his children. At least when he was there, which thank God wasn't often. But Father has always had very unreasonable expectations of my brothers, especially Rafe, because he's the oldest. Father wanted Rafe to succeed at everything, so he was punished severely if he was ever second best. But at the same time, Father didn't want to be overshadowed, so he took every opportunity to shame or degrade Rafe when he *was* the best."

"Oh," Hannah said softly, filled with sympathy for the boy that Rafe had been. "Did your mother do nothing to intervene?"

Lillian made a scoffing sound. "She's always been a silly creature who cares more for parties and social status than anything else. I'm sure she expended far more thought on her gowns and jewels than she did on any of her children. So whatever Father decided, Mother was more than willing to go along with it, as long as he kept paying the bills."

After a moment's pause, the contempt vanished from Lillian's tone, replaced by melancholy. "We rarely ever saw Rafe. Because my father wanted him to be a serious, studious boy, he was never allowed to play with other children. He was always with tutors, studying or being taught sports and riding . . . but he was never allowed one moment of freedom. One of Rafe's few escapes was his set of little soldiers—he would stage battles and skirmishes with them, and while he studied, he would line them up on his desk to keep him company." A faint smile came to her lips. "And Rafe would roam at night. Sometimes I would hear him sneaking along the hallway, and I knew he was going downstairs or outside, just for a chance to breathe freely."

The countess paused as they neared the library. "Let's stop here for a moment—it's not quite eight, and I'm sure the children are still gathering."

Hannah nodded wordlessly.

"One night," Lillian continued, "Daisy was ill, and they kept her in the nursery. I had to sleep in another room in case the fever was catching. I was frightened for my sister, and I woke in the middle of the night crying. Rafe heard me and came to ask what was the matter. I told him how worried I was for Daisy, and also about a terrible nightmare I'd had. So Rafe went to his room, and came back with one of his soldiers. An infantryman. Rafe put it on the table by my bed, and told me, 'This is the bravest and most stalwart of all my men. He'll stand guard over you during the night, and chase off all your worries and bad dreams.'" The countess smiled absently at the memory. "And it worked."

"How lovely," Hannah said softly. "So that's the significance of the soldier?"

"Well, not entirely. You see . . ." Lillian took a deep breath, as if she found it difficult to continue. "The very next day, the tutor told Father that he believed the toy soldiers were distracting Rafe from his studies. So Father got rid of all of them. Gone forever. Rafe never shed a tear—but I saw something terrible in his eyes, as if something had been destroyed in him. I took the infantryman from my nightstand and gave it to him. The only soldier left. And I think—" She swallowed hard, and a shimmer of tears appeared in her dark brown eyes. "I think he's carried it for all these years as if it were some fragment of his heart he wanted to keep safe."

Hannah wasn't aware of her own tears until she felt them

slide down both cheeks. She wiped at them hastily, blotting them with her sleeve. Her throat hurt, and she cleared it, and when she spoke, her voice was rusty. "Why did he give it to *me*?"

The countess seemed oddly relieved, or reassured, by the signs of her emotion. "I don't know, Hannah. It's left to you to find out the significance of it. But I can tell you this: it was *not* a casual gesture."

AFTER COMPOSING HERSELF, HANNAH WENT INTO THE library in something of a daze. The children were all there, seated on the floor, consuming sugar biscuits and warm milk. A smile tugged at Hannah's lips as she saw more children clustered beneath the library table as if it were a fort.

Seating herself in the large chair, she ceremoniously opened the book, but before she could read a word, a plate of biscuits was put in her lap, and a cup of milk was offered to her, and one of the girls put a paper silver crown on her head. After eating a biscuit and submitting to a minute or two of carryings-on, Hannah quieted the giggling children and began to read:

> "I am the Ghost of Christmas Present," said the Spirit. "Look upon me."

As Scrooge went on his travels with the second Spirit, and they visited the Cratchits' humble but happy home, Hannah was aware of Rafe Bowman's lean, dark form entering the room. He went to a shadowy corner and stood there, watching and listening. Hannah paused for a moment and looked back at him. She felt an anguished clutch of her heart, and a surge of ardent need, and a sense of remarkable foolishness as she sat there wearing a paper crown. She had no idea why Bowman would have come without Natalie to listen to the next part of the story. Or why merely being in the same room with him was enough to start her heart clattering like a mechanical loom.

But it had something to do with the realization that he was not the spoiled, heartless rake she had first believed him to be. Not entirely, at any rate.

And if that turned out to be true . . . had she any right to object to his marriage to Natalie?

For the next two days Hannah searched for an opportunity to return the toy soldier to Rafe Bowman, but with the manor so busy and Christmas drawing near, privacy was in short supply. It seemed that Bowman's courtship of Natalie was running smoothly: they danced together, went walking, and he turned the pages of music for Natalie as she played the piano. Hannah tried to be unobtrusive, keeping her distance whenever possible, staying quiet when she was required to chaperone them.

It seemed that Bowman was making a concerted effort to restrain himself around Hannah, not precisely ignoring her, but not paying her any marked attention. His initial interest in her had vanished, which certainly wasn't a surprise. He had Natalie's golden beauty dangling before him, along with the certainty of power and riches if he married her.

"I do like him," Natalie had told her privately, her blue eyes glowing with excitement. "He's very clever and amusing, and he dances divinely, and I don't think I've ever met a man who kisses half so well."

"Mr. Bowman kissed you?" Hannah asked, fighting to keep her tone even.

"Yes." Natalie grinned mischievously. "I practically had to corner him on the outside terrace, and he laughed and kissed me under the stars. There is no doubt he'll ask me to marry him. I wonder when and how he'll do it. I hope at night. I love getting proposals in the moonlight."

HANNAH HELPED NATALIE CHANGE INTO A WINTER DRESS of pale blue wool, the skirts heavy and flat pleated, the matching hooded cape trimmed with white fur. The guests were going on a massive afternoon sleigh ride, traveling across the newfallen snow to an estate in Winchester for a dinner and skating party. "If the weather stays clear," Natalie exclaimed, "we'll be riding home under the stars—can you imagine anything more romantic, Hannah? Are you certain you don't want to come?"

"Quite certain. I want to sit by the hearth and read my letter from Mr. Clark." The letter had been delivered that very morning, and Hannah was eager to peruse it in private. Besides, the last thing she wanted was to watch Natalie and Rafe Bowman snuggle together under a blanket on a long cold sleigh ride.

"I wish you would join the sleighing party," Natalie persisted. "Not only would you have fun, but you could do me the favor of keeping company with Lord Travers and diverting him. It seems that every time I'm with Mr. Bowman, Travers tries to barge in. It's dreadfully annoying."

"I thought you liked Lord Travers."

"I do. But he is so reticent, it drives me mad."

"Perhaps if you corner him, as you did Mr. Bowman—"

"I've already tried that. But Travers won't do anything. He said he *respects* me." Scowling, Natalie had gone to join her parents and Mr. Bowman for the sleigh ride.

Once the sleighs had departed, the horses' hooves tamping down the snow and ice, bells jingling on bridles, the manor and grounds were peaceful. Hannah walked slowly through the manor, enjoying the serenity of the empty hallways. The only sounds were the distant muffled conversations of servants. No doubt they, too, were glad that the mass of guests were gone for the rest of the day and evening.

Hannah reached the library, which was empty and inviting, the air lightly pungent with the scents of vellum and leather. The fire in the hearth cast a warm glow through the room.

Seating herself in the chair by the fire, Hannah removed her shoes and drew one foot up beneath her. She took the letter from Samuel Clark from her pocket, broke the seal, and smiled at his familiar penmanship.

It was easy to picture Clark writing this letter, his face still and thoughtful, his fair hair a bit mussed as he leaned over his desk. He asked after her health and that of the Blandfords, and wished her a happy holiday. He proceeded to describe his latest interest in the subject of inherited characteristics as described by the French biologist Lamarck, and how it meshed with Clark's own theories of how repeated sensory information might be stored in the brain tissue itself, thereby contributing to the future adaptation of species. As usual, Hannah only understood about half of it . . . he would have to explain it later in a way that she could comprehend more easily.

"As you see," he wrote, *"I require your good, sensible companionship. If only you were here to listen to my thoughts as I explain them, I could arrange them more precisely. It is only at times like this, in your absence, that I realize nothing is complete when you are gone, my dear Miss Appleton. Everything seems awry.*

"It is my fondest hope that when you return, we will sort out our more personal issues. During the course of our work you have come to know my character, and my temperament. Perhaps by now my meager charms have made some sort of impression on you. I have few charms, I know. But you have so many, my dear, that I think yours will atone for my lack.

Mr. Clark couldn't love me. But you're wrong. He sees
_."

Ordinary? Are you mad? You're the most insanely deli-
s girl I've ever met, and if I were Clark, I'd have done a
of a lot more than fondle your cranium by now—"

"Don't mock me!"

"I'd have seduced you ten times over." He deliberately
epped on the letter. "Don't lie to me, or yourself. You're not
appy. You don't want him. You're settling for this because
ou don't want to risk being an old maid."

"That's a fine accusation coming from you, you hypocrite!"

"I'm not a hypocrite. I've been honest with everyone, including Natalie. I'm not pretending to be in love. I don't
pretend to want her the way I want you."

Hannah froze, staring at him in astonished silence. That
he should admit it . . .

She realized she was breathing much too fast, and so
was he. Her fingers curled over his sleeves, against his hard-
muscled forearms. She wasn't certain if her grip was exerted
to keep him close or hold him away.

"Tell me you're in love with him," Bowman said.

Hannah couldn't speak.

More soft insistence. "Then say you desire him. You
should feel that much for him, at least."

A tremor ran all through her, spreading to the tips of her
fingers and toes. She took the deepest breath possible, and
managed a thin reply. "I don't know."

His expression changed, an odd half-smile coming to
his lips, his eyes hot and predatory. "You don't know how
to tell if you desire a man, sweetheart? I can help you with
that."

"*That* kind of help," Hannah said with asperity, "I do not
need." She stiffened as he brought her closer, his big hands

*I hope very much that you might do me the honor of becom-
ing my partner, helpmate, and wife . . ."*

There was more, but Hannah folded the letter and stared
blindly into the fire.

The answer would be yes, of course.

This is what you've wanted, she told herself. An honorable offer from a fine, decent man. Life would be interesting
and fulfilling. It would better her to be the wife of such a
brilliant man, to become acquainted with the people in his
educated circles.

Why, then, did she feel so miserable?

"Why are you frowning?"

Hannah started in surprise as she heard a voice from the
library threshold. Her eyes widened as she beheld Rafe Bowman standing there with his habitually negligent posture,
one leg slightly bent as he leaned against the doorframe. He
was in a perturbing state of undress, his vest unbuttoned,
his collarless shirt open at the throat, no cravat anywhere in
sight. Somehow the disarray only made him more handsome,
emphasizing the relaxed masculine vitality that she found so
disturbing.

"I . . . I . . . Why are you walking around half dressed?"
Hannah managed to ask.

One of his shoulders lifted in a lazy shrug. "No one here."

"*I'm* here."

"Why aren't you at the sleighing party?"

"I wanted a bit of peace and privacy. Why aren't *you* at
the sleighing party? Natalie will be disappointed—she was
expecting—"

"Yes, I know," Bowman said without a trace of remorse.
"But I'm tired of being watched like a bug under a magni-
fying glass. And more importantly, I had some business
matters to discuss with my brother-in-law, who also stayed
behind."

"Mr. Swift?"

"Yes. We went over contracts with a British heavy chemical company for sulphuric acid and soda supplies. Then we moved on to the fascinating topic of palm oil production." He came into the room, his hands tucked casually in his pockets. "We agreed that we'll eventually need to cultivate our own source by establishing a coco palm plantation." His brows lifted. "Care to go to the Congo with me?"

She stared directly into his sparkling eyes. "I wouldn't go with you to the end of the carriage lane, Mr. Bowman."

He laughed softly, his gaze sweeping over her as she stood to face him. "You didn't answer my earlier question. Why were you frowning?"

"Oh, it's nothing." Hannah fumbled nervously in the pocket of her skirts. "Mr. Bowman, I've been meaning to return this to you." Pulling out the little toy soldier, she extended her hand. "You must take him back. I think"—she hesitated—"you've been through many a battle together, you and he." She couldn't help glancing at his throat, where the skin looked smooth and golden. A bit lower, there was a shadow of hair where the open neck of his shirt parted. An unfamiliar, hot flourish of sensation went through her stomach. Dragging her gaze upward, she looked into eyes as rich and dark as exotic spices.

"If I take it back," he asked, "do I still owe you a forfeit?"

A smile struggled upward but didn't quite surface. "I'm not sure. I'll have to consider that."

Bowman reached out, but instead of taking the soldier from her, he closed his hand over hers, trapping the cool metal between their palms. His thumb moved in a gentle sweep over the back of her hand. The touch caused her to draw in a quick, severed breath. His fingers moved upward to close around her wrist, drawing her toward him. His head bent as he looked down at the letter still clasped in her fin-

gers. "What is it?" he asked quietly. "
Trouble at home?"

Hannah gave a wild little shake of h
smile. "Oh, nothing's worrying me. I've
news. I'm—I'm happy!"

A sardonic, slanting glance. "So I see."

"Mr. Clark wants to marry me," she blurte
reason, saying the words aloud sent a chill of
her.

His eyes narrowed. "Clark proposed by letter?
have troubled himself to come here and ask you

Although it was a perfectly reasonable question
felt defensive. "I find it very romantic. It's a love let

"May I see it?"

Her eyes turned round. "What makes you think I
show you something so personal, and—" She made a
sound of distress as he took the letter from her nerveless
gers. But she didn't try to take it back.

Bowman's face was expressionless as he glanced over th
neatly written lines. "This isn't a love letter," he muttered
tossing it contemptuously to the floor. "It's a damned science
report."

"How dare you!" Hannah bent to scoop the letter up, but
he wouldn't let her. The toy soldier dropped as well, bouncing
on the soft carpet as Bowman gripped her by the elbows.

"You're not actually considering it, are you? That cold-
blooded, pathetic excuse for a marriage proposal?"

"Of course I am." Her anger exploded without warning, fueled by some deep and treacherous longing. "He's everything
you're not, he's honorable and kind and gentlemanly—"

"He doesn't love you. He never will."

That hurt. In fact, the pain doubled and redoubled until
Hannah could hardly breathe. She twisted angrily in his hold.
"You think that because I'm poor and ordinary, someone

sliding from her elbows to hook beneath her arms. Her pulse had gone wild, heat thrumming in every part of her.

He bent to kiss her. She made a halfhearted attempt to wriggle away, causing his mouth to catch at her cheek instead of her lips. Bowman didn't appear to mind. He seemed amenable to kissing any part of her he could reach, her cheeks, chin, jaw, the lobe of her ear. Hannah went still, panting as the kisses slid and skimmed over her hot face. She closed her eyes as she felt his lips catch at hers. Another soft, glancing brush, and another, and finally he closed his mouth over hers, deep and secure.

He tasted her with his tongue, searching slowly, and the voluptuous sensation blotted out every thought or flicker of reason. One arm went around her, and his head turned, and he kissed her more urgently. His free hand came up to her jaw, cradling and angling her face. He withdrew just enough to play with her, the fever-glazed caresses of his mouth coaxing her into openness, licking into the vulnerable heat.

The trembling grew worse, insidious pleasure melting through her like boiling sugar. As he tried to soothe her, the tender parts of her body began to throb beneath her clothes, all the laces and seams and stays cinching and clinging with maddening tightness. She struggled a little, chafing against the artificial restrictions. He seemed to understand. His lips left hers, his warm breath fanning the curve of her ear as his fingers went to her bodice. She heard her own moan of relief as she felt him unfastening her collar, and his reassuring whispers that he would take care of her, he would never hurt her, she must relax and trust him, relax . . . all this while his hand moved stealthily along her front, tugging and unfastening.

He kissed her again, a burning velvet caress that caused her knees to give out entirely. But the slow collapse didn't seem to matter, he was holding her securely and lowering her to the carpeted floor. She found herself sprawled half across him while he knelt amid the abundant rumples of her dress. Her garments had fallen in perplexing disarray, buttons undone and skirts riding up. She made a dazed attempt to restore something, cover something, but the way he kissed her made it impossible to think. He gently arranged her beneath him, his arm a hard support beneath her neck. She relaxed helplessly as his wicked mouth took hers over and over, feasting on the taste of her.

"The sweetest skin . . ." he whispered, kissing her throat, easing her bodice open. "Let me see you, Hannah love . . ." He pulled at the top of her chemise, exposing a pale breast that had been pushed full and high by her underbust corset. It was then that Hannah comprehended that she was on the floor with him, and he was uncovering parts of her that no man had ever seen.

"Wait—I shouldn't—you shouldn't—" But her protest was silenced as he bent over the plush curve, his lips closing over a cold stiffening nipple. Her throat hummed with a low whimper as his tongue swept over her in raw-velvet strokes.

"Rafe," she moaned, the first time she had ever said his name, and he let out a shaking breath and cupped both her breasts.

His voice was deep and rough. "I wanted this the first time I met you. I watched you sitting there with that little teacup in your hand, and I couldn't stop wondering what you tasted like here . . . and here . . ." He suckled each breast in turn, his hands coasting over her writhing body.

"Rafe," she gasped. "Please, I can't—"

"No one's here," he whispered against her prickling flesh. "No one will know. Hannah, sweet love . . . let me touch you. Let me show you how it feels to want someone as much as I want you . . ."

And he waited for her answer, breathing against her quivering skin, a warm hand covering her breast. She couldn't seem to keep entirely still, her knees flexing, her hips rising in answer to a deep, demanding pulse. She was saturated with sweetness and shame and need. She would never have him, she knew that. His life was set on a far different path from hers. He was forbidden. Perhaps that was the reason for this reckless attraction.

Before she quite knew it, she had reached up and guided his head to hers. He responded immediately, taking her mouth in a ravishing, hard-plundering kiss. His hands slipped beneath her clothes, finding tender pale skin, caressing in ways that made her shiver. A muffled cry escaped her as she felt him pulling at the tapes of her drawers. He touched her taut stomach, a fingertip circling her navel. His hand slid over soft curls, cupped her sex, and gently parted her thighs. She felt herself being stroked, petted, lightly spread, his touch careful and clever as if he were drawing a pattern on a frosted window. Except that the surface beneath his fingertips was not icy glass but soft living skin, flushed and burning with desperate sensation.

She had one blurry glimpse of his dark face above hers, his expression intent with lust. He toyed with her, seeming to savor her writhing agitation, his own color high and fevered. She clutched at him, hips arching, lips parted in a wordless plea. One of his fingers pushed inside her, just past the entrance of her body, and she jerked in shock.

His touch withdrew, the wet fingertip making sly, lingering circles around the aching peak of her sex. He pushed her legs apart wider, and kissed the tips of her breasts. His whisper burned against her skin. "If I wanted to take you now, Hannah, you would let me, wouldn't you? You'd let me enter you, fill you . . . If I asked you to let me come inside

you, and ease you . . . what would you say, sweet darling?"
He began a light, torturous massage. "Say it," he murmured.
"Say it—"

"Yes." She clutched at him blindly, her breath coming in
sobs. *"Yes."*

Rafe smiled, his gaze smoldering. "Then here's your forfeit, sweetheart."

He stroked her in a quick, skillful rhythm, covering her
mouth with his to absorb her cries. He knew exactly what
he was doing, his fingers wicked and sure. It seemed she
might die of the annihilating release. She held and stiffened
against it even as the pleasure began to rush, and rush, gaining power and force until she was helpless and consumed and
shattered.

Slowly he brought her down, kissing and caressing her
twitching body. His finger slid inside her once more, this
time slipping easily into the wetness. The feel of the intimate
muscles grasping him so firmly seemed to cause him pain.
She lifted instinctively to take him, and he groaned and
withdrew his finger, leaving her swollen flesh to clench on
the emptiness.

Rafe's face was hard and sweat-misted as he took his hands
from her. He stared down at her with unconcealed hunger,
his eyes narrowed, his chest heaving. His hands trembled
as he reached for the top hooks of her corset busk, the buttons of her dress, the disheveled undergarments. But as one
of his knuckles brushed against her warm skin, he snatched
his hands back abruptly and rose to his feet. "Can't," he said
hoarsely.

"Can't what?" she whispered.

"Can't help with your clothes." An unsteady breath. "If I
touch you again . . . I won't stop until you're naked."

Staring up at him dizzily, Hannah comprehended that the
release, and relief, had been rather one-sided. He was dan-

gerously aroused, to the limit of his self-control. She pulled the chemise higher over her naked breasts.

Rafe shook his head, still staring at her. His mouth was a grim slash. "If you want Clark to do the things I just did to you," he said, "then go ahead and marry him."

And he left her there in the library, as if to stay there a moment longer would have resulted in disaster for them both.

Chapter Eleven

In Evie's opinion, the sleighing party had been enjoyable but too long. She was tired, her ears still ringing from all the noise and caroling. Evie had laughed and frolicked with the group, staying close to Daisy, whose husband had remained at the manor to discuss business matters with Rafe Bowman.

"Oh, I don't mind at all," Daisy had said cheerfully, when Evie had asked if she was disappointed that Swift had not accompanied them. "It's better to let Matthew clear away his business concerns first, and then he'll be free to give me all his attention later."

"Does he w-work very long hours?" Evie had asked with a touch of concern, knowing that the Bowmans' enterprise in Bristol was a massive project involving great responsibility.

"There are days when he must," Daisy had replied prosaically. "But there are other times when he stays home and we spend the day together." A grin had crossed her face. "I love being married to him, Evie. Although it's still all so new . . . sometimes it surprises me to wake up and find Matthew beside me." She had leaned closer and whispered, "I have to tell you a secret, Evie: I complained one day that I'd read all the books in the house, and there was nothing new at the bookshop, and Matthew challenged me to try writing one of my own. So I've started one. I have a hundred pages written already."

Evie had laughed in delight. "Daisy," she had whispered back, "are you going to be a f-famous novelist?"

Daisy shrugged. "It doesn't matter to me whether it's published or not. I'm enjoying writing it."

"Is it a respectable story or a naughty one?"

Daisy's brown eyes danced with mischief. "Evie, why would you even ask? Of *course* it's a naughty one."

Now back in the comfort of her room at Stony Cross Manor, Evie bathed in a small portable tub by the hearth, sighing in relief at the feel of the hot water against her stiff, aching limbs. Sleigh rides, she reflected, were one of those activities that always sounded better in theory than they turned out to be in reality. The seats on the sleigh had been hard and lumpy, and her feet had been cold.

She heard a tap at the door, and the sound of someone entering the room. Since she was shielded from view by a standing fabric screen, Evie leaned back and peeked around the screen's wooden frame.

A housemaid was hefting a dripping metal can with rags tied at the handles. "More hot water, milady?" she asked.

"Y-yes, please."

Carefully the maid poured the steaming water at the end near Evie's feet, and Evie sank deeper into the bath. "Oh, thank you."

"Shall I come back with a warming pan to take the chill from the bed, milady?" The long-handled covered pan was filled with live coals and run between the sheets just before bedtime.

Evie nodded.

The maid left, and Evie stayed in the bath until the heat

began to dissipate. Reluctantly she stepped from the tub and dried herself. The thought of going to bed alone—again— filled her with melancholy. She was trying not to pine for St. Vincent. But she woke up every morning searching for him, her arm stretched across the empty place beside her.

St. Vincent was the opposite of everything Evie was . . . elegant, dazzlingly articulate, cool and self-possessed . . . and so wicked that it had once been universally agreed he would be an absolutely terrible husband.

No one but Evie knew how tender and devoted he was in private. Of course, his friends such as Westcliff and Mr. Hunt were aware that St. Vincent had reformed his former villainous ways. And he was doing a remarkable job managing the gaming club she had inherited from her father, rebuilding a faltering empire while at the same time making light of the responsibilities he had assumed.

He was still a scoundrel, though, she thought with a private grin.

Standing from the bath, Evie dried herself and donned a velvet robe that buttoned along the front. She heard the door open again. "Back to w-warm the bed?" she asked.

But the voice that answered wasn't the maid's.

"As a matter of fact . . . yes."

Evie stilled at the sound of a deep, silky murmur.

"I passed the maid on the stairs and told her she wouldn't be needed tonight," he continued. "'If there's one thing I do well,' I told her, 'it's warming my wife's bed.'"

By this time Evie was fumbling to push the screen aside, nearly pushing it over.

St. Vincent reached her in a few graceful strides, folding her in his arms. "Easy, love. No need for haste. Believe me, I'm not going anywhere."

They stood together for a long, wordless moment, breathing, holding tight.

Eventually St. Vincent tilted Evie's head back and stared down at her. He was tawny and golden haired, his pale blue eyes glittering like gems in the face of a fallen angel. He was a long, lean-framed man, always exquisitely dressed and groomed. But he had not been sleeping well, she saw. There were faint shadows beneath his eyes, and signs of weariness on his face. The touches of human vulnerability, however, only served to make him more handsome, softening what might otherwise have been a gleaming, godlike remoteness.

"Your f-father," she began, staring at him in concern. "Is he . . ."

St. Vincent cast an exasperated glance heavenward. "He'll be fine. The doctors can't find a thing wrong with him, other than indigestion brought on by rich food and wine. When I left, he was leering and pinching the housemaids, and welcoming a score of obsequious relations who want to sponge off him for Christmas." His hands moved lightly over her velvet-covered back. His voice was very soft. "Have you been a good girl in my absence?"

"Yes, of course," she said breathlessly.

St. Vincent gave her a disapproving glance and kissed her with a seductive gentleness that sent her pulse racing. "We'll have to remedy that immediately. I refuse to tolerate proper behavior from my wife."

She touched his face, smiling as he nipped at her exploring fingertips. "I've missed you, Sebastian."

"Have you, love?" He unfastened the buttons of her robe, the light eyes glittering with heat as her skin was revealed. "What part did you miss the most?"

"Your mind," she said, and smiled at his expression.

"I was hoping for a far more depraved answer than that."

"Your mind is depraved," she told him solemnly.

He gave a husky laugh. "True."

She gasped as his experienced hand slipped inside her robe. "What part of m-me did you miss the most?"

"I missed you from head to toe. I missed every freckle. I missed the taste of you . . . the feel of your hair in my hands . . . Evie, my love, you are shamefully overdressed."

And he picked her up and carried her to bed. The velvet robe was stripped away, replaced by firelight and his caressing hands. He kissed the new rich curve of her stomach, fascinated by the changes in her fertile body. And then he kissed her everywhere else, and entered her with teasing skill. Evie jolted a little at the feel of him, so hard and heavy inside her.

Pausing, St. Vincent smiled down at her, his face flushed with desire. "Sweet little wife," he whispered. "What am I to do with you? Such a short time apart . . . and already you've forgotten how to accommodate me." Evie shook her head, straining to take him in, and her husband laughed softly. "Let me help you, love . . ." And he courted her body with careful, wicked thoroughness, until he had entered her fully and brought her, sighing and trembling, into helpless rapture.

Afterward, as Evie reclined on her side and tried to catch her breath, St. Vincent left the bed and returned with a large, rattling leather case. He set it on the nearby table. "I brought the family jewels," he told her.

"I know," she said languidly, and he laughed as he saw what she was staring at.

"No, love. The other family jewels. They're entailed to the future Duchess of Kingston. But I told my father I'm giving them to you now, since he'll obviously live for a damned eternity."

Her eyes widened. "Thank you, Sebastian. But I . . . I don't need jewelry . . ."

"You do. Let me see them on you." He pulled out ropes of priceless pearls, sparkling necklaces and bracelets and earrings wrought of gold and every imaginable jewel. To Evie's squirmy, giggling embarrassment, he sat beside her and began to adorn her, clasping a sapphire bracelet around her ankle, tucking a diamond into her navel.

"Sebastian—" she protested, while he weighted her naked body with enough gold and rare gemstones to purchase a small country.

"Be still." His mouth searched between strands of pearls, pausing here and there to lick and bite gently at her skin. "I'm decorating for Christmas."

Evie smiled and shivered. "You're not supposed to decorate *me*."

"Don't discourage my holiday spirit, darling. Now let me show you something interesting about these pearls . . ." And before long, her protests had faded into pleasured moans.

Chapter Twelve

Hannah!" Natalie was in bed, drinking her morning tea. A housemaid was stirring the coals and lighting the grate, giggling as if she and Natalie had just shared an irresistibly funny joke.

Having come in from a long walk outside, Hannah entered the room and smiled at her cousin fondly. "Good morning, dear. Finally awake?"

"Yes, I stayed up much too late last night." A group of the younger guests, including Natalie, had spent the evening playing parlor games. Hannah had neither asked nor wanted to know if Rafe . . . for that was how she now thought of Mr. Bowman . . . had been among them.

In the past few days since their astonishing interaction in the parlor, Hannah had avoided Rafe as much as possible, and she had tried not to speak to him directly. She had gone on many solitary walks and had done much soul-searching, unable to comprehend why Rafe had engaged in such an intimate act with her, why she had allowed it, and what her feelings were toward him.

Although Hannah knew little about physical desire, she understood that it resonated more strongly between some people than others. She couldn't perceive whether Rafe felt the same desire toward Natalie. It made her miserable to contemplate it. But she felt certain he had not made *that* kind of advance to Natalie, at least not yet, or Natalie would have told her.

Above all, she understood that ultimately none of this mattered. For a man in Rafe's position, feelings of desire and attachment would make no difference regarding the course he would take. When he married Natalie, he would no longer be the black sheep of the family. In one fell swoop he would please his father, secure his rightful position, and garner a large fortune.

If he chose someone else, he would lose everything.

A woman who cared about him would never ask him to make such a choice.

That afternoon when Hannah had picked herself up from the library floor and painstakingly restored her clothing, she had acknowledged that she was falling in love with him, and the more she knew of him, the deeper the feelings cut. She had retrieved the little toy soldier, and she carried it in her pocket, a small and private weight. It was her token now—she would not offer it to Rafe again. In the future she would be able to close the piece in her hand and remember the dashing American scoundrel and the attraction that had exploded in a passion she would never forget.

I'm a woman with a past now, she thought, amused and wistful.

Regarding Samuel Clark and his proposal . . . Rafe had been right. She did not love him. It would be unfair to Clark if she married him and forever compared him to someone else. Therefore Hannah resolved to write to Clark soon and turn down his offer of marriage, much as she was tempted by the safety of it.

Natalie's merry voice recalled her from her thoughts.

"Hannah! Hannah, are you listening? I have something *delicious* to tell you . . . a few minutes ago, Polly brought the most astonishing little note—" Natalie waved a scorched and half-crumpled bit of parchment in front of her. "You'll blush when you read it. You'll *faint*."

"What is it?" Hannah asked, slowly approaching the bed-side.

The young dark-haired housemaid, Polly, answered sheepishly. "Well, miss, it's part of my chores to polish the grates and clean the hearths in the bachelor's house behind the manor—"

"That's where Mr. Bowman is staying," Natalie interjected.

"—and after Mr. Bowman left this morning, I went to the hearth, and while I was sweeping out the ashes, I saw a bit of paper with writing on it. So I picked it up, and when I saw it was a love letter, I knew it was for Lady Natalie."

"Why did you assume that?" Hannah asked, nettled that Rafe's privacy should have been invaded in such a way.

"Because he's courting me," Natalie said, rolling her eyes, "and everyone knows it."

Hannah turned an unsmiling gaze to the housemaid, whose excitement had dimmed in the face of her disapproval. "You shouldn't snoop through the guests' things, Polly," she said gently.

"But it was in the hearth, half burnt," the maid protested, flushing. "He didn't want it. And I saw the words and thought it might be important."

"Either you thought it was rubbish, or you thought it was important. Which was it?"

"Am I going to get in trouble?" Polly whispered, turning a beseeching gaze to Natalie.

"No, of course not," Natalie said impatiently. "Now Hannah, don't turn all schoolma'amish. You're missing the point entirely, which is that this is a love letter from Mr. Bowman to me. And it's a rather dirty-minded and odd letter—I've never received anything like it before, and it's *very* entertaining and—" She broke off with a gasp of laughter as Hannah snatched it from her.

The letter had been crumpled up and tossed onto the grate. It had burned all around the edges, so the names at the top and bottom had gone up in smoke. But there was enough of the bold black scrawl to reveal that it had indeed been a love letter. And as Hannah read the singed and half-destroyed parchment, she was forced to turn away to hide the trembling of her hand.

—should warn you that this letter will not be eloquent. However, it will be sincere, especially in light of the fact that you will never read it. I have felt these words like a weight in my chest, until I find myself amazed that a heart can go on beating under such a burden.

I love you. I love you desperately, violently, tenderly, completely. I want you in ways that I know you would find shocking. My love, you don't belong with a man like me. In the past I've done things you wouldn't approve of, and I've done them ten times over. I have led a life of immoderate sin. As it turns out, I'm just as immoderate in love. Worse, in fact.

I want to kiss every soft place of you, make you blush and faint, pleasure you until you weep, and dry every tear with my lips. If you only knew how I crave the taste of you. I want to take you in my hands and mouth and feast on you. I want to drink wine and honey from you.

I want you under me. On your back.

I'm sorry. You deserve more respect than that.

But I can't stop thinking of it. Your arms and legs around me. Your mouth, open for my kisses. I need too much of you. A lifetime of nights spent between your thighs wouldn't be enough.

I want to talk with you forever. I remember every word you've ever said to me.

If only I could visit you as a foreigner goes into a new country, learn the language of you, wander past all borders into every private and secret place, I would stay forever. I would become a citizen of you.

You would say it's too soon to feel this way. You would ask how I could be so certain. But some things can't be measured by time. Ask me an hour from now. Ask me a month from now. A year, ten years, a lifetime. The way I love you will outlast every calendar, clock, and every toll of every bell that will ever be cast. If only you—

And there it stopped.

Aware of the silence in the room, Hannah endeavored to regulate her breathing. "Is there any more?" she asked in a controlled tone.

"I *knew* you would blush," Natalie said triumphantly.

"The rest was ashes, miss," Polly replied, more guarded.

"Did you show it to anyone else?" Hannah asked sharply, concerned for Rafe's sake. These words had not been meant for anyone to read. "Any of the servants?"

"No, miss," the girl said, her lower lip trembling.

"Heavens, Hannah," Natalie exclaimed, "there's no need to be so cross. I thought this would amuse you, not send you into a temper."

"I'm not in a temper." She was devastated, and aroused, and anguished. And most of all, confused. Hannah made her face expressionless as she continued. "But out of respect for Mr. Bowman, I don't think this should be put on display for others' amusement. If he is to be your husband, Natalie, you must protect his privacy."

"I, protect *him*?" Natalie asked roguishly. "After reading that, I rather think I shall need protection *from* him." She shook her head and laughed at Hannah's silence. "What a spoilsport you are. Go and burn what's left of it, if that will put you in a better mood."

SOME MEN, RAFE REFLECTED GRIMLY, WANTED NOTHING more for their sons than to carry on the same life *they* were having.

After a long and vicious argument that morning, it had become clear to him that Thomas would not yield in any way. Rafe must step into the life that his father had planned for him and become, more or less, a reflection of Thomas Bowman. Anything less and his father would regard him as a failure, both as a son and as a man.

The argument had begun when Thomas had told Rafe that he was expected to propose to Lady Natalie by Christmas Eve. "Lord Blandford and I want to announce the betrothal of our children at the Christmas Eve ball."

"What a wonderful idea," Rafe had marveled sarcastically. "But I haven't yet decided whether or not I want to marry her."

The predictable color had begun to rise in Thomas Bowman's face. "It's time to make a decision. You have all the necessary information. You've spent enough time with her to be able to assess her qualities. She's a daughter of the peerage. You know all the rewards that will come your way when you marry. Hell and damnation, why do you even hesitate?"

"I don't have any feelings for her."

"So much the better! It will be a steady marriage. It is time to take your place in the world as a man, Rafe." Thomas had made a visible effort to control his temper as he tried to make himself understood. "Love passes. Beauty fades. Life is not a romantic romp through a meadow."

"My God, that's inspiring."

"You've never done as I asked. You never even tried. I wanted a son who would be a help to me, who would understand the importance of what I was doing."

"I understand that you want to build an empire," Rafe had said quietly. "And I've tried to find a place for myself in your grand scheme. I could do a hell of a lot for the company, and you know it. What I don't understand is why you want me to prove myself this way first."

"I want you to demonstrate your commitment to me. As Matthew Swift did. *He* married the woman I chose for him."

"He happened to be in love with Daisy," Rafe snapped.

"And so could you be, with Lady Natalie. But in the end, love doesn't matter. Men like us marry women who will either further our ambitions, or at least not hinder them. You see what a long and productive marriage your mother and I have had."

"Thirty years," Rafe agreed. "And you and Mother can barely stand to be in the same room together." Sighing tautly, Rafe dragged his hand through his hair. He glanced at his father's round, obstinate face, with its bristling mustache, and he wondered why Thomas had always been compelled to exert such relentless control over the people around him. "What's all this for, Father? What reward do you have after all these years of building a fortune? You take no pleasure in your family. You have the temperament of a baited badger— and that's on your good days. You don't seem to enjoy much of anything."

"I enjoy being Thomas Bowman."

"I'm glad of it. But I don't think I would enjoy it."

Thomas stared at him for a long moment. His face softened, and for once, he spoke in a near-fatherly tone. "I'm trying to help you. I wouldn't ask you to do something I believed to be against your own interests. My judgment about Swift and Daisy was correct, wasn't it?"

"By some miracle of God, yes," Rafe muttered.

"It will all get better, easier, once you start making the right choices. You must build a good life for yourself, Rafe. Take your place at the table. There is nothing wrong with Blandford's daughter. Everyone wants this match. Lady Natalie has made it clear to all and sundry that she is amenable. And you led me to believe that you would go through with it as long as the girl was acceptable!"

"You're right. At first it didn't matter whom I married. But now I find myself unwilling to pick a wife with no more care than I would exert in choosing a pair of shoes."

Thomas had looked exasperated. "What has changed since you arrived in England?"

Rafe didn't answer.

"Is it that brown-haired girl?" his father prodded. "Lady Natalie's companion?"

He looked at his father alertly. "Why do you ask?"

"It seems you've gone more than once to listen to her read at night to a group of children. And you care nothing for children or Christmas stories." The heavy mustache twitched contemptuously. "She's common, Rafe."

"And we're not? Grandmother was a dockside washwoman, and the devil knows who your father was. And that was just on your side of the—"

"I have spent my life trying to elevate this blighted family into something more! Don't use this girl as a way to avoid your responsibilities. You can have as many of her kind as you desire after you've married Lady Natalie. No one would condemn you for it, especially in England. Seduce her. Make her your mistress. I'll even buy a house for her, if that will please you."

"Thank you, but I can afford my own mistresses." Rafe threw his father a glance of dark disgust. "You want this marriage so much that you're willing to finance the corruption of an innocent girl to accomplish it?"

"Everyone loses their innocence sooner or later." As Thomas saw Rafe's expression, his eyes had turned cold. "If you foil everyone's expectations, and embarrass me in the bargain, I will cut you off. No more chances. You will be disinherited, and renounced."

"Understood," Rafe had said curtly.

Chapter Thirteen

. . . and it was always said of him, that he knew how to keep Christmas well, if any man alive possessed the knowledge. May that be truly said of us, and all of us! And so, as Tiny Tim observed, God Bless Us, Every One!

Glancing upward as she finished reading *A Christmas Carol*, Hannah saw the rapt faces of the children, their eyes shining. There was a brief silence, the shared pleasure of a wonderful story tinged with the regret that it had to end. And then they were all standing, moving about the room, their faces sticky with milk and cookie crumbs, their small hands clapping enthusiastically.

There were two imps on her lap, and one hugging her neck from behind the chair. Hannah looked up as Rafe Bowman approached her. The rhythm of her heart went wild, and she knew her shortness of breath had nothing to do with the small arms clamped around her neck.

His gaze strayed to her disordered clothes and tousled coiffure. "Well done," he murmured. "You've made it feel like Christmas. For everyone."

"Thank you," she whispered, trying not to think of his hands on her skin, his mouth—

"I need to talk to you."

Carefully Hannah dislodged the children from her lap and disentangled the arms from her neck. Standing to face him, she tried in vain to straighten her dress and smooth her skirts. She took a deep breath, but her voice emerged with a dismaying lack of force. "I . . . I don't see how any good could come of that."

His gaze was warm and direct. "Nevertheless, I'm going to talk to you."

The words from his letter drifted through her mind. *"I want to kiss every soft place of you . . ."*

"Please not now," she whispered, with her face flushing and an ache rising in her throat.

Reading the signs of her distress, he relented. "Tomorrow?"

"I need too much of you . . ."

"Yes," she said with difficulty.

Comprehending how deeply his presence unnerved her, Rafe gave her a slight nod, his jaw firming. It seemed there were a dozen things he wanted to say, words hovering impatiently on his lips, but something . . . compassion or pity perhaps . . . afforded him the necessary self-restraint.

"Tomorrow," he repeated quietly, and left her.

NANNIES AND NURSERYMAIDS CAME TO COLLECT THE CHIL-dren, and Hannah went out into the hallway in a daze of misery.

No one had ever told her that love could make every cell in one's body hurt.

She was becoming fairly certain that she would not be able to attend Rafe and Natalie's wedding, that all the events of their married life, the births of children, the celebrations and rituals, would be impossible for her to tolerate. She would stew in jealousy and despair and resentment until she disintegrated. The common wisdom for a woman in her situation was that someday she would meet another man, and she would forget all about Rafe Bowman. But she didn't want another man. There was no one else like him.

I'm doomed, she thought.

With her head lowered, she plowed along the hallway, intending to go to her room, where she could mope and cry in private. Unfortunately, walking with one's head down meant one could not precisely see where one was going. She nearly collided with a woman approaching from the opposite direction, someone who walked with a distinctively long, free stride.

They both stopped abruptly, and the woman reached out to steady Hannah.

"My lady," Hannah gasped, recognizing Lillian. "Oh . . . I'm so sorry . . . I beg your pardon . . ."

"No harm done," the countess assured her. "My fault, actually. I was hurrying to tell the housekeeper something before I had to meet my sister, and—" She paused and stared at Hannah closely. "You look ready to cry," she said bluntly. "Is something the matter?"

"No," Hannah said brightly, and a few hot tears spilled out. She sighed and bent her head again. "Oh, *bollocks.* Forgive me, I must go—"

"You poor thing," Lillian said with genuine sympathy, seeming not at all shocked by the profanity. "Come with me. There's a private parlor upstairs where we can talk."

"I can't," Hannah whispered. "My lady, forgive me, but you're the last person I can confide in about this."

"Oh." The countess's eyes, the same velvet brown as her brother's, widened slightly. "It's Rafe, isn't it?"

More tears, welling up no matter how tightly she closed her eyes against them.

"Is there a friend you can talk to?" Lillian asked softly.

"Natalie is my best friend," Hannah said between sniffles. "So that's impossible."

"Then let me be your friend. I'm not sure I can help—but at least I can try to understand."

They went to a cozy parlor upstairs, a private receiving room decorated in a plush, feminine style. Lillian closed the door, brought Hannah a handkerchief, and sat beside her on the settee. "I insist that you call me Lillian," she said. "And before either of us says a word, let me assure you that everything in this parlor will remain completely private. No one will know."

"Yes, my—Lillian." Hannah blew her nose and sighed.

"Now, what happened to make you cry?"

"It's Mr. Bowman . . . Rafe . . ." She could not seem to put her words in the proper order, and so she let them tumble out, even knowing Lillian would never be able to make sense of them. "He is so . . . and I've never . . . and when he kissed me I thought *no,* it's merely infatuation, but . . . and then Mr. Clark proposed, and I realized I couldn't accept because . . . and I know it's too soon. Too fast. But the worst part is the letter, because I don't even know who he wrote it for!" She went on and on, trying desperately to make herself understood. Somehow, miraculously, Lillian managed to make sense of the mess.

While Hannah poured out the whole story, or at least an expurgated version, Lillian gripped her hands firmly. As Hannah paused to blow her nose again, Lillian said, "I'm going to ring for tea. With brandy."

She pulled the servants' bell, and when a maid came to the door, Lillian cracked it open and murmured to her. The maid went to fetch the tea.

Just as Lillian returned to the settee, the door opened, and Daisy Swift poked her head inside. She looked mildly surprised to see Hannah sitting there with Lillian. "Hello. Lillian, you were supposed to play cards."

"Hang it, I forgot."

Daisy's brown eyes were filled with curiosity and sympathy as she glanced at Hannah. "Why are you crying? Is there something I can do?"

"This is a very private and highly sensitive matter," Lillian told her. "Hannah's confiding in me."

"Oh, confide in me, too!" Daisy said earnestly, coming into the room. "I can keep a secret. Better than Lillian, as a matter of fact."

Without giving Hannah a chance to respond, Daisy closed the door and came to sit beside her sister.

"You are to tell *no one*," Lillian said to Daisy sternly. "Hannah is in love with Rafe, and he's going to propose to Lady Natalie. Except that he's in love with Hannah."

"I'm not sure about that," Hannah said in a muffled voice. "It's just . . . the letter . . ."

"Do you still have it? May I see it?"

Hannah regarded her doubtfully. "It's very private. He didn't want anyone to read it."

"Then he should have burned the damn thing properly," Lillian said.

"Do show us, Hannah," Daisy urged. "It will go no further, I promise."

Carefully Hannah pulled the scrap of parchment from her pocket and gave it to Lillian. The sisters bent over it intently.

"Oh, my," she heard Daisy murmur.

"He doesn't mince words, does he?" Lillian asked dryly, her brows lifting. She glanced at Hannah. "This is Rafe's handwriting, and I've no doubt he was the author. But it is unusual for him to express himself in such a manner."

"I'm sure he knows many pretty phrases to attract women," Hannah mumbled. "He's a rake."

"Well, yes, he's a rake, but to be so open and effusive . . . that's not like him. He's usually—"

"A rake of few words," Daisy finished for her.

"My point is, he was clearly moved by a very strong feeling," Lillian told Hannah. She turned to her younger sister. "What do you think, Daisy?"

"Well, reading such sentiments from one's brother is slightly revolting," Daisy said. "Wine and honey, et cetera. But regardless of that, it's clear that Rafe has fallen in love for the first time in his life."

"The letter may not have been meant for me—" Hannah began, when the door opened again.

It was Evie, Lady St. Vincent, her red hair arranged in a loose chignon. "I've been looking for you," she said.

"We haven't seen you for days," Lillian said. "Where have you been?"

Evie's color deepened. "With St. Vincent."

"What have you been . . . Oh, good God. Never mind."

Evie's gaze fell on Hannah. "Oh, dear. Are you all right?"

"We're discussing something *highly* private," Daisy told her. "Hannah's in love with Rafe. It's a secret. Come in."

Evie entered the room and sat in a nearby chair, while Lillian succinctly explained the situation. "May I see the letter?" she asked.

"I don't think—" Hannah began, but Daisy had already given it to her.

"Don't worry," Lillian murmured to Hannah. "Evie's better than anyone at keeping secrets."

After Evie had finished reading, looking up with round blue eyes, Hannah said morosely, "It may not have been intended for me. It could just as easily have been written for Natalie. Men adore her. They're *always* proposing to her, and she manages them so well, and I can't manage them at all."

"N-no one can manage men," Evie told her firmly. "They c-can't even manage themselves."

"That's right," Lillian said. "And furthermore, any woman who thinks she can manage men shouldn't be allowed to have one."

"Annabelle can manage them," Daisy said reflectively. "Although she would deny it."

There was a brief tap at the door.

"The tea," Lillian said.

However, it was not a maid, but Annabelle Hunt. "Hello," she said with a smile, her gaze sweeping across the group. "What are we doing?" As she looked at Hannah, her expression softened with concern. "Oh, you've been crying."

"She's in love with Rafe Bowman," Evie said. "It's a s-secret. Come in."

"Tell *no one,* Annabelle," Lillian said severely. "This is confidential."

"She's not very good with secrets," Daisy said.

"I am, too," Annabelle said, coming into the parlor. "At least, I am good at keeping big secrets. It's the little ones I seem to have a problem with."

"This is a big one," Lillian told her.

Hannah waited with resignation as the situation was explained to Annabelle.

Receiving the letter, Annabelle scanned the scorched parchment, and a faint smile came to her lips. "Oh, how lovely." She looked up at Hannah. "This was not meant for Lady Natalie," she said decisively. "Hannah, Rafe's attraction to you has not gone unnoticed. In fact, it has been discreetly remarked upon."

"She means everyone's gossiping about you," Daisy said to Hannah.

"I believe," Annabelle continued, "that Rafe likes Lady

Natalie—there is certainly much about her to like. But he loves *you*."

"But it's impossible," Hannah said, her face drawn with miserable tightness.

"Impossible that he could love you?" Daisy asked. "Or impossible because of the infernal deal that Father has set up for him?"

"Both," Hannah said dolefully. "First, I don't know if what he feels for me is merely infatuation . . ." She paused to blot her burning eyes.

"'Ask me an hour from now,'" Annabelle read softly from the letter. "'Ask me a month from now. A year, ten years, a lifetime . . .' That's not infatuation, Hannah."

"But even if it's true," Hannah said, "I would never accept him, because he would lose everything, including his relationship with his father. I would not want him to make such a sacrifice."

"Neither should Father," Lillian said darkly.

"Perhaps I should mention," Daisy volunteered, "that Matthew is determined to have it out with Father on this issue. He says Father can't be allowed to run to such excesses. Limits must be set, or he'll try to trample over *everyone*. And since Matthew has a great deal of influence with Father, it's very possible that he can make him retract his demands."

"But no matter what," Annabelle told Hannah, "you have nothing to do with the relationship between Rafe and his father. Your only obligation is to make your feelings known to Rafe. Out of love for him—and for your own sake as well—you must give Rafe a choice. He deserves to know your feelings before he makes important decisions about his future."

Hannah knew that Annabelle was right. But the truth was not exactly liberating. It made her feel hollow and small. She drew the toe of her shoe on a flowered medallion pattern on the carpet. "I hope I can be that brave," she said, more to herself than to the others.

"Love is worth the risk," Daisy said.

"If you don't tell Rafe," Lillian added, "you'll regret it forever. Because you'll never know what might have happened."

"Tell him," Evie said quietly.

Hannah took an unsteady breath, looking at the four of them. They were a peculiar group, all so bright and pretty, but . . . different. And she had the feeling that these women encouraged each other's eccentricities, and relished their differences. Anything could be said or done among them, and no matter what it was, they would accept and forgive. Sometimes, in some rare and wonderful friendships, the bond of sisterly love was much stronger than any blood tie.

It felt nice to be around them. She felt comforted in their presence, especially when she looked into the Bowman sisters' familiar dark eyes.

"All right," she told them, her stomach dropping. "I will tell him. Tomorrow."

"Tomorrow night is the Christmas Eve ball," Annabelle said. "Do you have a nice gown to wear?"

"Yes," Hannah replied. "A white one. It's very simple, but it's my favorite."

"I have a pearl necklace you could borrow," Annabelle offered.

"I have white satin gloves for her," Daisy exclaimed.

Lillian grinned. "Hannah, we'll adorn you more lavishly than the Christmas tree."

The maid brought in tea, and Lillian sent her back for extra cups. "Who wants tea with brandy?" Lillian asked.

"I do," said Daisy.

"I'll take m-mine without the brandy," Evie murmured.

"I'll take mine without the tea," Annabelle said.

Moving to the space beside Hannah, Daisy gave her a fresh handkerchief, and put her arm around her shoulders. "You know, dear," Daisy said, "you're our first honorary wallflower. And we've brought very good luck to each other. I have no doubt it will extend to you, too."

SLIGHTLY TIPSY FROM A GLASS OF STRAIGHT BRANDY, LILLIAN said good night to the wallflowers, including their newest member. They all left the Marsden parlor to go to their rooms. Wandering slowly toward the master's suite, Lillian pondered her brother's situation with a troubled frown.

Lillian was a straightforward, blunt-spoken woman, who far preferred to handle a problem by bringing it out into the open and dealing with it directly. But she understood that this matter must be handled with discretion and sensitivity. Which meant she needed to stay out of it. And yet she longed for Rafe to find the happiness he deserved. Even more, she longed to shake her stubborn ass of a father and command him to stop manipulating the lives of everyone around him.

She decided to talk to Westcliff, who could always be counted on for comfort and common sense. She could hardly wait to hear his opinions on the matter of Rafe and Hannah and Lady Natalie. Guessing that he would still be downstairs with the guests, she headed toward the grand staircase.

As she reached the top of the grand staircase and prepared to descend, she saw her husband standing in the entrance hall below, talking to someone.

Lady Kittridge . . . *again*.

"Marcus," she whispered, feeling a sick pang of jealousy. Followed swiftly by rage.

By God, this was not to be endured. She would not lose her husband's affections to someone else. Not without a fight. Her hands clenched into fists. Although every instinct screamed for her to storm downstairs and jump between her husband and the blond woman, she managed to restrain her-self. She was a countess. She would do the dignified thing, and confront Marcus in private.

First she went to the nursery to say good night to little Merritt, who was snuggled in a lace-trimmed crib, with a nurserymaid watching over her. The sight of her precious daughter calmed Lillian somewhat. She smoothed her hand lightly over the baby's dark hair, drinking in the sight of her. *I'm the mother of his child,* she thought vehemently, wish-ing she could hurl the words like daggers at the glamorous Lady Kittridge. *I'm his wife. And he hasn't fallen out of love with me yet!*

She went to the master bedroom, bathed and changed into a nightgown and velvet dressing robe, and brushed out her long sable hair.

Her heart began to thump madly as Marcus entered the room. He paused at the sight of her, the long locks of hair flowing down her back, and he smiled. Here in private, his autocratic demeanor faded away, and the all-powerful earl became a warm, loving, very mortal man.

He stripped off his coat and dropped it onto a chair. His cravat followed, and then he came to stand beside her.

Lillian closed her eyes as his hands came to her head, fin-gers sliding gently through her loose hair, and his fingertips massaged her temples. She was acutely aware of him, the coiled power of his body, and the dry, sweet outdoors scent of him, like fresh-cut hay. He fascinated her, this complex man with complex needs. Having been raised with the un-stinting criticism of her parents, it was no wonder that she occasionally doubted her ability to be enough for Marcus.

"Are you tired?" he asked in that gravel-wrapped-in-velvet murmur, so distinctive and pleasant.

"Just a little." She sighed as his hands slid to her shoul-ders, working the tension from them.

"You could just lie back and let me have my way with you," he suggested, his dark eyes glowing.

"Yes, but . . . there is something I must talk with you about first." Damn it, there was a quaver in her voice, despite her attempt to sound calm and dignified.

Marcus's expression changed as he heard the distress in her tone. He pulled her up to face him, and he stared down at her with instant concern. "What is it, my love?"

Lillian took a deep breath. Another. Her fear and anger and worry were so great, it was hard to force the words out. "I . . . I should not stand in the way of your . . . pursuits outside of marriage. I know that. I understand how it is with your kind . . . I mean, you've done it for centuries, and I suppose it was too much for me to expect that you—that I—would be enough. All I ask is that you be discreet. Because it isn't easy to watch you with her—the way you smile, and—" She stopped and covered her face with her hands, mortified to feel tears springing to her eyes. Bloody hell.

"My kind?" Marcus sounded bewildered. "What have I done for centuries? Lillian, what the hell are you talking about?"

Her woeful voice filtered out from behind her hands. "Lady Kittridge."

There was a short, shocked silence.

"Have you gone mad? Lillian, look at me. Lillian—"

"I can't look at you," she muttered.

He gave her a little shake. "Lillian . . . Am I to understand that you think I have a personal interest in her?"

The note of genuine outrage in his question made Lillian feel the tiniest bit better. No guilty husband could have feigned such baffled anger. On the other hand, it was never a good idea to provoke Marcus. He was usually slow to anger, but once it started, mountains trembled, oceans parted, and every creature with an instinct for self-preservation fled for cover.

"I've seen you talking with her," Lillian said, taking her hands down, "and smiling at her, and you've corresponded with her. And—" She gave him a look of miserable indignation. "You've changed the way you tie your cravat!"

"My valet suggested it," he said, looking stunned.

"And that new trick the other night . . . that new thing you did in bed . . ."

"You didn't like it? Damn it, Lillian, all you had to do was tell me—"

"I did like it," she said, turning scarlet. "But it's one of the signs, you see."

"Signs of what?"

"That you've tired of me," she said, her voice cracking. "That you want someone else."

Marcus stared at her and let out a string of curses that shocked Lillian, who had a fairly good command of filthy language herself. Seizing her arm, he pulled her with him out of the bedroom. "Come with me."

"Now? Like this? Marcus, I'm not dressed—"

"I don't give a bloody damn!"

I've finally driven him mad, Lillian thought in alarm, as he tugged and pulled her along with him, down the stairs and through the entrance hall past a few bemused-looking servants. Out into the biting December cold. What was he going to do? Toss her off the bluff? "Marcus?" she asked nervously, hurrying to keep pace with his ground-eating strides.

He didn't answer, only took her across the courtyard to the stables, with their central courtyard and drinking fountain for the horses, into the warm central space with rows of superbly appointed horse stalls. Horses stared at them with mild interest as Marcus pulled Lillian to the end of the first row. There was a stall with a large, cheerful red bow tacked at the top.

The stall contained an astonishingly beautiful Arabian mare about fourteen hands high, with a narrow, eloquent head and neck, large lustrous eyes, and what appeared to be perfect conformation.

Lillian blinked in surprise. "A white Arabian?" she asked faintly, having never seen such a creature before. "She looks like something out of a fairy tale."

"Technically she's registered as a gray," Marcus said. "But the shade is so light, it looks like pale silver. Her name is Misty Moonlight." He gave her a sardonic glance. "She's your Christmas present. You asked if we could work on your riding skills together—remember?"

"Oh." Lillian was suddenly breathless.

"It's taken me six damn months to make the arrangements," Marcus continued curtly. "Lady Kittridge is the best horse breeder in England, and very particular about whom she'll sell one of her Arabians to. And as this horse had been promised to someone else, I had to bribe and threaten the other buyer, and pay a bloody fortune to Lady Kittridge."

"And *that's* why you've been communicating so often with Lady Kittridge?"

"*Yes.*" He scowled at her.

"Oh, Marcus!" Lillian was overcome with relief and happiness.

"And in return for my pains," he growled, "I'm accused of infidelity! I love you more than life. Since I met you, I've never even thought of another woman. And how you think I could have the desire for someone else when we spend every bloody night together is beyond my powers of comprehension!"

Realizing that he had been mortally offended and his outrage was increasing by the second, Lillian offered him a placating smile. "I never thought you would actually betray me that way. I was just afraid that you found her tempting. And I—"

"The only thing I find tempting is the idea of taking you to the tack room and applying a saddle strap to your bottom. Repeatedly. With vigor."

Lillian backed away as her husband approached her menacingly. She was filled with a combination of giddy relief and alarm. "Marcus, everything's settled. I believe you. I'm not at all worried now."

"You should be worried," he said with chilling softness. "Because it's clear that unless there are consequences for this lack of faith in me—"

"*Consequences?*" she squeaked.

"—this problem may arise again in the future. So I'm about to remove all doubt about what I want, and from whom."

Staring at him with wide eyes, Lillian wondered if he was going to beat her, ravish her, or both. She calculated her chances of escaping. Not good. Marcus, with his powerful but agile build, was superbly fit and accomplished. He was as fast as lightning and could probably outmaneuver a hare. Watching her steadily, he removed his waistcoat and tossed it to the hay-covered floor. Picking up a horse blanket from a folded stack, he spread it over a pile of hay.

"Come here," he said quietly, his expression implacable.

Her eyes went huge. Wild, half-hysterical giggles rose in her throat. She tried to stand her ground. "Marcus, there are some things that shouldn't be done in front of children or horses."

"There are no children here. And my horses don't gossip."

Lillian tried to dart past him. Marcus caught her easily, tossing her onto the blanket-covered hay. And as she yelped and protested, he tore the nightgown from her. His mouth crushed over hers, his hands sliding over her body with insolent demand. A cry snagged in her throat as he bent to her breasts, clamping the tips gently with his teeth, then sooth-ing the little aches with his tongue. He did all the things that he knew would arouse her, his lovemaking gentle but ruth-less, until she gasped out a few words of surrender. Unfas-tening his trousers with a few deft tugs, he thrust deeply inside her with primitive force.

Lillian shivered in ecstasy and gripped his muscular flexing back. He kissed her, his mouth rough and greedy, his body moving in a powerful rhythm. "Marcus," Lillian gasped, "I'll never doubt you again . . . oh, *God* . . ."

He smiled privately against her hair and pulled her hips up higher against his. "See that you don't," he murmured. And long into the night, he had his way with her.

Chapter Fourteen

Hannah tried in vain to find an opportunity to talk to Rafe the next day. He was impossible to find. And so were Natalie and the Blandfords, and the Bowmans. She had the uneasy feeling that something was brewing.

Stony Cross Manor was swarming with activity, guests singing, eating, drinking, while the children put on productions with a huge toy theatre set up in one of the common rooms.

Quite late in the day, Hannah finally caught a glimpse of Rafe as she passed by Lord Westcliff's private study. The door had been left open, and he could be seen inside talking with Westcliff and Mr. Swift. As she paused uncertainly, Rafe glanced in her direction. Instantly he pushed away from the desk he had been leaning against, and murmured to the others, "One moment."

He came out to the hallway, his expression uncharacteristically sober. But a smile tipped the corners of his mouth as he looked down at her. "Hannah." The softness of his voice sent a ripple of awareness down her back.

"You . . . you said you wanted to talk with me," she managed to say.

"Yes, I did. I do. Forgive me—I've been occupied by a few matters." He reached out to touch her as if he couldn't help it, lightly fingering the loose fabric of one of her sleeves. "We'll need time and privacy for what I want to discuss—both of which seem to be in short supply today."

"Perhaps later tonight?" she suggested hesitantly.

"Yes. I'll find you." Letting go of her sleeve, he gave her a slight, gentlemanly bow. "Until tonight."

WHEN HANNAH WENT UPSTAIRS TO HELP NATALIE CHANGE into her ballgown, and then ready herself, she was mystified to discover that Natalie was already fully dressed.

Her cousin looked magnificent in a pale blue satin gown trimmed with bunches of matching blue tulle, her hair dressed in upswept golden curls. "Hannah!" Natalie exclaimed, leaving their room in the company of Lady Blandford. "I have something to tell you—something very important—"

"You may tell her later," Lady Blandford interrupted, seeming as distracted as her daughter. "Lord Blandford and Lord Westcliff are downstairs, Natalie. It will not do to keep them waiting."

"Yes, of course." Natalie's blue eyes sparkled with excitement. "We'll speak soon, Hannah."

Bemused, Hannah watched them hurry along the hallway. Something was definitely afoot, she thought, and a rush of worry caused a cool sweat to collect beneath the layers of her clothes.

A lady's maid waited for her inside the bedroom. "Miss Appleton. Lady Westcliff sent me to help you get ready for the ball."

"Did she? That is very kind. I don't usually require much help, but—"

"I'm very good at arranging hair," the maid said firmly. "And Lady Westcliff told me to use her very own pearl hairpins for you. Now, if you'll sit at the dressing table, miss . . . ?"

Touched by Lillian's generosity in sending her own maid, Hannah complied. It took an eternity to curl her hair with hot tongs, and arrange it in pinned-up curls, with gleaming white pearls scattered amid the dark locks of her hair. The maid helped her into the white ballgown, and gave her a pair of silver-embroidered silk stockings from Evie. After fastening a pearl necklace from Annabelle Hunt around Hannah's neck, the maid helped her to tug on a pair of long white satin gloves from Daisy Swift. The wallflowers, Hannah thought with a grateful smile, were her own group of fairy godmothers.

They finished with a dusting of powder on her nose and forehead, and some rose petal salve for her lips.

Hannah was vaguely startled by her own elegant reflection, her eyes wide and green, the elaborate coiffure contrasting pleasingly with the simplicity of the white gown.

"Very beautiful, miss," the maid pronounced. "You'd best hurry downstairs . . . the ball will be starting soon."

HANNAH WAS TOO NERVOUS TO BE TEMPTED BY THE MAG-nificent buffet of delicacies laid out on long tables. The refreshments would be enjoyed by the guests during the dance, and later in the evening a formal supper would be served. As soon as she appeared in the ballroom, she was joined by Lillian and Daisy, who exclaimed over her appearance.

"You are both so very kind," Hannah told them earnestly. "And to loan me the pearls and the gloves, it is beyond generous—"

"We have ulterior motives," Daisy replied.

Hannah gave her a perplexed glance.

"Very good ulterior motives," Lillian said with a grin. "We want you as our sister."

"Have you spoken to Rafe yet?" Daisy asked sotto voce.

Hannah shook her head. "I've hardly seen him all day. It seemed he was missing for a while, and then he was talking with a great many people."

"Something is brewing," Lillian said. "Westcliff was busy all day as well. And my parents were nowhere to be seen."

"The Blandfords as well," Hannah commented apprehensively. "What does all that mean?"

"I don't know." Lillian gave her a reassuring smile. "But I'm certain everything will be fine." She slipped her arm through Hannah's. "Come look at the tree."

With all the candles lit, the Christmas tree was a brilliant, spectacular sight, hundreds of tiny flames glowing amid the branches like fairy lights. The entire ballroom was decorated with greenery and gilt and red velvet swags. Hannah had never attended such a dazzling event. She looked around the room in wonder, watching couples swirling across the floor while the orchestra played Christmas music in waltz-time. Chandeliers shed sparkling light on the scene. Through the nearby row of windows, she saw the glow of torches that had been set in the gardens, glowing against a sky the color of black plums.

And then she saw Rafe across the room. Like the other men present, he was dressed in the traditional evening scheme of black and white. The sight of him, so charismatic and handsome, made her light-headed with yearning.

Their gazes caught across the distance, and he surveyed her intently, missing no detail of her appearance. His mouth curved with a slow, easy smile, and her knees turned to jelly.

"Here, miss." A servant had come with a tray of champagne. Glasses of the sparkling vintage were being passed out among all the guests. The orchestra finished a set and paused, and there was a clink of what sounded like silver on crystal.

"What's this?" Lillian asked, her brows lifting as she and Daisy took some champagne.

"Apparently someone is going to make a toast," Daisy commented.

Seeing Lord Blandford draw Natalie with him on the other side of the room, Hannah gripped the stem of her champagne glass tightly. Every nerve tensed with foreboding.

No . . . it couldn't be.

"My friends," Blandford said a few times, attracting the attention of the crowd. Guests quieted and looked at him expectantly. "As many of you know, Lady Blandford and I were blessed with only one child, our beloved Natalie. And now the time has come to give her into the keeping of a man who will be entrusted with her happiness and safekeeping, as they embark upon their life's journey together—"

"Oh, no," Hannah heard Lillian whisper.

The coldness concentrated in her chest until she felt it needling through her heart. Lord Blandford continued to speak, but she couldn't make out the words through the blood rush in her ears. Her throat closed on an anguished cry.

She was too late. She had waited too long.

Her hands had begun to shake too badly for her to hold the champagne. She thrust the glass blindly at Daisy. "Please take this," she choked. "I can't . . . I have to . . ." She turned in panic and anguish, and made her way to the nearest exit, one of the French doors that led outside.

"On this most joyous of holidays," Blandford continued, "I have the honor and pleasure of announcing a betrothal. Let us now make a toast to my daughter and the man to whom she will bestow her hand in marriage . . ."

Hannah slipped out the door and closed it, desperately pulling in huge lungfuls of cold winter air. There was the sound of a muffled cheer from inside.

The toast was done.

Rafe and Natalie were engaged.

She nearly staggered under the weight of her own grief. Wild thoughts coursed through her mind. She couldn't face it, any of it. She would have to leave tonight and go somewhere . . . back to her father and sisters . . . she could never see Natalie or Rafe or the Blandfords again. She hated Rafe for making her love him. She hated herself. She wanted to die.

Hannah, don't be an idiot, she thought desperately. *You're not the first woman with a broken heart, nor will you be the last. You will survive this.*

But the more she fought for self-control, the more it seemed to elude her. She had to find a place where she could fall apart. She headed out into the garden, following one of the torchlit paths. Reaching the little clearing with the mermaid fountain, she sat on one of the hard, freezing stone benches. As she covered her face with her hands, hot tears soaked into the white satin gloves. Each sob tore through her chest with knifelike sharpness.

And then through the wrenching gasps of misery, she heard someone say her name.

For anyone to see her like this was the ultimate humiliation. Hannah shook her head and curled into a ball of misery, managing to choke out helplessly, "Please leave me—"

But a man sat beside her, and she was gathered up in warm, strong arms. Her head was pulled against a hard chest. "Hannah, love . . . *no.* No, don't cry." It was Rafe's deep voice, his familiar scent. She tried to push him away, but Rafe gripped her firmly, his dark head bent over hers. Murmuring endearments, he smoothed her hair and pressed kisses against her forehead. His lips brushed her wet lashes. "Come. There's no need for this, sweet darling. Hush, everything is fine. Look at me, Hannah."

The exquisite pleasure of being held by him, comforted

by him, made her feel even worse. "You should be back there," she said, and let out a few coughing sobs. "With Natalie."

His palm stroked her back in firm circles. "Hannah. Sweetheart. Please calm yourself enough that we can talk."

"I don't want to talk—"

"I do. And you're going to listen to me. Take a deep breath. Good girl. One more." Rafe let go of her long enough to remove his evening coat, and he wrapped it around her shivering body. "I didn't think Blandford would have made the announcement so damned quickly," he said, pulling her close again, "or I would have made an effort to reach you first."

"It doesn't matter," she said, her despair congealing into sullenness. "Nothing matters. Don't even try to—"

Rafe put his hand over her mouth and looked down at her. Lit by the torches, his face was cast half in shadow, his eyes dark and bright. His voice was thick and warm, and tenderly chiding. "Had you stayed in the ballroom about thirty seconds longer, my impulsive love, you would have heard Blandford announcing Natalie's engagement to Lord Travers."

Hannah's entire body stiffened. She couldn't even breathe.

"With the exception of a brief errand in the village," Rafe continued, "I've been talking with people all damn day. With my parents, the Blandfords, Westcliff . . . and most importantly, Natalie." He took his hand from her mouth and rummaged in the pocket of his coat. Extracting a handkerchief, he wiped her wet cheeks gently. "I told her," he continued, "that as lovely and appealing as I found her, I could not marry her. Because I would never be able to care for her in the way that she deserved. Because I had fallen in love, deeply and forever, with someone else." He smiled into Hannah's dazed eyes. "I believe she went straight to Travers afterward, and in giving her comfort and counsel, he probably confessed his own feelings for her. I hope she hasn't rushed into an impulsive betrothal merely to save face. But that's not my concern."

Cradling Hannah's face in his hands, Rafe waited for her to say something. She merely shook her head, too overwhelmed to make a sound.

"That day in the library," he told her, "when I nearly made love to you, I realized afterward that I had wanted to get caught with you. I wanted to compromise you—anything that would allow me to be with you. And I knew then that no matter what, I wasn't going to be able to marry Natalie. Because a lifetime is too long to spend with the wrong woman."

His head and shoulders blotted out the torchlight as he bent over her, his mouth taking hers with a slow, penetrating kiss. He coaxed her trembling lips to part, exploring her with an ardent tenderness that caused her heart to thump with painful force. She gasped as she felt his hand slide inside the coat, caressing the fine skin exposed by the low-cut bodice of her ballgown.

"Darling Hannah," he whispered. "When I saw you crying just now, I thought 'Please, God, let it be because she cares for me, wicked scoundrel that I am. Let her love me even a little.'"

"I was crying," she managed to tell him unsteadily, "because my heart was breaking at the thought of you marrying someone else." She had to set her jaw against a quiver of emotion. "Because I . . . I wanted you for myself."

The flare of passion in his eyes sent her pulse rioting. "Then I have something to ask you, my love. But first you must understand . . . I'm not going to inherit Bowman's. That doesn't mean I can't provide for you, however. I'm a wealthy man in my own right. And I'm going to take my ill-gotten gains and put them to good use. There are opportunities everywhere."

Finding it difficult to think clearly, Hannah had to concentrate as if she were translating a foreign language. "You've been cut off?" she finally whispered in concern.

Pulling back a little, Rafe nodded. His face was sober and purposeful. "It's for the best. Some time in the future, my father and I may find a way to accept each other. But in the meantime, I won't live according to any man's dictates."

Her hand stole up to the side of his face, caressing his cheek gently. "I didn't want you to make such a sacrifice for me."

His lashes half lowered at her touch. "It wasn't a sacrifice. It was salvation. My father sees it as a weakness, of course. But I told him it doesn't make me less of a man to love someone this way. It makes me more of one. And you're under no obligation, you know. I don't want you to—"

"Rafe," she said unsteadily, "obligation is no part of what I feel for you."

His expression caused her insides to turn molten. Picking up one of her hands, he removed her glove in a leisurely manner, pulling gently at the fingertips to loosen them. After peeling off the white satin, he kissed the backs of her fingers and laid her palm against his warm, smooth-shaven cheek. "Hannah, I love you almost more than I can bear. Whether you want me or not, I'm yours. And I'm not at all certain what will happen to me if I have to spend the rest of my life without you. Please marry me so I can stop trying to be happy and finally just *be*. I know this has happened very fast, but—"

"Some things can't be measured by time," Hannah said with a tremulous smile.

Rafe went still and gave her a questioning glance.

"One of the housemaids found a half-burned love letter in the hearth in your room," Hannah explained, "and she brought it to Natalie, who showed it to me. Natalie assumed it was for her."

Even in the darkness, she saw Rafe's color heighten. "Well, hell," he said in a rueful tone. Bringing her close, he held her and whispered against her ear. "It was for you. Every word was about you. You must have known when you read it."

"I wanted it to be about me," Hannah said shyly. "And"—her own face flamed—"those things you wrote—I want all of that, too."

He gave a soft laugh and drew back to look at her. "Then give me your answer." He crushed a brief, impassioned kiss against her lips. "Say it, or I'll have to keep kissing you until you surrender."

"Yes," she said, breathless with joy. "Yes, I'll marry you. Because I love you too, Rafe, I love—"

He seized her mouth with his and kissed her hungrily, his hands coming up to her coiffure and disheveling it. She didn't care in the least. His mouth was so hot, delicious, consuming her with light sensual caresses, then ravaging deep and hard. She responded eagerly, shivering in his arms as her body tried to accommodate the surfeit of pleasure, too much, too fast.

Rafe dragged his parted lips slowly down her throat, exciting nerve endings, leaving a trail of fire in his wake. His mouth went down to her chest, and within the confinement of her bodice, she felt the tips of her breasts turn hard and sensitive. "Hannah," he whispered, spreading feverish kisses across her skin, "I've never wanted anyone this much before. You're so beautiful in every way . . . and everything I find out about you makes me love you more . . ." He lifted his head and gave it a rough shake as if to recall himself to where he was. A self-mocking grin came to his lips. "My God. We'd better make this a short betrothal. Here, give me your hand—no, the other." He searched one of the coat pockets and unearthed a shining circlet. It was a garnet set in silver. "This is why I went to the village today," he said, slipping the ring onto her fourth finger. "I'll buy you a diamond in London, but we had to start out with something."

"It's perfect," Hannah said, looking down at it with shining eyes. "A garnet means enduring love. Did you know that?"

He shook his head, staring at her as if she were a miracle.

Wrapping her arms around his neck, Hannah impulsively kissed him. Rafe angled his head over hers, possessing her lips with soft erotic demand. She ran her hands over the powerful lines of his body in a timid but ardent exploration, until she felt him shiver.

Gasping, he held her back from him. "Hannah . . . sweetheart, I'm . . . I've reached my limits. We have to stop."

"I don't want to stop."

"I know, love. But I have to escort you back inside before everyone notices that we're missing."

Everything in her rebelled at the thought of returning to the large, crowded ballroom. The talking, dancing, the long formal supper . . . it would be torture, when all she wanted was to be with him. Daringly, Hannah reached out to toy with the buttons of his waistcoat. "Take me to the bachelor's house. I'm sure it's empty. Everyone is at the manor."

He gave her a sardonic glance. "If I did that, sweetheart, there is no way you would get out of there with your innocence intact."

"I want you to compromise me," she told him.

"You do? Why, love?"

"Because I want to be yours in every way."

"You already are," he murmured.

"Not that way. Not yet. And even if you don't compromise me, I'm going to tell everyone that you did. So you may as well do it in actuality."

Rafe laughed at her threat. "In America," he told her, "we would say you're trying to seal the deal." Gently he framed her face in his hands, and stroked her cheeks with his thumbs. "But you don't have to, sweetheart. There's nothing on earth that will keep me from marrying you. You can trust me."

"I do trust you. But . . ."

His brows lifted. "But?"

The skin beneath his fingers warmed a few degrees. "I want you. I want to be close to you. As . . . as you wrote in the letter."

He gave her one of those slow smiles that sent hot and cold chills down her spine. "In that case . . . maybe I'll compromise you just a little."

PULLING HANNAH UP FROM THE BENCH, RAFE TOOK HER with him to the bachelor's house. He argued with himself every step of the way, knowing the right thing to do was to take her back to the manor without delay. And yet the desire to be alone with her, to hold her in privacy, was simply too powerful and all-encompassing to resist.

They went inside the bachelor's house, with its dark, stately furniture and paneled walls and luxurious rugs. Coals glowed in the bedroom hearth, spreading a pool of yellow and orange across the floor.

Rafe lit a bedside lamp and turned it low, and turned to look at Hannah. She had shed his coat and was reaching back to unfasten her ballgown. He saw her expression, how she was trying to appear nonchalant as if going to bed with a man were a normal occurrence for her. And he was filled with amusement and tenderness, and the most unholy ache of lust he'd ever experienced.

He went to her and reached around her, closing his hands over hers. "You don't have to do this," he said. "I'll wait for you. I'll wait as long as I have to."

Hannah tugged her hands free and slipped them behind

his neck. "I can't think of a thing I'd rather be doing," she told him.

He bent to kiss her compulsively, pausing only to murmur, "Oh, love, neither can I."

Slowly he removed layers of silk and linen, and unhooked her corset, and rolled the stockings from her legs. When every last garment was gone, and she was stretched blushing on the bed before him, he let his gaze wander along her slender body, and he let out a shaking sigh. She was so beautiful, so innocent and trusting. He touched her breast, molding the softness with fingers that held a slight tremor.

Her gaze lifted to his face. "Are you nervous?" she asked with a touch of surprise.

Rafe nodded, brushing the pad of his thumb over a pink nipple and watching it tighten. "It's never been an act of love for me before."

"Does that make it different?"

A wry smile curved his lips as he considered that. "I'm not certain. But there's one way to find out."

He undressed himself and lay beside her, gathering her carefully in his arms. Despite the desire raging through his body, he pressed her against him with controlled gentleness, letting her feel him. He slid one hand over her bottom, rubbing in a warm circle.

Her breath caught as she felt the length of him against her. A small hand came to the surface of his chest and explored delicately. "Rafe . . . how should I touch you?"

He smiled and kissed her throat, savoring the softness and female fragrance of her. "Anywhere, love. Any way you like." He held still as she played with the light pelt of hair on his chest.

Staring into his eyes, she let her palm drift to the muscles of his abdomen, stroking until they tightened reflexively. She fumbled a little as she grasped his aroused flesh, the hard satiny length alive and pulsing with masculine need. She gave him a few hesitant caresses. His response was so acute that he gasped at the sharply climbing sensation. "Hannah," he managed to say, reaching down to pull her hand away. "Change of plan. Next time"—he paused, struggling for self-control—"you can explore to your heart's content, but for now, let me make love to you."

"Did I do something wrong? Did you not like the way I—"

"I liked it too much. If I liked it any more, this would all be over in less than a minute." He rose above her and pressed kisses over her body, lingering at her breasts to tug and tease and softly bite. He delighted in the shocks of response he felt in her, the deepening color of arousal, the instinctive way she moved toward him to follow the source of pleasure.

Nudging her thighs open, he rested his hand between them, fitting his palm over the fleecy triangle. And he held her gently until she writhed and moaned, needing more. Sliding downward, Rafe kissed her stomach, letting his tongue trace delicate circles around her navel. He had never been so aroused, so completely absorbed in someone else's pleasure. The intimacy was nearly unbearable. His breathing was quick and frayed as he found the entrance of her body and teased around it with his fingertip.

"Hannah, darling," he whispered, "relax for me." He eased his finger inside the lush, clinging heat. The feel of her was so exquisite, he let out a groan. "I have to kiss you here. I have to taste you. No, don't be afraid . . . just let me . . . oh, Hannah, sweet love . . ." He dragged his mouth straight through the curls, and searched hungrily until he found the blunt silken peak. His senses were engulfed in radiant pleasure, all his muscles taut with lust. The taste of her, salt and female, was insanely arousing. He drew his tongue over her, flicked and circled, glorying in her helpless cries. He slid his finger deeper, and again, teaching her the rhythm.

She reached down with a low cry, her hands gripping his head. With tender skill he urged her into climax, luxuriating in the soft, pulsing warmth of her body. Long after her release had faded, he stayed with her, drawing his tongue through the rosy heat, easing her into a dreamy afterglow.

"Rafe," she said thickly, pulling him upward.

Smiling, he levered his body over hers, staring down into her dazed green eyes.

"More," she whispered, and wrapped her arms around his back, holding him to her. "I want more of you."

Murmuring her name, Rafe lowered his body into the cradle of her thighs. A rush of primitive satisfaction went through him as he felt the enticing softness parting for him. He pushed into the resisting flesh, so hot, so wet, and the deeper he went, the more tightly she closed around him. He thrust deep and held, trying not to hurt her. It was like nothing he had ever felt before, a pleasure beyond imagining. He took her head in his hands and kissed her mouth, while his senses swam in rapture. "I'm sorry, love," he said in a guttural voice. "So sorry to hurt you."

Hannah smiled and drew him down to her. "As a foreigner goes to a new country . . ." she whispered against his ear.

He let out a shaken laugh. "God. You'll never let me forget that letter, will you?"

"I never even read the whole thing," she said. "Parts of it were burned. And now I'll never know everything you said."

"The passages you missed were probably about this," he murmured, pushing gently inside her. They both caught their breath and held still, absorbing the feel of it. Rafe pressed a smile against her cheek. "I wrote quite a lot about this."

"Tell me what you wrote."

He whispered into her ear, love words and intimate praise, and all the longing he'd felt. And with each word he felt something opening inside him, a sense of freedom and power and perishing tenderness. She moved with him, welcoming him deeper, and the ecstasy of being joined with her roared through him, driving him to a piercing, brilliantly transcending release.

Indeed . . . love made it different.

RAFE HELD HER FOR A LONG TIME AFTERWARD, HIS HAND stroking gently over her back and hip. He couldn't seem to stop touching her. Hannah snuggled in the crook of his arm, her body feeling heavy and sated. "Is this real?" she whispered. "It feels like a dream."

Amusement rumbled in his chest. "It will seem real enough tomorrow morning when I take you back to the manor a fallen woman. If I hadn't already told Westcliff of my intentions to marry you, I daresay he'd greet me with a horsewhip."

"You aren't taking me back tonight?" she asked in pleased surprise.

"No. For one thing, I've ruined your coiffure. Second, I don't have the energy to leave this bed. Third . . . there's a distinct possibility that I'm not finished with you yet."

"Those are all very good reasons." She sat up and pulled the remaining pearl pins from her hair, and leaned over Rafe to deposit them on the bedside table. Catching her ribs in his hands, he held her over him and kissed her breasts as they were displayed before him. "Rafe," she protested.

Pausing, he looked up into her blushing face, and he grinned. "Modest?" he asked softly, and tucked her into the crook of his arm again. His lips pressed against her forehead. "Well. Being married to me will cure you of that soon enough."

Hannah leaned her face against his chest, and he felt the curve of her smile.

"What is it?" he asked.

"Our first night together. And our first morning will be Christmas."

Rafe patted her naked hip. "And I've already unwrapped my present."

"You're rather easy to shop for," she said, making him laugh.

"Always. Because Hannah, my love, the only gift I'll ever want"—he paused to kiss her smiling lips—"is you."

Epilogue

On Christmas morning Matthew Swift walked over to the bachelor's house, his shoes and the hem of his coat dusted with new snow. He knocked at the door and waited patiently until Rafe came to answer it. And with a wry smile, Swift told his brother-in-law, "All I can say is, everyone's talking. So you'd better marry her quickly."

There was, of course, no argument on Rafe's part.

Swift also told him that having been moved by the spirit of the holiday (and the combined pressuring of the entire family), Thomas Bowman had reconsidered his decision to disinherit Rafe, and wished to make peace. Later, over mugs of smoking bishop, a hot drink made with fruit, red wine, and port, the men came to an accord of sorts.

But Rafe did not consent to enter into the joint proprietorship with his father, realizing that the arrangement would undoubtedly be a source of future conflict between them. Instead, he entered into a highly lucrative partnership with Simon Hunt and Westcliff, and turned his abilities to the manufacturing of locomotive engines. This removed much of the burden from Hunt's shoulders, which made Annabelle happy, and allowed Rafe and Hannah to stay in England, to the pleasure of all.

In future years, Thomas Bowman would forget that Hannah was not the daughter-in-law he had originally wanted for Rafe, and a solid affection developed between them.

Natalie married Lord Travers and they were very happy together. She confided to Hannah that when she had gone to Travers for consolation that Christmas Eve, he had finally kissed her, and it had been a kiss worth waiting for.

Daisy eventually finished her novel, which was published with great popular success, if not critical acclaim.

Evie gave birth later that year to a high-spirited girl with flame-colored curls, leading St. Vincent to the conclusion that it was his destiny to be loved by many red-haired women. He was very pleased.

Hannah and Rafe were married by the end of January, but they always considered their true anniversary to be Christmas, and celebrated accordingly. And every Christmas Eve, Rafe wrote a love letter and left it on her pillow.

Samuel Clark hired a new secretarial assistant, a competent and pleasant young woman. Upon discovering her auspiciously shaped cranium, he married her without delay.

In 1848, a woodcut of the Queen and Prince Albert standing beside their Christmas tree was published in *The Illustrated London News,* popularizing the custom until soon every parlor was graced with a decorated tree. After viewing the illustration, Lillian rather smugly observed that her tree was much taller.

Thomas Bowman's toupee, alas, was never found. He was somewhat mollified by the gift of a very fine hat from Westcliff on Christmas Day.

Mine Till Midnight

To Cindy Blewett,
a wise, witty,
and much appreciated friend

Chapter One

Finding one person in a city of nearly two million was a formidable task. It helped if that person was a drunken sot whose behavior was predictable. Still, it wouldn't be easy. *Leo, where are you?* Miss Amelia Hathaway wondered desperately as the carriage wheels rattled along the cobbled street. Poor, wild, troubled Leo. Some people, when faced with intolerable circumstances, simply . . . broke. Such was the case with her formerly dashing and dependable brother. She feared he was beyond all hope of repair.

"We'll find him," Amelia said with an assurance she didn't feel. She glanced at the Rom who sat opposite her. As usual, Merripen showed no expression.

One could be forgiven for assuming Merripen was a man of limited emotions. He was so guarded, in fact, that even after living with the Hathaway family for fifteen years, he still hadn't told anyone his first name. They had known him simply as Merripen ever since he had been found, battered and unconscious beside a creek that ran through their property.

When Merripen had awakened to discover himself surrounded by curious Hathaways, he had reacted violently. It had required their combined efforts to keep him in bed, all of them exclaiming that he would make his injuries worse, he must lie still. Amelia's father had deduced the boy was the survivor of an attack by local landowners, who had ridden out on horseback to rid their properties of Romany encampments.

"The lad was probably left for dead," Mr. Hathaway had remarked gravely. As a scholarly and forward-thinking gentleman, he had disapproved of violence in any form. "I'm afraid it will be difficult to communicate with his tribe. They are probably long gone by now."

"Can we keep him, Papa?" Amelia's younger sister Poppy had asked.

Mr. Hathaway had smiled at her. "He may stay as long as he chooses. But I doubt he will remain here longer than a week or so. Roma tend to be a nomadic people."

However, Merripen had stayed and had grown at a near-alarming rate into a man of robust and powerful proportions. It was difficult to say exactly what Merripen was . . . not quite a family member, not quite a servant. Although he worked in various capacities for the Hathaways, acting as a driver and jack-of-all-trades, he also ate at the family table whenever he chose and occupied a bedroom in the main part of the cottage.

Now that Leo had gone missing and was possibly in danger, there was no question that Merripen would help find him.

It was hardly proper for Amelia to go unaccompanied in the presence of a man like Merripen. But at the age of twenty-six, she considered herself beyond any need of chaperonage.

"We shall begin by eliminating the places Leo would *not* go," she said. "Churches, museums, places of higher learning, and polite neighborhoods are naturally out of the question."

"That still leaves most of the city," Merripen grumbled.

Merripen was not fond of London. In his view, the workings of so-called civilized society were infinitely more barbaric than anything that could be found in nature. Given a choice between spending an hour in a pen of wild boars and a drawing room of elegant company, he would have chosen the boars without hesitation.

"We should probably start with taverns," Amelia continued.

Merripen gave her a dark glance. "Do you know how many taverns there are in London?"

"No, but I'm certain I will by the time the night is out."

"We're not going to start with taverns. We'll go where Leo is likely to find the most trouble."

"And that would be?"

"Jenner's."

Jenner's was an infamous gaming club where gentlemen went to behave in *un*gentlemanly ways. Originally founded by an ex-boxer named Ivo Jenner, the club had changed hands upon his death and was now owned by his son-in-law, Lord St. Vincent. The less-than-sterling reputation of St. Vincent had only enhanced the club's allure.

It was said that a membership at Jenner's cost a fortune. Naturally Leo had insisted on joining immediately upon inheriting his title two months ago.

"If you intend to drink yourself to death," Amelia had told Leo calmly, "I wish you would do it at a more affordable place."

"But I'm a viscount now," Leo had replied nonchalantly. "I have to do it with style, or what will people say?"

"That you were a wastrel and a fool, and the title might just as well have gone to a monkey?"

That had elicited a grin from her handsome brother. "I'm sure that comparison is quite unfair to the monkey."

Turning cold with increasing worry, Amelia pressed her gloved fingers to the aching surface of her forehead. This wasn't the first time Leo had ever disappeared, but it was definitely the longest. "I've never been inside a gaming club before," she said without looking at Merripen. "It will be a novel experience."

"They won't let you inside. You're a lady. And even if they did allow it, I wouldn't."

Lowering her hand, Amelia glanced at him in surprise. It was rare that Merripen forbade her to do anything. In fact, this may have been the first time. She found it annoying. Considering her brother's life might be at stake, she was hardly going to quibble over social niceties. Besides, she was curious to see what was inside the privileged masculine retreat. As long as she was doomed to remain a spinster, she might as well enjoy the small freedoms that came with it.

"Neither will they let *you* inside," she pointed out. "You're a Rom."

"As it happens, the manager of the club is also a Rom."

That was unusual. Extraordinary, even, for a Rom to be entrusted with the accounting of cash and credit, not to mention arbitrating controversies at the gambling tables. "He must be a rather remarkable individual to have assumed such a position," Amelia said. "I will allow you to accompany me inside Jenner's. It's possible your presence will induce him to be more forthcoming."

"Thank you." Merripen's voice was so dry one could have struck a match off it.

Amelia remained strategically silent as he drove the covered brougham through the highest concentration of attractions, shops, and theaters in the city. The poorly sprung carriage bounced with abandon along the wide thoroughfares, passing handsome squares lined with tidy fenced greens and

Georgian-fronted buildings. As the streets became more lavish, the brick walls gave way to stucco, which soon gave way to stone.

The West End scenery was unfamiliar to Amelia. Despite the proximity of their village, the Hathaways didn't often venture into town, certainly not to this area. Even now with their recent inheritance, there was little they could afford here.

Glancing at Merripen, Amelia wondered why he seemed to know exactly where they were going, when he was no more acquainted with town than she. But Merripen had always had an instinct for finding his way anywhere.

They turned onto King Street, which was ablaze with light from gas lamps. It was noisy and busy, congested with vehicles and groups of pedestrians setting out for the evening's entertainment. The sky turned dull red as the remaining light percolated through the haze of coal smoke that lay over the city. The crowns of lofty buildings broke the horizon, a row of dark shapes that protruded like a witch's teeth.

Merripen guided the horse to a narrow alley of mews behind a great stone-fronted building. Jenner's. Her stomach tightened. It was probably too much to ask that her brother would be found safely here, in the first place they looked.

"Merripen?" Her voice was strained.

"Yes?"

"You should probably know that if my brother hasn't already managed to kill himself, I plan to shoot him when we find him."

"I'll hand you the pistol."

Amelia smiled and straightened her bonnet. "Let's go inside. And remember—*I'll* do the talking."

An objectionable odor filled the alley—a city smell of animals and refuse and coal dust. In the absence of a good rain, filth accumulated quickly in the streets and tributaries. Glancing at the soiled ground, Amelia hopped out of the path of a pair of squeaking rats that ran alongside the wall of the building.

As Merripen gave the ribbons to a stableman at the mews, Amelia glanced toward the end of the alley.

A pair of street youths crouched near a tiny fire, roasting something on sticks. Amelia did not want to speculate on the nature of the objects being heated. Her attention moved to a group—three men and a woman—illuminated in the uncertain blaze. Two of the men were engaged in fisticuffs. However, they were so inebriated that their contest brought to mind nothing so much as a pair of dancing bears.

Judging from the woman's attire—a gown made of gaudily colored fabric, the bodice gaping wide to reveal the plump hills of her breasts—she was a prostitute. She seemed amused by the spectacle of two men battling over her, while a third attempted to break up the fracas.

"'Ere now, my fine jacks," the woman called out in a cockney accent, "I said I'd take ye both on—no need for a cockfight!"

"Stay back," Merripen murmured.

Amelia pretended not to hear and drew closer for a better view. It wasn't the sight of the brawl that was so interesting—even peaceful little Primrose Place had its share of fist fights. All men, no matter what their situation, occasionally succumbed to their lower natures. What attracted Amelia's notice was the third man, the would-be peacemaker, who darted between the drunken fools and attempted to reason with them.

He was black-haired and lean, moving with the swift grace of a cat as he avoided the swipes and lunges of his opponents.

"My lords," he was saying in an excessively reasonable

tone, sounding relaxed even as he blocked a heavy fist with his forearm. "I'm afraid you'll both have to stop this now, or I'll be forced to—" He broke off and dodged to the side just as the man behind him leapt.

The prostitute cackled at the sight. "They got you on the 'op tonight, Rohan," she exclaimed.

Dodging back into the fray, Rohan attempted to break it up once more. "My lords, surely you must know"—he ducked beneath the swift arc of a fist—"that violence"—he blocked a right hook—"never solves anything."

"Bugger you!" one of the men said, and butted forward like a deranged goat.

Rohan stepped aside and allowed him to charge straight into the side of the building. The attacker collapsed with a groan and lay gasping on the ground.

His opponent's reaction was singularly ungrateful. Instead of thanking the dark-haired man for putting a stop to the fight, he growled, "Curse you for interfering, Rohan! I would've knocked the stuffing from him!" He charged forth with his fists churning like windmill blades.

Rohan evaded a left cross and deftly flipped him to the ground. He stood over the prone figure, blotting his forehead with his sleeve. "Had enough?" he asked pleasantly. "Good. Please allow me to help you to your feet, my lord." As Rohan pulled the man upward, he glanced toward a club employee waiting at the threshold of a door that led into the club. "Dawson, escort Lord Latimer to his carriage out front. I'll take Lord Selway."

"No need," said the aristocrat who had just struggled to his feet, sounding winded. "I can walk to my own bloody carriage." Tugging his clothes back into place over his bulky form, he threw the dark-haired man an anxious glance. "Rohan, I will have your promise on something."

"Yes, my lord?"

"If word of this gets out—if Lady Selway should discover that I was fighting over the favors of a fallen woman—my life won't be worth a farthing."

Rohan replied with reassuring calm. "She'll never know, my lord."

"She knows *everything*," Selway said. "She's in league with the devil. If you are ever questioned about this minor altercation . . ."

"It was caused by a particularly vicious game of whist," came the bland reply.

"Yes. Yes. Good man." Selway patted the younger man on the shoulder. "And to put a seal on your silence—" He reached a beefy hand inside his waistcoat and extracted a small bag.

"No, my lord." Rohan stepped back with a firm shake of his head, his shiny black hair flying with the movement, then settling back into place. "There's no price for my silence."

"Take it," the aristocrat insisted.

"I can't, my lord."

"It's yours." The bag of coins was tossed to the ground, landing at Rohan's feet with a metallic thud. "There. Whether you choose to leave it lying on the street or not is entirely your choice."

As the gentleman left, Rohan stared at the bag as if it were a dead rodent. "I don't want it," he muttered to no one in particular.

"I'll take it," the prostitute said, sauntering over to him. She scooped up the bag and tested its heft in her palm. A taunting grin split her face. "Yer afraid o' blunt?"

"I'm not afraid of it," Rohan said sourly. "I just don't need it." Sighing, he rubbed the back of his neck with one hand.

She laughed at him and slid an openly appreciative glance over his lean form. "I 'ates to take something for noffing. Care for a little knock in the alley before I go back to Bradshaw's?"

"I appreciate the offer," he said politely, "but no."

She hitched a shoulder in a playful half-shrug. "Less work for me, then."

Rohan responded with a short nod, seeming to contemplate a spot on the ground with undue concentration, as if listening for some nearly imperceptible sound. Lifting a hand to the back of his neck again, he rubbed it as if to soothe a warning prickle. Slowly he turned and looked directly at Amelia.

A little shock went through her as their gazes met. Although they were standing several yards apart, she felt the full force of his notice. His expression was not tempered by warmth or kindness. In fact, he looked pitiless, as if he had long ago found the world to be an uncaring place and had decided to accept it on its own terms.

As his detached gaze swept over her, Amelia knew exactly what he was seeing: a woman dressed in serviceable clothes and practical shoes. She was fair-skinned and dark-haired, of medium height, with the rosy-cheeked wholesomeness common to the Hathaways. Her figure was sturdy and voluptuous when the fashion was to be reed slim and wan and fragile.

Without vanity, Amelia knew that although she wasn't a great beauty, she was sufficiently attractive to have caught a husband. However, she had always liked her independence too well to surrender it the kind of men who had been inclined to court her—practical men, who wanted a practical wife to manage their households efficiently. She didn't need them. God knew she was busy enough trying to manage the rest of the Hathaways.

Rohan looked away from her. Without a word or a nod of acknowledgment, he walked to the back entrance of the club. His pace was unhurried, as if he were giving himself time to think about something. There was a distinctive grace in his movements. His strides didn't measure out distance so much as flow over it like water.

Amelia reached the doorstep at the same time he did. "Sir . . . Mr. Rohan . . . I presume you're the manager of the club."

Rohan stopped and turned to face her. They were standing close enough for Amelia to detect the scents of male exertion and warm skin. His unfastened waistcoat, made of luxurious gray brocade, hung open at the sides to reveal a thin white linen shirt beneath. As Rohan moved to button the waistcoat, Amelia saw a quantity of gold rings on his fingers. A ripple of nervousness went through her, leaving unfamiliar heat in its wake. Her corset felt too tight, her high-necked collar constricting.

Flushing, she brought herself to stare at him directly. He was a young man, not yet thirty, with a face that had definitely been created for sin—the brooding mouth, the angular jaw, the golden-hazel eyes shaded by long, straight lashes. His hair needed cutting, the heavy black locks curling slightly over the back of his collar. Amelia's throat cinched around a quick, surprised breath as she saw the glitter of a diamond in his ear.

He accorded her a precise bow. "At your service, Miss . . ."

"Hathaway," she said precisely. She turned to indicate her companion, who had come to stand at her left. "And this is my companion, Merripen."

Rohan glanced at him alertly. "The Romany word for 'life' and also 'death'."

Was that what Merripen's name meant? Surprised, Amelia looked up at him. Merripen gave a slight shrug to indicate it was of no importance. Amelia turned back to Rohan. "Sir, we've come to ask you a question or two regarding—"

"I don't like questions."

"I am looking for my brother, Lord Ramsay," she continued doggedly, "and I desperately need any information you may possess as to his whereabouts."

"I wouldn't tell you even if I knew."

"I assure you, sir, I wouldn't put myself nor anyone else to the trouble were it not absolutely necessary. But this is the third day since my brother has gone missing—"

"Not my problem." Rohan turned toward the door.

"—he tends to fall in with bad company—"

"That's unfortunate."

"—he could be dead by now."

"I can't help you. I wish you luck in your search." Rohan pushed the door and made to enter the club.

He stopped as Merripen spoke.

Since Merripen had first come to the Hathaways, there had been only a handful of occasions on which Amelia had heard him speak in Romany. She sent him a questioning glance, but he didn't translate. Staring at Merripen intently, Rohan leaned his shoulder against the doorframe. "It's been years since I've heard that dialect," he said. "Who's the father of your tribe?"

"I have no tribe."

A long moment passed while Merripen remained inscrutable in the face of Rohan's regard.

Rohan's hazel eyes narrowed. "Come in," he said curtly. "I'll see what I can find out."

They were brought into the club without ceremony, Rohan directing an employee to show them to a private receiving room upstairs. Amelia heard the sounds of voices and music, and footsteps coming and going. It was a busy masculine hive, this place, forbidden to someone like herself.

The employee, a young man with an east London accent and careful manners, took them into a well-appointed room and bid them to wait there until Rohan returned. Merripen went to a curtained window overlooking King Street.

Amelia was surprised by the quiet luxury of her surroundings: the hand-knotted carpet done in shades of blue and cream, the wood-paneled walls and velvet-upholstered furniture. "Quite tasteful," she commented, removing her bonnet and setting it on a small mahogany claw-foot table. "For some reason, I had expected something a bit . . . well, tawdry."

"Jenner's is a cut above the typical establishment. It masquerades as a gentlemen's club, when its real purpose is to provide the largest hazard bank in London."

Amelia went to a built-in bookshelf and inspected the volumes as she asked idly, "Why is it, do you think, that Mr. Rohan was reluctant to take money from Lord Selway?"

Merripen cast a sardonic glance over his shoulder. "You know how Roma feel about material possessions."

"Yes, I know your people don't like to be encumbered. But from what I've seen, they're certainly willing to accept a few coins in return for a service."

"It's more than not wanting to be encumbered. For a *chal* to be in this position—"

"What's a *chal*?"

"A son of Roma. For him to wear such fine clothes, to stay under one roof so long, to reap such financial bounty—" He broke off and shook his head.

He was so stern and certain of himself, Amelia couldn't resist teasing him a little. "And what's your excuse, Merripen? You've stayed under the Hathaway roof for an awfully long time."

"That's different. For one thing, there's no profit in living with you."

Amelia laughed.

"For another . . ." Merripen's voice softened. "I owe my life to your family."

Amelia felt a surge of affection as she stared at his unyielding profile. "What a spoilsport," she said gently. "I try to mock you, and you ruin the moment with sincerity. You know you're not obligated to stay, dear friend. You've repaid your debt to us a thousand times over."

Merripen shook his head immediately. "It would be like leaving a nest of plover chicks with a fox nearby."

"We're not as helpless as all that," she protested. "I'm perfectly capable of taking care of the family . . . and so is Leo. When he's sober."

"When would that be?" His bland tone made the question all the more sarcastic.

Amelia opened her mouth to argue the point, but was forced to close it. Merripen was right—Leo had wandered through the past six months in a state of perpetual inebriation. She put a hand to her midriff, where worry had accumulated like a sack of lead shot. Poor, wretched Leo—she was terrified nothing could be done for him. Impossible to save a man who didn't want to be saved.

That wouldn't stop her from trying, however.

She paced around the room, too agitated to sit and wait calmly. Leo was out there somewhere, needing to be rescued. And there was no telling how long Rohan would have them bide their time here.

"I'm going to have a look around," she said, heading to the door. "I won't go far. Stay here, Merripen, in case Mr. Rohan should come."

She heard him mutter something beneath his breath.

Ignoring her request, he followed at her heels as she went out into the hallway.

"This isn't proper," he said behind her.

Amelia didn't pause. Propriety had no power over her now. "This is my one chance to see inside a gaming club—I'm not about to miss it." Following the sound of voices, she ventured toward a gallery that wrapped around the second story of a huge, splendid room.

Crowds of elegantly dressed men gathered around three large hazard tables, watching the play, while croupiers used rakes to gather dice and money. There was a great deal of talking and calling out, the air crackling with excitement. Employees moved through the hazard room, some bearing trays of food and wine, others carrying trays of chips and fresh cards.

Remaining half-hidden behind a column, Amelia surveyed the crowd from the upper gallery. Her gaze alighted on Mr. Rohan, who had donned a black coat and cravat. Even though he was attired similarly to the club members, he stood out from them like a fox among pigeons.

Rohan half-sat, half-leaned against the bulky mahogany manager's desk in the corner of the room, where the hazard bank was managed. He appeared to be giving directions to an employee. He used a minimum of gestures, but even so, there was a suggestion of showmanship in his movements, an easy physicality that drew the eye.

And then, somehow, the intensity of Amelia's interest seemed to reach him. He reached up to the back of his neck and looked directly at her. Just as he had done in the alley. Amelia felt her heartbeat awaken everywhere. A tide of uncomfortable color washed over her. She stood immersed in guilt and heat and surprise, red-faced as a child, before she could finally gather her wits sufficiently to dart behind the column.

"What is it?" she heard Merripen ask.

"I think Mr. Rohan saw me." A shaky laugh escaped her. "Oh, dear. I hope I haven't annoyed him. Perhaps we should go back to the receiving room."

Chapter Two

Cam Rohan pushed away from the mahogany desk and left the hazard room. As usual, he couldn't leave without being stopped once or twice. There was an usher, whispering that Lord so-and-so wished to have his credit limit raised, and an underbutler, asking if he should replenish the sideboard of refreshments in one of the cardrooms. He answered their questions absently, his mind occupied with the woman awaiting him upstairs.

An evening that had promised to be routine was turning out to be rather peculiar.

It had been a long time since a woman had aroused his interest as Amelia Hathaway had. The moment he had seen her standing in the alley, wholesome and pink cheeked, her voluptuous figure contained in a modest gown, he had wanted her. He had no idea why, when she was the embodiment of everything that annoyed him about Englishwomen.

It was obvious Miss Hathaway had a relentless certainty in her own ability to organize and manage everything around her. Cam's usual reaction to that sort of female was to flee in the opposite direction. But as he had stared into her pretty blue eyes, and seen the determined frown hitched between them, he had felt a nearly irresistible temptation to tease and play with her.

It had been a while since he'd wanted anyone like this. During the past year, he'd been uncharacteristically short-tempered, impatient, easily provoked. The things that had once given him pleasure were no longer satisfying. Worst of all, he'd found himself satisfying his sexual urges with the same lack of enthusiasm he was doing everything else these days.

Finding female companionship was never a problem—Cam had found release in the arms of many a willing woman, and had repaid the favor until they had purred with satisfaction. But there was no thrill in it. No excitement, no fire, no sense of anything other than having taken care of a bodily function as ordinary as sleeping or eating. Cam had been so troubled, he'd actually brought himself to discuss it with his employer, Lord St. Vincent.

Once a renowned skirt-chaser, now a devoted husband, St. Vincent knew as much about these matters as any man alive. When Cam had asked glumly if a decrease in physical urges was something that naturally occurred when a man entered his thirties, St. Vincent had choked on his drink.

"Good God, no," the viscount had said, coughing slightly as a swallow of brandy seared his throat. They had been in the manager's office of the club, going over account books in the early hours of the morning.

St. Vincent was a handsome man with wheat-colored hair and pale blue eyes. Some claimed he had the most perfect form and features of any man alive. The looks of a saint, the soul of a scoundrel. "What kind of women have you been taking to bed?"

"What do you mean, what kind?" Cam had asked.

"Do you usually choose a bed partner for her looks, or character?"

"Looks, I suppose."

"Well, there's your problem," St. Vincent said in a matter-of-fact tone. "Beautiful women—men too, for that matter—are rarely required to serve any purpose beyond the ornamental."

"Do you include yourself in that company?" Cam asked dryly.

"Oh, how I long to. But sadly, I was ripped away from my gloriously shallow existence by the necessity of working."

Cam had turned back to the account book. "Speaking of work . . ."

"But this is so much more entertaining." St. Vincent relaxed in his chair with a lazy smile and made a temple of his elegant hands. "Regarding your problem . . . you should try a woman who's interesting out of bed as well as in it. If your appetite has dulled, a bit of novelty may be just the thing to revive it."

Cam hadn't replied, only shrugged irritably.

In a moment, St. Vincent had stood and pushed his chair back. "If you'll pardon me, Rohan, I'll bid you good evening."

"What about the accounting?"

"I'll leave it in your capable hands." At Cam's scowl, St. Vincent shrugged innocently. "Rohan, one of us is an unmarried man with superior mathematical abilities and no prospects for the evening. The other is a confirmed lecher in an amorous mood with a willing and nubile young wife waiting at home. Who do *you* think should do the damned account books?" And, with a nonchalant wave, St. Vincent had left the office.

"Novelty" had been St. Vincent's recommendation—well, that word certainly applied to Miss Hathaway. Cam had always preferred experienced women who regarded seduction as a game and knew better than to confuse pleasure with emotion. He'd never cast himself in the role of tutor to an innocent. Nothing but pain for her, and the appalling possibility of tears and regrets afterward . . . he recoiled from the idea. No, there would be no pursuit of novelty with Miss Hathaway.

Hastening his pace, Cam went up the stairs to the room where the woman waited with the big *chal*. Merripen was a common Romany name. Yet the man was in a most uncommon position. It appeared he was acting as the woman's servant, a bizarre and repugnant situation for a freedom-loving Rom.

So the two of them, Cam and Merripen, had something in common. Both of them worked for *gadje*.

A Rom didn't belong indoors, enclosed in walls. Living in boxes, as all rooms and houses were, shut away from the sky and wind and sun and stars. Breathing in stale air scented with dust and floor polish. For the first time in years Cam felt a surge of mild panic. He fought it back and focused on the task at hand—getting rid of the peculiar pair in the receiving room.

Tugging at his collar to loosen it, he pushed at the half-open door and entered the room.

Miss Hathaway stood near the doorway, waiting with tightly leashed impatience, while Merripen remained a dark presence in the corner. As Cam approached and looked into her upturned face, the panic dissolved in a rush of warmth. Her blue eyes were smudged with faint lavender shadows, and her lips were pressed into a tight seam. Her hair had been pulled back and pinned, dark and shining against her head.

Cam found her delicious. He wanted to unwrap her like a long-awaited gift. He wanted her vulnerable and naked beneath him, that soft mouth swollen from hard, deep kisses, her skin flushed with desire. Startled by her effect on him, Cam made his expression blank as he studied her.

"Well?" Amelia demanded. "Have you discovered anything about my brother's whereabouts?"

"I have."

"And?"

"Lord Ramsay visited earlier this evening, lost some money at the hazard table—"

"Thank God he's alive," Amelia exclaimed.

"—and apparently decided to console himself by visiting the local brothel."

"Brothel?" She shot her companion an exasperated glance. "I swear, Merripen, he'll die at my hands tonight." She looked back at Cam. "How much did he lose at the hazard table?"

"Approximately fifty pounds."

The pretty blue eyes widened in outrage. "He'll die *slowly* at my hands. Which brothel?"

"Bradshaw's."

Amelia reached for her bonnet. "Come, Merripen. We're going there to collect him."

Both Merripen and Cam replied at the same time, "*No.*"

"I want to see for myself if he's all right," she said calmly. "I very much doubt he is." She gave Merripen a frosty stare. "I'm not returning home without Leo. You know me well enough to take me at my word."

Half-amused, half-alarmed by her force of will, Cam asked Merripen, "Am I dealing with stubbornness, idiocy, or some combination of the two?"

Amelia replied before Merripen had the opportunity. "Stubbornness, on my part. The idiocy may be attributed entirely to my brother." She settled the bonnet on her head and tied its ribbons beneath her chin.

Cherry-red ribbons, Cam saw in bemusement. That frivolous splash of red amidst her otherwise sober attire was an incongruous note. Becoming more and more fascinated by her, Cam heard himself say, "You can't go to Bradshaw's. Reasons of morality and safety aside, you don't even know where the hell it is."

Amelia didn't flinch at the profanity. "I assume a great deal of business is sent back and forth between your establishment and Bradshaw's. You say the place is local, which means all I have to do is follow the foot traffic from here to there. Goodbye, Mr. Rohan. Your help has been greatly appreciated."

Cam moved to block her path. "All you'll accomplish is making a fool of yourself, Miss Hathaway. You won't get past the front door. A brothel like Bradshaw's doesn't take strangers off the street."

"How I manage to retrieve my brother, sir, is no concern of yours."

She was correct. It wasn't. But Cam hadn't been this entertained in a long time. No sensual depravities, no skilled courtesan, not even a room full of unclothed women, could have interested him half as much as Miss Amelia Hathaway and her red ribbons.

"I'm going with you," he said.

She frowned. "No, thank you."

"I insist."

"I don't need your services, Mr. Rohan."

Cam could think of a number of services she was clearly in need of, most of which would be a pleasure for him to provide. "Obviously, it will be to everyone's benefit for you to retrieve Ramsay and leave London as quickly as possible. I consider it my civic duty to hasten your departure."

Chapter Three

Although they could have reached the brothel on foot, Amelia, Merripen, and Rohan went to Bradshaw's in the ancient barouche. They stopped before a plain Georgian-styled building. For Amelia, whose imaginings of such a place were framed with lurid extravagance, the brothel's facade was disappointingly discreet.

"Stay inside the carriage," Rohan said. "I'll go inside and inquire as to Ramsay's whereabouts." He gave Merripen a hard look. "Don't leave Miss Hathaway unattended, even for a second. It's dangerous at this time of night."

"It's early evening," Amelia protested. "And we're in the West End, amid crowds of well-dressed gentlemen. How dangerous could it be?"

"I've seen those well-dressed gentlemen do things that would make you faint to hear of them."

"I never faint," Amelia said indignantly.

Rohan's smile was a flash of white in the shadowed interior of the carriage. He left the vehicle and dissolved into the night as if he were part of it, blending seamlessly except for the ebony glimmer of his hair and the sparkle of the diamond at his ear.

Amelia stared after him in wonder. What category did one put such a man in? He was neither a gentleman, nor a lord, nor a common workingman. A shiver chased beneath her corset stays as she recalled the moment he had helped her up into the carriage. Her hand had been gloved, but his had been bare, and she had felt the heat and strength of his fingers. And there had been the gleam of a thick gold band on his thumb. She had never seen such a thing before.

"Merripen, what does it signify when a man wears a thumb ring? Is it a Romany custom?"

Seeming uncomfortable with the question, Merripen looked through the window into the damp night. A group of young men passed the vehicle, wearing fine coats and tall hats, laughing amongst themselves. A pair of them stopped to speak with a gaudily dressed woman. Still frowning, Merripen replied to Amelia's question. "It signifies independence and freedom of thought. Also a certain separateness. In wearing it, he reminds himself he doesn't belong where he is."

"Why would Mr. Rohan want to remind himself of something like that?"

He shrugged and gave her a blank look.

Amelia relaxed back against the worn upholstered seat. "I never thought I would be hoping so desperately to find my brother inside a house of ill repute. But between a brothel and floating facedown in the Thames—" She broke off and pressed the knuckles of her clenched fist against her lips.

"He's not dead," Merripen said.

Amelia was trying very hard to believe that. "We must get Leo away from London. He'll be safer out in the country . . . won't he?"

Merripen gave a noncommittal shrug, his dark eyes revealing nothing of his thoughts.

"There's far less to do in the country," Amelia pointed out. "And definitely less trouble for Leo to get into."

"A man who wants trouble can find it anywhere."

After minutes of unbearable waiting, Rohan returned to the brougham and tugged the door open.

"Where is my brother?" Amelia demanded as the Rom climbed inside.

"Not here. After Lord Ramsay went upstairs with one of the girls and, er . . . conducted the transaction . . . he left the brothel."

"Where did he go? Did you ask—"

"He told them he was going to a tavern called the Hell and Bucket."

"Lovely," Amelia said shortly. "Do you know the way?"

Seating himself beside her, Rohan glanced at Merripen. "Follow St. James eastward and turn left after the third crossing."

Merripen flicked the ribbons, and the carriage rolled past a trio of prostitutes.

Amelia watched the women with undisguised interest. "How young some of them are," she said. "If only some charitable institution would help them find respectable employment."

"Most so-called respectable employment is just as bad," Rohan replied.

She looked at him indignantly. "You think a woman would be better off working as a prostitute rather than taking an honest job that would allow her to live with dignity?"

"I didn't say that. My point is, some employers are far more brutal than pimps or brothel bawds. Servants have to endure all manner of abuse from their masters—female servants in particular. And if you think there's dignity in working at a mill or factory, you've never seen a girl who's lost a few fingers from cutting broom straw, or someone whose lungs are so congested from breathing in fluff and dust at a carding mill, she won't live past the age of thirty."

Amelia opened her mouth to reply, then snapped it shut. She adopted an expression of cool indifference and looked out the window. Although she didn't spare a glance for Rohan, she sensed he was watching her. She was unbearably aware of him. He wore no cologne or pomade, but there was something alluring about his smell, something smoky and fresh like green cloves.

"Your brother inherited the title quite recently," Rohan said.

"Yes."

"With all respect, Lord Ramsay doesn't seem entirely prepared for his new role."

Amelia couldn't restrain a rueful smile. "None of us are. It was a surprising turn of events for the Hathaways. There were at least three men in line for the title before Leo. But they all died in rapid succession, of varying causes. It appears becoming Lord Ramsay tends to shorten a man's life. And at this rate, my brother probably won't last any longer than his predecessors."

"One never knows what fate has in store."

Turning toward Rohan, Amelia discovered he was glancing over her in a slow inventory that spurred her heart into a faster beat. "I don't believe in fate," she said. "People are in control of their own destinies."

Rohan smiled. "Everyone, even the gods, are helpless in the hands of fate."

Amelia regarded him skeptically. "Surely you, being employed at a gaming club, know all about probability and odds. Which means you can't rationally give credence to luck or fate or anything of the sort."

"I know all about probability and odds," Rohan agreed. "Nevertheless, I believe in luck." He smiled, with a quiet smolder in his eyes that caused her breath to catch. "I believe in magic and mystery, and dreams that reveal the future. And

I believe some things are written in the stars . . . or even in the palm of your hand."

Mesmerized, Amelia was unable to look away from him. He was an extraordinarily beautiful man, with black hair falling over his forehead in a way that tempted her to push it back.

"Do *you* believe in fate too?" she asked Merripen.

A long hesitation. "I'm a Rom," he said.

Which meant yes. "Good Lord, Merripen. I've always thought of you as a sensible man."

Rohan laughed. "It's only sensible to allow for the possibility, Miss Hathaway. Just because you can't see or feel something doesn't mean it can't exist."

"There is no such thing as fate," Amelia insisted. "There is only action and consequence."

The carriage came to a halt, this time in a much shabbier place than St. James or King Street. There was a beer shop and a threepenny lodging house on one side, and a large tavern on the other. The pedestrians on this street had the appearance of sham gentility, rubbing elbows with costers, pickpockets, and more prostitutes.

A brawl took place near the threshold of the tavern, a writhing mixture of arms, legs, flying hats, and bottles and canes. Any time there was a fight, the greatest likelihood was that her brother had started it.

"Merripen," she said anxiously, "you know how Leo is when he's foxed. He's probably in the middle of the fray. If you would be so kind—"

Before she had even finished, Merripen made to leave the carriage.

"Wait," Rohan said. "You'd better let me handle it."

Merripen gave him a cold glance. "You doubt my ability to fight?"

"This is a London rookery. I'm used to the kind of tricks

they employ. If you—" Rohan broke off as Merripen ignored
him and left the carriage with a surly grunt. "So be it," Rohan said, exiting the carriage and standing beside it to watch.
"They'll slice him open like a mackerel at a Covent Garden
fish stand."

Amelia came out of the vehicle as well. "Merripen can
handle himself quite well in a fight, I assure you."

Rohan looked down at her, his eyes shadowed and catlike.
"You'll be safer inside the vehicle."

"I have you for protection, do I not?" she pointed out.

"Sweetheart," he said with a softness that undercut the
noise of the crowd, "I may be the one you most need protection from."

She felt her heart miss a beat. He met her wide-eyed glance
with a steady interest that caused her toes to curl inside her
practical leather shoes. Fighting for composure, Amelia
looked away from him. But she remained sharply aware of
him, the relaxed alertness of his posture, and the unknown
pulse secreted beneath the elegant layers of his clothing.

They both watched as Merripen waded into the chaos of
brawling men and sorted through a few of them. Before a half
minute had passed, he unceremoniously hauled someone out,
easily deflecting blows with his free arm.

"He's good," Rohan said in mild surprise.

Amelia was overwhelmed with relief as she recognized
Leo's disheveled form. "Oh, thank God."

Her eyes flew open, however, as she felt a gentle touch at
the edge of her jaw. Rohan's fingers were nudging her face
upward, his thumb brushing the tip of her chin. The unexpected intimacy sent a little shock through her. His flame-
bright gaze had seized hers again.

"Don't you think you're being a bit overprotective, chasing
your grown brother across London? He's not doing anything

all that unusual. Most men in his position would behave the same."

"You don't know him," Amelia said, sounding shaken to her own ears. She knew she should pull away, but her body remained perversely still, absorbing the pleasure of his touch. "It's far from usual behavior for him. He's in trouble. He—" She broke off.

Rohan's fingertip followed the shining trail of her bonnet ribbon to the place where it tied beneath her chin. "What kind of trouble?"

She jerked away from his touch and turned as Merripen and Leo approached the carriage. A rush of love and agonized worry filled her at the sight of her brother. He was filthy, battered, and grinning unrepentantly. Anyone who didn't know Leo would assume he hadn't a care in the world. But his eyes, once so warm, were dull and wintry. His formerly fit body was paunchy, and the visible portion of his neck was bloated. There was still a long way to go before Leo was in total ruins, but he seemed determined to hasten the process.

"How remarkable," Amelia said casually. "There's still something left of you." Plucking a handkerchief from her sleeve, she strode forward and tenderly wiped sweat and a smear of blood from his cheeks. Noticing his unfocused gaze, she said, "I'm the one in the middle, dear."

"Ah. There you are." Leo's head bobbed up and down like a string puppet's. He glanced at Merripen, who was providing far more support than Leo's own legs were. "My sister," he said. "Terrifying girl."

"Before Merripen puts you in the carriage," Amelia said, "are you going to cast up your accounts, Leo?"

"Certainly not," came the unhesitating reply. "Hathaways always hold their liquor."

Amelia stroked aside the dirty-brown locks that dangled

like strands of yarn over his eyes. "It would be nice if you would try to hold a bit less of it in the future, dear."

"Ah, but, sis . . ." As Leo looked down at her, she saw a flash of his old self, a spark in the vacant eyes, and then it was gone. ". . . I have such a powerful thirst."

Amelia felt the smart of tears at the corners of her eyes, tasted salt at the back of her throat. Swallowing it back, she said in a steady voice, "For the next few days, Leo, your thirst will be slaked exclusively by water or tea. Into the carriage with him, Merripen."

Leo twisted to glance at the man who held him steady. "For God's sake, you're not going to put me in *her* custody, are you?"

"Would you rather dry out in the care of a Bow Street gaolkeeper?" Merripen asked politely.

"He would be a damn sight more merciful." Grumbling, Leo lurched toward the carriage with Merripen's assistance.

Amelia turned to Cam Rohan, whose face was inscrutable. "May we take you back to Jenner's, sir? It will be tight quarters in the carriage, but I think we can manage."

"No, thank you." Rohan walked slowly around the carriage with her. "It isn't far. I'll go on foot."

"I can't leave you stranded in a London rookery."

Rohan stopped with her at the back of the carriage, where they were partially sheltered from view. "I'll be fine. The city holds no fears for me. Hold still."

Rohan turned her face up again, one hand cradling her jaw while the other descended to her cheek. His thumb brushed gently beneath her left eye, and with surprise she felt a smudge of wetness there.

"The wind makes my eyes water," she heard herself say unsteadily.

"There's no wind tonight." His hand remained at her jaw,

the smooth band of the thumb ring pressing lightly against her skin. Her heart had begun to thump until she could hardly hear through the blood rush in her ears. The clamor of the tavern was muted, the darkness thickening around them. His fingers slid over her throat with stunning delicacy, finding secreted nerves and stroking gently.

His eyes were over hers, and she saw that the light golden-hazel irises were rimmed with black. "Miss Hathaway . . . you're quite certain fate had no hand in our meeting tonight?"

She couldn't seem to breathe properly. "Qu-quite certain."

His head bent low. "And in all likelihood, we'll never meet again?"

"Never." He was too large, too close. Nervously, Amelia tried to marshal her thoughts, but they scattered like spilled matchsticks, and he set fire to them as his breath touched her cheek.

"I hope you're right. God help me if I should ever have to face the consequences."

"Of what?" Her voice was faint.

"This." His hand slid to the back of her neck and his mouth covered hers.

Amelia had been kissed before, but this mingling of heat and taste was so far removed from her experience it belonged in another category entirely. He kissed as if he had invented it, knowing how to hold her, how to tilt her head to just the right angle.

His mouth was firm but silken, nudging hers open, probing in soft strokes. One of his arms slid around her, lifting slightly as he pulled her against the hard contours of his body.

Her hands came up to his chest and slid around his neck as he continued to kiss her, exploring tenderly until she was weak all over and her knees threatened to buckle. With each breath she drew in a deeper scent of him . . . the sweetness of beeswax soap, the hint of salt. The supple power of his body was all around her, and she couldn't stop herself from relaxing into it, letting him support her. More kisses, one beginning before another had quite finished . . . moist and intimate caresses, secret strokes of pleasure and promise.

With a soft murmur Rohan took his mouth from hers. His lips wandered along the flushed curve of her neck, lingering on the most vulnerable spots. Her body felt swollen inside her clothes, the corset cinching around the desperate pitch of her lungs.

She quivered as he reached a place of exquisite sensation and touched it with the tip of his tongue as if the taste of her were some exotic spice. A pulse awakened in her breasts and stomach and between her thighs. She was filled with a dreadful urge to press against him. She wanted to fight free of the layers and layers of smothering fabric that made up her skirts. He was so careful, so gentle—

The crash of a bottle on the pavement, the sound of glass breaking, jolted her from the haze.

"No," she gasped, now struggling.

Rohan released her, his hands steadying her as she fought for equilibrium. Amelia turned blindly and staggered toward the open door of the carriage. Everywhere he had touched, her nerves stung with the desire for more. She kept her head low, grateful for the concealment of her bonnet.

Desperate for escape, Amelia ascended to the carriage step. Before she could climb in, however, Amelia felt Rohan's hands at her waist. He held her from behind, trapping her long enough to whisper near her ear, "*Latcho drom.*"

The Romany farewell. Amelia recognized it from the handful of words Merripen had taught the Hathaways. An intimate shock went through her as the heat of his breath collected in her ear. She didn't, couldn't, reply, only climbed into the carriage and awkwardly pulled the mass of her skirts away from the open doorway.

The door was closed firmly, and the vehicle started forward as the horse obeyed Merripen's guidance. The two Hathaways occupied their respective corners of the seat, one of them drunk, the other dazed. After a moment, Amelia reached to untie her bonnet with trembling hands, and discovered the ribbons were hanging loose.

One ribbon, actually. The other . . .

Removing her bonnet, Amelia regarded it with a perplexed frown. One of the red silk ribbons was gone except for the tiny remnant at the inside edge.

It had been neatly cut.

He had taken it.

Chapter Four

One week later, all five Hathaway siblings and their belongings had removed from London to their new home in Hampshire. Despite the challenges that awaited them, Amelia was strongly hopeful their new situation would benefit them all.

The house in Primrose Place held too many memories. Things had never been the same since both Hathaway parents had died—her father of a heart ailment, her mother of grief a few months afterward. It seemed the walls had absorbed the family's sorrow until it had become part of the paint and paper and wood. Amelia couldn't look at the hearth of the main room without remembering her mother sitting there with her sewing basket, or visit the garden without thinking of her father pruning his prized Apothecary roses.

Amelia had recently sold the house without compunction, not for lack of sentimentality but rather an excess. Too much feeling, too much sadness. And it was impossible to look forward when one was constantly being reminded of painful loss.

Her siblings hadn't offered a word of objection to selling their home. Nothing mattered to Leo—one could tell him the family intended to live on the streets, and he would have greeted the news with an indifferent shrug. Win, the next oldest sister, was too weak from prolonged illness to protest any of Amelia's decisions. And Poppy and Beatrix, both still in their teens, were eager for change.

As far as Amelia was concerned, the inheritance couldn't have come at a better time. Although, she had to admit, there was some question as to how long the Hathaways would manage to retain the title.

The fact was, no one wanted to be Lord Ramsay. For the previous three Lord Ramsays, the title had been accompanied by a streak of singular ill fortune capped by untimely death. Which explained, in part, why the Hathaways' distant relatives had been quite happy to see the viscountcy go to Leo.

"Do I get any money?" had been Leo's first question upon being informed of his ascendancy to the peerage.

The answer had been a qualified yes. Leo would inherit a modest annual sum that wouldn't begin to account for the cost of repairing the estate.

"We're still poor," Amelia had told her brother after poring over the solicitor's letter describing the estate and its affairs. "The house is shabby, the servants and most of the tenants have left, the land is unproductive, and the title is apparently cursed. Which makes the inheritance a white elephant, to say the least. However, we have a distant cousin who may arguably be in line before you—we can try to throw it all off on him. There's a possibility that our great-great-great-grandfather may not have been legitimate issue, which would allow us to apply for forfeiture of the title on the grounds of—"

"I'll take the title," Leo had said decisively.

"Because you don't believe in curses any more than I do?"

"Because I'm already so damned cursed, another one won't matter."

Having never been to the southern county of Hampshire before, all the Hathaway siblings—with the exception of Leo—craned their necks to view the scenery.

Amelia smiled at her sisters' excitement. Poppy and Beatrix, both dark-haired and blue-eyed like herself, were filled with high spirits. Her gaze alighted on Win and stayed for a moment, taking careful measure of her condition.

Win was different from the rest of the Hathaway brood, the only one who had inherited their father's pale blond hair and introspective nature. She was shy and quiet, enduring every hardship without complaint. When scarlet fever had swept through the village a year earlier, Leo and Win had fallen gravely ill. Leo had made a complete recovery, but Win had been frail and colorless ever since. The doctor had diagnosed her with a weakness of the lungs caused by the fever that he said might never improve.

Amelia refused to accept that Win would be an invalid forever. No matter what it took, she would make Win well again.

It was difficult to imagine a better place for Win and the rest of the Hathaways than Hampshire. It was one of the most beautiful counties in England, with intersecting rivers, great forests, meadows, and wet heathlands. The Ramsay estate was situated close to one of the largest market towns in the county. Stony Cross exported cattle, sheep, timber, corn, a plenitude of local cheeses, and wildflower honey . . . rich territory indeed.

"I wonder why the Ramsay estate is so unproductive?" Amelia mused as the carriage traveled alongside lush pastures. "The land in Hampshire is so fertile, one almost has to *try* not to grow something here."

"But our land is cursed, isn't it?" Poppy asked with mild concern.

"No," Amelia replied, "not the estate itself. Just the title-holder. Which would be Leo."

"Oh." Poppy relaxed. "That's fine, then."

Leo didn't bother responding, only huddled in the seat corner, looking surly and miserable. Although a week of enforced sobriety had left him clear-eyed and clearheaded, it had done nothing to improve his temper. With Merripen and the Hathaways watching over him like hawks, he'd had no opportunity to drink anything other than water or tea.

For the first few days, Leo had been given to uncontrollable shaking, agitation, and profuse sweating. Now that the worst of it was over, he looked more like his old self. But few people would believe Leo was a man of eight-and-twenty. The past year had aged him immeasurably.

The closer they came to Stony Cross, the lovelier the scenery was until it seemed nearly every view was worth painting. The carriage road passed tidy black-and-white cottages with thatched roofs, millhouses and ponds shrouded with weeping willows, and old stone churches dating back to the Middle Ages. Thrushes busily stripped ripe berries from hedgerows, while stonechats perched on blossoming hawthorns. Meadows were dense with yellow cowslips and buttercups, and the trees were dressed in autumn golds and reds. Plump white sheep grazed in the fields.

Poppy took a deep, appreciative breath. "How bracing," she said. "I wonder what makes the country air smell so different?"

"It must be the pig farm we just passed," Leo muttered.

Beatrix, who had been reading from a pamphlet describing the south of England, said cheerfully, "Hampshire is known for its exceptional pigs. They're fed on acorns and beechnut mast from the forest, and it makes the bacon quite lovely. And there's an annual sausage competition!"

Win, who had been reading from a thick tome about Hampshire and its environs, volunteered, "The history of Ramsay House is impressive."

"Our house is in a history book?" Beatrix asked in delight.

"It's only a small paragraph," Win said from behind the book, "but yes, Ramsay House is mentioned. Of course, it's nothing compared to that of our neighbor, the Earl of Westcliff, whose estate features one of the finest country homes in England. It dwarfs ours by comparison. And the earl's family has been in residence for nearly five hundred years."

"He must be awfully old, then," Poppy commented, straight-faced.

Beatrix snickered. "Go on, Win."

"Ramsay House," Win read aloud, "stands in a small park populated with stately oaks and beeches, coverts of bracken, and surrounds of deer-cropped turf. Originally an Elizabethan manor house completed in 1594, the building boasts of many long galleries representative of the period. Alterations and additions to the house have resulted in the grafting of a Jacobean ballroom and a Georgian wing."

"We have a ballroom!" Poppy exclaimed.

"We have deer!" Beatrix said gleefully.

Leo settled deeper into his corner. "God, I hope we have a privy."

It was early evening by the time the hired driver turned the carriage onto the private beech-lined drive that led to Ramsay House. Weary from the long journey, the Hathaways exclaimed in relief at the sight of the house, with its high roofline and brick chimney stacks.

"I wonder how Merripen is faring," Win said, her blue eyes

soft with concern. Merripen, the cook-maid, and the footman had gone to the house two days earlier to prepare for the Hathaways' arrival.

"No doubt he's been working ceaselessly day and night," Amelia replied, "taking inventory, rearranging everything in sight, and issuing commands to people who don't dare disobey him. I'm sure he's quite happy."

Win smiled. Even pale and drained as she was, her beauty was incandescent, her silvery-gold hair shining in the waning light, her complexion like porcelain. The line of her profile would have sent poets and painters into raptures. One was almost tempted to touch her to make certain she was a living, breathing being instead of a sculpture.

The carriage stopped at a much larger house than Amelia had expected. It was bordered by overgrown hedges and weed-clotted flower beds. With some gardening and considerable pruning, she thought, it would be lovely. The building was charmingly asymmetrical with a brick and stone exterior, a slate roof, and abundant lead glass windows.

The hired driver came to set out a moveable step and assist the passengers from the vehicle.

Descending to the crushed-rock surface of the drive, Amelia watched as her siblings emerged from the carriage. "The house and grounds are a bit unkempt," she warned. "No one has lived here in a very long time."

"I can't imagine why," Leo said.

"It's very picturesque," Win commented brightly. The journey from London had exhausted her. Judging from the slump of her narrow shoulders and the way her skin seemed stretched too tightly over her cheekbones, Win had little strength left.

As her sister reached for a small valise that had been set near the carriage step, Amelia rushed forward and picked it up. "I'll carry this," she said. "You are not to lift a finger. Let's go inside and find a place for you to rest."

"I'm perfectly well," Win protested as they all went up the front stairs into the house.

The entrance hall was lined with paneling that had once been painted white but now was brown with age. The floor was scarred and filthy. A magnificent curved stone staircase occupied the back of the hall, its wrought-iron balustrade clotted with dust and spider webs. Amelia noticed that an attempt had already been made to clean a section of the balustrade, but it was obvious the process would be painstaking.

Merripen emerged from a hallway leading away from the entrance room. He was in his shirtsleeves with no collar or cravat, the neck of the garment hanging open to reveal tanned skin gleaming with perspiration. With his black hair falling over his forehead, and his dark eyes smiling at the sight of them, Merripen cut a dashing figure. "You're three hours behind schedule," he said.

Laughing, Amelia pulled a handkerchief from her sleeve and gave it to him. "In a family of four sisters, there is no schedule."

Wiping at the dust and sweat on his face, Merripen glanced at all the Hathaways. His gaze lingered on Win for an extra moment.

Returning his attention to Amelia, Merripen gave her a concise report. He had found two women and a boy at the village to help clean the house. Three bedrooms had been made habitable so far. They had spent a great deal of time cleaning the kitchen and stove, and the cook-maid was preparing a meal—

Merripen broke off as he glanced over Amelia's shoulder. Unceremoniously, he brushed by her and reached Win in three strides.

Amelia saw Win's slight form swaying, her lashes lowering as she half-collapsed against Merripen. He lifted her easily in his arms, murmuring for her to put her head on his shoulder. Although his manner was as calm and unemotional as ever, Amelia was struck by the possessive way he held her sister.

"The journey was too much for her," Amelia said in concern. "She needs rest."

Merripen's face was expressionless. "I'll take her upstairs."

Win stirred and blinked. "Bother," she said breathlessly. "I was standing still, feeling fine, and then the floor seemed to rush up toward me. I'm sorry. I *despise* swooning."

"It's all right." Amelia gave her a reassuring smile. "Merripen will take you to bed. That is"—she paused uncomfortably—"he'll convey you to your bedroom."

"I can manage by myself," Win said. "I was just dizzy for a moment. Merripen, do put me down."

"You wouldn't make it past the first step," he said, ignoring her protests as he carried her to the stone staircase.

"Beatrix, will you go with them?" Amelia asked briskly, handing her the valise. "Win's nightgown is in here—you can help her change clothes."

"Yes, of course." Beatrix scampered toward the stairs.

Left in the entrance hall with Leo and Poppy, Amelia turned a slow circle to view all of it. "The solicitor said the estate was in disrepair," she said. "I think a more accurate word would have been 'shambles.' Can it be restored, Leo?"

Not long ago—though it seemed a lifetime—Leo had spent two years studying art and architecture at the Grand École des Beaux-Arts in Paris. He had worked as a draughtsman and painter for the renowned architect Rowland Temple. Leo had been regarded as an exceptionally promising student, and had even considered setting up a practice. Now all that ambition had been extinguished.

Leo glanced around the hall without interest. "Barring any structural repairs, we'll need about twenty-five to thirty thousand pounds, at least."

The figure caused Amelia to blanch. She lowered her gaze to the pockmarked floor at her feet and rubbed her temples. "Well, one thing is obvious. We need the advantage of wealthy in-laws. Which means you should start looking for available heiresses, Leo." She flicked a playful glance at her sister. "And you, Poppy—you'll have to catch a viscount, or at the very least, a baron."

Her brother rolled his eyes. "Why not you? I don't see why you should be exempt from having to marry for the family's benefit."

Poppy gave her sister a sly glance. "At Amelia's age, women are far beyond thoughts of romance and passion."

"One never knows," Leo told Poppy. "She may catch an elderly gentleman who needs a nurse."

Amelia tolerated their teasing with a smile and a slight shake of her head. "Thank you, but at this advanced state of life, I have no ambitions to marry."

Leo surprised her by bending to brush a light kiss on her forehead. "You haven't met a man worth giving up your independence for. But you will someday." He grinned before adding, "Despite your encroaching old age."

For a moment Amelia's mind chased back to the memory of the stranger's kiss in the shadows, his mouth slowly consuming hers . . .

As her brother turned to walk away, she asked with mild exasperation, "Where are you going? Leo, you can't leave when there's so much to be done."

He stopped and glanced back at her with a raised brow. "You've been pouring unsweetened tea down my throat for days. If you have no objection, I'd like to go out for a piss."

As Leo left the room, Amelia folded her arms and sighed.

"Despite that uncouth remark, he's generally pleasant when he's sober. A pity it doesn't happen more often. Come, Poppy, let's find the kitchen."

WITH THE HOUSE SO STALE AND DUST-RIDDLED, THE ATMO-sphere was hard on poor Win's lungs, causing her to cough incessantly through the night. Having awakened countless times to administer water to her sister, to open the windows, and to prop her up until the coughing spasms had eased, Amelia was bleary-eyed when morning came.

"It's like sleeping in a dustbox," she told Merripen. "She's better off sitting outside today, until we can manage to clean her room properly. The carpets must be beaten. And the windows are filthy."

The rest of the family was still abed, but Merripen, like Amelia, was an early riser. Dressed in rough clothes and an open-necked shirt, he stood frowning as Amelia reported on Win's condition.

"She's exhausted from coughing all night, and her throat's so sore, she can barely speak. I've tried to make her take some tea and toast, but she won't have it."

"I'll make her take it."

Amelia looked at him blankly. She supposed she shouldn't be surprised by his assertion. After all, Merripen had helped nurse both Win and Leo through the scarlet fever. Without him, Amelia was certain neither of them would have survived.

"In the meanwhile," Merripen continued, "make a list of supplies you want from the village. I'll go this morning."

Amelia nodded, grateful for his solid, reliable presence. "Shall I wake Leo? Perhaps he could help you—"

"No."

She smiled wryly, well aware that her brother would be more of a hindrance than a help.

Going downstairs, Amelia sought the help of Freddie, the boy from the village, to move an ancient chaise out to the back of the house. They set the furniture on a brick-paved terrace that opened onto a weed-choked garden bordered by beech hedges. The garden needed resodding and replanting, and the crumbling low walls would have to be repaired.

"There's work to be done, ma'am," Freddie commented, bending to pluck a tall weed from between two paving bricks.

"Freddie, you're a master of understatement." Amelia contemplated the boy, who looked to be about thirteen. He was robust and ruddy-faced, with a ruff of hair that stood up like a robin's feathers. "Do you like gardening?" she asked. "Do you know much about it?"

"I keeps a kitchen plot for my ma."

"Would you like to be Lord Ramsay's gardener?"

"How much does it pay, miss?"

"Would two shillings a week suffice?"

Freddie looked at her thoughtfully and scratched his wind-chapped nose. "Sounds good. But you'll have to ask my ma."

"Tell me where you live, and I'll visit her this very morning."

They shook hands on the deal, talked a moment more, and Freddie went to investigate the gardener's shed.

Turning at the sound of voices, Amelia saw Merripen carrying her sister outside. Win was dressed in a nightgown and robe and swathed in a shawl, her slim arms looped around Merripen's neck. With her white garments and blond hair and fair skin, Win was nearly colorless except for the flags of soft pink across her cheekbones and the vivid blue of her eyes.

". . . that was the most terrible medicine," she was saying cheerfully.

"It worked," Merripen pointed out, bending to settle her carefully on the chaise.

"That doesn't mean I forgive you for bullying me into taking it."

"It was for your own good."

"You're a bully," Win repeated, smiling into his dark face.

"Yes, I know," Merripen murmured, tucking the lap blankets around her with extreme care.

Delighted by the improvement in her sister's condition, Amelia smiled. "He really is dreadful. But if he manages to persuade some village women to come help clean the house, you will have to forgive him, Win."

Win's blue eyes twinkled. She spoke to Amelia, while her gaze remained on Merripen. "I have every faith in his powers of persuasion."

Coming from anyone else, the words might have been construed as a piece of flirtation. But Amelia was fairly certain that Win had no awareness of Merripen as a man. To her, he was a kindly older brother, nothing more.

The feelings on Merripen's side, however, were more ambiguous.

An inquisitive gray jackdaw flapped to the ground and made a tentative hop in Win's direction. "I'm sorry," she told the bird, "there's no food to share."

A new voice entered the conversation. "Yes, there is!" It was Beatrix, carrying a breakfast tray containing a plate of toast and a mug of tea. Her curly dark hair had been pulled back into an untidy bunch, and she wore a white pinafore over her berry-colored dress.

The pinafore was too young a style for a girl of fifteen, Amelia thought. Beatrix was now at an age when she should be wearing her skirts to the floor. And a corset, heaven help her. But in the past year of turmoil, Amelia hadn't given much thought to her youngest sister's attire. She needed to take Beatrix and Poppy to a dressmaker, and have some new frocks made for them. Adding that to the long list of expenditures in her head, Amelia frowned.

"Here's your breakfast, Win," Beatrix said, settling the tray on her lap. "Are you feeling well enough to butter the toast yourself, or shall I?"

"I will, thank you." Win moved her feet and gestured for Beatrix to sit at the other end of the chaise.

Beatrix obeyed promptly. "I'm going to read to you while you sit out here," she informed Win, reaching into one of the huge pockets of her pinafore. She withdrew a little book and dangled it tantalizingly. "This book was given to me by Philomena Parsons, my best friend in the entire world. She says it's a terrifying story filled with crimes and horrors and vengeful phantoms. Doesn't it sound lovely?"

"I thought your best friend in the world was Edwina Huddersfield," Win said with a questioning lilt.

"Oh, no, that was *weeks* ago. Edwina and I don't even speak now." Snuggling comfortably in her corner, Beatrix gave her older sister a perplexed glance. "Win? You have the oddest look on your face. Is something the matter?"

Win had frozen in the act of lifting a tea cup to her lips, her blue eyes round with alarm.

Following her sister's gaze, Amelia saw a small reptilian creature slithering up Beatrix's shoulder. A sharp cry escaped her lips, and she moved forward with her hands raised.

Beatrix glanced at her shoulder. "Oh, dear. You're supposed to stay in my pocket." She plucked the wriggling object from her shoulder and stroked him gently. "A spotted sand lizard," she said. "Isn't he adorable? I found him in my room last night."

Amelia lowered her hands and stared dumbly at her youngest sister.

"You've made a pet of him?" Win asked weakly. "Beatrix, dear, don't you think he would be happier in the forest where he belongs?"

Beatrix looked indignant. "With all those predators? Spot wouldn't last a minute."

Amelia found her voice. "He won't last a minute with me, either. Get rid of him, Bea, or I'm going to flatten him with the nearest heavy object I can find."

"You would *murder* my *pet*?"

"One doesn't murder lizards, Bea. One exterminates them." Exasperated, Amelia turned to Merripen. "Find some cleaning women in the village, Merripen. God knows how many other unwanted creatures are lurking in the house. Not counting Leo."

Merripen disappeared at once.

"Spot is the perfect pet," Beatrix argued. "He doesn't bite, and he's already house-trained."

"I draw the line at pets with scales."

Beatrix stared at her mutinously. "The sand lizard is a native species of Hampshire—which means Spot has more right to be here than we do."

"Nevertheless, we will not be cohabiting." Walking away before she said something she would regret later, Amelia wondered why, when there was so much to be done, Beatrix would be so troublesome. However, she reminded herself, fifteen-year-old girls didn't *choose* to be troublesome. They simply were.

Lifting handfuls of her skirts to pull them away from her legs, Amelia bounded up the grand central staircase. Since they would not be receiving guests or paying calls, she had decided not to wear a corset that day. It was a wonderful feeling to breathe as deeply as she wished and move freely about the house.

Filled with determination, she pounded on Leo's door. "Wake up, slugabed!"

A string of foul words filtered through the heavy oak panels.

Grinning, Amelia went into Poppy's room. She pulled the curtains open, releasing clouds of dust that caused her to sneeze. "Poppy, it's . . . *achoo!* . . . time to get out of bed."

The covers had been completely drawn over Poppy's head. "Oh, not yet," came her muffled protest.

Sitting on the edge of the mattress, Amelia eased the covers away from her nineteen-year-old sister. Poppy was groggy and sleep-flushed, her cheek imprinted with a line left by a fold of the bedclothes. Her brown hair, a warmer, ruddier tint than Amelia's, was a wild mass of tangles.

"I hate morning," Poppy mumbled. "And I'm sure I don't like being awakened by someone who looks so pleased about it."

"I'm so sorry." Continuing to smile, Amelia stroked her sister's hair away from her face repeatedly.

"Mmmn." Poppy kept her eyes closed. "That's the way Mama used to smooth my hair. Feels nice."

"Does it?" Amelia laid her hand gently over the curve of Poppy's skull. "Dear, I'm going to walk to the village, to ask Freddie's mother if we can hire him as our gardener." She went to Poppy's valise in the corner and picked up the bonnet poised atop it. "May I borrow this? Mine still hasn't been repaired."

"Of course, but . . . you're going right now?"

"I won't be long. I'll cover the territory quickly."

"Would you like me to go with you?"

"Thank you, dear, but no. Dress yourself and have some

breakfast—and keep a close watch on Win. She's in Beatrix's care at the moment."

"Oh." Poppy's eyes widened. "I'll hurry."

Chapter Five

It was a pleasantly cool, nearly cloudless day, the southern climate far milder than London's. Amelia walked briskly through a fruit orchard beyond the garden. The tree branches were weighted with large green apples. Some of the fallen fruit had been half-eaten by deer and other animals, left to ferment and spoil.

Pausing to tug an apple from a low-hanging branch, Amelia polished it on her sleeve and took a bite. The flavor was intensely acidic.

A honeybee buzzed close by, and Amelia jerked back in alarm. She had always been terrified of bees. Although she had tried to reason herself out of her fear, she couldn't seem to control the panic that overcame her whenever one of the dratted beasts was in the vicinity.

Hurrying from the orchard, Amelia followed a sunken lane that led past a wet meadow. Despite the lateness of the season, heavy beds of watercress flourished everywhere. Known as "poor man's bread," the delicate pepper-flavored leaves were eaten in bunches by local villagers, and made into everything from soup to goose stuffing. She would gather some on her way back, she decided.

The shortest route to the village crossed through a corner of Lord Westcliff's estate. As Amelia passed the invisible boundary between the Ramsay estate and Stony Cross Park, she could almost feel a change in the atmosphere. She walked on the outskirts of a rustling forest too dense for daylight to penetrate the canopy. The land was luxurious, secretive, the ancient trees anchored deeply into dark and fertile ground. Amelia removed her bonnet, held it by the brim, and enjoyed the breeze against her face.

This had been Westcliff's land for generations. She wondered what kind of people the earl and his family were. Terribly proper and traditional, she guessed. It would not be welcome news that Ramsay House was now occupied with an ill-mannered, red-blooded lot like the Hathaways.

Heading up a well-worn footpath that cut through the forest, she disrupted a pair of wheatears, who flapped away with indignant chirps. Life abounded everywhere, including butterflies of almost unnatural color and beetles as bright as sparks. Taking care to stay on the footpath, Amelia picked up her skirts to keep them from dragging through the leaf litter of the forest floor.

She emerged from a copse of hazel and oak into a broad dry field. It was empty. And ominously quiet. No voices, no cheep of finches, no drone of bees or rattle of grasshoppers. Something about it filled her with the instinctive tension that warned of an unknown threat.

As she reached the brow of a stunted hill, she paused in bewilderment at the sight of a towering contraption made of metal. It appeared to be a chute propped up on legs, tilted at a steep angle.

Her attention was caught by a minor commotion farther afield. Two men emerging from behind a small wooden shelter were shouting and waving their arms at her.

Amelia instantly realized she had stumbled into danger,

even before she saw the smoldering trail of sparks move, snakelike, along the ground toward the metal chute.

A *fuse*?

Although she didn't know much about explosive devices, she was aware that once a fuse had been lit, nothing could be done to stop it. Dropping to the sun-warmed grass, Amelia covered her head with her arms, having every expectation of being blown to bits. A few heartbeats passed, and she let out a startled cry as she felt a large, heavy body fall on hers . . . no, not fall, *pounce*. He covered her completely, his knees digging into the ground on either side of her as he made a shelter of his body.

At the same moment, a deafening explosion pierced the air. There was a violent *whoosh* over their heads. A shock went through the ground beneath them. Too stunned to move, Amelia tried to gather her wits. Her ears were filled with a high-pitched buzz.

Her companion remained motionless over her, breathing heavily in her hair. The air was sharp with smoke, but even so, Amelia was aware of a pleasant masculine scent, skin-salt and soap and an intimate spice she couldn't quite identify. The noise in her ears faded. Raising up on her elbows, feeling the solid reach of his chest against her back, she saw shirtsleeves rolled up over forearms cabled with muscle . . . and there was something else . . .

Her eyes widened as she saw a small, stylized design inked on his arm. A tattoo of a black winged horse with eyes the color of brimstone. It was an Irish design, of a nightmare horse called a pooka: a malevolent mythical creature who spoke in a human voice and carried people away at midnight.

Her heart stopped as she saw the heavy, rounded band of a thumb ring.

Wriggling beneath him, Amelia tried to turn to her back. The strong hand curved around her shoulder, helping to ease her over. His voice was low and familiar. "Are you all right? I'm sorry. You were in the path of—"

He stopped as Amelia rolled to her back. The front of her hair had come loose, pulled free of a strategically anchored pin. The lock fanned over her face, obscuring her vision. Before she could reach up to push it away, he did it for her, and the brush of his fingertips sent ripples of liquid fire along intimate pathways of her body.

"You," he said softly.

Cam Rohan.

It can't be, she thought dazedly. *Here, in Hampshire?* But there were the unmistakable eyes, gold and hazel and heavy lashed, the midnight hair, the wicked mouth, and the glitter of the diamond on his ear.

His expression was perturbed, as if he'd been reminded of something he had wanted to forget. But as his gaze slid over her bewildered face, his mouth curved a little, and he settled into the cradle of her body with an insolent familiarity that temporarily robbed her breath.

"Mr. Rohan . . . how . . . why . . . what are you doing here?"

He replied without moving, as if he were planning to lie there and converse all day. His infinitely polite tone was an unsettling contrast to the intimacy of their position. "Miss Hathaway. What a pleasant surprise. As it happens, I'm visiting friends. And you?"

"I live here."

"I don't think so. This is Lord Westcliff's estate."

Her heart thundered in her breast as her body absorbed the details of him. "I didn't mean *precisely* here. I meant over there, on the other side of the woods. The Ramsay estate. We've just taken up residence." She couldn't seem to stop herself from chattering in the aftermath of nerves and fright. "What was that noise? What were you doing? Why do you have that tattoo on your arm? It's a pooka—an Irish creature—isn't it?"

That last question earned her an arrested stare. Before Rohan could reply, the other two men approached. From her prone position, Amelia had an upside-down view of them. Like Rohan, they were in their shirtsleeves, with waistcoats left unbuttoned.

One of them was a portly old gentleman with a shock of silver hair. He held a small wood-and-metal sextant, which had been strung around his neck on a lanyard. The other, a black-haired man who looked to be in his late thirties. He wasn't as tall as Rohan, but he had an air of authority tempered with aristocratic arrogance.

Amelia made a helpless movement, and Rohan lifted away from her with fluid ease. He helped her stand, his arm steadying her. "How far did it go?" he asked the men.

"Devil take the rocket," came a gravelly-voiced reply. "What is the woman's condition?"

"Unharmed."

The silver-haired man remarked, "Impressive, Rohan. You covered a distance of fifty yards in no more than five or six seconds."

"I would hardly miss a chance to leap on a beautiful woman," Rohan said, causing the older man to chuckle.

Rohan's hand remained at the small of Amelia's back, the light pressure causing her blood to simmer. Easing away from his distracting touch, Amelia raised her hands to the dangling front locks of her hair and tucked them behind her ears. "Why are you shooting rockets? And more to the point, why are you shooting them at my property?"

The stranger nearby gave her a sharp, assessing glance. "*Your* property?"

Rohan interceded. "Lord Westcliff, this is Miss Amelia Hathaway. Lord Ramsay's sister."

Frowning, Westcliff executed a precise bow. "Miss Hathaway. I was not informed about your arrival. Had I been aware of your presence, I would have notified you about our rocket experiments, as I have everyone else in the vicinity."

Clearly Westcliff was a man who expected to be informed about everything. He looked annoyed that the new neighbors had dared to move into their own residence without telling him first.

"We arrived only yesterday, my lord," Amelia replied. "I had intended to call on you after we settled in." Under ordinary circumstances, she would have left it at that. But she was still off-balance, and there was no stopping the flow of comments from her own mouth. "Well, I must say, the guidebook didn't warn adequately about the occurrence of rocket fire amid the peaceful Hampshire scenery." She reached down and whacked at the dust and bits of leaf that clung to her skirts. "I'm sure you don't know the Hathaways well enough to shoot at us. Yet. When we become better acquainted, however, I have no doubt you'll find ample reason to declare war and bring out the artillery."

Over her head, she heard Rohan laugh. "Considering our issues with aim and accuracy, you have nothing to fear, Miss Hathaway."

The silver-haired gentleman spoke then. "Rohan, if you wouldn't mind finding out where that rocket landed—"

"Of course." Rohan took off at an easy lope.

"Agile fellow," the older man said approvingly. "Fast as a leopard. Not to mention steady of hands and nerves. What a sapper he'd make."

After introducing himself as Captain Swansea, formerly of the Royal Engineers, the man explained to Amelia that he was a rocketry enthusiast who was continuing his scientific work in a civil capacity. As a friend of Lord Westcliff, who shared his interest in engineering science, Swansea had come to experiment with a new rocket design in the country, where there was sufficient land to do so. Lord Westcliff had enlisted Cam Rohan to help with the flight equations and other mathematical calculations necessary to evaluate the performances of the rockets. "Quite extraordinary, really, his facility with numbers," Swansea said. "You'd never expect it to look at him."

Amelia couldn't help but agree. In her experience scholarly men such as her father were pale from spending much of their time indoors, and they had paunches and spectacles and rumpled, tweedy appearances. Not handsome, incredibly athletic young men.

"Miss Hathaway," Lord Westcliff said, "to my knowledge, there hasn't been a Ramsay in residence in nearly a decade. I find it difficult to believe the house is habitable."

"Oh, it's in fine condition," Amelia lied brightly, her pride rising to the fore. "Of course, some dusting is needed—and a few minor repairs—but we're quite comfortable."

She thought she'd spoken convincingly, but Westcliff looked skeptical. "We're having a large supper at Stony Cross Manor this evening," he said. "You will bring your family. It will be an excellent opportunity for you to meet some local residents, including the vicar."

A supper with Lord and Lady Westcliff. Heaven help her.

Had the Hathaway family been well-rested, had Leo been a bit further on the path of sobriety, had they all possessed suitable formal attire, and had they been given enough time to study etiquette, Amelia might have considered accepting the invitation. But as things were . . . no. "You are very kind, my lord, but I must decline. We've only just arrived in Hampshire, and most of our clothes are still packed away—"

"The occasion is informal."

Amelia doubted his definition of "informal" matched hers. "It's not merely a matter of attire, my lord. One of my sisters is somewhat frail, and it would be too taxing for her. She needs a great deal of rest after the long journey from London."

"Tomorrow night, then. It will be a much smaller affair, and not at all taxing."

In light of his insistence, there was no way to refuse. Cursing herself for not staying at Ramsay house that morning, Amelia forced a smile to her lips. "Very well, my lord. Your hospitality is much appreciated."

Rohan returned, his breath quickened from exertion. A mist of sweat had accumulated on his skin until it gleamed like bronze. "Right on course," he said to Westcliff and Swansea. "The stabilizing fins worked. It landed at a distance of approximately two thousand yards."

"Excellent!" Swansea exclaimed. "But where is the rocket?"

A grin flashed across Rohan's face. "Buried in a deep, smoking hole. I'll go back to dig it up later."

"Yes, we'll want to see the condition of the casing and the inner core." Swansea was red-faced with satisfaction. He used a handkerchief to blot his steaming, wrinkled countenance. "It's been an exciting morning, eh?"

"Perhaps it's time to return to the manor, Captain," Westcliff suggested.

"Yes, quite." Swansea bowed to Amelia. "A pleasure, Miss Hathaway. And may I say, you took it rather well, being the target of a surprise attack."

"The next time I visit, Captain," she said, "I'll remember to bring my white flag."

He chuckled and bid her farewell.

Before turning to join the captain, Lord Westcliff glanced at Cam Rohan. "I'll take Swansea back to the manor, if you'll see to it that Miss Hathaway is delivered home safely."

"Of course," came the unhesitating reply.

"Thank you," Amelia said, "but there's no need. I know the way, and it isn't far."

Her protest was ignored. She was left to stare uneasily at Cam Rohan, while the other two men departed.

"I'm hardly some helpless female," she said. "I don't need to be *delivered* anywhere. Besides, in light of your past behavior, I'd be safer going alone."

A brief silence. Rohan tilted his head and regarded her curiously. "Past behavior?"

"You know what I—" She broke off, flushing at the memory of the kiss in the darkness. "I'm referring to what happened in London."

He gave her a look of polite perplexity. "I'm afraid I don't follow."

"You're not going to pretend you don't remember," she exclaimed. Perhaps he had kissed so many legions of women, he couldn't possibly recollect them all. "Are you also going to deny you stole one of my bonnet ribbons?"

"You have a vivid imagination, Miss Hathaway." His tone was bland. But there was a flare of provoking laughter in his eyes.

"I have no such thing. The rest of my family is *steeped* in imagination—I'm the one who clings desperately to reality." She turned and began to walk at a brisk pace. "I'm going home. There's no need for you to accompany me."

Ignoring her, Rohan fell easily into step beside her, his relaxed stride accounting for every two of hers. He let her set their pace. In the openness of their surroundings, he seemed even larger than she had remembered. "When you saw my arm," he murmured, "the tattoo . . . how did you know it was a pooka?"

Amelia hesitated before replying. As they walked, the shadows of nearby branches crossed their faces. A red-tailed hawk glided across the sky and disappeared into the heavy wood. "I've read some Irish folklore," she finally said. "A wicked, dangerous creature, the pooka. Invented to give people nightmares. Why would you choose such a design?"

"It was given to me as a child. I don't remember when it was done."

"For what purpose? What significance does it have?"

"My family would never explain." Rohan shrugged. "Perhaps they might now. But it's been years since I've seen them."

"Could you ever find them again, if you wished?"

"Given enough time." Casually he fastened his waistcoat and rolled down his sleeves, concealing the heathen symbol. "I remember my grandmother telling me about the pooka. She encouraged me to believe it was real—I think she half-believed it herself. She practiced the old magic."

"What is that? Do you mean fortune telling?"

Rohan shook his head and slid his hands into the pockets of his trousers. "No," he said, looking amused, "although she did tell fortunes to *gadje* at times. The old magic is a belief that all of nature is connected and equal. Everything is alive. Even the trees have souls."

Amelia was fascinated. It had always been impossible to coax Merripen to say anything about his past or his Romany beliefs, and here was a man who seemed willing to discuss anything. "Do you believe in the old magic?"

"No. But I like the idea of it." Rohan reached for her elbow to guide her around a rough patch of ground. Before she could object to his touch, it was gone. "The pooka isn't always wicked," he said. "Sometimes it acts out of mischief. Playfulness."

She gave him a skeptical glance. "You call it playful for a creature to toss you on its back, fly up to the sky, and drop you into a ditch or bog?"

"That's one of the stories," Rohan admitted with a grin. "But in other accounts, the pooka just wants to take you on an adventure . . . fly you to places you can only see in dreams. And then he returns you home."

"But the legends say that after the horse takes you on his midnight travels, you're never the same."

"No," he said softly. "How could you be?"

Without realizing it, Amelia had slowed their pace to a relaxed amble. It seemed impossible to walk with brisk efficiency on a day like this, with so much sun and soft air. And with this unusual man beside her, dark and dangerous and charming.

"Of all the places to see you again," she said, "I would never have expected Lord Westcliff's estate. How did you come to be acquainted? He's a member of the gaming club, I suppose."

"Yes. And friends with the owner."

"Are Lord Westcliff's other guests accepting of your presence at Stony Cross Manor?"

"You mean because I'm a Rom?" A sly smile touched his lips. "I'm afraid they have no choice but to be polite. First, out of respect for the earl. And then there's the fact that most of them are obliged to come to me for credit at the club—which means I have access to their private financial information."

"Not to mention private scandals," Amelia said dryly, remembering the alley fight.

His smile lingered. "A few of those, too."

"Nevertheless, you must feel like an outsider at times."

"Always," he said in a matter-of-fact tone.

Amelia wondered what it must be like for him, caught between two cultures, belonging to neither. And yet there was no trace of self-pity in his tone.

"The Hathaways are outsiders as well," she said. "It's obvious we're not suited to a position in polite society. None of us have the education or breeding to carry it off. Supper at

Stony Cross Manor should be a spectacle—I'm sure it will end with us being tossed out on our ears."

"You may be surprised. Lord and Lady Westcliff don't usually stand on formality. And their table includes a great variety of guests."

Amelia was not reassured. To her, upper society resembled the fish bowls in fashionable parlors, filled with glittering creatures who darted and circled in patterns she had no hope of understanding. The Hathaways might as well have attempted to live underwater as to belong in such elevated company. And yet, they had no choice but to try.

Spying a heavy growth of watercress on the bank of a wet meadow, Amelia went to examine it. She grasped a bunch and pulled until the delicate stems snapped. "Watercress is plentiful here, isn't it? I've heard it can be made into a fine salad or sauce."

"It's also a medicinal herb. My grandmother used to put it in poultices for sprains or injuries. And it's a powerful love tonic. For women, especially."

"A what?" The delicate greenery fell from her nerveless fingers.

"If a man wishes to reawaken his lover's interest, he feeds her watercress. It's a stimulant of the—"

"Don't tell me! Don't!"

Rohan laughed, a mocking gleam in his eyes.

Giving him a warning glance, Amelia brushed a few stray watercress leaves from her palms and continued on her way.

Her companion followed readily. "Tell me about your family," he coaxed. "How many of you are there?"

"Five in all. Leo—that is, Lord Ramsay—is the oldest, and I am the next, followed by Winnifred, Poppy, and Beatrix."

"Which sister is the frail one?"

"Winnifred."

"Has she always been that way?"

"No, Win was quite healthy until a year ago, when she nearly died from scarlet fever." A long hesitation, while her throat tightened a little. "She survived, thank God, but her lungs are weak. She has little strength, and she tires easily. The doctor says Win may never improve, and in all likelihood, she won't be able to marry or have children." Amelia's jaw hardened. "We will prove him wrong, of course. Win will be completely well again."

"God help anyone who stands in your way. You do like to manage other peoples' lives, don't you?"

"Only when it's obvious I can do a better job of it than they can. What are you smiling at?"

Rohan stopped, obliging her to turn to face him. "You. You make me want to—" He stopped as if thinking better of what he'd been about to say. But the trace of amusement lingered on his lips.

She didn't like the way he looked at her, the way he made her feel hot and nervous and giddy. All her senses informed her that he was a thoroughly untrustworthy man. One who abided by no one's rules but his own.

"Tell me, Miss Hathaway . . . what would you do if you were invited on a midnight ride across the earth and ocean? Would you choose the adventure, or stay safe at home?"

She couldn't seem to tear her gaze from his. His topaz eyes were lit by a glint of playfulness—not the innocent mischief of a boy, but something far more dangerous.

"Home, of course," she managed in a sensible tone. "I don't want adventure."

"I think you do. I think in a moment of weakness, you might surprise yourself."

"I don't have moments of weakness. Not *that* kind, at any rate."

His laughter curled around her like a drift of smoke. "You will."

Amelia didn't dare ask why he was so certain of that. Perplexed, she lowered her gaze to the top button of his waistcoat. Was he flirting with her? No, it must be that he was mocking her, trying to make her look foolish. And if there was one thing she feared in life more than bees, it was appearing foolish.

Gathering her dignity, which had scattered like bits of dandelion fluff in a high wind, she frowned at him. "We're nearly at Ramsay house." She indicated the outline of a roof rising from the forest. "I would prefer to go the last part of the distance alone. You may tell the earl that I was safely delivered. Good day, Mr. Rohan."

He gave a nod, took her in with one of those bright, disarming glances, and stayed to watch her progress as she walked away. With each step Amelia put between them, she should have felt safer, but the sense of disquiet remained. And then, she heard him murmur something, his voice shadowed with amusement, and it sounded as if he had said, "Some midnight . . ."

Chapter Six

The news that they were to have supper at the home of Lord and Lady Westcliff was received with a variety of reactions from the Hathaways. Poppy and Beatrix were pleased and excited, whereas Win, who was still trying to regain her strength after the journey to Hampshire, was merely resigned. Leo was looking forward to a lengthy repast accompanied by fine wine.

Merripen, on the other hand, flatly refused to go.

"You're part of the family," Amelia told him, watching as he secured loose paneling boards in one of the common rooms. Merripen's grip on a carpenter's hammer was deft and sure as he expertly sank a handmade nail into the edge of a board. "No matter how you may try to deny all connection to the Hathaways—and one could hardly blame you for that—the fact is, you're one of us, and you should attend."

Merripen methodically pounded a few more nails into the wall. "My presence won't be necessary."

"Well, of course it won't be *necessary*. But you might enjoy yourself."

"No, I wouldn't," he replied with grim certainty and continued his hammering.

"Why must you be so stubborn? If you're afraid of being treated badly, you should recall that Lord Westcliff is already acting as host to a Rom and seems to have no prejudice—"

"I don't like *gadje*."

"My entire family—*your* family—are *gadje*. Does that mean you don't like us?"

Merripen didn't reply, only continued to work. Noisily.

Amelia let out a taut sigh. "Merripen, you're a dreadful snob. And if the evening turns out to be terrible, it's your obligation to endure it with us."

Merripen reached for another handful of nails. "That was a good try," he said. "But I'm not going."

THE PRIMITIVE PLUMBING AT RAMSAY HOUSE, ITS POOR lighting, and the dinginess of the few looking glasses available made it difficult to prepare for the visit to Stony Cross Manor. After laboriously heating water in the kitchen, the Hathaways hauled buckets up and down the stairs for their own baths. Everyone except Win, of course, who was resting in her room to preserve her strength.

Amelia sat with unusual submissiveness as Poppy styled her hair, pulling it back, making thick braids, then pinning it into a heavy chignon that covered the back of her head. "There," Poppy said with pleasure. "At least you're fashionable from the ears upward."

Like the other Hathaway sisters, Amelia was dressed in a serviceable bombazine gown of twilled blue silk and worsted. Its design was plain with a moderately full skirt, the sleeves long and tightly fitted.

Poppy's gown was a similar style, only in red. She was an uncommonly pretty girl, her fine features lit with vivacity and intelligence. If a girl's social popularity were based on merit rather than fortune, Poppy would have been the toast of London. Instead, she was living in the country in a rattletrap house, wearing old clothes, hauling water and coal like a maidservant. And she had never once complained.

"We'll have some new dresses made very soon," Amelia said earnestly, feeling her heart twist with remorse. "Things will improve, Poppy. I promise."

"I hope so," her sister said lightly. "I'll need a ball gown if I'm to catch a rich benefactor for the family."

"You know I only said that in jest. You don't have to look for a rich suitor. Only one who will be kind to you."

Poppy grinned. "Well, we can hope that wealth and kindness are not mutually exclusive, can't we?"

Amelia smiled back at her. "Indeed."

As the siblings assembled in the entrance hall, Amelia felt even more remorseful on seeing Beatrix turned out in a green dress with ankle-length skirts and a starched white pinafore, an ensemble far more appropriate for a girl of twelve than of fifteen.

Making her way to Leo's side, Amelia muttered to him, "No more gambling, Leo. The money you lost at Jenner's would have been better spent on proper clothes for your younger sisters."

"There's more than enough money for you to have taken them to the dressmaker," Leo said coolly. "Don't make me the villain when it's your responsibility to clothe them."

Amelia gritted her teeth. As much as she adored Leo, no one could make her as angry as he, and so quickly. She longed to administer some heavy clout on the head that might restore his wits. "At the rate you've been going through the family coffers, I didn't think it would be wise of me to go on a spending spree."

The other Hathaways watched, wide-eyed, as the conversation exploded into a full-on argument.

"You may choose to live like a miser," Leo said, "but I'll be damned if I have to. You're incapable of enjoying the moment because you're always intent on tomorrow. Well, for some people, tomorrow never comes."

Her temper flared. "*Someone* has to think of tomorrow, you selfish spendthrift!"

"Coming from an overbearing shrew—"

Win stepped between them, resting a light hand on Amelia's shoulder. "Hush, both of you. It serves no purpose to make yourselves cross just before we're to leave." She gave Amelia a sweet quirk of a smile. "Don't frown like that, dear. What if your face stayed that way?"

"With prolonged exposure to Leo," Amelia replied, "it undoubtedly would."

Her brother snorted. "I'm a convenient scapegoat for you, aren't I? If you were honest with yourself, Amelia—"

"Merripen," Win called out, "is the carriage ready now?"

Merripen came through the front door, looking rumpled and surly. It had been agreed that he would drive the Hathaways to the Westcliffs' residence and return for them later. "It's ready." As he glanced at Win's golden beauty, it seemed his expression turned even surlier, if such a thing were possible.

As if a word puzzle had just solved itself in her brain, that stolen glance made a few things clear to Amelia. Merripen wasn't attending the dinner that evening because he was trying to avoid being in a social situation with Win. He was trying to keep a distance between them, while at the same time, he was desperately worried about her health.

It troubled Amelia, the notion that Merripen, who never displayed strong feelings about anything, might be entertaining a secret longing for her sister. Win was too delicate, too refined, too much his opposite in every way. And Merripen knew that.

Feeling sympathetic and maudlin and rather worried herself, Amelia climbed into the carriage after her sisters.

The occupants of the vehicle were silent as they proceeded along the oak-lined drive to Stony Cross Manor. None of them had ever seen grounds so richly tended or imposing. Every leaf on every tree seemed to have been affixed with careful forethought. Surrounded by gardens and orchards that flowed into dense woods, the house sprawled over the land like a drowsing giant. Four lofty corner towers denoted the original dimensions of the European-styled fortress, but many additions had given it a pleasing asymmetry. With time and weathering, the house's honey-colored stone had mellowed gracefully, its outlines dressed with tall, perfectly trimmed hedges.

The residence was fronted by a massive courtyard—a distinctive feature—and sided by stables and a residential wing. Instead of the usual understated design of stables, these were fronted by wide stone arches. Stony Cross Manor was a place fit for royalty—and from what they knew of Lord Westcliff, his bloodlines were even more distinguished than the Queen's.

As the carriage stopped before the porticoed entrance, Amelia wished the evening were already over. In these stately surroundings, the Hathaways' faults would be magnified. They would appear no better than a group of vagabonds. She glanced over her siblings. Win had donned her usual mask of irreproachable serenity, and Leo looked calm and slightly bored—an expression he must have learned from his recent acquaintances at Jenner's. The younger girls were filled with a bright exuberance that drew a smile from Amelia. They, at least, would have a good time, and heaven knew they deserved it.

Merripen helped the sisters from the carriage, and Leo emerged last. As he stepped to the ground, Merripen checked him with a brief murmur, an admonition to keep a close watch on Win. Leo shot him a vehement glance. Enduring

Amelia's criticism was bad enough—he wouldn't tolerate it from Merripen. "If you're so bloody concerned about her," Leo muttered, "*you* go inside and play nanny."

Merripen's eyes narrowed, but he didn't reply.

The relationship between the two men had never been what one could describe as brotherly, but they'd always maintained a cool cordiality.

Merripen had never tried to assume the role of second son, in spite of the Hathaway parents' obvious fondness for him. And in any situation which might have lent itself to a competition between the two boys, Merripen had always drawn back. Leo, for his part, had been reasonably pleasant to Merripen, and had even deferred to Merripen's opinions when he'd judged them better than his own.

When Leo had fallen ill with scarlet fever, Merripen had helped care for him with a mixture of patience and kindness that had surpassed even Amelia's. Later she had told Leo that he owed Merripen his life. Instead of being grateful, however, Leo seemed to hold it against Merripen.

Please, please don't be an ass, Leo, Amelia longed to beg, but she held her tongue and went with her sisters to the brightly lit entrance of Stony Cross Manor.

A pair of massive double doors opened into a cavernous hall hung with priceless tapestries. A grand stone and marble staircase curved up to the lofty second-floor gallery. Even the most distant corners of the hall, and the entrances of several passages leading away from the great room, were lit by a massive crystal chandelier.

If the outside grounds had been well-tended, the interior of the manor was nothing short of immaculate, everything swept and sparkling and polished. There was nothing of newness in their surroundings, no sharp edges or modern touches to disrupt the atmosphere of easeful splendor.

It was, Amelia thought bleakly, exactly the way Ramsay House should look.

Servants came to take hats and gloves, while an elderly housekeeper welcomed the new arrivals. Amelia's attention was immediately drawn to the sight of Lord and Lady Westcliff, who were crossing the hall toward them.

Clad in precisely tailored evening clothes, Lord Westcliff moved with the physical confidence of a seasoned sportsman. His expression was reserved, his austere features striking rather than handsome. Everything about his appearance indicated he was a man who demanded a great deal of others and even more of himself.

There was no doubt that someone as powerful as Westcliff should have chosen the perfect English bride, a woman whose icy sophistication had been instilled in her since birth. It was with surprise, then, that Amelia heard Lady Westcliff speak in a distinctly American voice, the words tumbling out as if she couldn't be bothered to think everything over before speaking.

"You can't know how often I've wished for new neighbors. Things can get a bit dull in Hampshire. You Hathaways will do nicely." She surprised Leo by reaching out and shaking hands in the way men did. "Lord Ramsay, a pleasure."

"Your servant, my lady." Leo didn't seem to know quite what to make of this singular woman.

Amelia reacted automatically as she was accorded a similar handshake. Returning the firm pressure of Lady Westcliff's hand, she stared into tip-tilted eyes the color of gingerbread.

Lillian, Lady Westcliff, was a tall, slender young woman with gleaming sable hair, fine features, and a raffish grin. Unlike her husband, she radiated a casual friendliness that instantly put one at ease. "You are Amelia, the one they fired upon yesterday?"

"Yes, my lady."

"I'm so glad the earl didn't murder you. His aim is hardly ever off, you know."

The earl received his wife's impudence with a slight smile, as if he were well accustomed to it. "I wasn't aiming at Miss Hathaway," he said calmly.

"You might consider a less dangerous hobby," Lady Westcliff suggested. "Bird-watching. Butterfly-collecting. Something a bit more dignified than setting off explosions."

Amelia expected the earl to frown at this irreverence, but he only looked amused. And as his wife's attention moved to the rest of the Hathaways, he stared at her with covert fascination. Clearly there was a powerful attraction between the two.

Amelia introduced her sisters to the unconventional countess. Thankfully, they all remembered to curtsey and managed polite responses to her forthright questions: Did they like to ride, did they enjoy dancing, had they tried any of the local cheeses yet, and did they share her dislike of slimy English fare such as eels and jellied hog loaf?

Laughing at the droll face the countess had made, the Hathaway sisters went with her to the receiving room, where approximately two dozen guests had gathered in anticipation of going in to supper. "I like her," she heard Poppy whisper to Beatrix as the two of them walked behind her. "Do you think all American women are so dashing?"

Dashing . . . yes, that was an appropriate word for Lady Westcliff.

"Miss Hathaway," the countess said to Amelia in a tone of friendly concern, "the earl says Ramsay House has been unoccupied for so long, it must be in shambles."

Mildly startled by the woman's directness, Amelia shook her heard firmly. "Oh no, 'shambles' is too strong a word.

All the place wants is a good thorough cleaning, a few small repairs, and . . ." she paused uncomfortably.

Lady Westcliff's gaze was frank and sympathetic. "That bad, is it?"

Amelia hitched her shoulders in a slight shrug. "There's a great deal of work to be done at Ramsay House," she admitted. "But I'm not afraid of work."

"If you need assistance or advice, Westcliff has infinite resources at his disposal. He can tell you where to find—"

"You are very kind, my lady," Amelia said hastily, "but there is no need for your involvement in our domestic affairs." The last thing she wanted was for the Hathaways to appear as a family of cheapjacks and beggars.

"You may not be able to avoid our involvement," Lady Westcliff said with a grin. "You're in Westcliff's sphere now, which means you'll get advice whether or not you asked for it. And the worst part is, he's almost always right." She sent a fond glance in her husband's direction. Westcliff was standing in a group at the side of the room.

Becoming aware of his wife's gaze, Westcliff's head turned. Some voiceless message was delivered between them, and he responded with an almost indiscernible wink.

A chuckle rustled in Lady Westcliff's throat. She turned to Amelia. "We'll have been married three years, come September," she said rather sheepishly. "I had supposed I would have stopped mooning over him by now, but I haven't." Mischief danced in her dark eyes. "Now, I'll introduce you to some of the other guests. Who do you want to meet first?"

Amelia's gaze had moved from the earl to the group of men around him. A ripple of awareness went down her spine as her attention was caught by Cam Rohan. He was dressed in black and white, identical to the other gentlemen, but the formal attire couldn't conceal the power and grace of his lean form. Catching sight of her, Rohan bowed, which she acknowledged with a curtsey.

"You've already met Mr. Rohan, of course," Lady Westcliff commented, observing the exchange. "An interesting fellow, don't you think? Usually, I find mysterious people somewhat annoying, but Mr. Rohan is charming and very nice."

Amelia tore her gaze from Rohan with effort, her heart thrumming erratically. "How long have you known Mr. Rohan?"

"Only since Lord St. Vincent took possession of the gambling club. Since then, Mr. Rohan has become a sort of protégé of both Westcliff's and St. Vincent's." She gave a quick laugh. "Rather like having an angel on one shoulder and a devil on the other. Rohan seems to manage them both quite well."

"Why have they taken such an interest in him?"

"He's an unusual man. I'm not certain anyone knows what to make of him. According to Westcliff, Rohan has an exceptional mind. But at the same time, he's superstitious and unpredictable. Have you heard about his good luck curse?"

"His what?"

"It seems no matter what Rohan does, he can't help making money. A *lot* of money. Even when he tries to lose it. He claims it's wrong for one person to own so much. Against his will, Mr. Rohan has been given a percentage of the profits at the club, and no matter how many charitable donations or unsound investments he makes, he keeps getting massive windfalls. First, he bought an old racehorse with short legs—Little Dandy—who won the Grand National last April. Then there was the rubber debacle, and—"

"The what?"

"It was a small, failing rubber manufactory on the east side of London. Just as the company was about to go under,

Mr. Rohan made a large investment in it. Everyone, including Lord Westcliff, told him not to, that he was a fool and he'd lose every cent—"

"Which was his intention," Amelia said.

"Exactly. But to Rohan's dismay, the whole thing turned around. The company's director used his investment to acquire the patent rights for the vulcanization process, and they invented these little stretchy scraps of tubing called rubber bands. And now the company is a blazing success. I could tell you more, but it's all variations on the same theme—Mr. Rohan throws the money away, and it comes back tenfold."

"I wouldn't call that a curse," Amelia said.

"Neither would I." Lady Westcliff laughed softly. "But Mr. Rohan does. That's what makes it so amusing. You should have seen him sulking earlier in the day when he received the latest report from one of his stockjobbers in London. All good news. He was gnashing his teeth over it."

Taking Amelia's arm, Lady Westcliff led her across the room. "Although we have a sad lack of eligible gentlemen tonight, I promise we'll have quite an array visiting later in the season. They come to hunt and fish—and there's usually a high proportion of men to women."

"That's good news," Amelia replied. "I have high hopes that my sisters will find suitable men to marry."

Not missing the implication, Lady Westcliff asked, "But you have no such hopes for yourself?"

"No, I don't expect ever to marry."

"Why?"

"I have a responsibility to my family. They need me." After a brief pause, Amelia added frankly, "And the truth is, I'd hate to submit to a husband's dictates."

"I used to feel the same way. But I warn you, Miss Hathaway . . . life has a way of fouling up our plans. I speak from experience."

Amelia smiled, unconvinced. It was a simple matter of priorities. She would devote all her time and energies to creating a home for her siblings and seeing them all healthy and happily married. There would be nieces and nephews aplenty, and Ramsay House would be filled with the people she loved.

No husband could offer her more.

Catching sight of her brother, Amelia noticed a peculiar expression on his face, or rather a lack of expression that indicated he was concealing some strong emotion. He came to her at once, exchanged a few pleasantries with Lady Westcliff, and nodded politely as she asked leave to attend to an elderly guest who had just arrived.

"What is it?" Amelia whispered, looking up as Leo cupped her elbow in his hand. "You look as though you'd just gotten a mouthful of rotten cork."

"Don't let's trade insults just now." Leo gave her a glance that was more concerned than any he'd given her in recent memory. His tone was low and urgent. "Bear up, sis—there's someone here you don't want to see. And he's coming this way."

She rolled her eyes. "If you mean Mr. Rohan, I assure you, I'm perfectly—"

"No. Not Rohan." His hand went to her waist as if anticipating the need to steady her.

And she understood.

Before she even turned to see who was approaching, Amelia knew the reason for Leo's strange reaction, and she went cold and hot and unsteady. But somewhere in the internal havoc, a certain resignation lurked.

She had always known she'd see Christopher Frost again someday.

He was alone, which was a small mercy, as one would have expected him to have his new wife in tow. Amelia was fairly certain she couldn't have tolerated being introduced to the woman Christopher had abandoned Amelia for. As it was, she stood stiffly with her brother and tried desperately to resemble an independent woman who was greeting her former love with polite indifference. But she knew there was no disguising the whiteness of her face—she could feel the blood shooting straight to her overstimulated heart.

If life were fair, Frost would have appeared smaller, less handsome, less desirable than she had remembered. But life, as usual, wasn't fair. He was as lean and graceful and urbane as ever, with alert blue eyes and thick, close-trimmed hair, too dark to be blond, too light to be brown. That shining hair contained every shade from champagne to fawn.

"My old acquaintance," Leo said. Although his tone held no rancor, neither did it evince pleasure. Their friendship had been shattered the moment Frost had left Amelia. Leo had his faults, certainly, but he was nothing if not loyal.

"My lord," Frost said, bowing to them both. "And Miss Hathaway." It seemed to cost him something to meet her gaze. Heaven knew it cost her to return it. "It's been far too long."

"Not for some of us," Leo returned, not flinching as Amelia surreptitiously stepped on his foot. "Are you staying at the manor?"

"No, I'm visiting some old family friends—they own the village tavern."

"How long will you hang about?"

"I have no firm plans. I'm mulling over a few commissions while enjoying the calm and quiet of the countryside." His gaze strayed briefly to Amelia and returned to Leo. "I sent a letter when I learned of your ascendancy to the peerage, my lord."

"I received it," Leo said idly. "Although for the life of me, I can't remember its contents."

"Something to the effect that while I was pleased for your

sake, I was disappointed to have lost a worthy rival. You always drove me to reach beyond the limits of my abilities."

"Yes," Leo said sardonically, "I was a great loss to the architectural firmament."

"You were," Frost agreed without irony. His gaze remained on Amelia. "May I remark on how well you look, Miss Hathaway?"

How odd it was, she thought dazedly, that she had once been in love with him, and now they were speaking to each other so formally. She no longer loved him, and yet the memory of being held by him, kissed, caressed . . . it tinted every thought and emotion, like tea-dyed lace. One could never fully remove the stain. She remembered a bouquet of roses he had once given her . . . he had taken one and stroked the petals over her cheeks and parted lips. *My little love*, he'd whispered—

"Thank you," she said. "In turn, may I offer my congratulations on your marriage?"

"I'm afraid no felicitations are in order," Frost replied carefully. "The wedding didn't take place."

Amelia felt Leo's hand tighten at her waist. She leaned against him imperceptibly and looked away from Christopher Frost, unable to speak. *He isn't married.* Her thoughts were in anarchy.

"Did she come to her senses," she heard Leo ask casually, "or did you?"

"It became obvious we didn't suit as well as one would have hoped. She was gracious enough to release me from the obligation."

"So, you got the boot," Leo said. "Are you still working for her father?"

"Leo," Amelia protested in a half-whisper. She looked up in time to see Frost's wry grin, and her heart twisted at the painful familiarity of it.

"You were never one to mince words, were you? Yes, I'm still employed by Temple." Frost's gaze moved slowly over Amelia, taking measure of her brittle guardedness. "A pleasure to see you again, Miss Hathaway."

She sagged a little as he left them, turning blindly toward her brother. Her voice was tattered at the edges. "Leo, I would very much appreciate it if you could cultivate just a little delicacy of manner."

"We can't all be as suave as your Mr. Frost."

"He's not my Mr. Frost." A pause, and she added dully, "He never was."

"You deserve a hell of a lot better. Just remember that if he comes sniffing around your heels again."

"He won't," Amelia said, hating the way her heart leapt behind her well-manufactured defenses.

Chapter Seven

From the moment Amelia Hathaway had entered the room, Cam's attention had been riveted. In a crowd of elaborately dressed women, she stood out in her simple gown and unadorned throat and ears. She looked as wholesome and sweet as a fresh apple. He wanted to be alone with her, outside in the open air, his hands free upon her body. Cam dragged his gaze from her, knowing better than to entertain such thoughts about a respectable young woman.

He watched the tense little scene involving Amelia, her brother, Lord Ramsay, and the architect, Mr. Christopher Frost. Although he couldn't hear their conversation, he read their postures—the subtle way Amelia leaned into her brother's support. Clearly there was some kind of history between Amelia and Frost . . . and not a happy one. He imagined them together, Amelia and Frost. It provoked him far more than he would have liked. Tamping down the surge of inappropriate curiosity, he dragged his attention away from them.

Contemplating the long supper to come, Cam sighed heavily. He had learned the social choreography of these situations, the rigid boundaries of propriety. He had grown tired of hovering at the edge of the *gadje* world, but there seemed to be no other place for him.

It had all started approximately two years earlier, when St. Vincent had thrown a bank passbook at him in the casual manner he might have used to toss a rounders ball.

"I've established an account for you at the London Banking House and Investment Society," St. Vincent had told him. "It's on Fleet Street. Your percentage of Jenner's profits will be deposited monthly. Manage them if you wish, or they'll be managed for you."

"I don't want a percentage of the profits," Cam had said, thumbing through the passbook without interest. "My salary is fine."

"Your salary wouldn't cover the annual cost of my bootblacking."

"It's more than enough. And I wouldn't know what to do with this." Cam had been appalled by the figures listed on the balance page. Scowling, he tossed the book to a nearby table. "Take it back."

St. Vincent had looked amused and vaguely exasperated. "Damnation, man, now that I own the place, I can't have it said that you're paid pauper's wages. Do you think I'll tolerate being called a skinflint?"

"You've been called worse," Cam had pointed out.

"I don't mind being called worse when I deserve it. But that isn't the case here." St. Vincent had stared at him in a considering way. And, with one of those damnable flashes of intuition you would never expect from the former profligate, he'd murmured, "It means nothing, you know. It doesn't make you any less a Rom."

"I've compromised too much already. Since I first came to London, I've stayed under one roof, I've worn *gadje* clothes, I've worked for a salary. But I draw the line at this."

"I've just given you an investment account, Rohan,"

St. Vincent had said acidly, "not a pile of manure." He had gestured to the discarded bank passbook. "Do something with it. Whatever pleases you."

Cam had resolved to get rid of every cent by scattering it in a series of lunatic investments. That was when he'd begun to comprehend the curse that had befallen him. His growing fortune had begun to open doors that should never have been open to him. It was starting to change him. He had forgotten things; words, stories, the songs that had lulled him to sleep as a child. The faces of his family were a distant blur. He wasn't certain he would know them if he met them now.

The company proceeded as a whole into the dining hall. The informal nature of the gathering meant they would not have to be arranged in order of precedence. A line of footmen clad in black, blue, and mustard moved forward to attend the guests, pulling out chairs, pouring wine and water. The long table was covered by an acre of pristine white linen. Each place setting, bristling with silverware, was surmounted with a hierarchy of crystal glasses in assorted sizes.

Cam wiped all expression from his face as he discovered he had been seated next to the vicar's wife, whom he had met on previous visits to Stony Cross Park. The woman was terrified of him. Whenever he tried to talk to her, she cleared her throat incessantly, like a tea kettle with an ill-fitting lid.

No doubt the vicar's wife had heard one too many stories of Roma stealing children, placing curses on people, and attacking helpless females in a frenzy of uncontrolled lust. Cam was tempted to inform the woman that, as a rule, he never kidnapped or pillaged before the second course. But he kept silent and tried to look as unthreatening as possible, while she shrank in her chair and made desperate conversation with the man at her left.

Turning to his right, Cam found himself staring into

Amelia Hathaway's amused blue eyes. They had been seated next to each other. Pleasure unfolded inside him.

"If you're trying to look meek," she said, "it's not working."

"I assure you, I'm harmless."

She smiled at that. "No doubt it would suit you for everyone to think so."

He relished her nearness, the light powdered-rose scent of her, the charming pitch of her voice. He wanted to touch the fine skin of her cheeks and throat. Instead, he held still and watched as she adjusted a linen napkin over her lap.

A footman came to fill their wine glasses. Cam noticed Amelia kept stealing glances at her siblings like a mother hen with chicks gone astray. Even her brother, seated only two places away from the head of the table, was subjected to the same relentless concern.

"At the first formal supper I attended in London," he told her, "I expected to come away hungry."

"Why?"

"Because I thought the little side plates were what *gadje* used for their main course. Which meant I wasn't going to get much to eat."

Amelia laughed. "You must have been relieved when the large plates were brought out."

He shook his head. "I was too busy learning the rules of the table."

"Such as?"

"Always drink your soup from the side of the spoon, and never offer someone food from your plate."

"Roma share food from each other's plates?"

"Some do." He stared at her steadily. "If we were eating together, I would offer you the choicest bites of meat. The soft inside of the bread. The sweetest sections of fruit."

The color heightened in her cheeks, and she reached for her wine glass.

Footmen and underbutlers worked in perfect harmony to present huge steaming tureens of mushroom soup laced with sour cream and brandy.

After soup was ladled into a shallow china bowl in front of Cam, he turned to speak to Amelia again. To his disgruntlement, she was now being monopolized by the man on her other side, who was enthusiastically describing his collection of Far East porcelain.

Cam took a quick inventory of the other conversations around him, all featuring mundane subjects. He waited patiently until the vicar's wife had bent her attention to the soup bowl in front of her. As she raised a spoon to her papery lips, she became aware that Cam was looking at her. Another throat-clearing noise while the spoon quivered in her hand.

He tried to think of something that would interest her. "Horehound," he said to her in a matter-of-fact manner.

Her eyes bulged with alarm, and a pulse throbbed visibly in her neck. "H-h-h . . ." she whispered.

"Horehound, licorice root, and honey. It's good for getting rid of phlegm in the throat."

The word "phlegm" nearly caused her eyes to roll back in her head.

"It's also good for coughs and snake bites." Cam continued helpfully.

Her face drained of color, and she set her spoon on her plate. Turning away from him blindly, she gave her attention to the diners on her left.

His attempt at polite discussion having been rebuffed, Cam sat back as the soup was removed and the second course was brought out. Sweetbreads in béchamel sauce, partridges nestled in herb beds, pigeon pies, roast snipe, and vegetable soufflé laced the air with a cacophony of rich scents. The guests exclaimed appreciatively as their plates were filled.

Amelia Hathaway barely seemed aware of what was being served. Her attention focused on a conversation at the end of the table between Lord Westcliff and her brother Leo. Her face was calm, but her fingers clenched tightly around a fork handle.

". . . obvious you possess a large acreage of arable land that's gone unused . . ." Westcliff was saying, while Leo listened without apparent interest. "If you like, I'll make my own estate agent available to you to apprise you of the standard terms of tenancy here in Hampshire."

"Thank you," Leo said after downing half his wine in an expedient gulp, "but I'll deal with my tenants in my own time, my lord."

"I'm afraid time has run out for some of them," Westcliff replied. "Many of the tenant houses on your land have run to ruins."

"Then it's time they learn my one consistency is neglecting the people who depend on me." Leo flicked a laughing glance at Amelia, his eyes hard. "Isn't that right, sis?"

With visible effort, Amelia forced her fingers to unclench from the fork. "Pray don't be misled by my brother's attempts to be amusing, my lord," she said. "He intends to make the necessary land improvements and study modern agricultural methods—"

"If I study anything," Leo drawled, "it will be the bottom of a good bottle of port. The Ramsay tenants have proven their ability to thrive on neglect—they clearly don't need my involvement."

Tension thickened the air.

If Leo was deliberately trying to make an enemy of Westcliff, he couldn't have chosen a better way of doing it. Westcliff had a deep concern for those less fortunate than himself, and an active dislike for self-indulgent noblemen who failed to live up to their responsibilities.

But just as Westcliff parted his lips to deliver a withering speech to the insolent young viscount, one of the female guests gave an earsplitting shriek. Two other ladies jumped up from their chairs along with several of the gentlemen, all of them staring in white-eyed horror at the center of the table.

All conversation had stopped. Following the guests' collective gazes, Cam saw something—a lizard?—wriggling and slithering its way past sauceboats and salt cellars. Without hesitation he reached out and captured the small creature, cupping it in closed hands. The lizard squirmed furiously in the space between his palms.

"I have it," he said mildly.

The vicar's wife half-fainted, slumping back in her chair with a low moan.

"Don't hurt him!" Beatrix Hathaway called out anxiously. "He's a family pet!"

The assembled guests glanced from Cam's closed hands to the Hathaway girl's apologetic face.

"A pet? What a relief!" Lady Westcliff said calmly, staring down the length of the table at her husband's blank countenance. "I thought it was some new English delicacy we were serving."

A swift wash of color darkened Westcliff's face, and he looked away from her with fierce concentration. To anyone who knew him well, it was obvious he was struggling not to laugh.

"You brought Spot to supper?" Amelia asked her youngest sister in disbelief. "Bea, I told you to get rid of him yesterday!"

"I tried to," came Beatrix's contrite reply, "but after I left him in the woods, he followed me home."

"Bea," Amelia said sternly, "reptiles do not follow people home."

"Spot is no ordinary lizard. He—"

"We'll discuss it outside." Amelia rose from her chair, obliging the gentlemen to hoist themselves courteously out of their seats. She threw Westcliff an apologetic glance. "I beg your pardon, my lord. If you will excuse us . . ."

The earl gave her a decisive nod.

"I'll come with you," Cam offered, still holding the squirming reptile, and he accompanied the Hathaway sisters from the room.

Chapter Eight

Cam led them away from the dining hall through a pair of French doors that opened to a conservatory. The outdoor room was sparsely furnished with cane-back chairs and a settee. White columns around the edge of the conservatory were interspersed with lush hanging plants.

As soon as the doors were closed, Amelia went to her sister with her hands raised. At first, Cam thought she intended to shake her, but instead Amelia pulled Beatrix close, her shoulders trembling. She could barely breathe from laughing.

"Bea . . . you did it on purpose, didn't you? I couldn't believe my eyes . . . that blasted lizard running along the table . . ."

"I had to do *something*," the girl explained in a muffled voice. "Leo was behaving badly—I didn't understand what he was saying, but I saw Lord Westcliff's face—"

"Oh . . . oh . . ." Amelia choked with giggles. "Poor Westcliff . . . one moment he's defending the local population from Leo's tyranny, and then Spot comes s-slithering past the bread plates . . ."

"Where is Spot?" Twisting away from her sister, Beatrix approached Cam, who deposited the lizard in her outstretched palms. "Thank you, Mr. Rohan. You have very quick hands."

"So I've been told." He smiled at her. "The lizard is a lucky animal. Some people say it causes prophetic dreaming."

"Really?" Beatrix stared at him in fascination. "Come to think of it, I *have* been dreaming more often lately—"

"Please," Amelia interrupted, her eyes sparkling, "my sister needs no encouragement." She gave Beatrix a meaningful glance. "It's time to say farewell to Spot, dear."

"Yes, I know." Beatrix heaved a sigh and peered inside the loose cage of her fingers at her erstwhile pet. "I'll let him go now. I think Spot would rather live here than at the Ramsay estate."

"Who wouldn't?" Amelia asked dryly. "Go find a nice place for him, Bea. I'll wait for you here."

As her sister scampered off, Amelia turned and gazed at the dim verge of the house, its outline melding into an iron-stone wall set along the bluff overlooking the river.

"What are you doing?" Cam asked, approaching her.

"I'm taking a last look at Stony Cross Manor, since this is the last time I'll ever see it."

He smiled. "I doubt that. The Westcliffs have welcomed back guests who've done far worse."

"Worse than setting wild creatures loose at the supper table?"

"They have great tolerance for eccentricity." He paused before adding quietly, "What they don't take well, I'm afraid, is callousness."

The reference to her brother caused a delicate play of emotions on her face, chagrin chased by worry. "Leo was never callous before." She wrapped her arms tightly across her chest as if she wanted to tie herself into a self-protective bundle. "He's not himself these days."

"Because he inherited the title?"

"No, it's—" Looking away from him, she swallowed hard. He heard a nervous tapping from a foot half-concealed beneath her skirts. "Leo lost someone," she finally said. "The fever struck many people in the village, including a girl he . . . well, he was betrothed to her. Laura." The name seemed to stick in her throat. "She was my best friend, and Win's too. A beautiful girl. She liked to sketch and paint. She had a laugh that would make you laugh too, just to hear it . . ."

Amelia was silent for a moment, lost in her memories. "Laura was one of the first to fall ill," she said. "Leo stayed with her every possible moment. No one expected her to die . . . but it happened so quickly. After three days she was so feverish and weak, you could barely feel her pulse. Finally she lost consciousness and died a few hours later in Leo's arms. He came home and collapsed, and we realized he had caught the fever. And then Win had it, too."

"But the rest of you didn't?"

Amelia shook her head. "I had already sent Beatrix and Poppy away. And for some reason, neither I nor Merripen were susceptible. He helped me nurse them both through it. Without his help, they would both have died. Merripen made a syrup with some kind of toxic plant . . ."

"Deadly nightshade," Cam said. "Not easy to find. The trick is to administer enough to counteract the poison in the blood, but not enough to kill the patient."

"Well, both of them came through it, thank God. But Win is quite fragile, as you can probably see, and Leo . . . now he cares for nothing and no one. Not even himself." Her foot resumed its nervous tapping. "I don't know how to help him. I was in love once, but . . . not like that."

"You mean Mr. Frost," he said.

Amelia gave him a sharp glance. "How did you know?"

"I saw it when you talked to him earlier." He watched her closely. "Why didn't you marry?"

"He fell in love with someone else. A prettier, younger woman who happened to be his employer's daughter. It would have been a very advantageous marriage for him."

"You're wrong."

Amelia gave him a perplexed glance. "I assure you, it would have been an enormously advantageous—"

"She couldn't possibly have been prettier than you."

Her eyes widened at the compliment. "Oh," she whispered.

Approaching her, Cam touched her vibrating foot with his own. The tapping stopped.

"A bad habit," Amelia said sheepishly, ducking her head. "I can't seem to rid myself of it."

Cam smiled, thoroughly charmed. "A hummingbird will do that in spring. She hangs on the side of the nest and uses her other foot to tamp down the floor."

Her gaze chased around as if she couldn't decide where to look.

"Miss Hathaway," he said gently. "Do I make you nervous?"

She brought herself to look up at him. "No," she said immediately. "No, of course you—*yes*. Yes, you do."

The night deepened—one of the torches had burned out—and the conversation devolved into something halting and broken and delicious, like pieces of barley sugar melting on the tongue.

"I would never hurt you," Cam said.

"I know. It's not that—"

"It's because I kissed you, isn't it?"

She took an unsettled breath. "You said you didn't remember."

He smiled faintly. "I remember."

Their conversation was checked by the reappearance of Beatrix. "Spot's gone," she reported. "He's very happy to live at Stony Cross Park."

Seeming relieved by her sister's return, Amelia went to her, brushed at the crumbs of soil on her sleeve, and straightened her hair bow. "Good luck to Spot. Are you ready to go back in to supper, dear?"

"No."

"Oh, everything will be fine. Just remember to look chastened while I grimace in an authoritative manner, and I'm certain they'll allow us to stay through dessert."

"I don't want to go back," Beatrix moaned. "It's so dreadfully dull, and I don't like all that rich food, and I've been sitting beside the vicar, who only wants to talk about his own religious writings. It's so *redundant* to quote oneself, don't you think?"

"It does bear a certain odor of immodesty," Amelia agreed with a grin, smoothing her sister's dark hair. "Poor Bea. You don't have to go back, if you don't wish it. I'm sure one of the servants can recommend a nice place for you to wait until supper is done. The library, perhaps."

"Oh, *thank you*." Beatrix heaved a sigh of relief. "Only . . . who will create another distraction if Leo starts being disagreeable again?"

"I will," Cam assured her gravely. "I can be shocking at a moment's notice."

"I'm not surprised," Amelia said, "In fact, I'm fairly certain you would enjoy it."

Chapter Nine

The company at Westcliff's table had been relieved by the news that Beatrix had elected to spend the rest of the evening alone in quiet contemplation. No doubt they feared another interruption by another pocket-sized pet, but Amelia had assured them there would be no more unexpected visitors at the table.

Only Lady Westcliff had seemed genuinely perturbed by Beatrix's absence. The countess excused herself somewhere between the fourth and fifth courses and reappeared after a quarter hour. Amelia later learned that Lady Westcliff had sent for a supper tray to be brought to Beatrix in the library and had visited her there.

"Lady Westcliff told me a few stories of when she was a girl, and how she and her younger sister used to misbehave," Beatrix recounted the next day. "She said bringing a lizard to supper was *nothing* compared to the things they had done—in fact, she said they were both diabolical and rotten to the core. Isn't that wonderful?"

"Wonderful," Amelia said sincerely, reflecting on how much she liked the American woman, who seemed relaxed and fun-loving. Westcliff was another matter. The earl was more than a little intimidating. And after Leo's callous dismissal of Westcliff's concerns over the Ramsay tenants, it was doubtful the earl would be kindly disposed toward the Hathaways.

Thankfully, Leo had managed to steer clear of further controversies during supper, mostly because he had been drawn into flirtation with the attractive woman beside him. Although women had always been beguiled by Leo, with his height and good looks and intelligence, he had never been as ardently pursued as he was now.

"I think it says something odd about women's tastes," Win told Amelia privately as they stood in the Ramsay House kitchen, "that Leo wasn't chased by nearly as many women when he was nice. It seems the more odious he is, the more they like him."

"They're welcome to have him," Amelia replied grumpily. "I fail to see the appeal of a man who goes through each day looking as if he's either just gotten out of bed or is preparing to get back in it." She wrapped her hair in a protective cloth and tucked the ends under turban-style.

They were preparing for another day of cleaning, and the ancient house dust tended to cling obstinately to the skin and hair. Since Leo was still abed after a night of heavy drinking, and probably wouldn't arise until noon, Amelia was feeling particularly cross with him. It was Leo's house and estate—the least he could do was help restore it.

"His eyes have changed," Win murmured. "Have you noticed?"

Amelia went still. She took a long time to reply. "I thought it might have been my imagination."

"No. They were always dark blue like yours. Now they're light."

"I'm certain the color of some people's eyes change as they mature."

"It's because of Laura."

A heaviness pressed against Amelia from all sides as she thought about the friend she had lost, and the brother she seemed to have lost along with her. But she couldn't dwell on any of that now. There was too much to be done.

"I don't think such a thing is possible. I've never heard of—" She broke off as she saw Win wrapping her long braids in a cloth identical to hers. "What are you doing?"

"I'm going to help today," Win said. Although her tone was placid, her delicate jaw was set like a mule's. "I'm feeling quite well and—"

"Oh, no you're not! You'll work yourself into a collapse, and then you'll take days to recover. Just find some place to sit, while the rest of us—"

"I'm tired of sitting. I'm tired of watching everyone else work. I can set my own limits, Amelia. Let me do as I wish."

"No." Amelia watched incredulously as Win picked up a broom from the corner. "Win, put that down and stop being silly." Annoyance whipped through her. Win was not going to help anyone by expending all her reserves on menial tasks.

"I can do it," Win insisted, gripping the broom handle with both hands, as if she sensed Amelia was on the verge of wrenching it away from her. "I won't overtax myself."

"Put down the broom."

"Leave me alone," Win cried. "Go dust something!"

"Win, if you don't—" Amelia's attention was diverted as she saw her sister's gaze fly to the kitchen threshold.

Merripen stood there, his broad shoulders filling the doorway. Although it was early morning, he was already dusty and perspiring, his shirt clinging to the powerful contours of his chest and waist. He wore an expression they knew well—the implacable one that meant one could move a mountain with a teaspoon sooner than change his mind about something.

Approaching Win, he extended a broad hand in a wordless demand.

They were both motionless. But even in their stubborn opposition, Amelia saw a singular connection, as if they were locked in an eternal stalemate from which neither wanted to break free.

Win gave in with a helpless scowl. "I have nothing to do." It was rare for her to sound so peevish. "I'm sick of sitting and reading and staring out the window. I want to be useful. I want . . ." Her voice trailed away as she saw his stern face. "Fine, then. Take it!" She tossed the broom at Merripen, and he caught it reflexively. "I'll just find a corner somewhere and quietly go mad. I'll—"

"Come with me," Merripen interrupted calmly. Setting the broom aside, he left the room.

Win exchanged a perplexed glance with Amelia. "What is he doing?"

"I have no idea."

The sisters followed him down a hallway to the dining room, which was spattered with rectangles of light from the tall multi-paned windows that lined one wall. A scarred table ran down the center of the room, every available inch covered with dusty piles of china—towers of cups and saucers, plates of assorted sizes sandwiched together, bowls wrapped in tattered scraps of gray linen. There were at least three different patterns all jumbled together.

"It needs to be sorted," Merripen said, nudging Win toward the table. "Many pieces are chipped—they must be separated from the rest."

It was the perfect task for Win, enough to keep her busy but not so strenuous that it would exhaust her. Filled with gratitude, Amelia watched as her sister picked up a teacup and held it upside down. The husk of a tiny dead spider dropped to the floor.

"What a mess," Win said, beaming. "I'll have to wash it, too, I suppose."

"If you'd like Poppy to help—" Amelia began.

"Don't you dare send for Poppy," Win said. "This is my project, and I won't share it." Sitting at a chair that had been placed beside the table, she began to unwrap pieces of china.

Merripen looked down at Win's turbaned head, his fingers twitching as if he were sorely tempted to touch a blond tendril that had slipped from beneath the cloth. His face was hard with the patience of a man who knew he would never have what he truly wanted. Using a single fingertip, he pushed a saucer away from the edge of the table. The china rattled subtly across the battered wood.

Amelia followed Merripen back to the kitchen. "Thank you," she said when they were out of her sister's hearing. "In my worry over making certain Win didn't tire herself, it hadn't occurred to me that she might go mad from boredom."

Merripen picked up a heavy, clattering box of discarded odds and ends, and hoisted it to his shoulder with ease. A subtle smile crossed his face. "She's getting better." He strode to the door and shouldered his way outside.

It was hardly an informed medical opinion, but Amelia was certain he was right. Looking about the dilapidated kitchen, she felt a surge of happiness. It had been the right thing to come here. A new place offering new possibilities. Perhaps the Hathaways' bad luck had finally changed.

Armed with a broom, mop, dustpan, and a stack of rags, Amelia went upstairs to one of the rooms that hadn't yet been explored. She used her full weight to open the first door, which gave way with a cracking sound and a shriek of unoiled hinges. It appeared to be a private receiving room, with built-in wooden bookcases.

There were two volumes on one shelf. Examining the dust-coated books, their aged leather covers shot with spidery cracks, Amelia read the first title: *Fine Angling: A Symposium on the Fisherman's Art with Much on Roach and Pike.* No wonder the book had been abandoned by its previous owner, she thought. The second title was far more promising: *Amorous Exploits of the Court of England in the Reign of King Charles the Second.* Hopefully it would contain some ribald revelations she and Win could giggle over later.

Replacing the books, Amelia went to open the shrouded windows. The draperies' original color had faded to gray, their velvet nap ragged and moth-eaten.

As Amelia labored to pull one drape to the side, the entire brass rod came loose from the ceiling and clattered heavily to the floor. A cloud of dust enveloped her, and she sneezed and coughed in the clotted air. She heard an inquiring shout from downstairs, probably from Merripen.

"I'm all right," she called back. Picking up a clean rag, she wiped her face and unlatched the filthy window. The casing stuck. She pushed hard against the frame to loosen it. Another push, harder, and then a determined shove with all her weight behind it. The window gave way with astonishing suddenness, unsettling her balance. She pitched forward and caught the edge of the window in an attempt to find purchase, but it swung outward.

In the flash of forward-falling panic, she heard a muffled sound behind her.

Before another heartbeat had passed, she was snatched, pulled back with such force that her bones protested the abrupt reversal of momentum. She staggered, fetching hard against something solid and yet supple. Helplessly, she tumbled to the floor in a tangle of limbs—some of them not her own.

Sprawled over a sturdy masculine chest, she saw a dark face below her, and she muttered in confusion, "Merri—"

But these were not Merripen's sable eyes. They were light, glowing amber. A jolt of pleasure went through her stomach.

"You know, if I have to keep rescuing you like this," Cam Rohan remarked casually, "we really should discuss some kind of reward."

He reached up to tug off her hair covering, which was askew, and her braids tumbled down. Mortification swept away every other feeling. Amelia knew how she must look, disheveled and dust stippled. Why did he never miss an opportunity to catch her at a disadvantage?

Gasping out an apology, she struggled to get off him, but the weight of her skirts and the stiffness of her corset made it difficult.

"No . . . wait . . ." Cam inhaled sharply as she squirmed against him, and he rolled them both to their sides.

"Who let you into the house?" Amelia managed to ask.

Cam gave her an innocent glance. "No one. The door was unlocked and the entrance hall was empty." He kicked his legs free of her clinging skirts and pulled her to a sitting position. She had never known anyone who possessed such ease of movement, almost feline in nature.

"Have you had this place inspected?" he asked. "The house is ready to fall off its timbers. Let me help you up."

He tugged Amelia to her feet, not letting go until her balance was secured.

"Why *are* you here?" she asked.

Cam shrugged. "Just paying a call. There isn't much to do at Stony Cross Park. It's the first day of foxhunting season."

"You didn't want to take part?"

He shook his head. "I only hunt for food, not sport. And I tend to sympathize with the fox."

"Mr. Rohan," she said awkwardly, "I wish I could be a proper hostess and show you to the parlor and offer refreshments. But I don't have refreshments. I really don't even have a parlor. Everything around here needs repairing. Please excuse me for sounding rude, but this isn't a good time to call—"

"I can help." He leaned a shoulder against the wall, smiling. "I'm good with my hands."

His tone was free of innuendo, but her color deepened nonetheless. "No, thank you." Anxious to demonstrate her competence, she went to the other window and began jerking at the closed draperies. "As you can see, I have the situation under control."

"I think I'll stay. Having just stopped you from falling through one window, I'd hate for you to go out the other."

"I won't. I'll be fine. I don't need any—" She tugged harder, and the rod clattered to the floor, just as the other had done. But unlike the other curtain, which had been lined with aged velvet, this one was lined with some kind of shimmering rippling fabric, some kind of—

Amelia froze in horror. The underside of the curtain was covered with bees. *Bees*. Hundreds, no, thousands of them, their iridescent wings beating in an angry relentless hum. They lifted in a mass from the crumpled velvet, while more flew from a crevice in the wall, where an enormous hive simmered. The insects swarmed like tongues of flame around Amelia's paralyzed form.

She felt the blood drain from her face. "Oh God—"

"Don't move." Cam's voice was astonishingly calm. "Don't swat at them."

She had never known such primal fear, welling from beneath her skin, leaking through every pore. No part of her body seemed to be under her control. The air was boiling with them, bees and more bees.

It was not going to be a pleasant way to die. Closing her eyes tightly, Amelia willed herself to be still when every muscle strained and screamed for action. The air moved in sinuous patterns around her, tiny bodies touching her sleeves, hands, shoulders.

"They're more afraid of you than you are of them," she heard Rohan say.

Amelia highly doubted that. "These are not f-frightened bees." Her voice didn't sound like her own. "These are *f-furious* bees."

"They do seem a bit annoyed," Rohan conceded, approaching her slowly. "It could be the dress you're wearing—they tend not to like dark colors." A short pause. "Or it could be the fact that you just ripped down half their hive."

"If you h-have the nerve to be *amused* by this—" She broke off and covered her face with her hands, trembling all over.

His soothing voice undercut the buzzing around them. "Be still. Everything's fine. I'm right here with you."

"Take me away," she whispered desperately. Her heart was pounding too hard, making her bones shake, driving every coherent thought from her head. She felt him brush a few inquisitive insects from her hair and back. His arms went around her, his shoulder hard beneath her cheek.

"I will, sweetheart. Put your arms around my neck."

She groped for him blindly, feeling sick and weak and disoriented. The flat muscles at the back of his neck shifted as he bent toward her, gathering her up as if she were a child. "There," he murmured. "I have you." Her feet left the floor, and she was floating and cradled at the same time. Still shaking with fear, she turned her face into his shoulder and let him carry her.

His breath fell in a warm, even rhythm on the curve of her cheek. "Some people think of the bee as a sacred insect," he told her. "Its presence in your home is a sign of good things to come."

Her voice was buried in the fine wool of his coat. "Wh-what does it mean if there are *thousands* of bees in one's home?"

He shifted her higher in his arms, his lips curving gently against the cold rim of her ear. "Probably that we'll have plenty of honey for teatime. We're going through the doorway now. In a moment, I'm going to set you on your feet."

Amelia kept her face against him, her fingertips digging into the layers of his clothes. "Are they following?"

"No. They want to stay near the hive. Their main concern is to protect the queen from predators."

"She has nothing to fear from me!"

There was a catch of laughter in his throat. With extreme care, he lowered Amelia's feet to the floor. Keeping one arm around her, he reached with the other to close the door. "There. We're out of the room. You're safe." His hand passed over her hair. "You can open your eyes now."

Clutching the lapels of his coat, Amelia waited for a feeling of relief that didn't come. Her heart was racing too hard, too fast. Her chest ached from the strain of her breathing. Her lashes lifted, but all she could see was a shower of sparks.

"Amelia . . . easy. You're all right." His hands chased the shivers that ran up and down her back. "Slow down, sweetheart."

She couldn't. Her lungs were about to burst. No matter how hard she worked, she couldn't get enough air. Bees . . . the sound of buzzing was still in her ears. The sparks danced and collided, and when they faded, there was nothing around her but layers of gray softness. She sank into the quiet billows without a sound.

After what could have been a minute or an hour, pleasant sensations filtered through the haze. A tender pressure moved over her forehead. The gentle brushes touched her eyelids,

slid to her cheeks. Strong arms held her against a comfortingly hard surface, while a clean, salt-edged scent tickled her
nostrils. Her lashes fluttered, and she turned into the warmth
with confused pleasure.

"There you are," came a low murmur.

Opening her eyes, Amelia saw Cam's face above her. They
were on the hallway floor—he was holding her in his lap. As
if the situation weren't mortifying enough, the front of her
bodice was gaping, and her corset was unhooked. Only her
crumpled chemise was left to cover her chest.

Amelia stiffened. Until that moment, she had never known
there was a feeling beyond embarrassment, that made one
wish one could crumble into a pile of ashes. "My . . . my
dress . . ."

"You weren't breathing well. I thought it best to loosen
your corset."

"I've never fainted before," she said groggily, struggling
to sit up.

"You were frightened." His hand came to the center of her
chest, gently pressing her back down. "Rest another minute."
His gaze moved over her pale features. "So. You don't like
bees."

"I've hated them ever since I was seven."

"Why?"

"One day I was playing outside with Win and Leo. A
bee flew at my face and stung me right here." She touched a
spot just below her right eye, high on the crest of her cheek.
"The side of my face swelled until my eye closed. I couldn't
see from it for almost two weeks—"

His fingertips smoothed over her cheek as if to soothe the
long-ago injury.

"—and my brother and sister called me Cyclops." She
watched him struggle not to smile. "They still do, whenever
a bee flies too near."

He regarded her with friendly sympathy. "Everyone's afraid of something."

"What are you afraid of?"

"Ceilings and walls, mostly."

She stared at him in puzzlement, her thoughts still coursing too slowly. "You mean . . . you'd rather live outside?"

"Yes. At least, more than I do now. Have you ever slept outside before?"

"On the ground?"

Her bewildered tone made him grin. "On a pallet beside a fire."

Amelia tried to imagine it, lying undefended on the hard ground, at the mercy of every creature that crawled, crept, or flew. "I don't think I could fall asleep that way."

She felt his hand playing slowly in the loose locks of her hair. "You could." His voice was soft. "I'd help you."

She had no idea what he meant by that, and she was afraid to speculate. All she knew was that as his fingertips reached her scalp, she felt a sensual shiver run down her spine. Clumsily, she reached for her bodice, trying to pull the reinforced fabric together.

"Let me do that. You're still unsteady." His hands brushed hers aside and he began to hook her corset deftly. Obviously, he was familiar with the intricacies of a woman's undergarments. Amelia didn't doubt there had been more than a few ladies willing to let him practice.

Flustered, she asked, "Was I stung anywhere?"

"No." Mischief flickered in his eyes. "I checked thoroughly."

Amelia suppressed a little moan of distress. She was tempted to push his hands away from her, except that he was restoring her clothing far more efficiently than she would have. She closed her eyes, trying to pretend she wasn't sprawled in a man's lap while he fastened her corset.

"You'll need a local beekeeper to remove the hive," Cam said.

Thinking of the enormous colony in the wall, Amelia asked, "How will he kill them all?"

"He may not have to. If possible, he'll sedate them with smoke and transfer the queen to a movable frame hive. The rest will follow. But if he can't manage that, he'll have to kill the colony with soap water. The larger problem is how to remove the comb and the honey. If you don't take it all out, it will ferment and attract all kinds of vermin."

Her eyes opened, and she looked up at him in worry. "Will the entire wall have to be removed?"

Before Cam could reply, a new voice entered the conversation. "What's this?"

It was Leo, who had just arisen from bed and pulled on his clothes. He came barefoot from the direction of his bedroom. His bleary gaze moved over the pair of them. "Why are you on the floor with your buttons undone?"

Amelia considered the question. "I decided to have a spontaneous tryst in the middle of the hallway with a man I hardly know."

"Well, try to be quieter next time. A fellow needs his sleep."

Amelia stared at him quizzically. "For heaven's sake, Leo, aren't you worried I may have been compromised?"

"Were you?"

"I . . ." Her face turned hot as she glanced into Cam's vivid topaz eyes. "I don't think so."

"If you're not sure about it," Leo said, "you probably weren't." He came to Amelia, sank to his haunches, and stared at her steadily. His voice gentled. "What happened, sis?"

She pointed an unsteady finger at the closed door. "There are *bees* in there, Leo."

"Bees. Good God." Her brother gave her an affectionately mocking smile. "What a coward you are, Cyclops."

Amelia scowled, lifting herself from Cam's lap. He braced her automatically, his arm firm behind her back. "Go see for yourself."

Leo sauntered lazily to the room, opened it, and stepped inside.

In two seconds, he sped out, slammed the door, and lodged his shoulders against it. "Christ!" His eyes were wide and glazed. "There must be thousands of them!"

"I'd estimate at least two hundred thousand," Cam said. Finishing the last of Amelia's buttons, he helped her to her feet. "Slowly," he murmured. "You may be a bit light-headed."

She let him support her while she assessed her uncertain balance. "I'm all right now. Thank you." She turned her attention to her brother. "Mr. Rohan saved my life twice today. First, I nearly fell out the window, and then I found the bees."

"This house," Leo muttered, "should be torn down and used for matchsticks."

"You should order a full structural inspection," Cam said. "The house has settled badly. Some of the chimneys are leaning, and the entrance hall ceiling is sagging. You have damaged joinery and beams."

"I know what the problems are." The calm appraisal had annoyed Leo. He'd retained enough of his past architectural training to assess the house's condition accurately.

"It may not be safe for the family to stay here."

"But that's my concern," Leo said, adding with a sneer, "isn't it?"

Sensitive to the brittle disquiet in the atmosphere, Amelia made a hasty attempt at diplomacy. "Mr. Rohan, Lord Ramsay is convinced the house poses no immediate danger to the family."

"I wouldn't be so easily convinced," Cam replied. "Not with four sisters in my charge."

"Care to take them off my hands?" Leo asked. "You can have the lot of them." He smiled without amusement at Cam's silence. "No? Then pray don't offer unwanted advice."

Despondent worry swept over Amelia as she saw the bleakness of her brother's face. He was becoming a stranger, this man who harbored despair and fury so deep inside that it had begun to eat at his foundations. Until, like the house, he would eventually collapse as the weakest parts of the structure gave way.

Unruffled, Cam turned to Amelia. "In lieu of advice, let me offer some information. Two days hence, there'll be a Mop Fair held at the village."

"What is that?"

"It's a hiring fair, attended by all the local residents in need of work. They wear tokens to signify their trade—a servant girl will carry a mop, a thatcher carries a tuft of straw, and so forth. Give the ones you want a shilling to seal the contract, and you'll have them for a year's employment."

Amelia darted a cautious glance at her brother. "We do need servants, Leo."

"Go, then, and hire whomever you please. I don't give a damn."

Amelia gave a troubled nod and raised her hands to her upper arms, rubbing them over her sleeves.

It was cold, she thought, even for autumn. Icy draughts crept around her stockinged ankles, beneath the edges of her cuffs, across the sweat-dampened back of her neck. Her muscles tensed against the strange, raw chill.

Both men had fallen silent. Leo's face was blank, his gaze focused inward.

It felt as if the space around them was folding in on itself, thickening until the air was as heavy as water. Colder, tighter, closer . . . instinctively, Amelia stepped away from her brother until she felt Cam's chest against her shoulders. His hand came up to her arm, gently cupping her elbow. Shivering, she leaned harder against the warm, vital strength of his body.

Leo had not moved. He waited, his gaze unfocused, as if he were intent on absorbing the chill. As if he welcomed it, wanted it. His averted face was harsh and shadow-crossed.

Something divided the space between her and Leo. She felt the resonance of movement, softer than a breeze, more delicate than eiderdown . . .

"Leo?" Amelia murmured uncertainly.

The sound of her voice seemed to bring him back to himself. He blinked and stared at her with nearly colorless eyes. "Show Rohan out," he said curtly. "That is, if you've been sufficiently compromised for one day." He walked away rapidly. Reaching his room, he closed the door with a clumsy swipe of his arm.

Amelia was slow to move, bewildered by her brother's behavior, and even more so by the splintering coldness in the hallway. She turned to face Cam, who was staring after Leo with a level, thoughtful gaze.

He glanced down at her, keeping his expression carefully impassive. "I hate to leave you." There was a gentle, mocking edge to his tone. "You need someone to follow you around and keep you safe from mishaps. On the other hand, you also need someone to find a beekeeper."

Realizing he was not going to talk about Leo, Amelia followed his lead. "Will you do that for us? I would consider it a great favor."

"Of course." Reaching out, Cam smoothed back her hair, letting the heel of his hand graze the edge of her cheekbone. The brush of his skin was light and erotic, causing her to swallow hard. "Goodbye, Miss Hathaway. I'll see myself out." He flashed a smile at her and advised, "Stay away from the windows."

On the way down the stairs, Cam passed Merripen, who was ascending at a measured pace.

Merripen's face darkened at the sight of the visitor. "What are you doing here?"

"It seems I'm helping with pest eradication."

"Then you can begin by leaving," Merripen growled.

Cam grinned nonchalantly and continued on his way.

After informing the rest of the family about the perils of the upstairs parlor, which was promptly dubbed "the bee room," Amelia investigated the rest of the upstairs with extreme caution. There were no more hazards to be found, only dust and decay and silence.

But it wasn't an unwelcoming house. When the windows were opened and light spilled across floors that had been untouched for years, it seemed the place was eager to open and breathe and be restored. Ramsay House was a charming place, really, with eccentricities, secret corners, and unique features that only needed some polish and attention. Not unlike the Hathaway family itself.

IN THE AFTERNOON, AMELIA COLLAPSED IN A CHAIR DOWNstairs, while Poppy made tea in the kitchen. "Where is Win?"

"Napping in her room," Poppy replied. "She was exhausted after the busy morning. She wouldn't admit it, but you can always tell when she gets all pale and drawn."

"Was she content?"

"She certainly seemed to be." Pouring hot water into a chipped pot filled with tea leaves, Poppy chatted about some of her discoveries. She had found a lovely rug in one of the bedrooms, and after she had beaten it for an hour, it had turned out to be richly colored and in good condition.

"I think most of the dust was transferred from the carpet to you," Amelia said. Since Poppy had covered the lower half of her face with a handkerchief during the carpet beating, the dust had settled on her forehead, eyes, and the bridge of her nose. When the handkerchief was removed, it had left Poppy's face oddly two-toned, the top half gray, the lower half white.

"I enjoyed it immensely," Poppy replied with a grin. "There's nothing like whacking a carpet with a rug beater to vent one's frustrations."

Amelia was about to ask what Poppy's frustrations were, when Beatrix entered the kitchen.

The girl, usually so lively, was quiet and downcast.

"Tea will be ready soon," Poppy said, busy slicing bread at the kitchen table. "Will you have some toast too, Bea?"

"No, thank you. Not hungry." Beatrix sat in a chair beside Amelia's, staring at the floor.

"You're always hungry," Amelia said. "What's the matter, dear? Aren't you feeling well? Are you tired?"

Silence. A violent shake of her head. Beatrix was definitely upset about something.

Amelia settled a gentle hand on her youngest sister's narrow back and leaned over her. "Beatrix, what is it? Tell me. Are you missing your friends? Or Spot? Are you—"

"No, it's nothing like that." Beatrix ducked her head until only the reddened arc of her cheek was visible.

"Then what?"

"Something's wrong with me." Her voice roughened with misery. "It's happened *again*, Amelia. I couldn't help myself. I barely remember doing it. I—"

"Oh, no," came Poppy's whisper.

Amelia kept her hand on Beatrix's back. "Is it the same problem as before?"

Beatrix nodded. "I'm going to kill myself," she said vehemently. "I'm going to lock myself in the bee room. I'm going to—"

"Hush. You'll do no such thing." Amelia rubbed her rigid back. "Quiet, dear, and let me think for a moment." Her worried gaze met Poppy's over Beatrix's downbent head.

"The problem" had occurred on and off for the past four years, ever since the Hathaways' mother had died. Every now and then, Beatrix suffered an irresistible impulse to steal something, either from a shop or someone's home. Usually, the objects were insignificant—a tiny pair of sewing scissors, hairpins, a pen nib, a cube of sealing wax. But every so often, she took something of value, like a snuff box or an earring. As far as Amelia could tell, Beatrix never planned these small crimes—in fact, the girl often wasn't even aware of what she had done until later. And then she suffered an agony of remorse, and no small amount of fear. It was alarming to discover one wasn't always in control of one's actions.

The Hathaways kept Beatrix's problem a secret, of course, all of them conspiring to return the stolen objects discreetly and protect her from the consequences. Since it hadn't happened for nearly a year, they had all assumed Beatrix was cured of her odd compulsion.

"I assume you took something from Stony Cross Manor," Amelia said with forced calm. "That's the only place you've visited."

Beatrix nodded miserably. "It was after I let Spot go. I went to the library, and looked in a few rooms on the way, and . . . I didn't mean to, Amelia! I didn't want to! I—"

"I know." Amelia wrapped her arms around her in a consoling hug. "We'll fix it, Bea. We'll put everything back and no one will know. Just tell me what you took, and try to remember which rooms the things came from."

"Here . . . this is everything." Reaching into the pockets of her pinafore, Beatrix dumped a small collection of objects in her lap.

Amelia held up the first item. It was a carved wooden horse, no bigger than her fist, with a silk mane and a delicately painted face. The object was worn from much handling, and there were teeth marks along the horse's body. "The Westcliffs have a daughter, still quite small," she murmured. "This must belong to her."

"I took a toy from a baby," Beatrix moaned. "It's the lowest thing I've ever done. I should be in prison."

Amelia picked up another object, a card with two similar images printed side by side. She guessed it was meant to be inserted into a stereoscope, a device that would merge the two images into a picture of three dimensions.

The next stolen item was a household key, and the last . . . *oh, dear*. It was a sterling silver seal with an engraved family crest on one end. One would use it to stamp a blob of melted wax and close an envelope. The object was heavy and quite costly, the kind of thing that was passed down from generation to generation.

"From Lord Westcliff's private study," Beatrix muttered. "It was on his desk. He probably uses it for his official correspondence. I'll go hang myself now."

"We must return this immediately," Amelia said, passing a hand over her dampening brow. "When they realize it's missing, a servant may be blamed."

The three women were silent with horror at the thought.

"We'll pay a morning call to Lady Westcliff," Poppy said, sounding a bit breathless from anxiety. "Is tomorrow a receiving day?"

"Irrelevant," Amelia said, striving to sound calm. "There's no time to wait. You and I are calling tomorrow, whether or not it's a proper day."

"Shall I go too?" Beatrix asked.

"*No*," both Amelia and Poppy answered simultaneously.

"Thank you." Beatrix seemed relieved. "Although I'm sorry you have to undo my wrongs. I should be punished somehow. Perhaps I should confess and apologize—"

"We'll resort to that if we're caught," Amelia said. "First let's try covering it up."

"Do we have to tell Leo or Win or Merripen?" Beatrix asked sheepishly.

"No," Amelia murmured, gathering her close and pressing her lips to her sister's unruly dark curls. "Poppy and I will take care of everything, dear."

"All right. Thank you." Beatrix relaxed and nestled against her with a sigh. "I only hope you can do it without getting caught."

"Of course, we can," Poppy said brightly. "Don't you worry for one minute."

"Problem solved," Amelia added.

But above Beatrix's head, Amelia and Poppy looked at each other in shared panic.

Chapter Ten

I don't know why Beatrix does these things," Poppy said the next morning, as Amelia held the ribbons of the barouche. They were on their way to Stony Cross Manor with the stolen objects secreted in the pockets of their best day gowns.

"I'm certain she doesn't mean to," Amelia replied. "If it were intentional, Beatrix would steal things she truly wanted, like hair ribbons or gloves or candy, and she wouldn't confess afterward." She sighed. "It seems to happen when there's been a significant change in her life. When Mother and Father died, and when Leo and Win fell ill . . . and now, when we've uprooted ourselves and moved to Hampshire. We'll smooth this over as best we can, and try to ensure that Beatrix is in a calm and serene atmosphere."

"There is no such thing as 'calm and serene' in our household," Poppy said glumly. "Oh, Amelia, why must our family be so *odd*?"

"We're not odd."

Poppy batted her hands in a dismissive gesture. "Odd people never think they're odd."

"I'm perfectly ordinary," Amelia protested.

"Ha."

Amelia glanced at her in surprise. "Why in heaven's name would you say 'Ha' to that?"

"You try to manage everything and everyone. And you don't trust anyone outside the family. You're like a hedgehog. No one can get past the quills."

"Well, I like that," Amelia said indignantly. "Being compared to a large prickly rodent, when I've decided to spend the rest of my entire life looking after the family—"

"No one's asked that of you."

"Someone has to do it. And I'm the oldest Hathaway."

"Leo's the oldest."

"I'm the oldest *sober* Hathaway."

"That still doesn't mean you have to martyr yourself."

"I'm not a martyr, I'm merely being responsible. And you're ungrateful!"

"Do you want gratitude or a husband? Personally, I'd take the husband."

They bickered all the way to Stony Cross Manor. By the time they arrived, they were both cross and surly. However, as a footman came to assist them out, they pasted false smiles on their faces and linked tense arms as they walked to the front door.

They waited in the entrance hall as the butler went to announce their arrival. To Amelia's vast relief, he showed them to the parlor and informed them that Lady Westcliff would be with them directly.

Venturing farther into the airy parlor, with its vases of fresh flowers and light-blue silk upholstery, and the cheerful blaze in the white marble fireplace, Poppy exclaimed, "Oh, it's so pretty in here, and it smells so lovely, and look how the windows sparkle!"

Amelia was silent, but she couldn't help agreeing. Seeing this immaculate parlor, so far removed from the dust and squalor of Ramsay House, made her feel guilty and sullen.

"Don't take off your bonnet," she said as Poppy untied her ribbons. "You're supposed to leave it on during a formal call."

"Only in town," Poppy argued. "In the country, etiquette is more relaxed. And I hardly think Lady Westcliff would mind."

A woman's voice came from the doorway. "Mind what?" It was Lady Westcliff, her slender form clad in a pink gown, her dark hair gathered at the back of her head in shining curls. Her smile was wrought of mischief and easy charm. She held hands with a dark-haired toddler in a blue dress, a miniature version of herself with big, round eyes the color of ginger-bread.

"My lady . . ." Amelia and Poppy both bowed. Deciding to be frank, Amelia said, "Lady Westcliff, we were just debating whether or not we could remove our bonnets."

"Good God, don't bother with formality," Lady Westcliff exclaimed, coming in with the child. "Off with the bonnets, by all means. And do call me Lillian. This is my daughter, Merritt. She and I are having some playtime before her morning nap."

"I hope we're not interrupting—" Poppy began apologetically.

"Not at all. If you can tolerate our romping during your visit, we're more than happy to have you. I've sent for tea."

Before long, they were all chatting easily. Merritt quickly lost all vestige of shyness and showed them her favorite doll named Annie and a collection of pebbles and leaves from her pocket. Lady Westcliff—Lillian—was an openly affectionate and playful mother, showing no compunction about kneeling on the floor to look for fallen pebbles beneath the table.

Lillian's interactions with the child were quite unusual for an aristocratic household. Children were hardly ever brought out to see visitors unless it was a brief presentation, accompanied by a pat on the head and a quick departure. Most women of the countess's exalted position wouldn't see their own offspring more than once or twice a day, leaving the majority of child-rearing to the nanny and nurserymaids.

"I can't help wanting to see her," Lillian explained candidly. "So the nursery servants have learned to tolerate my interference."

When the tea tray arrived, Annie the doll was propped up on the settee between Poppy and Merritt. The little girl pressed the edge of her tea cup against the doll's painted mouth. "Annie wants more sugar, Mama," Merritt said.

Lillian grinned, knowing who was going to drink the highly sweetened tea. "Tell Annie we never have more than two lumps in a cup, darling. It will make her ill."

"But she has a sweet tooth," the child protested. She added ominously, "A sweet tooth and a *temper*."

Lillian shook her head with a *tsk tsk*. "Such a headstrong doll. Be firm with her, Merritt."

Poppy, who had been watching the exchange with a grin, adopted a perplexed look and wriggled slightly on the settee. "Dear me, I do believe I'm sitting on something . . ." She reached behind her and produced the little wooden horse, pretending she had found it lodged between the settee cushions.

"That's my horsie," Merritt exclaimed, her small fingers closing around the object. "I thought he'd run away!"

"Thank goodness," Lillian said. "Horsie is one of Merritt's favorite toys. The entire household has been searching for it."

Amelia's smile wavered as she met Poppy's gaze, both of them wondering if it had been discovered that other things were missing. The stolen objects, especially the silver seal, must be returned as soon as possible. She cleared her throat. "My lady . . . that is, Lillian . . . if you wouldn't mind . . . I should like to know where the convenience is."

"Oh, certainly. Shall I have a housemaid show you the way, or—"

"No, thank you," Amelia said hastily.

After receiving Lillian's matter-of-fact instructions, Amelia excused herself from the parlor, leaving the three of them to continue their tea.

The first room she had to find was the library, where the stereoscope card and the key belonged. Recalling Beatrix's description of the main floor plan, Amelia hurried along the quiet hallway. She slowed her pace as she saw a maid sweeping the carpet, and tried to look as if she knew where she was going. The maid stopped sweeping and stood aside respectfully as she passed.

Rounding a corner, Amelia found an open door revealing a large library with upper and lower galleries. Better yet, it was empty. She rushed inside and saw a stereoscope on the massive library table. There was a wooden box nearby, stuffed with cards just like the one in her pocket. Tucking the card in with the others, she hurried out of the library, pausing only to insert the key into the empty lock case of the door.

Only one task left—she had to find Lord Westcliff's private study and return the silver seal. The weight of it bounced uncomfortably against her leg as she walked. *Please don't let Lord Westcliff be there*, she thought desperately. *Please let it be empty. Please don't let me be caught.*

Beatrix had said the study was close to the library, but the first door Amelia tried turned out to be the music room. Spying another door across the hallway, she discovered a supplies closet filled with pails, brooms, rags, and pots of wax and polish.

"Blast, blast, *blast*," she muttered, rushing to another open doorway.

It was a billiards room. And it was occupied by a half-dozen gentlemen involved in a game. Worse, one of them was Christopher Frost. His handsome face was devoid of expression as his gaze met hers.

Amelia stopped, color flaring in her face. "Do excuse me," she murmured, and fled.

To her dismay, Christopher Frost moved as if to follow her. She was so intent on making her escape that she didn't see someone cut in front of Frost, neatly blocking him.

"Miss Hathaway."

Amelia whirled around to discover Cam Rohan had followed her. "Sir."

He was in his shirtsleeves, and his collar was a bit loose. His jet-black hair was casually disordered, as if he'd recently dragged his fingers through the shining layers. Her heart quickened as he approached.

"Have you lost your way?" he asked, his eyes smiling.

Abandoning caution in favor of expediency, Amelia seized a fold of his rolled-up sleeve. "Do you know where Lord Westcliff's study is?"

"Yes, of course."

"Please show me."

He gave her a quizzical glance. "Why?"

"There's no time to explain. Just take me there now. Please, let's hurry!"

Obligingly, Cam led her across the hallway, two doors down, into a small rosewood-paneled room. A gentleman's study. The only ornamentation was a row of rectangular stained glass windows along one wall. Here was where Marcus, Lord Westcliff, conducted most of his estate business.

Cam closed the door behind them.

Fumbling in her pocket, Amelia retrieved the heavy silver seal. "Where does this go?"

"On the right side of his desk, near the inkwell. How did you come by it?"

"I'll explain later. I beg you, don't tell anyone." She went to place the silver seal on the desk. "I only hope he didn't notice it was missing."

"Why would you want it in the first place?" Cam asked idly. "Resorting to forgery, are we?"

"Forgery?" Amelia turned pale. A letter in Westcliff's name, sealed with his family emblem, would be a powerful instrument indeed. What other interpretation could be drawn from the borrowing of the sterling seal? "Oh, no, I wouldn't have—that is, I didn't want—"

She was interrupted by the heart-stopping sound of the doorknob turning. In that one instant, she was pierced with simultaneous anguish and resignation. It was over. She had been so close, and now she'd been caught, and God knew what the repercussions would be. There was no way to explain her presence in Westcliff's office other than to divulge Beatrix's problem, which would bring shame on the family and ruin the girl's future in polite society. A pet lizard was one thing. Thievery was another matter entirely.

All these thoughts flashed through Amelia's mind. But as she stiffened and waited for the ax to fall, Cam came to her in two long strides. Before she could move or think or even breathe, he had jerked her full length against him and pulled her head to his.

His arms were firm around her, keeping her steady while his mouth caught hers at just the right angle. He was the only solid thing in a kaleidoscopic world, his body strong, foreign, and yet intensely familiar. The way he had kissed her before . . . she had relived it a thousand times in her dreams. She just hadn't realized it until now.

Graceful masculine fingers cupped around her neck and jaw, turning her face upward. The tips of his fingers found the silken edge of her hairline. And all the while, he continued to fill her with concentrated fire until the inside of her mouth prickled sweetly, and her legs shook beneath her.

His mouth lifted, his breath a hot caress against her damp lips. He turned his head as he spoke to whoever had entered the room. "I beg your pardon, my lord. We wanted a moment of privacy."

Amelia turned crimson as she followed his gaze to the doorway, where Lord Westcliff stood with an unfathomable expression.

An electric moment passed while Westcliff appeared to marshal his thoughts. A smile flickered in his dark eyes. "I intend to return in approximately a half hour. It would probably be best if my study were vacated by then." Giving them a courteous nod, he took his leave.

As soon as the door closed behind him, Amelia dropped her forehead to Rohan's shoulder with a groan. She would have pulled away, but she didn't trust her knees to hold. "Why did you do that?"

He didn't look at all repentant. "I had to come up with a reason for both of us to be in here. It seemed the most expedient option."

Amelia shook her head slowly, still resting her forehead against him. The dry sweetness of his scent reminded her of a sun-warmed meadow. "Do you think he'll tell anyone?"

"No," he said immediately, reassuring her. "Westcliff won't say a word to anyone, except . . ."

"Except?"

"Lady Westcliff. He might tell her."

Amelia considered that, thinking perhaps it wasn't so terrible. Lady Westcliff didn't seem like the kind of person who would condemn her for this.

"Of course," Rohan continued, "if Lady Westcliff knows, there's a high probability she'll tell Lady St. Vincent, who's due to arrive with Lord St. Vincent by the end of the week. And since Lady St. Vincent tells her husband everything, he'll know about it too. Other than that, no one will find out. Unless . . ."

Her head jerked upward like a string puppet's. "Unless what?"

"Unless Lord St. Vincent mentions it to Mr. Hunt, who would undoubtedly tell his wife Mrs. Hunt, and then . . . basically everyone would find out."

"Oh no. I can't bear it."

He gave her an alert glance. "Because you were caught kissing a Rom?"

"No, because I'm not the kind of woman who is caught kissing *anyone*. When everyone finds out, I'll have no dignity left. No reputation. No— What are you smiling at?"

"You. I wouldn't have expected such melodrama."

That annoyed Amelia, who was not the kind of woman who indulged in theatrics. She wedged her arms more firmly between them. "My reaction is perfectly reasonable—" she began.

"You're not bad at it."

She blinked in confusion. "Melodrama?"

"Kissing. With a little practice, you'd be exceptional. But you need to relax."

"I don't want to relax. I don't want to . . . oh, dear." He had bent his head to her throat, his lips warm and searching.

Her hands went to his shoulders. "Mr. Rohan, you mustn't—"

"This is how to kiss, Amelia." He cradled her head in his palms, deftly tilting it to the side. "Noses go here." A disorienting brush of his mouth, a wash of sensual heat. "You taste like sugar and tea."

"I h-have to go back."

"Not yet." His thumb passed over her kiss-heated lips, urging them to part. "Let me in, Amelia," he whispered.

Never in her life had she thought a man would say something so outrageous to her . . . and if the words were improper, the gleam in his eyes was positively immolating.

"I . . . I'm a spinster." She offered the word as if it were a talisman.

A covert smile deepened the corners of his mouth. "Are you? Well, I've just reconsidered my entire policy on spinsters."

His mouth possessed hers again, while his fingers caressed the taut edge of her jaw, coaxing her to relax. The taste of him was so compelling that she found herself yielding, letting him search her with slow, erotic forays of his tongue. The kisses were melting sweet like boiling candy syrup, soaking into her, sinking deep and simmering.

Her legs turned unsteady, and he gathered her into the firm support of his body. His hands moved in restive paths over her back and shoulders, while his lips broke from hers to explore the soft slope of her neck. He found a place that made her writhe, teasing gently until she gasped and twisted against him.

Cam's head lifted. His eyes glowed as if brimstone were contained within their dark-rimmed irises. He spoke slowly as if he were collecting words like fallen leaves from the ground. "This is probably a bad idea."

Amelia nodded shakily. "Yes, Mr. Rohan."

His fingertips teased a fresh surge of color to the surface of her cheeks. "My name is Cam."

"I can't call you that."

"Why not?"

"You know why," came her unsteady reproach. A long breath was neatly rifted as she felt his mouth descend to her cheek, exploring the heat-polished skin. "What does it mean?"

"My name? It's the Romany word for sun."

Amelia could scarcely think. "As in . . . the offspring of a father, or the one in the sky?"

"Sky." He moved to the arch of her eyebrow, kissing the outward tip. "Did you know a Rom has three names?"

She shook her head slowly while his mouth slid across her forehead. He pressed a warm veil of words against her skin. "The first is a secret name a mother whispers into her child's ear at birth. The second is a tribal name used only by Roma. The third is the name we use with *gadje*."

His scent was all around her, spare and fresh and delicious. "What . . . what is your tribal name?"

He smiled slightly, the shape of his mouth a burning motif against her cheek. "I can't tell you. I don't know you well enough yet."

Yet. The tantalizing promise embedded in that word shortened her breath. "Let me go," she whispered.

"Yes. Just one more. Just—" He bent and took her mouth hungrily.

Suffused with pleasure, Amelia groped for his hair, finding acute satisfaction in the slide of heavy silk through her fingers. As he felt her touch him, he gave a low mutter of encouragement. The pattern of his breath changed, roughened, his kisses turning hard and languorous.

He took what she offered—more—sinking his tongue deeper, gathering sensation. And she responded until her soul was scorched at the edges, and her thoughts had vanished like sparks leaping from a bonfire.

Abruptly, Cam took his mouth from hers and held her tightly, too tightly, against the hard contours of his body. She felt herself straining in a subtle pendulum sway, needing friction, pressure, release. He let her go by gradual degrees until he was finally able to push her away completely.

"Sorry," he eventually said. "I don't usually have such a difficult time stopping."

Amelia nodded blindly and wrapped her arms around

herself. She wasn't aware of her foot's nervous tapping until Cam came to her and slid one of his feet beneath her skirts to still her drumming toes.

"Hummingbird," he whispered. "You'd better go now. If you don't, I'm sure I'll keep compromising you."

Amelia was never quite certain how she returned to the parlor without getting lost. She moved as if through the layers of a dream.

Reaching the settee where Poppy sat, Amelia accepted another cup of tea and smiled at little Merritt, who was fishing around in her own cup for a dropped sugar biscuit, and responded noncommittally to Lillian's suggestion that the entire Hathaway family join them on a picnic in a few days.

"I do wish we could have accepted her invitation," Poppy said wistfully on the way home. "But I suppose that would be asking for trouble since Leo would probably be objectionable and Beatrix would steal something."

"And there's far too much for us to do at Ramsay House," Amelia added, feeling distracted and distant.

Only one thought was clear in her mind. Cam Rohan would return to London soon. For her own sake—and perhaps his as well—she would have to avoid Stony Cross Park until he was gone.

PERHAPS IT WAS BECAUSE THEY WERE ALL EXHAUSTED FROM cleaning, repairing and organizing, but the entire Hathaway family was in a desultory mood that evening. Everyone but Leo gathered around the hearth in one of the downstairs rooms, lounging while Win read aloud from a Dickens novel. Merripen occupied a distant corner of the room, near the family but not quite part of it, listening intently. No doubt Win could have read names from an insurance register, and he would have found it enthralling.

Poppy was busy with needlework, stitching a pair of men's slippers with bright wool threads, while Beatrix played solitaire on the floor near the hearth. Noticing the way her youngest sister was riffling through the cards, Amelia laughed. "Beatrix," she said after Win had finished a chapter, "why in heaven's name would you cheat at solitaire? You're playing against yourself."

"Then there's no one to object when I cheat."

"It's not whether you win but *how* you win that's important," Amelia said.

"I've heard that before," Beatrix said, "and I don't agree at all. It's much nicer to win."

Poppy shook her head over her embroidery. "Bea, you are positively shameless."

"*And* a winner," Beatrix said with satisfaction, laying down the exact card she wanted.

"Where did we go wrong?" Amelia asked of no one in particular.

Win smiled. "Her pleasures are few, dear. A game of solitaire isn't going to hurt anyone."

"I suppose not." Amelia was about to say more, but she was diverted by a cold waft of air that slipped around her ankles and turned her toes numb. She shivered and pulled her knitted blue shawl more snugly around herself. "My, it's chilly in here."

"You must be sitting in a draught," Poppy said in concern. "Come sit by me, Amelia—I'm much closer to the fire."

"Thank you, but I think I'll go to bed now." Still shivering, Amelia yawned. "Good night, everyone." She left as Beatrix asked Win to read one more chapter.

As Amelia walked along the hallway, she passed a small room that, as far as they had been able to tell, had been intended as a gentlemen's room. It featured an alcove just large enough for a billiards table and a dingy painting of a

hunting scene on one wall. An overstuffed chair was posi-
tioned between the windows, its velvet nap eroded. Light
from a standing lamp slid across the floor in a diluted wash.

Leo was drowsing in the chair, one arm hanging loosely
over the side. An empty bottle stood on the floor near the
chair, casting a spear-like shadow to the other side of the
room.

Amelia would have continued on her way, but something
about her brother's undefended posture caused her to stop.
He slept with his head slumped over one shoulder, lips
slightly parted, just as he had in childhood. With his face
wiped clean of anger and grief, he looked young and vulnerable. She was reminded of the gallant boy he had once been,
and her heart contracted with pity.

Venturing into the room, Amelia was shocked by the
abrupt change of temperature, the biting air. It was far colder
in here than it was outside. And it wasn't her imagination—
she could see the white puffs of her breath. Shivering, she
drew closer to her brother. The coldness was concentrated
around him, turning so bitter that it made her lungs hurt
to breathe. As she hovered over his prone form, she was
swamped in a feeling of bleakness, a sorrow beyond tears.

"Leo?" His face was gray, his lips dry and blue, and when
she touched his cheek, there was no trace of warmth. "Leo!"

No response.

Amelia shook him, pushed hard at his chest, took his stiff
face in her hands. As she did so, she felt some invisible force
pulling at her. She held on doggedly, knotting her fists in the
loose folds of his shirt. "Leo, *wake up!*"

To her infinite relief, he stirred and gasped, and his lashes
flickered upward. The irises of his eyes were as pale as ice.
His palms came to her shoulders, and he muttered groggily,
"I'm awake. I'm awake. Jesus. Don't scream. You're making
enough noise to wake the dead."

"For a moment I thought that was exactly what I was doing." Amelia half-collapsed onto the arm of the chair, her nerves thrilling unpleasantly. The chill was receding now. "Oh, Leo, you were so still and pale. I've seen livelier-looking corpses."

Her brother rubbed his eyes. "I'm only a bit tap-hackled. Not dead."

"You wouldn't wake up."

"I didn't want to. I . . ." He paused, looking troubled. His tone was soft and wondering. "I was dreaming. Such vivid dreams . . ."

"About what?

He wouldn't answer.

"About Laura?" Amelia persisted.

His face closed, deep lines weathering the surface like fissures made by the expansion of ice inside rock. "I told you never to mention her name to me."

"Yes, because you didn't want to be reminded of her. But it doesn't matter, Leo. You never stop thinking about her whether you hear her name or not."

"I'm not going to talk about her."

"Well, it's fairly obvious avoidance isn't working." Her mind spun desperately with the question of what tack to take, how best to reach him. She tried determination. "I won't let you fall to pieces, Leo."

The look he gave her made it clear that determination had been a bad choice. "Someday," he said, "you may be forced to acknowledge there are some things beyond your control. If I want to go to pieces, I'll do it without asking your bloody permission."

She tried sympathy next. "Leo . . . I know what you've gone through since Laura died. I'm so sorry—"

"No you don't. You've never loved anyone that way."

Amelia blinked, taken aback. "I've loved many people in my life."

"Not the way we're speaking of. You don't understand anything."

"I know that other people have recovered from loss, and they've gone on to find happiness again—"

"There's no more happiness," Leo said roughly. "There's no peace in any damn corner of my life. She took it all with her. For pity's sake, Amelia, go meddle in someone else's affairs, and leave me the hell alone."

Chapter Eleven

The morning after Amelia Hathaway's visit, Cam went to visit Lord Westcliff's private study, pausing at the open doorway. "My lord."

He suppressed a smile as he noticed a child's porcelain-head doll under the mahogany desk, propped in a sitting position against one of the legs, and the remains of what appeared to be a honey tart. Knowing of the earl's adoration for his three-year-old daughter, Cam guessed he found it impossible to defend against Merritt's invasions.

Looking up from the desk, Westcliff gestured for Cam to enter. "Is it Brishen's tribe?" he asked without prelude.

Cam took the chair he indicated. "No—it's headed by a man named Danior. They saw the marks on the trees."

That morning, one of Westcliff's tenants had reported that a Romany camp had been set by the river. Unlike other landowners in Hampshire, Westcliff tolerated the presence of Roma at his estate as long as they made no mischief and didn't outstay their welcome.

On past occasions, the earl had sent food and wine to visiting Roma. In return, they had carved marks on trees by the river to indicate this was friendly territory. They usually stayed only a matter of days and left without causing damage to the estate.

Upon learning of the camp, Cam had volunteered to go talk to the newcomers and ask about their plans. Westcliff had agreed at once, welcoming the opportunity of sending an intermediary.

It had been a good visit. The tribe was a small one, its leader an affable man who had assured Cam they would make no trouble.

"They intend to stay a week, no more," Cam told Westcliff.

"Good."

The earl's decisive reply caused Cam to smile. "You don't like being visited by Roma."

"It's not something I would wish for," Westcliff admitted. "Their presence makes the villagers and my tenants nervous."

"But you allow them to stay. Why?"

"For one thing, proximity makes it easier to know what they're doing. For another . . ." Westcliff paused, seeming to choose his words with unusual care. "One can't punish them for living as men of nature. It harms no one."

Cam raised his brows, impressed. It was rare for anyone, let alone an aristocrat, to deal with Roma in a fair manner. He rested a hand on the arm of the chair, his gold rings glinting against the rich mahogany. Unlike the earl, who was precisely dressed in tailored clothes and a deftly knotted necktie, Cam wore boots and breeches and an open-necked shirt. It wouldn't have been appropriate to visit the tribe in the formal stiff-necked attire of a *gadjo*.

Westcliff watched him closely. "What was said between you? I would imagine they expressed some surprise upon meeting a Rom who lives with *gadje*."

"Surprise," Cam agreed, "along with pity."

"Pity?"

"For any man who leads this kind of life." Cam gestured loosely at their refined surroundings. "Burdened by possessions. Having a schedule. Carrying a pocket watch. All of it's unnatural."

He fell silent, thinking of the moment he had set foot in the camp, the sense of ease that had stolen over him. The sight of the wagons with dogs lazing between the front wheels, the contented cob horses tethered nearby, the smells of wood smoke and ashes—all of it had evoked warm childhood memories.

"It's man's nature to organize his surroundings," Westcliff said. "Otherwise, society would disintegrate, and there would be nothing but chaos and war."

"And *gadje*, with their clocks and farms and fences—they have no war?"

The earl frowned. "One can't view these matters simplistically."

Cam studied the tips of his boots, the worn leather coated with a dry film of river mud. "They asked me to go with them when they leave," he said almost absently.

"You refused, of course."

"I wanted to say yes. If not for my responsibilities in London, I would have."

Westcliff's face went blank. A speculative pause. "You surprise me."

"Why?"

"You're a man of unusual abilities and intelligence. You have wealth and the prospect of acquiring much more. There's no logic in letting all that go to waste."

A smile touched Cam's lips. "Why would it be a waste?"

The earl picked up the silver letter seal from the corner of his desk, examining the engraved base of it with undue concentration. He used the edge of his thumbnail to remove a hardened droplet of sealing wax that had marred the polished surface. Cam was not deceived by Westcliff's sudden diffidence.

"One can't help but notice," Westcliff murmured, "that while you're considering a change in your entire way of life, you also seem to have taken a conspicuous interest in Miss Hathaway."

Cam's expression didn't change, the barrier of his smile firmly fixed. "She's a beautiful woman. I'd have to be blind not to notice her. But that's hardly going to change my future plans."

"Yet."

"Ever," Cam returned, pausing as he heard the unnecessary intensity of his own voice. He adjusted his tone at once. "I've decided to leave in two days, after St. Vincent and I confer on a few matters regarding the club. It's not likely I'll see Miss Hathaway again." *Thank God*, he added privately.

Cam couldn't recall when, if ever, he had been so affected by a woman. He wasn't one to involve himself in other peoples' affairs. He was loath to give advice, and he spent little time considering problems that didn't directly concern him. But he was irresistibly drawn to Amelia.

The tenacious connections she had formed with the others in her family, the extent she would go to take care of them . . . That appealed to him on an instinctual level. Roma were like that. Tribal. And yet Amelia was his opposite in the most essential ways, a creature of domesticity who would insist on putting down roots. Ironic, that he should be so fascinated by someone who represented everything he needed to escape from.

IT SEEMED THE ENTIRE COUNTY HAD TURNED OUT FOR THE Mop Fair, which according to tradition, had been held every October 12 for at least a hundred years. The village, with its tidy shops and white and black thatched cottages, was almost absurdly charming. Crowds milled about the distinctive oval village green or strolled along the main thoroughfare where a multitude of temporary stalls and booths had been erected. Vendors sold penny toys, foodstuffs, bags of salt from Lymington, glassware and fabrics, and pots of local honey.

The music of singers and fiddlers was punctuated by bursts of applause as entertainers performed tricks for passersby. Most of the work hiring had been done earlier in the day, with hopeful laborers and apprentices standing in lines on the village green, talking to potential employers. After an agreement was made, a fasten-penny was given to the newly hired servant, and the rest of the day was spent in merry-making.

Merripen had gone in the morning to find two or three suitable servants for Ramsay house. With that business concluded, he returned to the village in late afternoon, accompanied by the entire Hathaway family. They were all delighted by the prospect of music, food, and entertainment. Leo promptly disappeared with a pair of village women, leaving his sisters in Merripen's charge.

Browsing among the stalls, the sisters feasted on hand-sized pork pies, leek pasties, apples and pears, and to the girls' delight, "gingerbread husbands." The gingerbread had been pressed into wooden man-shaped molds, baked, and gilded. The baker at the stall assured them that every unmarried maiden must eat a gingerbread husband for luck if she wanted to catch the real thing someday.

A laughing mock argument sprang up between Amelia and the baker as she flatly refused one for herself, saying she had no wish to marry.

"But of course, you do!" the baker declared with a sly grin. "It's what every woman hopes for."

Amelia smiled and passed the gingerbread men to her sisters. "How much for three, sir?"

"A farthing each." He attempted to hand her a fourth. "And this for no charge. It would be a sad waste for a lovely blue-eyed lady to go without a man."

"Oh, I couldn't," Amelia protested. "Thank you, but I don't—"

A new voice came from behind her. "She'll take it."

Discomfiture and pleasure seethed low in her body, and Amelia saw a dark masculine hand reaching out, dropping a silver piece into the baker's upturned palm. Hearing her sisters' giggling exclamations, Amelia turned and looked up into a pair of bright golden-hazel eyes.

"You need the luck," Cam Rohan said, pushing the gingerbread husband into her reluctant hands. "Have some."

She obeyed, deliberately biting off the head, and he laughed. Her salivary glands spiked at the rich flavor of molasses and the melting chewiness of the gingerbread on her tongue.

Her eyes were dazzled as she looked at Cam. There should have been at least one or two flaws, some irregularity of skin or structure. But his complexion was as smooth as velvet, and his features were strong and fine. As he bent his head toward her, the sun struck brilliant spangles in the dark waves of his hair.

Managing to swallow the gingerbread, Amelia mumbled, "I don't believe in luck."

Cam smiled. "Or husbands, apparently."

"Not for myself, no. But for others—"

"It doesn't matter. You'll marry anyway."

"Why do you say that?"

Before replying, Cam cast a look of askance at the Hathaway sisters, who were smiling benevolently upon them. Merripen, on the other hand, was scowling.

"May I steal your sister away?" Cam asked the rest of

the Hathaways. "I need to speak with her on some apiary matters."

"What does that mean?" Beatrix asked, taking the head-less gingerbread husband from Amelia.

"I suspect Mr. Rohan is referring to our bee room," Win replied with a grin, gently urging her sisters to come away with her. "Come, let's see if we can find a stall with embroidery silks."

"Don't go far," Amelia called after them, more than a little amazed by the speed at which her family was abandoning her. "Bea, don't pay for something without bargaining first, and Win . . ." Her voice trailed away as they scattered among the stalls without listening. Only Merripen gave her a backward glance, glowering over his shoulder.

Seeming to enjoy the sight of Merripen's annoyance, Cam offered Amelia his arm. "Walk with me."

She could have objected to the soft-voiced command, except this was probably the last time she would see him for a long while, if ever. And it was difficult to resist the beguiling gleam of his eyes.

"Why did you say I would marry?" she asked as they moved through the crowd at a relaxed pace.

"It's written on your hand."

"Palm-reading is a sham. And men don't read palms. Only women."

"Just because we don't," Cam replied cheerfully, "doesn't mean we can't. And anyone could see your marriage line. It's as clear as day."

"Marriage line? Where is it?" Amelia took her hand from his arm and scrutinized her own palm.

Cam drew her with him beneath the shade of a bulky beech tree on the edge of the green. Crowds milled across the cropped oval, while the last few swags of sunlight crumpled beneath the horizon. Torches and lamps were already being lit in anticipation of the evening.

"This one," Cam said, taking her left hand, turning it palm upward.

Amelia's fingers curled as a wave of embarrassment went through her. She should have been wearing gloves, but her best pair had been stained, and her second-best pair had a hole in one of the fingers, and she hadn't yet managed to buy new ones. To make matters worse, there was a scab on the side of her thumb where the edge of a metal pail had gashed it, and her nails had been filed childishly short after she'd broken them. It was the hand of a housemaid, not a lady. For one wistful moment, she wished she had hands like Win's, pale, long-fingered and elegant.

Cam stared for a moment. As Amelia tried to pull away, he closed his hand more firmly around hers. "Wait," he murmured.

She had no choice but to let her fingers relax into the warm envelope of his hand. A blush raced over her as she felt his thumb nuzzle into her palm and stroke outward until all her fingers were lax and open.

"Here," he said quietly, his fingertip brushing over a horizontal line at the base of her little finger. "Only one marriage. It will be a long one. And these . . ." He traced a trio of small vertical notches that met the marriage line. "It means you'll have at least three children." He squinted in concentration. "Two girls and a boy. Elizabeth, Jane, and . . . Ignatious."

She couldn't help smiling. "Ignatious?"

"After his father," he said gravely. "A very distinguished bee farmer."

The spark of teasing in his eyes made her pulse jump. She took his hand and inspected the palm. "Let's see yours."

Rohan kept his hand relaxed, but she felt the power of it.

His fingers were well-tended, the nails scrupulously clean and pared nearly to the quick. "You have an even deeper marriage line than I do," Amelia said.

He responded with a single nod, his gaze not moving from her face.

"And you'll have three children as well . . . or is it four?" She touched a nearly imperceptible line etched near the side of his hand.

"Only three. That one on the side means I'll have a very short betrothal."

She studied him. "I find it difficult to imagine you as a husband. You seem too solitary."

"Not at all. I'll take my wife everywhere with me." His fingers caught playfully at her thumb, as if he'd caught a wisp of dandelion thistle. "We'll travel in a *vardo* from one side of the world to the other. I'll put gold rings on her fingers and toes, and bracelets on her ankles. At night I'll wash her hair and comb it dry by the firelight. And I'll kiss her awake every morning."

Amelia averted her gaze from him, her cheeks turning hot. She moved away, needing to walk, anything to break the intimacy of the moment. He fell into step beside her as they traversed the village green.

"Mr. Rohan, why did you leave your tribe?"

"I've never been quite certain."

She glanced at him in surprise.

"I was ten years old," he said. "For as long as I could remember, I traveled with the tribe in my grandparents' wagon. I never knew my parents—my mother died giving birth to me, and my father was a *gadjo*. His family rejected his marriage and convinced him to abandon my mother. I don't think he ever knew she'd had a child." He paused. "One day, my grandmother dressed me in a new shirt she had made, and told me I had to leave the tribe. She said I was in danger and could no longer live with them."

"What kind of danger? From what source?"

"She wouldn't say. An older cousin of mine—Noah—took me to London and helped me find a situation and a job. He promised to come back for me someday and tell me when it was safe to go home."

"And in the meantime, you worked at the gaming club?"

"Yes, old Jenner hired me as a listmaker's runner." Rohan's expression softened with reminiscent fondness. "In many ways, he was like a father to me. Of course, he was quick-tempered and a bit too ready with his fists. But he was a good man. He looked out for me."

"It couldn't have been easy for you," Amelia said, feeling compassion for the boy he had been, obliged to make his own way in the world. "I wonder that you didn't try to run back to your tribe."

"I'd promised I wouldn't." Seeing a leaf fluttering down from an overhead tree branch, Cam reached upward, his clever fingers plucking it from the air as if by sleight of hand. He brought the leaf to his nose, inhaled its sweetness, and gave it to her.

"I stayed at the club for years," he said in a matter-of-fact tone. "Waiting for Noah to come back for me."

Amelia chafed the crisply pliant skin of the leaf between the pads of her fingers. "But he never did."

"No. Then Jenner died, and his daughter and son-in-law took possession of the club."

"You've been treated well in their employ?"

"Too well." A frown chased across his forehead. "They started my good luck curse."

"Yes, I've heard about that." She smiled at him. "But since I don't believe in luck or curses, I'm skeptical."

He looked morose. "No matter what I do, money comes to me."

"That must be very trying for you."

"It's damned embarrassing," he muttered with a sincerity she couldn't doubt.

Half-amused, half-envious, Amelia asked, "Had you ever experienced this problem before?"

Cam shook his head. "But I should have seen it coming. It's fate." Stopping with her, he showed her his palm, where a cluster of star-shaped intersections glimmered at the base of his forefinger. "Financial prosperity," came his glum explanation. "And it won't end any time soon."

"You could give your money away. There are countless charities and many people in need."

"I intend to. Soon." Taking her elbow, he guided her carefully around an uneven patch of ground. "The day after tomorrow, I'm returning to London to find a replacement factotum at the club."

"And then what will you do?"

"I'll find some tribe to travel with. No more account books or salad forks or shoe polish. I'll be free." He brought her to a stall set up by the village wine shop and bought two cups of plum wine. She drank the tart, slightly sweet vintage in thirsty gulps, making Cam laugh quietly. "Not so fast," he cautioned. "This stuff is stronger than you realize. Any more and I'll have to haul you home over my shoulders like a felled deer."

"It's not that strong," Amelia protested, unable to taste any alcohol in the fruit-heavy wine. It was delicious, the dry plummy richness lingering on her tongue. She held out her cup to the wine seller. "I'll take another."

Although proper women didn't ordinarily eat or drink in public, the rules were cast aside at rural fairs and festivals, where gentry and commoners rubbed elbows and ignored the conventions.

Looking amused, Cam finished his own wine, and waited patiently as she drank more. "I found a beekeeper for you," he said. "I described your problem to him. He said he would go to Ramsay House tomorrow, or perhaps the next day. One way or another, you'll be rid of the bees."

"Thank you," Amelia said fervently. "I am indebted to you, Mr. Rohan. Will it take long for him to remove the hive?"

"There's no way of knowing until he sees it. With the house having gone unoccupied for so long, the colony could be quite large. He said he'd once encountered a hive in an abandoned cottage that harbored a half million bees, by his estimate."

Her eyes turned enormous. "A half million—"

"I doubt yours is that bad," Cam said. "But it's almost certain part of the wall will have to be removed after the bees are gone."

More expense. More repairs. Amelia's shoulders slumped at the thought. She spoke without thinking. "Had I known Ramsay House was in such terrible condition, I wouldn't have moved the family to Hampshire. I shouldn't have taken the solicitor's word that the house was suitable. But I was in such a hurry to remove Leo from London—and I wanted so much for all of us to make a new start—"

"You're not responsible for everything. Your brother is an adult. So are Winnifred and Poppy. They agreed with your decision, didn't they?"

"Yes, but Leo wasn't in his right mind. He still isn't. And Win is frail, and—"

"You like to blame yourself, don't you? Come walk with me."

She set her empty wine cup at the corner of the stall, feeling lightheaded. The second cup of wine had been a mistake. And going somewhere with Cam, with night deepening and revelry all around them, would be yet another. But as she looked into his hazel eyes, she felt absurdly reckless. Just a few stolen minutes . . . she couldn't resist the lawless mischief of his smile. "My family will worry if I don't rejoin them soon."

"They know you're with me."

"That's why they'll worry," she said, making him laugh.

They paused at a table bearing a collection of magic lanterns, small embossed tin lamps with condensing lenses at the front. There was a slot for a hand painted glass slide just behind the lens. When the lamp was lit, an image would be projected on a wall. Cam insisted on buying one for Amelia, along with a packet of slides.

"But it's a child's toy," she protested, holding the lantern by its wire handle. "What am I to do with it?"

"Indulge in pointless entertainment. Play. You should try it sometime."

"Playing is for children, not adults."

"Oh, Miss Hathaway," he murmured, leading her away from the table. "The best kind of playing is for adults."

They hemmed the edge of the crowd, weaving in and out like an embroiderer's needle until finally, they drifted free of the torchlight and movement and music, and reached the dark, luminous quiet of a beech grove.

"Are you going to tell me why you had that silver seal from Westcliff's study?" he asked.

"I would rather not, if you don't mind."

"Because you're trying to protect Beatrix?"

Her startled glance cut through the shadows. "How did you . . . that is, why did you mention my sister?"

"The night of the supper party, Beatrix had the time and opportunity. The question is, why did she want it?"

"Beatrix is a good girl," Amelia said quickly. "A wonderful girl. She would never deliberately do anything wrong, and—you didn't tell anyone about the seal, did you?"

"Of course not." His hand touched the side of her face. "Easy, hummingbird. I wouldn't betray your secrets. I'm your friend. I think . . ." A brief, electrifying pause. "In another lifetime, we would be more than friends."

Her heart turned in a painful revolution behind her ribs. "There's no such thing as another lifetime."

"Why can't there be?"

"Occam's razor," she said.

He was silent as if her answer had surprised him, and then a wondering laugh slipped from his throat. "The medieval scientific principle?"

"Yes. When formulating a theory, eliminate as many assumptions as possible. In other words, the simplest explanation is the best."

"And that's why you don't believe in magic or fate or reincarnation? Because they're too complicated, theoretically speaking?"

"Yes."

"How did you learn about Occam's razor?"

"My father was a medieval scholar." She shivered a little as she felt his hand glide along the side of her neck, finding every sensitive nerve. "Sometimes we studied together."

Cam pried the wire handle of the magic lantern from her shaky grip, and set it near their feet. "Did he also teach you that the complicated explanations are sometimes more accurate than the simpler ones?"

She shook her head, unable to speak as he took her shoulders, fitting her against himself with extreme care. Her pulse ran riot. She shouldn't allow him to hold her. Someone might see, even secreted in the shadows as they were. But as her muscles drew in the warm pressure of his body, the pleasure of it made her dizzy, and she stopped caring about anyone or anything outside his arms.

Cam's fingertips drifted with stunning delicacy over her throat, behind her ear, pushing into the satiny warmth of her hair. "You are an interesting woman, Amelia."

Gooseflesh rose wherever his breath touched. "I can't f-fathom why you would think so."

His playful mouth traced the wing of her brow. "I find you thoroughly, seriously, deeply interesting. I want to open you like a book and read every page." A smile curled the corners of his lips as he added huskily, "Footnotes included." Feeling the stiffness of her neck muscles, he coaxed the tension out of them, kneading lightly. "I want you. I want to lie with you beneath constellations and clouds and shade trees."

Before she could answer, he covered her mouth with his. She felt a jolt of heat, her blood igniting, and she could no more withhold her response than stop her own heart from beating. She reached up to his hair, the beautiful ebony locks curling slightly over her fingers. Touching his ear, she found the faceted diamond stud in the lobe. She fingered it gently, then followed the taut satin skin with innocent curiosity down to the edge of his collar. His breath roughened as he deepened the kiss, his tongue penetrating with silky demand until she bent in his arms like an unfurling flower.

The white moon sent shards of light through the beech boughs, outlining the silhouette of Cam's head, touching her own skin with an unearthly glow. Supporting her with one hand, he cradled her face with the other, his breath hot and scented of sweet wine as it fell against her mouth.

A curt voice shot through the humid darkness. "Amelia." It was Christopher Frost, standing a few yards away, his posture rigid and combative. He gave Cam a long, hard stare.

"Don't make a spectacle of her. She's a lady, and deserves to be treated as such."

"I don't need advice from you on how to treat her," Rohan said softly.

"You know what it will do to her reputation if she is seen with you."

It immediately become apparent the confrontation would turn ugly if Amelia didn't do something about it. She pulled away from Cam. "This isn't seemly," she said. "I must go back to my family."

"I'll escort you," Frost said at once.

Cam's eyes flashed dangerously. "Like hell you will."

"Please." Amelia reached up to touch her cool fingers to Cam's parted lips. "I think it's better that we part here. I want to go with him. There are things that must be said between us. And you . . ." She managed to smile at him. "You have many roads to travel." Clumsily, she bent and retrieved the magic lantern at her feet. "Goodbye, Mr. Rohan. I hope you find everything you're looking for. I hope . . ." She broke off with a crooked smile, and felt a peculiar stinging pain in her throat and swallowed the bittersweet taste of longing. "Goodbye, Cam," she whispered.

He didn't move or speak. She felt him watching as she went to Christopher Frost, his gaze penetrating her clothes, lingering against her skin. And as she walked away, a sense of loss rushed through her.

THEY WANDERED SLOWLY, SHE AND CHRISTOPHER, FALLING into a familiar harmony. It reminded her of their courtship, when they'd gone for long walks and chaperoned drives. To Amelia, it had seemed magical, unbelievable, that someone so handsome and perfect would want her. In fact, Amelia had put him off at the beginning for that very reason, telling him with a laugh that she was sure he meant to trifle with her. But Christopher had said he was hardly going to trifle with his best friend's sister, and he was certainly not some London rake who would play her false.

"For one thing, I don't dress nearly well enough to be a rake," Christopher had pointed out with a grin.

"You're right," Amelia had agreed, looking him over with mock solemnity. "In fact, you don't even dress well enough to be an architect."

"And," he'd continued, "I have a respectable history with women. Hearts and reputations all left intact. No rake would make such a claim."

"You're very convincing," Amelia had observed, a bit breathless as he'd moved closer.

"Miss Hathaway," Christopher had whispered, engulfing her cool hand with both of his warm ones, "take pity. At least let me write to you. Promise you'll read my letter. And if you still don't want me after that, I'll never bother you again."

Intrigued, Amelia had consented. And what a letter it had been, charming and eloquent and fairly blistering in parts. They'd begun a correspondence, and Christopher had visited Primrose Place whenever he could.

Amelia had never enjoyed any man's company so much. They'd shared similar opinions on a variety of issues, which was pleasant. But when they disagreed, it had been even more enjoyable. Christopher seldom became heated on a subject—his approach was analytical, scholarly, rather like her father. And if Amelia became annoyed with him, he laughed and kissed her until she forgot what had started the argument.

Christopher had never tried to seduce Amelia—he respected her too much for that. Even when she'd encouraged him to go beyond mere kisses, he'd refused. "I want you," he'd whispered, his breath unsteady, his eyes bright with passion. "But not until it's right. Not until you're my wife."

That was as close to a proposal as he'd ever come. There had been no official betrothal, although Christopher had led her to expect one. There had only been a mysterious silence for almost a month, and then Leo had gone to find him on Amelia's behalf. Her brother had come back from London looking angry and troubled.

"There are rumors," Leo had told Amelia gruffly, taking her against his shirtfront, drying her tears with his handkerchief. "He's been seen with Rowland Temple's daughter. They say he's courting her."

Soon another letter had come from Christopher, so devastating that Amelia wondered how mere scratches of ink on paper could rip someone's soul to shreds. How could she could feel so much pain and still survive? She'd gone to bed for a week, not venturing from her darkened room, crying until she was ill, and then crying some more.

Ironically, the thing that had saved her was the scarlet fever that had struck Win and Leo. They had needed her, and caring for them had pulled her out of the depths of melancholy. She hadn't shed a tear for Christopher Frost after that.

But the absence of tears wasn't the same as an absence of feeling. Amelia was surprised now to discover that underneath the bitterness and caution, all the things she had once found appealing about him were still there.

"I'm the last person who should remark on how you conduct your personal affairs," Christopher said, offering an arm as they walked. "However, you know what people will say if you're seen with him."

"I appreciate your concern for my reputation." Amelia's tone was lightly salted with sarcasm. "But Mr. Rohan is leaving for London soon. I doubt I'll ever see him again. And I can't fathom why you'd care one way or another."

"Of course I care," Christopher said gently. "Amelia, I regret having hurt you, more than you could ever know.

I certainly don't wish to see you endure further harm from yet another ill-advised love affair."

"Why aren't you married?" she asked abruptly.

The question was met with a long sigh. "She accepted my proposal to please her father, rather than out of any sincere attachment to me. As it happened, she was in love with someone else, a man her father didn't approve of. Eventually they eloped to Gretna Green."

"There's some justice in that," Amelia said. "You abandoned someone who loved you, and then you were abandoned in turn."

"Would it please you to know I never loved her? I liked and admired her, but it was nothing compared to what I felt for you."

"No, that doesn't please me in the least. It's even worse that you put ambition before all else."

"I'm a man who's trying to support himself—and someday a family—with an uncertain career. I don't expect you to understand."

"Your career was never uncertain," Amelia shot back. "You had every promise of advancement, even without marrying Rowland Temple's daughter. Leo told me your talent would have taken you far."

"Would that talent were enough. But it's naïve to think so."

"Well, naïveté seems to be a common failing of the Hathaways."

"Amelia," he murmured. "It's not like you to be cynical."

She bent her head. "You don't know what I'm like now."

"I want the chance to find out."

That drew a glance of startled disbelief from her. "There's nothing to be gained by a renewed acquaintance, Christopher. I'm no wealthier, nor am I more advantageously connected. Nothing has changed since we last met."

"Perhaps I have. Perhaps I've come to realize what I lost."

"Threw away," she corrected, her heart thumping painfully.

"Threw away," he acknowledged in a soft tone. "I was a fool and a cad, Amelia. I would never ask you to overlook what I did. But at least give me the opportunity to make amends. I want to be of service to your family, if at all possible. And to help your brother."

"You can't," Amelia said. "You see what's become of him."

"He's a man of remarkable talents. It would be criminal to waste them. Perhaps, if I could befriend him again—"

"I don't think he would be receptive to that."

"I want to help him. I have influence with Rowland Temple now. His daughter's elopement left him with a sense of obligation toward me."

"How convenient for you."

"I might be able to interest Leo in working for him again. It would benefit them both."

"But how would it benefit you?" she asked. "Why would you go to trouble on Leo's behalf?"

"I'm not a complete villain, Amelia. I have a conscience. It's not easy to live with the memories of the people I hurt in the past. Including you and your brother."

"Christopher . . . I don't know what to say. I need some time to consider things."

"Take all the time you wish," he said gently. "If I can't be what I once was to you, I would be satisfied with friendship." He smiled slightly. "And if you should ever want more, a single word is all it will take."

Chapter Twelve

Ordinarily, Cam would have been pleased by the arrival of Lord and Lady St. Vincent at Stony Cross Park. However, Cam wasn't looking forward to the prospect of telling St. Vincent about his decision to quit the club. St. Vincent wouldn't like it. Not only would it be inconvenient to have to find a replacement manager, but the viscount wouldn't understand Cam's desire to live as a Rom. St. Vincent was nothing if not an enthusiastic advocate of fine living.

Many people feared St. Vincent for his lethal way with words and calculating nature, but Cam was not one of them. In fact, he had challenged the viscount on more than one occasion, both of them arguing with a vicious articulateness that would have sliced anyone else to ribbons.

The St. Vincents arrived with their daughter Phoebe, a red-haired infant with an alarmingly changeable temperament. One moment, the child was placid and adorable. The next, she was a squalling devil-spawn who could only be soothed by the sound of her father's voice. "There, darling," St. Vincent had been known to coo into the infant's ear. "Has someone displeased you? Ignored you? Oh, the insolence. My poor princess shall have anything she wants . . ." And,

appeased by her father's outrageous spoiling, Phoebe would settle into hiccupping smiles.

The baby was duly admired and passed around in the parlor. Evie and Lillian chattered without stopping, frequently hugging and linking arms in the way of old friends.

After a while Cam, St. Vincent, and Lord Westcliff withdrew to the back terrace, where an afternoon breeze diffused the scents of the river and reed sweetgrass and marsh marigold. Raucous honks of greylag geese punctuated the peace of the Hampshire autumn along with the lowing of cattle being driven down a well-worn path to a dry meadow.

The men sat at an outside table. Cam, who disliked the taste of tobacco, waved his hand in dismissal as St. Vincent offered him a cigar.

Under Westcliff's interested regard, Cam and St. Vincent discussed the progress of the club's renovations. Then, seeing no reason to tiptoe around the issue, Cam told St. Vincent of his decision to quit the club as soon as the work was completed.

"You're leaving me?" St. Vincent asked, looking perturbed. "For how long?"

"For good, actually."

As St. Vincent absorbed the information, his pale blue eyes narrowed. "What will you do for money?"

Relaxed in the face of his employer's displeasure, Cam shrugged. "I already have more money than anyone could spend in a lifetime."

St. Vincent glanced heavenward. "Anyone who says such a thing obviously doesn't know the right places to shop." He sighed shortly. "Rohan, you're a wealthy bachelor with all the advantages of modern life. If you have *ennui*, do what every other man of means does."

Cam's brows lifted. "And that would be . . ."

"Gamble! Drink! Buy a horse! Take a mistress! For God's

sake, have a little imagination. Can you think of no better option than to throw it all away and put me to great inconvenience? How the devil am I to replace you?"

"No one's irreplaceable."

"You are. No other man in London can do what you do. You're a walking account book, you have eyes in the back of your head, you have the mind of a banker, and you can put down a fight in a matter of seconds. I'd need to hire at least a half-dozen men for your job."

"I don't have the mind of a banker," Cam said indignantly.

"After all your investment coups, you can't deny—"

"That wasn't on purpose!" A scowl settled on Cam's face. "It was my good luck curse."

Looking satisfied to have unsettled Cam's composure, St. Vincent drew on his cigar. He exhaled a smooth, elegant stream of smoke and glanced at Westcliff. "Say something," he told his old friend. "You can't approve of this any more than I."

"It's not for either of us to approve."

"Thank you," Cam muttered.

"However," Westcliff continued, "I urge you, Rohan, to reflect adequately on the fact that half of you is Irish—a race renowned for its fierce love of land. Which leads me to doubt you'd be as content in your wandering as you seem to expect."

The point rattled Cam. He had always tried to ignore the *gadjo* half of his nature, lugging it around like a piece of baggage he would have liked to set aside but could never find a convenient place.

"If your point is that I'm damned whatever I do," Cam said tersely, "I'd rather err on the side of being free."

"All men of intelligence must eventually give up their freedom," St. Vincent replied. "Bachelorhood is far too easy,

which makes it tedious. The only real challenge left is marriage."

Marriage. Respectability. Cam regarded his companions with a skeptical smile, thinking they resembled a pair of birds trying to convince themselves of how comfortable their cage was. No woman was worth having his wings clipped.

"I'm leaving for London tomorrow," he said. "I'll stay at the club until it reopens. After that, I'll be gone for good."

St. Vincent's clever mind circumvented the problem, analyzing it from various angles. "Rohan, you've led a more or less civilized existence for years, and yet suddenly it's intolerable. Why?"

Cam remained silent. The truth wasn't something he was readily able to admit to himself, let alone say it aloud.

"There has to be *some* reason you want to leave," St. Vincent persisted.

"Perhaps I'm off the mark," Westcliff said, "but I suspect it has to do with Miss Hathaway."

Cam sent him a damning glare.

St. Vincent looked alertly from Cam's stony face to Westcliff's. "You didn't tell me there was a woman."

Cam stood so quickly the chair nearly toppled backward. "She has nothing to do with it."

"Who is she?" St. Vincent always hated being left out of gossip.

"One of Lord Ramsay's sisters," came Westcliff's reply. "They reside at the estate next door."

"Well, well," St. Vincent said. "She must be quite something to provoke such a reaction in you, Rohan. Tell me about her."

To remain silent or to deny the attraction would have been to admit the full extent of his weakness. Cam lowered back into his chair and strove for an offhand tone. "Dark-haired. Pretty. And she has . . . quirks."

St. Vincent's eyes glinted with enjoyment. "How charming. Go on."

"She's read obscure medieval philosophy. She's afraid of bees. Her foot taps when she's nervous." And there were other, more personal things he couldn't reveal . . . like the beautiful skin of her throat and chest, the weight of her hair in his hands, the way strength and vulnerability were pleated inside her like two pieces of fabric folded together.

Aware that Westcliff and St. Vincent had exchanged a significant glance, Cam said sourly, "If you're assuming my plans to leave are nothing more than a reaction to Miss Hathaway . . . I've been considering this for a long time. I'm not an idiot. Nor am I inexperienced with women."

"To say the least," St. Vincent commented dryly. "But in your pursuit of women—or perhaps I should say, their pursuit of you—you seem to have regarded them all as interchangeable. Until now. If you're taken with this Miss Hathaway, don't you think it bears investigating?"

"God, no. There's only one thing it could lead to."

"Marriage," the viscount said rather than asked.

"Yes. And that's impossible."

"Why?"

The fact that they were discussing Amelia and the subject of marriage was enough to make Cam blanch in discomfort. "I'm not the marrying kind—"

St. Vincent snorted. "No man is. Marriage is a female invention."

After a moment, Westcliff stubbed out his cigar methodically. "Obviously you've made up your mind," he said to Cam. "Further debate would be pointless."

St. Vincent followed his lead with a resigned shrug and a facile smile. "I suppose now I'm obliged to wish you happiness in your new life. Although happiness in the absence of indoor plumbing is a debatable concept."

Cam was undeceived by the show of resignation. He had never known Westcliff or St. Vincent to lose an argument easily. Each, in his own way, would hold his ground long after the average man would have collapsed to his knees. Which made Cam fairly certain he hadn't heard the last word from either of them yet.

"I'm leaving at dawn," was all he said.

Nothing could change his mind.

Chapter Thirteen

Beatrix, whose imagination had been captured by the magic lantern, could hardly wait for evening so she could view the selection of glass slides again. Many of the images were amusing, featuring animals wearing human clothes as they played piano or sat at writing desks or stirred soup in a pot.

Other slides were more sentimental: a train passing through a village square, winter scenes, children at play. There were even a few scenes of exotic animals in the jungle. One of them, a tiger half-hidden in leaves, was particularly striking. Beatrix had experimented with the lantern, moving it closer to the wall then farther away, trying to make the tiger's image as distinct as possible.

Now Beatrix had taken to the idea of writing a story, recruiting Poppy to paint some accompanying slides. It was decided they would put on a show someday, with Beatrix narrating while Poppy operated the magic lantern.

As her younger sisters lounged by the hearth and discussed their ideas, Amelia sat with Win on the settee. She watched Win's slender, graceful hands as she embroidered a delicate floral pattern, the needle flashing as it dove through the cloth.

At the moment, her brother was lolling on the carpet near the girls, slouched and half-drunk. Once he had been a kind and caring older brother, sympathetically bandaging one of the children's hurt fingers, or helping to look for a lost doll. Now he treated his younger sisters with the polite indifference of a stranger.

Absently, Amelia reached up to rub the pinched muscles at the back of her neck. She glanced at Merripen as he sat in the corner of the room, every line of his body lax with the exhaustion of heavy labor. His gaze was distant as if he, too, were consumed with private thoughts.

Beatrix pulled a glass slide from the front of the lamp casing, laid it aside carefully, and reached for another. "This one's my favorite," she was saying to Poppy as she slid the next image in place.

Having lost interest in the succession of pictures on the wall, Amelia did not look up. Her attention remained on Win's embroidering. But Win made an uncharacteristic slip, the needle jabbing into the soft flesh of her forefinger. A scarlet drop of blood welled.

"Oh, Win—" Amelia murmured.

Win, however, didn't react to the pinprick. She didn't even seem to have noticed it. Frowning, Amelia glanced at her sister's still face and followed her gaze to the opposite wall.

The image cast by the magic lantern was a winter scene, with a snow-blurred sky and the dark cache of forest beneath. It would have been an unremarkable scene, except for the delicate outline of a woman's face that seemed to emerge from the shadows.

A familiar face.

As Amelia stared, transfixed, the spectral features seemed to gain dimension and substance until it seemed almost as if she could reach out and shape her fingers against the waxing contours.

"Laura," she heard Win breathe.

It was the girl Leo had loved. The face was unmistakable. Amelia's first coherent thought was that Beatrix and Poppy must be playing some horrid joke. But as she looked at the pair on the floor, chatting together innocently, she perceived at once that they didn't even see the dead girl's image. Nor did Merripen, who was watching Win with a questioning frown.

By the time Amelia's gaze shot once more to the projection, the face had disappeared.

Beatrix pulled the slide from the magic lantern. She fell back with a little cry as Leo charged toward her and made a grab for the slide.

"Give it to me," Leo said, more an animal growl than a human voice. His face was blanched and contorted, his body knotted with panic. He hunched over the little piece of painted glass and stared through it as if it were a tiny window into hell. Fumbling with the magic lantern, Leo nearly overset it as he tried to jam the slide back in.

"Don't! You'll break it!" Beatrix cried in bewilderment. "Leo, what are you doing?"

"Leo," Amelia managed to say, "you'll cause a fire. Careful."

"What is it?" Poppy demanded, looking bewildered. "What's happening?"

The glass fell into place, and the winter scene flickered on the wall once more.

Snow, sky, forest.

Nothing else.

"Come back," Leo muttered feverishly, rattling the lantern. "Come back. Come back."

"You're frightening me, Leo," Beatrix accused, hopping up and speeding to Amelia. "What's the matter with him?"

"Leo's foxed, that's all." Amelia said distractedly. "You know how he is when he's had too much to drink."

"He's never been like *this* before."

"It's time for bed," Win remarked. Worry seeped through her voice like a watermark on fine paper. "Bea . . . Poppy . . . let's go upstairs." She glanced at Merripen, who stood at once.

"But Leo's going to break my lantern," Beatrix exclaimed. "Leo, *do* stop. You're bending the slides!"

Since their brother was apparently beyond hearing or comprehension, Win and Merripen efficiently whisked the younger girls from the room. A questioning murmur from Merripen, and Win replied softly that she would explain in a moment.

When everyone had gone, and the sounds of voices had faded from the hallway, Amelia spoke carefully.

"I saw her too, Leo. So did Win."

Her brother didn't look at her, but his hands stilled on the lantern. After a moment he removed the slide and put it back in again. His hands were shaking. The sight of such raw misery was difficult to bear. Amelia stood and approached him. "Leo, please talk to me. Please—"

"Leave me alone." He half-shielded his face from her regard, palm turned outward.

"Someone has to stay with you." The room was getting colder. A tremor began at the top of Amelia's spine and worked downward.

"I'm fine." A few stunted breaths. With a titanic effort, Leo lowered his hand and stared at her with strange, light eyes. "I'm fine, Amelia. I just need . . . I want . . . a little time alone."

"But I want to talk about what we saw right in front of us."

"It was nothing." He was sounding calmer by the second. "It was just an illusion."

"It was Laura's face. You and Win and I all saw it!"

"We all saw the same shadow." The barest hint of wry amusement edged his lips. "Come, sis, you're too rational to believe in ghosts."

"Yes, but . . ." She was reassured by the familiar mockery in his tone, but she didn't like the way he kept one hand on the side of the lamp as if his skin had been fused to the perforated metal.

"Go on," he urged gently. "As you said, it's late. You need to rest. I'll be all right."

Amelia hesitated, her arms chilled and stinging beneath the sleeves of her gown. "If you really want—"

"Yes. Go on."

She did, reluctantly. A draught from somewhere seemed to rush past her as she left the room. She hadn't intended to close the door fully, but it snapped shut like the jaws of a hungry animal.

It was difficult to make herself walk away. She wanted to protect her brother from something.

She just didn't know what it was.

AFTER REACHING HER ROOM, AMELIA CHANGED INTO HER favorite nightgown. The white flannel was thick and shrunken from many washings, the high collar and long sleeves textured with white work embroidery that Win had done. The chill she had taken downstairs was slow to fade, even after she had crawled beneath the bedclothes and curled tightly into a ball. She should have thought to light a fire at the hearth. She should do it now to make the room warmer, but the idea of climbing out of bed was too daunting.

Instead, she occupied her mind with thoughts of hot things: a cup of tea, a woolen shawl, a steaming bath, a foot-warming brick. Gradually, body heat accumulated around her, and she relaxed enough to sleep.

But it was a troubled rest. She had the impression of arguing with people in her dreams, back-and-forth conversations that made no sense. Shifting, rolling to her stomach, her side, her back, she tried to ignore the bothersome dreams.

Now there were voices . . . Poppy's voice, actually . . . and no matter how she tried to ignore it, the sound persisted.

"Amelia. Amelia!"

She heaved herself up on her elbows, blind and confused from the sudden awakening. Poppy was by her bed.

"What is it?" Amelia mumbled, scraping back a tangled curtain of hair from her face.

At first, Poppy's face was disembodied in the darkness, but as Amelia's eyes adjusted, the rest of her became dimly visible.

"I smell smoke," Poppy said.

Such words were never used lightly, nor could they ever be dismissed without investigation. Fire was an ever-present concern no matter where one lived. It could start in any number of ways, from overturned candles, lamps, sparks that leapt from the hearth or embers from coal-burning ovens. And fire in a house this old would be nothing less than disaster.

Struggling from the bed, Amelia hunted for the slipper box near the end of the bed. She stubbed her toe and hopped and cursed.

"Here, I'll fetch them." Poppy lifted the tin lid of the slipper box and took the shoes out, while Amelia found a shawl.

They linked arms and made their way through the dark room with the caution of elderly cats.

Reaching the top of the stairs, Amelia sniffed hard but could detect nothing other than the familiar accumulation of cleaning soap, wax, dust, and lamp-oil. "I don't smell any smoke."

"Your nose isn't awake. Try again."

This time, there was a definite stench of something burning. Alarm speared through her. She thought of Leo, alone with the lantern . . . and she knew instantly what had happened.

"Merripen!" The whip-crack force of her voice caused Poppy to jump. Amelia gripped her sister's arm to steady her. "Get Merripen. Wake everyone up. Make as much noise as you can."

Poppy obeyed at once, scampering toward her siblings' bedrooms while Amelia made her way downstairs. A sullen glow came from the direction of the parlor, ominous light bleeding beneath the door.

"Leo!" She flung the door open and recoiled at a furnace blast that struck her entire body. One entire wall was covered in flame, rippling and curling upward in hot tentacles. Through a bitter haze of smoke, her brother's bulky form was visible on the floor. She ran to him, grasped the folds of his shirt, and tugged so hard that the cloth began to give and the seams crackled. "Leo, get up, get up *now!*" But Leo was insensible.

Shrieking at him to wake up and gather his wits, Amelia tugged and dragged without success. Frustrated tears sprang to her smoke-stung eyes. But then Merripen was there, pushing her aside none too gently. Bending, he picked Leo up and hoisted him over a broad shoulder with a grunt. "Follow me," he said brusquely to Amelia. "The girls are already outside."

"I'll come out in just a moment. I have to run upstairs and fetch some things—"

He gave her a dangerous glance. "No."

"But we have no clothes—it's all going to go up—"

"*Out!*"

Since Merripen had never raised his voice to her in all the years they had known each other, Amelia was startled into obeying. Her eyes continued to smart and water from the smoke even after they had gone through the front door and out to the waiting darkness of the graveled drive. Win and Poppy were there, both huddled around Leo and trying to coax him into waking and sitting up. Like Amelia, the girls were dressed only in nightgowns, shawls, and slippers.

"Where's Beatrix?" Amelia asked. At the same moment, the estate bell began to peal, its high, clear tone traveling in every direction.

"I told her to ring it," Win said. The sound would bring neighbors and villagers to help, although by the time people reached them, Ramsay House would probably be consumed in flames.

Merripen went to lead the horse from the stable, in case that went up too.

"What's happening?" Amelia heard Leo ask hoarsely. Before anyone could reply, he was seized by a spasm of coughing. Win and Poppy remained beside their brother, murmuring gently to him. Amelia, however, stood a few yards apart from them, knotting her shawl more tightly around her shoulders.

She was filled with bitterness and fury and fear. There was no doubt in her mind Leo had started the fire, that he had cost them the house and had nearly succeeded in killing them all. It would be a long time before she could trust herself to speak to him, this sibling she had once loved so dearly, who now seemed to have transformed into someone else entirely.

At this point, there was little left of Leo to love. At best he was an object to be pitied, at worst a danger to himself and his family. They would all be better off without him, Amelia thought. Except that if he died, the title would pass to some distant relative or expire, and they would be left with no income whatsoever.

Watching Merripen illuminated in the cloud-blunted moonlight as he worked to pull first the horse and then the barouche from the stables, Amelia felt a surge of gratitude. What would they ever have done without him? When her father had taken in the homeless boy so long ago, it had always been regarded by the residents of Primrose Place as an act of charity. But the Hathaways had been infinitely repaid by Merripen's quiet, steady presence in their lives.

People had already begun to arrive on horseback—some from the village, some from the direction of Stony Cross Manor. The villagers had brought a handpump cart pulled by a sturdy draught horse. The wheeled card was sided by troughs that would be filled with river water by people carrying buckets back and forth. Cranking a wooden lever would push the water through a leather hose and expel it through a metal nozzle. By the time the process was underway, the fire would probably be raging out of control, but the handpump might help to save at least a portion of the house.

Amelia ran to the approaching villagers to describe the shortest route to the nearby river. Immediately a group of men, accompanied by Merripen, set off at a run toward the water, buckets swinging from the yokes on their shoulders.

As she turned to go back to her sisters, Amelia bumped into a big, dark form behind her. Gasping, she felt a familiar pair of hands close over her shoulders.

"Christopher." Relief flooded her at his presence, despite the fact that he could do nothing to save her home. She twisted to look up at him, his handsome features bathed in erratic light.

He pulled her close. "Thank God you're not hurt. How did the fire start?"

"I don't know." Amelia went still against him, thinking dazedly that she had never expected to be held by him again. But remembering that he'd betrayed her, she wriggled free and pushed her hair from her eyes.

Christopher released her reluctantly. "Stay away from the house. I'm going to help with the handpump."

Another voice came from the darkness. "You'll be of more use over there."

Amelia and Christopher both turned with a start, for the voice seemed to have come from nowhere. With his dark clothes and black hair, Cam Rohan seemed to emerge like a shadow from the night. His gaze ran over Amelia in swift assessment. "Have you been hurt?"

"No, but the house—" Her throat clenched on a sob.

Cam shrugged off his coat and settled it around her, pulling the edges together at the front. The wool was permeated with warmth and his comforting masculine scent. "We'll see what we can do." He gestured for Christopher Frost to come with him. "Two canisters are being unloaded near the stairs. You can help me carry them inside."

Amelia's eyes turned round at the sight of the two large metallic vessels. "What are they?"

"An invention of Captain Swansea's. They're filled with pearl ash solution. We're going to use it to keep the fire from spreading until they've primed the water pump." Rohan slid a glance toward Christopher Frost. "Since Swansea is too old to carry the containers, I'll take one and you take the other."

Amelia knew Christopher well enough to sense his dislike of taking orders, especially from a man he considered his inferior. But he surprised her by acceding without protest, and followed Cam to the burning house.

Chapter Fourteen

Amelia watched as Cam and Christopher Frost lifted the ungainly copper containers, which had been fitted with leather hosing, and hauled them past the front door. Captain Swansea remained on the steps, shouting instructions after them.

The windows were shot with lurid flashes as fire began to digest the interior of the house. Soon, Amelia thought bleakly, nothing would be left but a blackened skeleton.

Making her way back to her sisters, Amelia stood beside Win, who was cradling Leo's head in her lap. "How is he?"

"He's ill from the smoke." Win ran a gentle hand over her brother's disheveled head. "But I think he'll be all right."

Glancing down at Leo, Amelia muttered, "The next time you try to kill yourself, I'd appreciate it if you'd leave the rest of us out of it."

He gave no indication of having heard, but Win, Beatrix, and Poppy glanced at her in surprise.

"Not now, dear," Win said in gentle reproof.

Amelia stifled the hot words that rose to her lips and stared stonily at the house.

More people were arriving, some forming a line to pass

water buckets back and forth from the river to the handpump. There was no sign of activity from within the building. She wondered what Cam and Christopher were doing.

Win seemed to read her mind. "Captain Swansea finally has a chance to test his invention," she said.

"What invention?" Amelia asked. "And how do you know about it?"

"I sat next to him at supper, at Stony Cross Manor," Win replied. "He told me that during his experiments with rock-etry design, he had the idea for a device that would extinguish fires by spraying them with pearl ash solution. When the copper canister is upended, a vial of acid mixes with the solution, and it creates enough pressure to force the liquid from the canister."

"Would that work?" Amelia asked doubtfully.

"I certainly hope so."

They both flinched at the sound of breaking windows. The handpump crew was making an opening large enough to direct a stream of water into the burning room.

Becoming more worried by the moment, Amelia watched intently for any sign of Cam or Christopher, who had gone into a burning house with an untested device that could explode in their faces. Confronted by chemicals, smoke, and heat, they might have become disoriented or overwhelmed. Just as her anxiety rose to an unbearable level, they emerged from the house with the emptied canisters and were approached by Captain Swansea. She hurried forward with a cry of gladness, fully intending to stop once she reached them. Which was why it was a surprise when her legs insisted on carrying her forward.

Cam dropped the canister and caught her tightly. "Easy, hummingbird."

She had lost his coat and her shawl somewhere amid the impetuous dash. The cold night air pierced the thin layer of her gown, causing her to shiver. He gripped her more closely. His heartbeat was steady beneath her ear, his hand making circles on her back.

"The extinguishers were even more effective than I'd anticipated," she heard Captain Swansea say to Christopher. "Two or three more canisters, and I do believe we could have put it down by ourselves."

Collecting herself, Amelia looked out from the circle of Cam's arms. Christopher stared at her with disapproval and something that might have been jealousy. She knew she was making a spectacle of herself with Cam. Again. But she couldn't make herself leave the comforting shelter of his arms yet.

Captain Swansea was smiling, pleased with the results of his efforts. "The fire's under control now," he told her. "I should think they'll have it out quite soon."

"Captain, I'll never be able to thank you enough," she managed to say.

"I've been waiting for an opportunity like this," Swansea declared. "Although I certainly wouldn't have wished for your home to serve as the testing site." He turned around to view the progress with the handpump, which was now operating at full capacity.

"I'd like to go in and see what can be salvaged," Amelia said.

"Later," Cam interrupted calmly. "Right now, I'm taking you and the others to Stony Cross Park."

Before Amelia could reply, Christopher said, "I'm staying with the Shelsher family at the village tavern. The Hathaways can go there with me."

"Westcliff's home is closer," Cam said. "Miss Hathaway and her sisters are standing outside in the cold, dressed in little more than their nightgowns. Their brother needs to be seen by a doctor, and if I'm not mistaken, so does Merripen."

"What?" Amelia asked in concern. "Where is he?"

Cam turned her in his arms. "Over there, beside your sisters."

She gasped at the sight of Merripen huddled on the ground. Win was with him, attempting to pull the thin fabric of his shirt away from his back. "Oh, no." She hurried toward her family, ignoring Christopher as he called out her name. "What happened?" she asked, dropping to the damp ground beside Win. "Has he been burned?"

"Yes, on his back." Win ripped a makeshift bandage from the hem of her own gown. "Beatrix, would you take this, please, and soak it in water?"

Without a word, Beatrix scampered to the trough at the handpump.

Win stroked Merripen's thick, black hair as he rested his head on his forearms. His breath hissed through his teeth.

Win kept her hand on the nape of Merripen's neck as she spoke to Amelia. "He went too close to the eaves of the house. The heat from the fire caused the flashing on the shingles to melt. Some molten lead fell on his back." She glanced up as Beatrix returned with a dripping cloth. "Thank you, dear." Lifting Merripen's shirt, she laid the wet cloth over the burn, and he let out a low growl of pain. Losing all sense of pride or decorum, he let Win pillow his head on her lap while he shook uncontrollably.

Amelia realized Cam was right—she needed to take her family to Stony Cross Park and immediately send for a doctor.

She made no protest as Cam and Captain Swansea came to load the Hathaways into the carriage. Leo had to be lifted bodily into the vehicle, as did Merripen, who was unsteady and disoriented. Captain Swansea handled the ribbons deftly as he drove the family to Stony Cross Manor.

Upon their arrival, the Hathaways were greeted with considerable excitement and sympathy, servants running in all directions, houseguests volunteering extra clothes and personal items. After bathing and washing her hair, Amelia dressed in a white nightgown and blue velvet robe that a housemaid had brought. She braided her damp hair into a neat plait behind each ear and went to check on her siblings, starting with her brother.

A servant in the hallway directed her to Leo's room. The doctor, an elderly man with a neatly trimmed gray beard, was just leaving. He paused, bag in hand, as she asked about her brother's condition.

"All in all, Lord Ramsay is doing well," the doctor replied. "There is minor swelling of the throat—due to the smoke inhalation, of course—but it's mere tissue irritation rather than serious damage."

"Thank God. What about Merripen?"

"His condition is more serious. It's a nasty burn. But I've treated it and applied a honey dressing which should keep the bandage from sticking as it heals. I will return tomorrow to check on his progress."

"Thank you. Sir, I don't wish to trouble you—I know the hour is late—but could you spare a moment to visit one of my sisters? She has weak lungs, and even though she wasn't exposed to the smoke, she was out in the night air—"

"You're referring to Miss Winnifred."

"Yes."

"She was in Merripen's room. Apparently, he shared your concern over your sister's health. Both of them were arguing quite strenuously over which one of them I should see first."

"Oh." A faint smile came to her lips. "Who won? Merripen, I suppose."

He smiled back at her. "No, Miss Hathaway. Your sister may have weak lungs, but she has no end of resolve." He bowed to her. "I wish you good evening. My sympathies on your misfortune."

Amelia nodded in thanks and went into Leo's room, where the lamps had been turned down low. He was laying on his side, eyes open, but he didn't spare her a glance as she approached. Sitting on the side of the mattress with care, she reached out and smoothed his matted hair.

His voice was a soft croak. "Have you come to finish me off?"

She smiled wryly. "You seem to be doing an excellent job of that all by yourself." Her hand shaped tenderly over his skull. "How did the fire start, dear?"

He looked at her then, his eyes so bloodshot they resembled two tiny coaching road maps. "I don't remember. I fell asleep. I didn't set the fire on purpose. I hope you believe that."

"Yes." She leaned over and kissed his head as if he were a young boy. "Rest, Leo. Everything will be better in the morning."

"You always say that," he mumbled, closing his eyes. "Maybe someday it'll be true." And he fell asleep with startling quickness.

Hearing a noise at the door, Amelia looked up to see the housekeeper, who had brought a tray laden with brown glass bottles and bundles of dried herbs. Cam was just behind her, carrying a small open kettle filled with steaming water. He hadn't yet washed the smoke from his clothes and hair and skin. Although he must have been tired from the night's exertions, he showed no signs of it. He took Amelia in with an all-encompassing glance, his eyes as bright as brimstone in his smudged, sweat-streaked face.

"The steam will help Lord Ramsay breathe more comfortably during the night," the housekeeper explained. She proceeded to light the candles beneath a bedside holder, onto which the kettle was placed. "We've also brought morphine to help him sleep," she continued. "I'll leave it by the bedside, and if he awakens later—"

"No," Amelia said quickly. The last thing Leo needed was unsupervised access to a large bottle of morphine. "That won't be necessary."

"Yes, miss." The housekeeper departed with a quiet murmur to ring if anything was needed.

Cam remained in the room, casually leaning a shoulder against one towering bedpost. He watched as Amelia investigated the contents of the steam kettle.

"You must be exhausted," she said, picking up a sprig of dried leaves to smell them. "It's very late."

"I've spent most of my life in a gaming club. By now, I'm more or less nocturnal." He paused, his gaze sweeping over her. "You should go to bed."

Amelia shook her head. Somewhere beneath the clamor of her pulse and the raffle of worries in her mind, there was a great ache of weariness. But any attempt to sleep would be useless—she would simply lie there and stare at the ceiling. "My head is spinning like a carousel. The thought of sleep . . ." She shook her head.

"Would it help," he asked gently, "to have a shoulder to cry on?"

"Thank you, but no." Carefully she dropped the herbs into the kettle. "Crying's a waste of time."

He studied her, seeing too much, reading what simmered beneath the forced calm. "You have friends to help you through this, Amelia. I'm one of them."

Amelia was terrified for him to see her as an object of pity. She would avoid that at all cost. She couldn't lean on him, or anyone. If she did, she might never be able to stand on her own again. She moved away from him, around him, her hands fluttering as if to bat away any attempt to reach her. "You mustn't trouble yourself about the Hathaways. We'll manage. We always have."

"Not this time." Cam watched her steadily. "Your brother is beyond helping anyone, including himself. Your sisters are too young, except for Winnifred. And now even Merripen is bedridden."

"If you're trying to console me," she said dryly, "that's not helping." She reached for a length of toweling draped at the foot of the bed and folded it neatly. "You're leaving for London in the morning, aren't you? You should probably take your own advice and go to bed."

The light eyes turned flinty. "Why do you have to be stubborn? Is it pride or fear?"

"Neither. It's just that I don't want anything from you. And you deserve to find the freedom you've been deprived of for so long."

"Are you concerned about my freedom, or just terrified of admitting you need me?"

He was right—but she would rather have died than admit it. "I don't need anyone."

His voice was no less blistering for being soft. "You have no idea how much I want to prove you wrong." He began to reach for her and checked the movement.

"Maybe next lifetime," she whispered, somehow managing a crooked smile. "Please go. Please, Cam."

She waited tensely until he had left the room, and then her shoulders sagged with relief.

NEEDING TO ESCAPE THE SMOTHERING CONFINES OF THE house, Cam went outside. The night threaded weak moonlight through a weft of infinite darkness. He wandered to the ironstone wall that edged a bluff overlooking the river.

Hoisting himself easily to the top of the wall, he sat with his feet dangling over the edge and listened to the water and the night sounds. Smoke hung in the air, mingling with the scents of earth and forest.

Cam tried to sort through a tangle of emotions.

He had never known jealousy before, but when he had seen Amelia and Christopher Frost embracing earlier, he'd experienced a violent urge to strangle the bastard. Every instinct raged that Amelia was his, his alone to protect and comfort.

He should leave Hampshire, he thought. Amelia would make her own decision about Frost, and Cam would follow his destiny. No compromises or sacrifices on either side. He would never be anything more to Amelia than a brief episode in her life.

Lowering his head, he scrubbed his hands through his unruly hair. His chest ached in the way it always had when he yearned for freedom. But for the first time, he wondered if he was right about what he wanted. Because it didn't seem as if the pain would be cured when he left. In fact, it threatened to become a good deal worse.

The future spread before him in a great lifeless void. Thousands of nights without Amelia. He would hold and make love to other women, but none of them would ever be the one he truly wanted.

He thought of Amelia living as a spinster. Or worse, reconciling with Frost, perhaps marrying him, but always living with the knowledge that Frost had betrayed her once and might again. She deserved so much more than that. She deserved passionate, heart-scalding, overwhelming, consuming love. She deserved . . .

Oh, hell. He was thinking too much.

He forced himself to face the truth. Amelia was his, whether he stayed or left, whether they walked the same path or not. They could live on opposite sides of the world, and she would still be his.

THE HOUSEHOLD EVENTUALLY SETTLED INTO A RESTIVE SI-lence, with questions and tasks and decisions to be faced on the morrow. For now, however, all that could wait.

Amelia's bed was soft and luxurious, but it might as well have been made of bare wood planks. She rolled, turned, sprawled, but she could find no comfortable position for her aching body, and no peace for her tortured brain.

The room was still and stuffy, the air turning thicker by the minute. Craving a breath of clear, cold air, she slipped from the bed, went to the window, and pushed it open. A gasp of relief escaped her as a light breeze swept over her. She closed her sore eyes and used her knuckles to rub at her wet lashes.

It was strange, but with all the problems she faced, the thing that kept her from sleeping was the question of whether or not Christopher Frost had ever really loved her. She had wanted to think so, even after he had abandoned her. She had told herself that love was a luxury for most people, that Christopher's career was a difficult one, and he'd been faced with an impossible choice. He had done what he'd thought best at the time. Perhaps it had been wrong of her to expect him to choose her and damn the consequences.

To be wanted, needed, desired above all else . . . that would never happen to her.

The door opened in a well-oiled arc. She saw the shadows change, felt a presence in the room. Turning with a start, she saw Cam standing just inside the door. Her heart began to drum with furious force.

He approached her slowly. The closer he came, the more it seemed everything around her was unraveling, falling away, leaving her exposed and vulnerable. His breathing wasn't quite steady. Neither was hers.

After a long pause, he spoke. "Roma believe you should take the road that calls to you, because you never know what adventures await." He reached for her slowly, giving her every opportunity to object. Through the cottony gauze of her nightgown, he touched the curve of her hips. He brought her close into his hard weight. "Let's take this road," he murmured, "and see where it leads." He waited for a signal, some syllable of objection or encouragement. And she found herself reaching for him.

He smoothed her hair, whispering for her not to fear him, he would take care of her, please her. His fingers found the sensitive curve of her scalp, cradling her head as he kissed her. He dragged his mouth across hers, again and again, and when her lips were open and damp, he sealed them with his.

Excitement flooded her, and she opened to the penetrating strokes of his tongue, struggling to capture the silkiness. His hands gently urged her backward until she lay on the tumbled bed. Bending over her, Cam kissed her throat. There was a series of quick tugs at the front of her gown, and the edges of the garment parted.

She felt his urgency, the heat radiating from his body, but every movement was careful, lingering, as he reached beneath the fragile cotton and caressed her breast. Her knees drew up, her entire body arching to contain the pleasure of his touch. With a wordless sound, Cam coaxed her to relax, his hand gliding from her chest to her knees. His parted lips brushed the naked tip of her breast, toying with the hardening bud, his tongue skimming wetly. She brought her hands to his hair, tangling her fingers in the ebony locks, trying to hold him to her.

In a moment, she reached for his shirt with trembling hands. It was loose cut and collarless, the kind that lifted over the head instead of unbuttoning. Cam moved to help her, pulling the garment off and tossing it aside. Moonlight gilded the supple, muscular lines of his body, his chest taut and smooth.

Flattening her palms against the hard flesh, she drew them gently downward to his sides and around his back. He shivered at her touch and lowered to the place beside her, one leg sliding between hers. The gown fell open to expose her chest completely, the hem bunching high on her thighs.

His lips descended to her breast again while he cupped and kneaded the firm flesh. Arching up to him, she struggled to press closer, to bring his weight more fully over her. He resisted, his hands traveling over her in caresses meant to calm her. She quivered at his gentleness, her hands gripping his back. She couldn't think clearly, couldn't find words. Twisting against him, she felt the desire sharpen to unbearable intensity.

The kisses turned harder, longer, sweeter. Grasping her hand in his, Cam brought it down his body to the urgent thrust of his erection. Shocked and fascinated, Amelia eased her hand along the length of him, her fingers molding hesitantly over the hardness. Cam groaned as if in pain, and she snatched her hand back at once.

"I'm terribly sorry," Amelia said, flushing. "I didn't mean to hurt you."

"You didn't hurt me." There was a flick of tender amusement in his voice. He caught her hand and brought it back down.

She explored him slowly, her curiosity stirred by the heat and suggestion of movement beneath the taut fabric of his breeches. He seemed to revel in her touch, nearly purring as he moved over her to nuzzle and lick at her throat.

Both his legs were between hers now, widening the space between them. The nightgown crumpled around her waist.

Exposed, embarrassed, excited, she felt one of his hands roaming low on her stomach. Soon there would be pain and possession, all mysteries solved. She thought perhaps now would be an opportune time to mention something.

"Cam?"

His head lifted. "Yes?"

"I've heard there are ways—that is, since this can lead to—and I certainly don't want—I hope you know how to do this without—"

"You don't want me to give you a baby." His fingertips played gently through her intimate dark curls.

She nodded, her breath tangling around a moan.

"I won't. Although . . . there's always a chance." He found a place so alive with sensation that she jerked and drew her knees up. His fingers were light and gentle, parting the soft flesh. "The question, love, is whether you want me enough to take the risk."

Amelia pulled in several deep, quick breaths, her senses swimming in shame and pleasure at the way he touched her. Her entire existence had dwindled to the sly teasing of one fingertip. And Cam knew exactly what he was doing. Artful and tender, he toyed with her while his wicked mouth descended to her breast.

"Yes," she said unsteadily. "I want you."

The pad of his thumb stroked downward, away from where she most wanted it, and she wriggled in mute objection. But she went still as she felt his touch gliding through a patch of inexplicable wetness. Before she could say a word, he had pressed into the moisture with his thumb, invading her slightly.

His lashes lowered. "Do you want this?" he whispered.

She nodded and tried to say *yes*, but all that came out was a low whimper.

Deeper, a gently inquiring stroke, until she felt the hard

ridge of his thumb ring press against the entrance of her body. He made slow circles inside her, the smooth ring teasing and rubbing until she felt faint and hot, ripples of delight running through her. Another swirl, another, each one coiling the pleasure tighter until her heart was thundering and her hips nudged rhythmically against the heel of his hand. But then, the exquisite invasion was withdrawn, and her body clasped desperately around the emptiness. "Cam . . . oh, please . . ."

Cam had the effrontery to laugh softly. "Easy, sweetheart. There's no need to hurry through it." He kissed the inside of her elbow, working his way down to her wrist. "The point is to make it last as long as possible."

"Why?"

"It's better that way. For both of us." He pried her clenched fingers apart and kissed the palm of her hand. "You'll find out."

After pulling her nightgown back into place, he buttoned the front with meticulous care. "What are you doing?" she asked.

"Taking you for a ride." As she sputtered with questions, he touched a gentle forefinger to her lips.

Amelia complied in a daze as he pulled her from the bed, wrapped the velvet robe around her, and tucked her feet into soft slippers.

Clasping her hand firmly in his, Cam led her from the room. The house was still and soundless, the walls hung with portraits of aristocrats with disapproving faces.

They went out the back of the house to the great stone terrace, its wide curving steps leading down to the gardens. The moonlight was crossed with shredded clouds that glowed against a sky the color of black plums. Puzzled but willing, Amelia went with Cam to the bottom of the steps.

He stopped and gave a short whistle.

"What—" Amelia blinked in bewilderment as she heard

the sound of approaching hooves. It was a sleek black horse, his breaths rising like wraiths in the raw air. "Is this really happening?" she asked doubtfully.

Cam reached in his pocket, fed the horse a sugar lump, and ran his hand over the sleek midnight neck. "Have you ever had a dream like this?"

"Never."

"Then it must be happening."

"This is your horse?" At Cam's nod, she asked, "What's his name?"

"Can't you guess?"

Amelia thought for a moment. "Pooka?" The horse turned his head to look at her as if he understood. "Pooka," she repeated with a faint smile.

Walking to the horse's side, Cam swung up onto the pack-saddle in a graceful movement. He sidled close to the step on which Amelia was standing and reached down to her. She took his hand, managing to gain a foothold on the stirrup. She was lifted easily onto the saddle in front of him. Momentum carried her a little too far, but Cam's arm locked around her, keeping her in place.

Amelia leaned back into the hard cradle of his chest and arm. Her nostrils were filled with the scents of autumn, damp earth, horse, and man.

"You knew I'd come with you," she said.

Cam leaned over her, kissing her temple. "I only hoped." His thighs tightened, setting the horse to a gallop, and then a smooth canter. And when Amelia closed her eyes, she could have sworn they were flying.

Chapter Fifteen

Cam rode to the abandoned river encampment where the Romany tribe had stayed. The remains of the camp were still there: the ruts left by the wheels of the *vardos*, circles of grass eaten where the cobs had been tethered, the shallow fire pit filled with ash. And everywhere there was the sound of the sloshing, rushing river, pushing at the banks, soaking the yielding earth.

Earlier, Amelia had said she could manage without him. Cam believed her. But that didn't mean she didn't need him. And when he'd thought about leaving, knowing what she would face without him, every part of him had revolted.

He dismounted and helped Amelia to the ground. At his direction, she sat on a fallen birch log while he set up a makeshift camp. She waited with her hands folded neatly in her lap, watching his every movement as he pulled a bundle of thick blankets from the packsaddle. In a few minutes, he had made a fire in the stone-circled pit and laid out a pallet beside it.

As soon as he'd spread the blankets, Amelia hurried to it and burrowed beneath the layers of wool and quilted cotton. "Are we safe out here?" she asked in a muffled voice.

"You're safe from everything but me." Smiling, Cam lowered himself beside her. After removing his boots, he joined her beneath the blankets and pulled her against him. Reminding himself of the rewards to be gained by patience, he cuddled her close and waited.

The fire flicked and snapped its yellow ribbons, lapping at broken birch and oak until its heat blistered the air. Despite the cold night, it soon became warm beneath the blankets, and Amelia's inquisitive hands crept beneath the loose hem of his shirt. The small, cool fingers roamed over his skin, and it felt so good that Cam let out a faint groan against her hair. She grasped loose handfuls of the shirt and tugged upward. Without hesitation, he sat up, stripped the garment off, and tossed it aside.

Amelia crawled into his lap, her hair streaming over his naked chest and shoulders in a silken net. Entranced, Cam held still as she pressed her mouth to his chest, his shoulders, and the base of his throat in a frolic of kisses.

His pulse began a hard, rolling drum, the heat thickening between every beat. He cradled her face in his hands, guiding her to look at him. "*Monisha.* I won't do anything you don't want. I only want to give you pleasure."

Her face was glowing in the firelight, her lips slightly swollen from his kisses. He couldn't stop staring at her mouth, the soft color of red currant wine.

"What does that word mean?" she asked.

"*Monisha*? An endearment." Cam lowered her to the blankets in a pool of dancing firelight. He opened her robe and gown, dreamily pulling the soft fabric away from the deep curves of her breasts and waist. She was so beautifully made, lush and firm, shadowed in the places he yearned to touch and taste. He followed her spreading blush with his mouth, and she shivered beneath him, her hands gripping the bulging muscles of his upper arms.

Cupping her breasts, he teased the peaks with his breath and tongue until they were hard and silken. Softly, he drew one between his teeth and held it there until she whimpered and lifted upward. He tugged at the tangled layer of her gown between them and slid lower to kiss her stomach.

"Cam . . . oh, wait . . ." She was squirming now, pushing at him in earnest. He caught her hands and gripped them close against her body.

Fighting for self-control, he laid his cheek against her skin with all the gentleness he was capable of. "I won't hurt you," he whispered. He let his fingers drift over her hip and thigh, into the soft curls. "I want to know every part of you, *monisha* . . . Hold still for me and . . . yes, love, yes . . ." He nuzzled between her thighs, shaking with hunger at the intimate scent of her. He licked the seam of softly closed lips, stroking her open, delving into the heat and silkiness.

Amelia was silent except for her broken gasps, her legs clamping hard against his sides. Helplessly, she followed the sinuous movements of his tongue, her entire body arching and yearning. He slid a finger inside her, thrusting in counterpoint, the rhythm steady and even.

She made a sound of distress as she lost all self-control, and he gloried in it. He drew out the torment, licking at every twitch and throb. After a while, she reached down to the fastenings of his breeches and worked at them until the garment was loose around his hips. The hard length of his erection sprang free. Her hand curled around the shaft as she tried to guide him in place, while instinctively making an open cradle of her hips and legs.

Murmuring gently, he fit his hips to hers and thrust inside her.

Amelia flinched and cried out. Cam tried to soothe away the pain, stroking her, kissing her throat and breasts. Taking a nipple into his mouth, he sucked lightly and ran his tongue over it until she relaxed and began to moan. He couldn't stop from moving then, easing deeper into the gently gripping flesh, beginning a rhythm. Release approached swiftly, and he let it happen, not wanting to make her any more sore than necessary. Just before the culmination, he withdrew and thrust against her stomach. Heat jetted and slid between them. Cam buried his head in the crook of her neck and shoulder, groaning. No feeling had ever come close to this, he thought dizzily. Nothing ever would, unless it was with her.

It took a long time for his heartbeat to return to normal. Amelia had gone lax beneath him, drowsing and sighing. He had had to force himself to withdraw, when all he wanted was to linger and revel in the feel of her. After using a hand-kerchief to clean the blood and moisture from her body, he dressed her in her nightgown, and went to replenish the fire. When he returned to settle beneath the blankets, Amelia snuggled in the crook of his arm.

Relishing the trusting weight of her head on his shoulder, Cam watched over her while she slept. He pulled a quilt higher over her shoulder and stroked back a curl that had looped over her ear. Everything had changed, he thought. And there was no going back.

Chapter Sixteen

Daybreak.

A perfect word for the way the morning had entered the bedroom in pieces—a shard of light falling across her bed, another on the floor between the window and the small hearth.

Amelia blinked and lay for a while in a torpor. There was a fire in the hearth—she must have slept right through the maid lighting the grate.

Fire . . . Ramsay House . . . the memory fell on her with an unpleasant thud, and she closed her eyes. They flew open again, however, as she thought of darkness and blue moonlight and warm male flesh. Goose bumps raised all over her.

What had she done?

She was in her bed with only a murky recollection of riding back when it was still dark, Cam carrying her, tucking the soft mass of bedclothes around her as if she were a child . . . *"Go to sleep,"* he had murmured, his hand a comforting pressure on her skull. And she had slept and slept. Now as she squinted at the cheerfully ticking mantel clock, she saw that it was nearly noon.

Panic thrashed inside her until she reminded herself that

it was impractical to panic. Nevertheless, her heart pumped something that seemed too hot and light to be blood, and her breath turned choppy.

She would have liked to persuade herself that it had all been a dream, but her body still retained the feel of him, the invisible map he had drawn all over her with his lips, tongue, teeth, hands.

Raising her fingertips to her lips, Amelia felt that they were puffier, smoother than usual . . . they had been licked and abraded by his mouth. Every inch of her body felt sensitive, the most tender places still harboring an ache of pleasure.

The night had been so extraordinary, so rich and dark and sweet, she would hoard it in some distant corner of her memory forever. It had been an experience not to be missed, with a man unlike anyone she had ever known or would ever meet again.

She rang for a maid, and fumbled to fasten her robe. In less than a minute, a sturdy light-haired maid with apple cheeks appeared.

"May I have some hot water?" Amelia asked.

"Aye, miss. I can bring some up. If tha like, I can draw a bath for thee."

"Yes, please." Amelia followed the maid out of the room. "How are my sisters and brothers? And Mr. Merripen?"

"Miss Winnifred, Miss Poppy, and Miss Beatrix have all gone downstairs for breakfast," the maid reported. "The two gentlemen are still in their rooms."

"How is Merripen? Does he have a fever?"

"I don't know, miss."

Amelia resolved to check on Merripen as soon as she was presentable. Burn wounds were dangerous and unpredictable— she was still quite worried for his sake.

They entered a room with walls covered in pale blue tiling.

There was a chaise longue in one corner and a large porcelain tub in another. The bath water was heated by some kind of gas apparatus, with taps for cold, hot or tepid water, and pipes leading outside.

The housemaid opened the taps and adjusted the water temperature. She laid out bath linens across the chaise longue in a precise row. "Shall I attend while thee bathe, miss?"

"No, thank you," Amelia said at once. "I'll manage by myself. If you wouldn't mind bringing—" She broke off as she realized everything she owned had been burned in the fire. "I have nothing to wear," she muttered.

"Lady St. Vincent had some of her dresses put in your room, miss—she and thee are of a size, more or less. There's a lovely red woolen—I'll fetch it for thee."

"How generous of her. Thank you." After the maid shut off the taps and left, Amelia began to undress, and paused in surprise as she saw a flash of gold on her left forefinger. It was a small signet ring with an elaborate engraved initial. Cam must have put it on her last night while she was sleeping. Had he meant it as a parting gift?

She tried to pull it off and discovered it was firmly stuck. With a sigh, she finished undressing, picked up a cake of soap, and brought it into the bath with her. The hot water was lovely, soothing her aching body and easing the soreness between her thighs.

Amelia soaped her hand and tried to remove the ring, but it still wouldn't budge. Soon the surface of the bath water was covered with soap froth, and she was cursing with frustration. She couldn't let anyone see her wearing one of Cam's rings. How in God's name was she supposed to explain it?

After pulling and twisting until the knuckle was swollen, Amelia gave up and finished her bath. She dried herself with a Turkish towel, its pile loose and soft against her skin. Entering the adjoining dressing room, she found Betty waiting for her with an armload of soft wine-colored wool and crisp white undergarments.

"Here is the frock, miss. It will look right pretty on thee, with thy dark hair."

After dressing in the soft, beautifully made clothes, Amelia sat while the maid arranged her hair in a braided coil at the back of her head. "How long has Lady St. Vincent been acquainted with Mr. Rohan?" Amelia asked casually.

"Since childhood, miss. That Mr. Rohan, he's a fine doorful of man, aye? Tha should see the carryings-on when he visits. Every last one of us fighting for a turn at the keyhole, just to gawp at him."

"I wonder . . ." Amelia strove for a casual tone. "Do you think the relationship between Mr. Rohan and Lady St. Vincent was ever . . ."

"Oh, nay, miss. They were raised like brother and sister. But she's fair fond of him." With a wry smile, Betty added, "She has warned me and the other maids to keep ourse'en far away from him. She says no good could come of it, and we'd be tupped and left." Finishing Amelia's hair, Betty viewed her with satisfaction and went to collect the used linens that had been heaped by a chair, including the discarded nightgown.

The maid paused for the measure of two, three seconds, with the nightgown in hand. "Shall I make a pad of clean rags, miss?" she asked carefully. "For thy monthly courses?"

Still pondering the disagreeable phrase "tupped and left," Amelia shook her head. "No, thank you. It's not time for—" She stopped with a little shock as she saw what the maid had noticed—a few rusty spots of blood on the nightgown. She blanched.

"Aye, miss." Folding the gown tightly into the bundle of bedlinens, Betty gave her a neutral smile. "Tha has only to ring, and I'll come." She went to the door and let herself out carefully.

Amelia propped her elbows on the dressing table, and rested her forehead on her fists. Heaven help her, there would be talk belowstairs. And until now she had never done anything worthy of gossip.

"Please, *please* let him be gone," she whispered.

As Amelia headed downstairs, she decided she did believe in luck after all. It seemed as good a word as any to describe a consistent pattern of things. A dependable, predictable outcome for nearly every situation.

And hers happened to be *bad* luck.

As she reached the entrance hall, she saw Lady St. Vincent coming in from the back terrace, her cheeks wind brightened, the hem of her gown littered with bits of leaves and grass. She looked like an untidy angel with her lovely, calm face, rippling red hair, and the playful spray of light-gold freckles across her nose.

"How are you feeling today?" Lady St. Vincent asked warmly. "You look lovely. Your sisters are walking outside, except for Winnifred, who's having tea on the terrace. Have you eaten yet?"

Amelia shook her head.

"Come to the back terrace, we'll have a tray brought out."

"If I'm interrupting—"

"N-not at all," Lady St. Vincent, who had a slight stammer, said gently. "Come."

Amelia went with her.

"My lady," she said, "Thank you for letting me wear one of your dresses. I'll return it as soon as possible—"

"Call me Evie. And you must k-keep the dress. It is very becoming on you, and not at all on me. That shade of red clashes with my hair."

"You're too kind," Amelia said, wishing she didn't sound

so stiff, wishing she could accept the gift without feeling the weight of obligation.

But Evie didn't seem to notice her awkwardness, just reached for her hand and drew it through her arm as they walked, as if Amelia needed to be led like a young girl. "Your sisters will be relieved to see you up and about. They said it was the f-first time they could ever remember you staying abed so long."

"I'm afraid I didn't sleep well. I was . . . preoccupied." Color climbed up the pale slopes of Amelia's cheeks as she thought of lying next to Cam's body, their clothes disheveled to reveal places of bareness and heat, lips and hands delicately investigating.

"Yes, I'm sure you—" A quick hesitation, then Evie continued in a bemused tone. "I'm s-sure you had much to think about."

Following her gaze, Amelia realized that Evie had glanced down at the hand that rested on her sleeve.

She'd seen the ring.

Amelia's fingers curled. She looked up into the countess's curious blue eyes, and her mind went blank.

"It's all right," Evie said, catching Amelia's hand when she would have withdrawn it, pressing it back to her arm. She smiled. "I thought he wasn't qu-quite himself today. Now I understand why."

There was no need to clarify who "he" was.

"My lady . . . Evie . . . there is nothing between Mr. Rohan and myself. Nothing." Her cheeks burned with agitated color. "I don't know what you must think of me."

They paused before the French doors that opened onto the back terrace, and Amelia withdrew her hand from Evie's arm to tug frantically at the ring. It remained stubbornly clamped on her finger.

"I think you're a capable young woman," Evie said, "who

loves her family and bears a great deal of r-responsibility for them. I think that's a heavy burden for a woman to carry alone. I also think you have a gift for accepting people as they are, no matter what their eccentricities. And Cam knows how rare that is."

"Is he still here?"

"He's talking with my husband and Lord Westcliff. They rode to Ramsay House early this morning to see what was left of it and make some early assessments."

Amelia didn't like the thought of them visiting the property without consulting her first. She squared her shoulders. "That was very kind of them, but I can manage the situation now. I expect part of Ramsay House is still habitable, which means we won't need to prevail on Lord and Lady Westcliff's hospitality any longer."

"Oh, you mustn't leave," Evie said quickly. "Lillian has already said you are w-welcome to stay here until Ramsay House is fully restored. This is such a large place, you would never intrude on anyone's privacy. And the Westcliffs are leaving for Bristol soon—along with my husband and I—to visit Lillian's younger sister Daisy, who's expecting a child. So you'll have the manor to yourselves."

"We'd reduce the place to a heap of rubble by the time they return."

Evie smiled. "I suspect your family isn't as dangerous as all that."

"You don't know the Hathaways." Feeling a strong need to assert control over the situation, Amelia said, "After breakfast, I'll ride to Ramsay House and make my own assessments."

"Perhaps you sh-should speak to Cam first," Evie suggested.

"He has nothing to do with my decisions."

"Forgive me. I shouldn't make assumptions. It's just that

the ring on your finger . . . Cam's worn it since he was twelve years old." She pushed the French doors open for Amelia. "Your sisters are outside," she said. "I'll have a tray sent out."

It was a damp, brisk day, the air saturated with the scents of mulch and roses and late flowering grasses. The back terrace overlooked acres of meticulously tended gardens, all connected by graveled pathways. Tables and chairs had been set upon the flagstone floor. Since most of Lord Westcliff's guests had departed at the conclusion of the latest hunting party, the terrace was largely unoccupied.

Seeing Win, Poppy, and Beatrix at a table, Amelia went to them eagerly. "How are you?" she asked Win. "Did you sleep well? Did you cough?"

"I'm quite well. We were worried about you—I've never known you to sleep so long, unless you are ill."

"Oh no, not ill, couldn't be better." Amelia glanced at her other sisters, who were both wearing new gowns, Poppy in yellow and Beatrix in green. "Why, Beatrix . . . how pretty you look."

Smiling, Beatrix stood and executed a slow turn for her. The pale green dress, with its intricately pleated bodice and dark green corded trim, fit almost perfectly, the skirts falling down to the floor. "Lady Westcliff gave it to me," she said. "It belonged to her younger sister who can't wear it any longer because she's in confinement."

"Oh, Bea . . ." Seeing her sister's pleasure in the grown-up dress, Amelia felt a pang of regret. Beatrix should attend a finishing school, where she would learn French and flower arranging and all the social graces the rest of the Hathaways lacked. But there was no money for that—and at this rate, there never would be.

She felt Win's hand slip into hers and give it a small squeeze.

"Amelia," Win murmured, "sit by me. I want to ask you something."

Amelia lowered herself in the chair, which gave her a perfect vantage of the gardens. There was a sharp pang of recognition in her chest as she saw a trio of men walking slowly along a yew hedge, Cam's dark and graceful form among them. Like his companions, Cam wore riding breeches and tall leather boots. But instead of the traditional riding coat and waistcoat, he wore a white shirt topped with a jerkin, an open collarless vest made of thin leather. A breeze played in the black layers of his hair, lifting the glossy locks and letting them settle.

As the three men walked, Cam interacted with his surroundings in a way the other two didn't, picking a stray leaf from the hedge, running his palm across the coppery tails of maiden grass. But Amelia was certain he didn't miss a word of the conversation.

Although nothing could possibly have alerted him to Amelia's presence, he paused and looked over his shoulder in her direction. Even across the distance of twenty yards, meeting his gaze gave her a small shock. Every hair on her body lifted.

"Amelia," Win asked, "Have you come to some kind of arrangement with Mr. Rohan?"

Amelia's mouth went dry. She buried her left hand, the one with the ring, in the folds of her skirt. "Of course not. Where would you get such an idea?"

"He and Lord Westcliff and Lord St. Vincent have been talking ever since they returned from Ramsay House this morning. I couldn't help overhearing some of their conversation when they were on the terrace. And the things that were said—the way Mr. Rohan phrased himself—it sounded as if he were speaking for us."

"What do you mean, speaking for us?" Amelia asked indignantly. "No one speaks for the Hathaways except me. Or Leo."

"He seems to be making decisions about what needs to be done, and when." Win added in an abashed whisper, "As if he were the head of the family."

Amelia was flooded with indignation. "But he has no right . . . I don't know why he would think . . . oh, Lord."

This had to be stopped right away.

"Are you all right, dear?" Win asked in concern. "You look distressed. Here, have some of my tea."

Aware that all three of her sisters were staring at her with round eyes, Amelia took the china cup and drained it in a few gulps.

"How long are we going to stay here, Amelia?" Beatrix asked. "I like it much better than our house."

Before Amelia could answer, Poppy joined in with, "Where did that pretty ring come from?"

Amelia stood abruptly. "Excuse me, dears." She strode across the terrace and hurried down the curving steps to the garden walk.

As she approached the three men, who had paused beside a stone urn filled with dahlias, Amelia overheard a few snatches of conversation, such as ". . . extend the existing foundation . . ." and ". . . the remainder of quarried stone from Jenner's and have it carted here . . ."

Surely they couldn't be talking about Ramsay House, she thought with increasing alarm. Her family couldn't afford the materials and labor to rebuild.

Becoming aware of her presence, the three men turned. Cam's face was unreadable, his gaze traveling over her in a quick, thorough sweep.

"Good day, gentlemen." Amelia steeled herself not to blush as she stared up at Cam. "Mr. Rohan, I had thought you would have been gone by now."

"I'll be leaving for London soon. But I'll return within a week with an architect and engineer to appraise the condition of Ramsay House."

Amelia was shaking her head even before he had finished. "Mr. Rohan, I don't wish to sound ungrateful, but that won't be necessary. My brother and I will decide how to proceed."

"Your brother's in no condition to decide anything."

Lord Westcliff broke in. "Miss Hathaway, you're welcome to stay at Stony Cross Manor indefinitely."

"You're very generous, my lord. But if Ramsay House is no longer habitable, we'll move into the gatehouse on the approach road."

"That place is too small for the lot of you," Cam said. "And it's in bad condition."

"That's none of your business, Mr. Rohan."

Cam stared at her intently. "We need to talk privately," he said.

"No, we don't." All her nerves shrilled in warning as she saw the glances the three men exchanged.

"With your permission," Lord Westcliff murmured, "St. Vincent and I will take our leave."

"No," Amelia said swiftly, "you don't have to go, really, there's no need . . ." Her voice faded as they walked away.

"I told them we're betrothed," Cam said, taking her arm and guiding her to the other side of the yew, where they couldn't be observed from the house.

"Why?"

"Because we are."

"*What?*"

They stopped in the concealment of the hedge. Aghast, Amelia looked up into the heathen depths of his eyes. "Are you mad?" she asked faintly.

Taking her hand, Cam lifted it until the ring gleamed in the daylight. "You're wearing my ring. You slept with me.

Many Roma would say that constitutes full-blown marriage. But to make certain it's legal, we'll do it the *gadje* way as well."

"We'll do no such thing." Amelia snatched her hand from his and backed away. "I'm only wearing this ring because it's stuck on my finger."

"But you did sleep with me," he pointed out.

She flushed and turned to walk along a graveled path. "That didn't mean anything."

Cam kept pace with her. "It meant something to me. The sexual act is sacred to a Rom."

"What about all the ladies you seduced in London?" she asked dryly. "Was it sacred when you slept with them, too?"

"For a while, I fell into the impure ways of *gadje*," he said innocently. "Now I've reformed."

She rolled her eyes. "You don't want this. You don't want me."

He caught her from behind and eased her to a halt. "Please, *monisha*. Stop running and listen. I do want you. I want you even knowing if I marry you, I'll have an instant family, complete with a suicidal brother-in-law and a Romany houseboy with the temperament of a poked bear."

"Merripen isn't a houseboy."

"Call him what you like. He comes along with the Hathaways. I accept that."

"It would be disastrous." Heat climbed in her breasts and throat and face. "You'd resent me for taking away your freedom . . . and I'd resent you for taking mine. I can't promise to obey you, accept your decisions, and never again be entitled to my own opinions—"

"It doesn't have to be that way."

"Oh? Would you swear never to command me to do anything against my will?"

Cam turned her to face him, his fingers gentle on the burning surface of her cheek. He considered the question for a long moment. "I would never command you," he said flatly. "But I wouldn't keep silent if I thought something was for your own good."

"I've always been the one to decide what's for my own good. I won't yield that right to you, nor to anyone."

His gaze held hers. "We'll learn to compromise, then." As he saw the indecision in her face, he urged softly, "Let me help you, sweetheart. Your family's in trouble."

"That's nothing new. We're *always* in trouble." She stared at him in bewilderment. "Why would you possibly want to marry a woman with so many problems?"

"You're my fate," he said simply. One hand slid to the back of her head. "Marry me, Amelia." He nibbled at her lips, licked at them, opened them as he sealed his mouth over hers. He kissed her until her pulse was racing. "Say yes, and save me from ever having to spend a night with another woman. I'll sleep indoors. I'll get a haircut. God help me, I think I'd even carry a pocket watch if it pleased you."

Amelia felt dizzy, unable to think. She leaned helplessly into the hard support of his body. Everything was him, every breath, beat, blink, quiver. He said her name, and his voice seemed to come from a distance.

"Amelia . . ." Cam shook her a little, asking something, and she gathered he wanted to know when she had eaten last.

"Yesterday," she managed to reply.

Cam didn't look sympathetic so much as annoyed. "No wonder you're ready to faint. You've had no food and hardly any sleep."

Fitting a hard arm around her back, he propelled her back to the house and took her to her sister's table. She sank gratefully into a chair and sat with her eyes closed until a plate of ham and salad was set before her. As she ate slowly, Cam sat beside her and talked with Win, Beatrix, and Poppy. They asked him about the condition of Ramsay House and what was left of it. A chorus of groans greeted the revelation that the bee room had been left intact.

"The hive is still busy and thriving," Cam said.

"The bees didn't leave even with all the smoke?" Beatrix asked in amazement.

Cam smiled. "No, it only calmed them." He reached for a basket of bread rolls and set it closer to Amelia. "Will you have one of these?" he asked in a low voice, making no effort to hide his concern.

She took one and smiled faintly. "I'm feeling better," she told him, and lifted a teacup to her lips.

"Good."

"Mr. Rohan," she heard Beatrix ask, "are you going to marry my sister?"

Amelia choked on her tea and set the cup down. She sputtered and coughed into her napkin.

"Hush, Beatrix," Win murmured.

"But she's wearing his ring—"

Poppy clamped her hand over Beatrix's mouth. "*Hush!*"

They were all distracted as a set of French doors flew open, accompanied by the sound of breaking glass. Everyone on the back terrace looked up in startlement, the men rising from their chairs.

"No," came Win's soft cry.

Merripen stood there, having dragged himself from his sickbed. He was bandaged and disheveled, but he looked far from helpless. His stare, promising death, was firmly fixed on Cam.

There was no mistaking the bloodlust of a Rom whose kinswoman had been dishonored.

"Oh God," Amelia muttered.

Cam, who stood beside her chair, glanced down at her with a question in his eyes. "Did you say something to him?"

"No." Amelia turned red as she recalled her blood-spotted nightgown and the maid's expression. "It must have been servants' talk."

Cam stared at the enraged giant with resignation. "You may be in luck," he said in an aside to Amelia. "It looks as if our betrothal is going to end prematurely." Holding Merripen's gaze, he moved slowly away from the table. "Is there something you'd like to discuss, *chal*?" he asked with admirable self-possession.

Merripen replied in Romany. Although no one save Cam understood what he said, it was clearly not encouraging.

"I'm going to marry her," Cam said, as if to pacify him.

"That's even worse!" Merripen moved forward, murder in his eyes.

"Not in front of *gadje*." Cam told him coolly, and jerked his head in the direction of the back gardens. "Come, we'll talk out there."

And after a brief hesitation, Merripen followed.

Chapter Seventeen

When the pair was out of sight, Lord Westcliff spoke to St. Vincent. "Perhaps we should follow at a distance to prevent them from killing each other."

St. Vincent shook his head, relaxing in his chair. He reached for his Evie's hand and began to play with her fingers. "Believe me, Rohan has the situation well in hand. His opponent may be larger, but Rohan is accustomed to dealing with criminals and violent brutes." Smiling at his wife, he added, "And those are just our employees."

"Merripen has been injured," Win said. "He should be resting, not chasing about after Mr. Rohan."

"It's not my fault he left his sickbed!" Amelia protested in an indignant whisper.

Win's blue eyes narrowed. "You've done *something* to stir everyone up. And it's fairly obvious that whatever you did, Mr. Rohan was involved."

Poppy, who was listening avidly, couldn't resist adding, "*Intimately* involved."

The two older sisters glanced at her and said in unison, "Shut up, Poppy."

Poppy frowned. "I've been waiting my entire life for

Amelia to stray from the straight and narrow. Now that it's happened, I'm going to enjoy it."

"I'd enjoy it too," Beatrix said plaintively, "if I only knew what we're talking about."

CAM LED THE WAY ALONG THE YEW HEDGE, GOING AWAY from the manor until they reached a sunken lane stretching toward the wood. They stopped beside a thicket of St. John's wort, its golden flowers in full bloom, and sedge spiked with blue bottlebrush. Deceptively relaxed, Cam folded his arms loosely across his chest. He was puzzled by the large, irate *chal* with the air of a loner. The mysterious Merripen had no affiliation with a tribe, but had instead chosen to make himself the watchdog of a *gadje* family. Why? What did he owe them?

"You took advantage of Amelia," Merripen said.

"Not that it matters," Cam countered, "but how did you find out?"

Merripen's huge hands flexed as if longing to rip him apart. "The maids were talking about it," Merripen replied. "I heard them standing outside my door. You dishonored one of my family."

"Yes, I know," Cam said quietly.

"You're not good enough for her."

"I know that too." Watching him intently, Cam asked, "Do you want her for yourself, *chal*?"

Merripen looked mortally offended. "She's a sister to me."

"That's good to hear. Because I want her for my wife. And as far as I can see"—Cam gestured wide with his hands—"there aren't exactly queues forming to help the Hathaways."

"They don't need your money. Ramsay has an income."

"Ramsay will be dead soon. We both know it. And after that, the title will go to the next poor bastard in line, and there'll be four unmarried Hathaway sisters with few practical skills to speak of. What do you think will become of them? What about Win? She'll need medical care—"

"Don't talk about her." Merripen made his face expressionless, but not before Cam had seen a flash of extraordinary emotion, something ferocious and dark and tormented.

Apparently, Cam thought wryly, not *all* of the Hathaways were like sisters to him. "Merripen," he said slowly, "you're going to have to tolerate me. Because there are things I can do for the Hathaways that you can't." He continued in a level tone despite the look on Merripen's face, which would have terrified a lesser man. "I'm not going to battle you every step of the way. If you want what's best for them, either leave or find a way to accept this. I'm here to stay."

As the huge Rom glared at him, Cam could almost see the progression of his thoughts, the weighing of options, the violent desire to mow down his enemy, all of it overshadowed by the urge to do what was right for his family.

"Besides," Cam added, "if Amelia doesn't marry me, the *gadjo* will be after her again. And you know she'll be better off with me."

Merripen's eyes narrowed. "Frost broke her heart. You took her innocence. Why does that make you any better?"

"Because I'm not going to leave her. Unlike *gadje*, Roma are faithful to our women."

"If you hurt her in any way," Merripen said, "I'm going to kill you."

"I won't."

"I may kill you anyway."

Cam smiled slightly. "You'd be surprised how many people have said that to me before."

"No," Merripen said, "I wouldn't."

AMELIA PAUSED NERVOUSLY AT THE DOOR OF CAM'S ROOM. There were sounds of movement within, drawers opening and

closing, objects being moved. She realized he must be preparing to leave for London.

Glancing up and down the hallway, she made certain she
was unobserved before she gave a feather-light rap at the
door and let herself into the room.

Cam pushed a stack of neatly folded garments into a small
gentleman's trunk at the foot of the bed. He glanced at her.
A spill of black silk fell down to his eyes. He was so vibrant
and beautiful. Amelia was seized by the despairing recognition that he would haunt every dream until the last day of
her life.

Her voice came unevenly from her constricted throat. "I
was afraid Merripen would bring you back in pieces."

Cam smiled as he approached her. "All still here." He
reached out for her slowly, his hands closing over her shoulders. "Are you going to marry me, Amelia?"

"I can't," she said weakly. "I just can't. We don't suit. It's
obvious we're not at all alike. You're impetuous. You make
life-altering decisions in the blink of an eye, whereas I
choose one course and don't stray from it."

"You strayed last night. And look how well it turned out."
Cam smiled at her expression. "I'm not impetuous. It's just
that I know when something is too important to be decided
according to logic."

"And marriage is one of those things?"

"Of course." Cam settled a hand high on her chest, over
her heart. "You have to decide it in here."

Amelia's chest felt tight beneath the warmth of his hand.
"I can't entrust the future of my family to a man I don't even
know."

"You know the important things already."

As Cam's foot slid beneath Amelia's skirts and gently
touched hers, she realized she was doing her blasted toe-
tapping again. With an effort, she went still.

Sliding one arm around her, Cam picked up her left hand and brought it to his mouth. His lips brushed over the chafed red patch on her knuckle where she'd tried to pull the ring off.

"It's too tight," she grumbled.

"Relax your hand and it will come off."

"My hand is relaxed."

Cam's head bent, his mouth finding hers. He explored slowly, enticing her to open for him, hunting for the shy tip of her tongue. At the same time, he began to unfasten her dress.

"Wait," she whispered, her face turning scarlet. "Lock the door."

A quick smile crossed his face. He went to the door, stripping off his jerkin and shirt along the way. After turning the key in the lock, he took his time about returning to Amelia, seeming to enjoy the sight of her undressing for him.

He stood before her half-naked, the trousers riding low on his hips. Amelia dragged her gaze away from the sleek, tightly muscled surface of his torso and climbed hastily into bed. "You're putting me in a difficult position," she said.

Cam shed his trousers and coaxed her into the bed. "Let's find one you like better."

She was pulled against him full-length, his body large and startlingly warm. He ran his hands over her, discovering she was still wearing garters and silk stockings. With a smoothness that left her gasping, Cam disappeared beneath the covers, his broad shoulders tenting the layers of linen, wool, and velvet.

Amelia tried to struggle to a sitting position but fell back with a whimper as she felt his mouth against the soft skin inside her thigh. He untied the garter, letting it fall away, and began to roll the stocking down her leg with torturous slowness. His tongue ventured into the crease behind her knee, glided over the clenched muscle of her calf, and delved into the throbbing hollow on the side of her ankle. The silk was gently tugged away from her foot. She quivered and gasped as she felt his hot, wet mouth closing over her toes, one at a time, sucking and tickling.

By the time the second stocking was removed, Amelia was steaming. She fought to push the covers back, the tips of her breasts contracting as they were exposed to the cool air. Cam spread her thighs and pulled her legs over his shoulders. His fingers sifted through the springy curls, and he kissed her tenderly, licking into the heat and tension until Amelia strained beneath him.

He settled a hand over her stomach, rubbing in soothing circles. "Lie easy, sweetheart."

"I can't. Oh, please hurry."

Cam laughed softly against her sensitive flesh. He traced her with his tongue, making her wet, and blew against the damp curls. She moaned as he teased the stiff bud of her clitoris, flicking gently, until she was shaking from head to toe and her inner muscles were clenching desperately on emptiness. A sob of relief escaped her as he moved upward to fit himself into the taut slip of her thighs. He entered carefully and began to ride her deep and slow, stretching her with each thrust.

She began to lift eagerly, anticipating each wet, grinding slide, panting for it, sensation building on sensation until it culminated in a blinding swell of delight. He groaned as her body gripped and stroked the hard length of him, his teeth gritting with the effort to hold back his own pleasure. When at last she went limp, he withdrew and shuddered with the force of his own release.

They rolled to their sides, their bodies loosely entwined, and Cam reached for her left hand. Taking the signet ring between his fingers, he drew it off easily. "Here," he said, giving it to her. "Although I'd rather you left it on."

Amelia's mouth fell open. "How did you do that?"

"I helped you relax." He ran a coaxing hand along her spine. "Put it back on, Amelia."

Her lips twitched. She shook her head and slid the ring onto his smallest finger. "I can't. That would mean I've accepted your proposal, and I haven't."

Stretching like a cat, Cam rolled her flat again, his weight partially supported on his elbows. Amelia drew in a quick breath of surprise as she felt him nudge inside her again. "You can't lie with me twice and then refuse to marry me." Cam lowered his head to kiss her ear and worked his way to the little hollow behind her earlobe. "I'll feel so cheap."

Despite the seriousness of the matter, Amelia had to bite back a smile. "I'm doing you a favor by refusing you. You'll thank me for it someday."

"I'll thank you right now if you'll put the ring back on."

She shook her head.

Cam pressed deeper inside her, making her gasp. He felt harder inside her, thicker, his desire gaining new momentum. "But we just finished," she protested, twisting beneath him.

Cam lifted his head. "Rom," he said, as if by way of explanation, and settled back over her. If there was a hint of apology in his tone, there was none in the insistent rhythm of his thrusts. His beautiful sleek body moved over her, inside her, muscles bunching at her touch.

Amelia wrapped her arms and legs around him, while the steady, rocking thrusts brought her to the edge of release. But he withdrew before she could reach it, and turned her over, and for an agonizing moment, she thought he had decided to stop. Covering her with his body, Cam used his knees to push hers wide, and she whispered *yes, yes*. He slid impossibly deep, his hands steadying her hips.

Her head dropped, her gasps muffled against the linen-covered mattress. His teasing hand slid to her sex. Pleasure shimmered through her in waves, each one stronger, higher, until she was shuddering, drowning, sighing. Cam's sudden withdrawal was a shock of unwelcome emptiness as he made his last thrust against the sheets and groaned. Stunned and disoriented, Amelia remained with her hips propped high, her flesh pulsing with the need to have him back inside. His hand came to her bottom, patting gently before he pushed her back down.

"You'll have me, hummingbird," Cam whispered. "You know I'm your fate—even if you won't admit it yet."

Chapter Eighteen

With Cam gone, Amelia was relieved to be free of the distractions and arguments that occurred whenever he was near. Her relief lasted approximately two hours, after which she found herself wandering despondently through the large manor.

It was strangely quiet in the house, everyone having retired to their rooms for afternoon naps. Preparations were being made for the earl and countess, and Lord and Lady St. Vincent, to leave for Bristol in the morning.

"Will you and the others be all right in our absence?" Lillian had asked. "I hate to leave with things so unsettled and Mr. Merripen under the weather."

"I expect Merripen will heal very quickly," Amelia said with utter confidence. "He has a robust constitution."

"I've asked the doctor to visit daily," Westcliff said. "And if you have any difficulties, send word to Bristol. It isn't far, and I'll come at once."

Now, as Amelia made her way through the art gallery, her gaze moving over paintings and sculptures, she became aware of an unfamiliar feeling, a terrible hollowness. She couldn't think how to make it go away. It wasn't hunger, fear, or anger, it wasn't exhaustion or dread.

It was loneliness.

Nonsense, she scolded herself, striding to a long row of windows that overlooked a side garden. It had begun to rain, a cold soaking glitter that fell steadily over the grounds and rushed in muddy streams toward the bluff and the river. *You can't be lonely. Cam has only been gone for half a day. And your entire family is in the same house.*

It was the first time she had ever felt the kind of loneliness that couldn't be cured with just any available company.

Sighing, she pressed her nose against the cold surface of a window pane while thunder vibrated the glass.

Her brother's voice came from the other side of the gallery. "Mother always said that would flatten your nose."

Pulling back, Amelia smiled as Leo approached her. "She only said that because she didn't want me to smudge the glass."

Her brother looked drawn and hollow-eyed, the pastiness of his complexion a striking contrast to Cam Rohan's clover-honey tan. Leo was dressed in borrowed clothes so fine and precisely tailored, they must have been donated by Lord St. Vincent. But instead of hanging gracefully as they did on St. Vincent's elegantly spare frame, the garments strained over Leo's bloated waist and puffy neck.

"One can only hope you feel better than you look," Amelia said.

"I'll feel better once I can find some decent refreshment. I've asked several times for wine or spirits, and the servants are all damnably absent-minded."

As Amelia stared at her brother, who seemed so lost beneath his brittle facade, she felt a rush of compassion. Walking forward, she put her arms around him and hugged him. And wondered how to save him.

Startled by the impulsive gesture, Leo remained still, not returning the embrace but not pulling away, either. His hands came to her shoulders, easing her away.

"I should have known you'd be maudlin today," he said.

"Yes, well . . . finding one's brother nearly roasted to death tends to make a woman rather emotional."

"I'm just a bit charred, that's all." He stared at her with those strange, light eyes, not at all the eyes of the brother she had known all her life. "And not so altered as you, it seems."

Amelia knew immediately what he was leading to. Warily, she turned away from him and pretended to inspect a nearby landscape of hills and clouds and a silvery lake. "Altered? I've no idea what you mean, Leo."

"I'm referring to the game of hide-the-slipper you've been playing with Rohan."

"Who told you that? The servants?"

"Merripen."

"I can't believe he dared—"

"For once he and I agree on something. We're going back to London as soon as Merripen is well enough. We'll stay at the Rutledge Hotel until we can find a suitable house to lease—"

"The Rutledge costs a fortune," she exclaimed. "We can't afford—"

"Don't argue, Amelia. I'm the head of this family, and I've made the decision. With Merripen's full support, for what that's worth."

"The two of you can go to blazes! I don't take orders from you, Leo."

"You will in this instance. Your brief-lived affair with Rohan is over."

Feeling bitter and outraged, Amelia turned away from

him. She didn't trust herself to speak. In the past year, there had been countless times she had longed for Leo to assume his place as the head of the family, to have an opinion about *anything*, to show concern for someone other than himself. And yet *this* was the issue that had provoked him to take action? Her relationship with Cam was no one's business but her own, and she would be damned if she'd allow it to be used to manipulate her.

"I'm so glad," she said with ominous quietness, "you've taken such an interest in my personal affairs, Leo. Now perhaps you might expand your interest to other topics of importance, such as how and when Ramsay House will be rebuilt, and what we're going to do about Win's health, and Beatrix's education, and Poppy's— "

"You won't distract me that easily. Good God, sis, couldn't you find someone of your own class to dally with? Have your prospects really sunk so low that you've taken a Rom to your bed?"

Amelia's mouth dropped open. She spun to face him. "I can't believe you would say such a thing. Our brother is a Rom, and he—"

"Merripen isn't our brother. And he happens to agree with me. This is beneath you."

"Beneath me," Amelia repeated dazedly, backing away from him until her shoulders flattened against the wall. "Until this moment, I had no intention of marrying Cam," she said. "But now I'm seriously considering the merits of having at least one rational man in the household."

"*Marriage?*"

Amelia almost enjoyed the look on his face. "I suppose Merripen forgot to mention that minor detail. Yes, Cam has proposed to me. And he's rich, Leo. *Rich* rich, which means no matter what you do, the girls and I would be taken care of. Nice, isn't it, that someone's concerned about our future?"

"I forbid it."

She gave him a scornful glance. "Forgive me if I'm less than impressed by your authority, Leo. Perhaps you should practice on someone else."

And she left him in the gallery while thunder rumbled and rain cascaded down the windows.

CAM STOPPED THE DRIVER ON THE WAY TO LONDON, wanting another look at Ramsay House before he departed Hampshire. He was in a quandary as to what should be done with the place. It would have to be restored, of course. As part of an aristocratic entailment, the estate had to be maintained in a decent condition. And Cam liked the place. There were possibilities in it. If the slopes of the surrounding grounds were altered and landscaped, and the building itself was properly redesigned and rebuilt, the Ramsay estate would be a jewel.

But it was doubtful the Ramsay title and its entailments would remain in the Hathaways' possession much longer. Not if everything depended on Leo, whose health and future existence were very much in question.

Cam bid the driver to wait and went into the ramshackle house, heedless of the rain that dampened his hair and coat. It didn't especially matter to him whether Leo lived or died, but Amelia's feelings mattered very much indeed. Cam would do whatever was necessary to spare her grief. If that meant helping preserve her brother's worthless life, so be it.

The interior of the house sagged like a creature that had been beaten into submission. He wondered what a builder would make of the place, and how much of the structure could be preserved. Cam imagined what it might look like when it was fully restored and painted. Bright, charming, a touch eccentric. Like his Hathaways.

A smile tugged at the corners of his lips at the thought. It was strange, how the idea of settling on this land, becoming part of this family, had become so appealing.

He stopped at the side of the entrance hall as he heard a noise from upstairs. A thump, a tapping, as if someone were hammering at wood. The nape of his neck crawled. Who the hell could be here? Superstition struggled with reason as he wondered if the intruder were mortal or spectral. He made his way up the stairs with extreme care, his feet swift and silent.

Pausing at the top of the stairs, he listened intently. The sound came again, from one of the bedrooms. He made his way to a half-open door and looked inside.

The presence in the room was most definitely human. Cam's eyes narrowed as he recognized Christopher Frost. It appeared he was trying to pry a piece of paneling from the wall using an iron pry bar. The wood defied his efforts, and, after a few seconds of exertion, Frost dropped the pry bar and swore.

"Need help?" Cam asked.

Frost nearly leapt out of his shoes. "What the devil—" He whirled around, his eyes huge. "What are you doing there?"

"I was going to ask you the same thing." Leaning against the doorjamb, Cam folded his arms and stared at the other man speculatively. "I decided to stop here on my way to London. What's behind the panel?"

"Nothing," the architect snapped.

"Then why are you trying to remove it?"

Collecting himself, Frost bent to retrieve the pry bar. He held it casually, but with the slightest change in his grip, the iron bar could easily be turned into a weapon. Cam kept his posture relaxed, not taking his gaze from Frost's face.

"How much do you know about construction and design?" Frost asked.

LISA KLEYPAS

"Not much. I've done some woodworking now and then."

"Yes. Your people sometimes work as tinkers and bodgers. Perhaps even roofing. But never building. You would never stay long enough to complete the project, would you?"

Cam kept his tone immaculately polite. "Are you asking about me specifically or Roma in general?"

Frost approached him, the pry bar firmly in his grasp. "It doesn't matter. To answer your previous question—I'm inspecting the house to make an estimate of the damage and to develop ideas for the new design. On behalf of Miss Hathaway."

"Did she ask you to inspect the house?"

"As an old friend of the family—and particularly Miss Hathaway—I've taken it upon myself to help them."

The hint of ownership in his utterance of the phrase "particularly Miss Hathaway" made Cam instantly hostile. "Maybe," he said, "you should have asked first. As it turns out, your services aren't needed."

Frost's face darkened. "What gives you the right to speak for Miss Hathaway and her family?"

Cam saw no reason to be discreet. "I'm going to marry her."

Frost nearly dropped the iron bar. "Don't be absurd. Amelia would never marry you."

"Why not?"

"Good God," Frost exclaimed incredulously, "how can you ask that? You're a mongrel."

"All the same, I'm going to marry her."

"I'll see you in hell first!" Frost cried, taking a step toward him.

"Either drop that bar," Cam said quietly, "or I'll dislocate your arm." To his disappointment, Frost set the bar on the ground.

The architect glared at him. "After I talk to her, she'll want nothing more to do with you. I'll make certain she understands what people would say. She'd be better off with a peasant. A dog. A—"

"Point taken," Cam said. He gave Frost a bland smile designed to infuriate.

"You selfish bastard," Frost said. "You'll ruin her. You think nothing of bringing her down to your level. If you cared for her at all, you would disappear for good." He brushed by Cam without another word. Soon his footsteps could be heard as he descended the stairs.

Cam stayed in the empty doorway for a long time, seething with anger, concern for Amelia, and even worse, guilt. He couldn't change what he was, nor would he be able to shield Amelia from the arrows that would be aimed at the wife of a Rom.

But he'd be damned if he let her make her way through a merciless world without him.

Supper was a somber and quiet affair that evening, with the Westcliffs and St. Vincents having departed for Bristol, and Leo having purportedly gone to the village tavern for amusement. It was a miserable night. Amelia found it hard to imagine there would be much revelry in the cold and wet, but Leo was probably desperate for more sympathetic company than he could find at Stony Cross Manor.

Merripen had remained in his room, sleeping most of the day, which was so unlike him that the Hathaways were all worried.

"I suppose it's good for him to rest," Poppy ventured, brushing idly at a few crumbs on the tablecloth. A footman came hurriedly to remove the crumbs for her with a napkin and a silver implement. "It will help him heal faster, won't it?"

"Has anyone had a look at Merripen's shoulder?" Amelia asked, glancing at Win. "It's probably time for the dressing to be changed."

"I'll do it," Win said at once. "And I'll take him a supper tray."

"Beatrix will accompany you," Amelia advised.

"I can manage the tray," Win protested.

"It's not that . . . I meant it's not proper for you to be alone with Merripen in his room."

Win looked surprised, and made a face. "I don't need Beatrix to come. It's only Merripen, after all."

After Win left the dining hall, Poppy looked at Amelia. "Do you think," she asked, "that Win really doesn't know how he—"

"I have no idea. And I've never dared to broach the subject, because I don't want to put ideas into her head."

"I hope she doesn't know," Beatrix ventured. "It would be dreadfully sad if she did."

Amelia and Poppy both glanced at their younger sister quizzically. "Do you know what we're talking about, Bea?" Amelia asked.

"Yes, of course. Merripen's in love with her. I knew it a long time ago, from the way he washed her window."

"Washed her window?" both older sisters asked at the same time.

"Yes, when we lived in the cottage at Primrose Place. Win's room had a casement window that looked out onto the big maple tree—do you remember? After the scarlet fever, when Win couldn't get out of bed for the longest time, and she was too weak to hold a book, she would just lie there and watch a birds' nest on one of the tree limbs. She saw the baby swallows hatch and learn to fly. One day, she complained that the window was so dirty, she could barely see through it, and it made the sky look grayish. So from then on, Merripen always kept the glass spotless. Sometimes he climbed a ladder to wash the outside, and you know how afraid of heights he is. You never saw him do that?"

"No," Amelia said with difficulty, her eyes stinging. "I didn't know he did that."

"Merripen said the sky should always be blue for her," Beatrix said. "And that was when I knew he . . . Are you crying, Poppy?"

Poppy used a napkin to dab at the corners of her eyes. "No. I just inh-haled some pepper."

"So did I," Amelia said, blowing her nose.

WIN CARRIED A LIGHT BAMBOO TRAY LADEN WITH BROTH, bread, and tea to Merripen's room. It hadn't been easy to persuade the kitchen maids that she could take the tray herself. They had felt strongly that no guest of Lord and Lady Westcliff should carry anything. However, Win knew Merripen's dislike of strangers, and in his vulnerable state, he would be contrary and obstinate.

Finally, a compromise had been reached: a housemaid would bring the tray to the top of the stairs, and Win could take it from there.

As she neared his room, Win heard the sounds of something hitting a wall with a thud, and a few threatening growls that could only have come from Merripen. She frowned, her pace quickening as she proceeded along the hallway. An indignant housemaid was departing from Merripen's room.

"Well, I never," the maid exclaimed, red and bristling. "I went to stir the coals and add wood to the fire—and that nasty man shouted and threw his cup at me!"

"Oh, dear. I'm so sorry. You weren't injured, were you? I'm sure he didn't intend—"

"No, his aim was off," the maid said with dark satisfaction. "The tonic's made him higher than a Cable Street constable."

The reference was to a mile-long road in London known for harboring a quantity of opium dens. "I wouldn't go in there if I were you, miss. He'd snap you in two as soon as you got within arm's length of him."

Win frowned in concern. "Yes. Thank you. I'll be careful." Tonic . . . the doctor must have left something extremely potent to dull the agony of a burn wound. It was probably laced with opiate syrup and spirits. Since Merripen never took medicine and rarely even drank a glass of wine, he would be highly susceptible to intoxicants.

Entering the room, Win used her back to close the door and went to set the tray on the bedside table. She started a little at the sound of Merripen's voice.

"I told you to get out!" he barked. "Told you—" He broke off as she turned to face him.

Win had never seen him like this before, flushed and disoriented, his dark eyes slightly unfocused. He lay on his side, his white shirt falling open to reveal the edge of a heavy bandage and muscles gleaming like polished bronze.

"Kev," she said gently, using his first name.

They'd made a bargain once, after she'd gotten scarlet fever, when he'd wanted her to take some medicine. Win had refused until he offered to tell her his name. She'd promised never to tell anyone, and she hadn't. Perhaps he had even thought she had forgotten.

"Lie still," she urged gently. "There's no need to work yourself into a temper. You frightened the poor housemaid half to death."

Merripen watched her sluggishly, having trouble keeping his gaze focused. "They're poisoning me," he told her. "Pouring medicine down my throat. My head's muddled. Don't want any more."

Win assumed the role of implacable nurse, when all she

wanted was to baby and coddle him. "You'd be much worse off without it." She sat on the edge of the mattress and reached for his wrist. His forearm was hard and heavy as it lay across her lap. Pressing her fingers to his wrist, she kept her face expressionless. "How much of that tonic have they given you?"

His head lolled. "Too much."

Win agreed silently, feeling how weak his pulse was. Releasing his wrist, she felt his forehead. He was very warm. Was it the beginnings of a fever? Her worry sharpened. "Let me see your back." She tried to ease away, but he had reached up to press her cool hand harder against his forehead. He wouldn't let go.

"Hot," he said and closed his eyes.

Win sat very still, absorbing the feel of him, the heavy body beside hers, the smooth burning skin beneath her hand.

"Stay out of my dreams," Merripen whispered in the humid stillness. "Can't sleep when you're here."

Win let herself caress him, the heavy black hair, the handsome face devoid of its usual sullen sternness. She could smell his skin, his sweat, the sweet opiated breath, the pungent whiff of honey. Merripen was always clean shaven, but now his bristle was softly scratchy on her palm. She wanted to take him into her arms.

"Kev . . . let me look at your back."

Merripen moved, swift and powerful even now, more aggressive in his drugged state than he normally would ever have permitted himself to be. He'd always handled Win with a sort of exaggerated gentleness, as if she would blow away like dandelion floss. But at this moment, his grip was hard and sure as he pinned her to the mattress.

Breathing heavily, he glared down at her with glassy belligerence. "I said stay out of my dreams."

Win was amazed, excited, the tiniest bit frightened . . . but this was Merripen . . . and as she stared at him, the edge of fear melted. She drew his head down to hers, and he kissed her.

She had always imagined there would be roughness, urgency, impassioned pressure. But his lips were soft, grazing over hers with the heat of sunshine, the sweetness of summer rain. She opened to him in wonder, heat filling her chest, the solid weight of him in her arms, his body pressing into the crumpled layers of her skirts. Forgetting everything in the passionate tumult, Win reached around his shoulders, until he winced and she felt the bulk of his bandage against her palm.

"Kev," she said breathlessly, "I'm so sorry, I . . . no, don't . . . be still. Be still." She curled her arms loosely around his head, shivering as he kissed her throat. He nuzzled against the gentle rise of her breast, pressed his cheek against her bodice, and sighed.

After a long, motionless minute, while her chest rose and fell beneath his heavy head, Win spoke hesitantly. "Kev?"

A slight snore was his reply.

The first time she had ever kissed a man, she thought ruefully, and she'd put him to sleep.

Struggling out from beneath him, Win turned back the covers and grasped the hem of his shirt. The linen clung to the powerful slope of his back. Pulling the hem all the way up, she tucked it into the collarless neck of the shirt. Carefully, she lifted the edge of the bandage, the cotton gauze sticky and reeking of honey. She blinked at the sight of the burn wound, which was angry and inflamed. The doctor had said a scab would form, but the oozing crust of the wound didn't remotely resemble healing.

Seeing a black mark on the other side of his back, Win

frowned curiously and pushed his shirt a little higher. What she discovered caused her breath to catch, and her eyes widened. "Kev," she murmured in wonder, her fingers tracing the pattern on his shoulder. "What secrets are you hiding?"

Chapter Nineteen

The next morning, Amelia awakened to the unwelcome news delivered by Poppy that Leo had not slept in his bed the previous night and couldn't be found anywhere, and Merripen had taken a turn for the worse.

"Bother Leo," Amelia grumbled, climbing out of bed and reaching for her robe and slippers. "He started drinking yesterday afternoon and doubtless didn't stop. I couldn't care less where he is, or what's happened to him."

"What if he wandered out of the house and . . . oh, I don't know . . . stumbled over a tree branch or something? Shouldn't we ask some of the gardeners and groundsmen to look for him?"

"God. How mortifying." Amelia pulled the robe over her head and buttoned it hastily. "I suppose so. Yes, although make it clear they're not to go on an all-out search. I should hate for their work to be interrupted just because our brother has no self-control."

"He's grieving, Amelia," Poppy said quietly.

"I know. But God help me, I'm tired of his grieving. And it makes me feel horrid to say so."

Poppy stared at her compassionately and reached out to

hug her. "You shouldn't feel horrid. It always falls to you to pick up the pieces of his muck-ups, not to mention everyone else's. I'd be tired, too, if I were you."

Amelia returned the hug, and stepped back with a sigh. "We'll worry about Leo later. Right now, I'm more concerned about Merripen. Have you seen him this morning?"

"No, but Win has. She says he's definitely feverish and the wound isn't healing. I think she stayed up with him most of the night."

"And now she'll probably faint from exhaustion," Amelia said in exasperation.

Poppy hesitated and frowned. "Amelia . . . I can't decide whether this is the best or worst time to tell you . . . but there's a minor to-do belowstairs. It seems some of the silver flatware has gone missing."

Amelia went to the window and stared beseechingly up at the cloud-heavy sky. "Dear Merciful Lord, please don't let it be Beatrix."

"Amen," Poppy said. "But it probably is."

Feeling overwhelmed, Amelia thought in despair, *I've failed. The house is gone, Leo is missing or dead, Merripen is injured, Win is ill, Beatrix is going to prison, and Poppy is doomed to spinsterhood.* But what she said was, "Merripen first," and strode briskly from the room with Poppy at her heels.

Win was at Merripen's bedside, so exhausted she could barely sit up straight. Her face was blanched, her eyes blood-shot, her entire body drooping. She had so few reserves, it took very little to deplete them. "He has fever," she said, wringing out a wet cloth and draping it over the back of his neck.

"I'll send for the doctor." Amelia came to stand beside her. "Go to bed."

Win shook her head. "Later. He needs me now."

"The last thing he needs is for you to make yourself ill over him," Amelia replied shortly. She softened her tone as she saw the anguish in her sister's gaze. "Please go to bed, Win. Poppy and I will take care of him while you sleep."

Slowly Win lowered her face until their foreheads were touching. "It's going all wrong, Amelia," she whispered. "His strength has gone too quickly. And the fever shouldn't have come this fast."

"We'll get him through this." Even to her own ears, Amelia's words rang false. She forced a reassuring smile to her lips. "Go and rest, dear."

Win obeyed reluctantly while Amelia bent over the patient. Merripen's healthy color had been leached by ashen paleness, the black slashes of his brows and the fans of his lashes standing out in sharp contrast. He slept with his mouth partially open, shallow breaths rushing over the chapped surface of his lips. It didn't seem possible that Merripen, always so rugged and sturdy, could have sunk so fast.

Touching the side of his face, Amelia was shocked by the heat coming from his skin. "Merripen," she murmured. "Wake up, dear. Poppy and I are going to clean your wound. You must hold still for us. All right?"

He swallowed and nodded, his eyes cracking open.

Murmuring in sympathy, the sisters worked in tandem, folding back the covers to his waist, lifting the hem of his shirt to his shoulders, and laying out clean rags, pots of salve and honey, and fresh bandages.

Amelia went to ring the servants' bell, while Poppy removed the old dressing. She wrinkled her nose at the mildly unpleasant scent of the exposed raw flesh. The sisters exchanged worried glances.

Working as gently and quickly as possible, Amelia cleaned the exudate from the oozing wound, applied fresh salve, and covered it. Merripen was quiet and rigid, although his back flinched beneath the treatment. He couldn't stifle an occasional hiss of pain. By the time she had finished, he was trembling.

Poppy wiped his sweating face with a dry cloth. "Poor Merripen." She brought a cup of water to his lips. When he tried to refuse, she slid an arm beneath his head and raised it insistently. "Yes, you must. I should have known you'd be a terrible patient. Drink, dear, or I'll be forced to sing something."

Amelia stifled a grin as Merripen complied. "Your singing isn't that terrible, Poppy. Father always said you sang like a bird."

"He meant a parrot," Merripen said hoarsely, leaning his head on Poppy's arm.

"Just for that," Poppy informed him, "I'm going to send Beatrix in here to look after you today. She'll probably put one of her pets in bed with you and spread her jacks all over the floor. And if you're very lucky, she'll bring in her glue pots, and you can help make paper doll clothes."

Merripen gave Amelia a glance rife with muted suffering, and she laughed.

"If that doesn't inspire you to get well quickly, dear, nothing will."

But as the next two days passed, Merripen only worsened. The doctor seemed powerless to do anything except offer more of the same treatment. The wound was turning sour, he admitted. One could tell by the way it was bleeding white and the skin around it was blackening, an inevitable process that would eventually poison Merripen's blood and his entire body.

Merripen dropped weight faster than one would have thought humanly possible. It was often that way with burn injuries, the doctor said. The body consumed itself in its efforts to heal the wounds. What troubled Amelia even more than Merripen's appearance was the increasing listlessness that even Win couldn't seem to penetrate. "He can't stand being helpless," Win told Amelia, holding Merripen's hand as he slept.

"No one likes to be helpless," Amelia replied.

"It's not a question of liking or not liking. I think Merripen literally can't tolerate it. And so, he withdraws." Win gently stroked the lax fingers, so powerful and calloused from work.

Watching the tender absorption of her sister's expression, Amelia couldn't help asking softly, "Do you love him, Win?"

And her sister, unreadable as a sphinx, turned mysterious blue eyes to her. "Why, of course. We all love Merripen, don't we?"

Which wasn't at all an answer.

A matter of increasing worry was Leo's continued absence. He'd taken a horse but had packed no belongings. Would he have gone on the long ride to London on horseback? Knowing her brother's dislike of travel, Amelia didn't think so. It was likely Leo had remained in Hampshire, although where he could be staying was a mystery. He wasn't at the village tavern, nor was he at Ramsay House, nor was he anywhere on the Westcliff estate.

To Amelia's relief, Christopher Frost came to call one afternoon, dressed in somber attire. Handsome and scented of expensive cologne water, he brought a perfectly arranged bouquet of flowers wrapped in parchment lace.

Amelia met him in the downstairs parlor. In her distress over Merripen's illness and Leo's disappearance, all the constraint she might have felt toward Christopher was gone. The past hurts had receded to the back of her mind, and at the moment, she needed a sympathetic friend.

Taking both her hands in his, Christopher sat with her on a plush settee. "Amelia," he murmured in concern. "I can see the state of your spirits. Don't say Merripen's condition is worse?"

"A great deal worse," she said, grateful for the sustaining grip of his hands. "The doctor seems to have no other treatment, nor does he think any of the local folk cures would have any effect other than to cause Merripen further discomfort. I'm so afraid we'll lose him."

His thumbs rubbed gently over her knuckles. "I'm sorry. I know what he means to your family. Shall I send for a doctor from London?"

"I don't think there's time." She felt tears rising and held them back with effort.

"If there is any help I can give, you have only to ask."

"There is something . . ." She told him about Leo's absence and that she felt certain he was somewhere in Hampshire. "Someone has to find him," she said. "I'd look for him myself, but I'm needed here. And he tends to go to places where . . ."

"Where respectable people don't go," Christopher finished wryly. "Knowing your brother as I do, sweet, it's probably best to let him stay wherever he is until he's slept it off and the fog has lifted."

"But he could be hurt, or in danger. He . . ." She perceived from his expression that the last thing Christopher wanted to do was search for her scapegrace of a brother. "If you would ask some of the townspeople if they have seen him, I'd be very grateful."

"I will. I promise." He surprised her by reaching out for her, his arms closing around her. She stiffened but allowed him to draw her near. "Poor sweet," he murmured. "You have so many burdens to carry."

There had been a time when Amelia had passionately

longed for a moment such as this. Being held by Christopher, soothed by him. Once this would have been heaven.

But it didn't feel the same as before.

She turned away from him as his mouth sought hers. "No, Christopher."

"Of course." He pressed his lips to her hair. "Now isn't the proper time. I'm sorry."

"I'm so concerned about my brother and Merripen, I can't think of anything else—"

"I know, sweet." He turned her face back to his. "I'm going to help you and your family. There's nothing I want more than your safety and happiness. And you need my protection. With your family in turmoil, you could easily be taken advantage of."

She frowned. "No one's taking advantage of me."

"What about the Gypsy?"

"You're referring to Mr. Rohan?"

Christopher nodded. "I chanced to meet him on his way to London, and he spoke of you in a way that . . . well, suffice it to say, he's no gentleman. I was offended for your sake."

"What did he say?"

"He went so far as to claim that you and he were going to marry." A scornful laugh escaped him. "As if you'd ever lower yourself to that."

Amelia felt a rush of defensive anger. She looked into the face of the man she had once loved so desperately. He was the embodiment of everything a young woman should want to marry. Not all that long ago, she might have compared him to Cam Rohan and found Christopher superior. But she was no longer the woman she had been, and Christopher wasn't the knight in shining armor she'd believed him to be.

"I wouldn't consider it lowering myself," she said. "Mr. Rohan is a gentleman, and highly esteemed by his friends."

"They find him entertaining enough for social occasions,

but he'll never be their equal. And never a gentleman. That's understood by everyone, my dear, even Rohan himself."

"It's neither understood nor accepted by me," she said. "There's more to being a gentleman than fine manners."

Christopher stared intently into her indignant face. "Very well, we won't discuss him. But your faith in him is misplaced, Amelia. I only hope you haven't entrusted your family's business or legal affairs to him."

"My family's affairs will remain in the hands of Lord Ramsay and myself."

"Then Rohan won't be returning from London? Your connection with him is severed?"

"He will return," she admitted reluctantly, "to bring some professional men who'll advise what can be done with Ramsay House."

"Ah." There was just enough condescension in his tone to set her teeth on edge. Christopher shook his head and was silent for a long moment. "Is it only his counsel you'll accept on the matter?" he finally asked. "Or will I be allowed to make recommendations on a subject of which I have a fair amount of expertise and he has none?"

"I'd welcome your recommendations, of course."

"Then I may visit Ramsay House to make professional assessments of my own?"

"If you like. That's very kind of you. Although . . ." She paused uncertainly. "I wouldn't wish for you to spend too much of your time there."

"Any time in your service is well spent." He leaned forward and brushed his lips against hers before she had the chance to pull back.

"Christopher, I'm far more concerned about my brother than the house—"

"Of course," he said reassuringly. "I'll ask after him. If there's any news, I'll relay it to you at once."

"Thank you."

But somehow, she knew Christopher's search for Leo would be halfhearted at best. Despair crept through her in a cold, heavy tide.

THE NEXT MORNING, AMELIA AWAKENED FROM A NIGHT-mare with her arms and legs thrashing, her heart pounding. She had dreamed of finding Leo floating face-down in a pond, and as she had swum to him and tried to pull him to the edge, his body had begun to sink. She couldn't keep him afloat, and as he retreated further into the black water, she was pulled down with him . . . choking on water, unable to see or breathe . . .

Trembling, she climbed out of bed and hunted for her slippers and robe. It was early yet, the house still dark, the atmosphere quiet. She headed for the door, then paused with her hand on the doorknob. Fear was pumping through her veins. She didn't want to leave the room. She was afraid of finding out that Merripen had died during the night . . . afraid, too, that her brother had met with tragedy . . . and afraid most of all that she wouldn't be able to accept the worst, if the worst should come.

It was only the thought of her sisters that caused her to grip the knob and turn it. For their sakes, she could act with strength and confidence. She would do whatever needed to be done.

Hurrying along the hallway, she pushed at the half-open door of Merripen's room and went to the bedside. The exhausted light of dawn barely leavened the darkness, but it was enough for Amelia to see two people in the bed. Merripen was on his side, the formerly strong lines of his body collapsed and sprawling. And there was the slim, neat shape of Win sleeping beside him, fully clothed, her feet tucked beneath the skirts of her house dress. Though it seemed laughable that such a delicate creature could protect someone so much larger, Win's body was curved as if to shelter him.

Amelia stared at them in wonder, understanding more from the tableau than any words could have conveyed. Their position conveyed longing and restraint, even in sleep.

She realized her sister's eyes were open—there was the shine of her eyes. Win stared at her, making no sound, no movement, her expression grave as if she were absorbed in collecting each second with him.

Overwhelmed with compassion and shared sorrow, Amelia tore her gaze from her sister's and left the room. She nearly bumped into Poppy, who was also walking through the hallway, her robe a ghostly white.

"How is he?" Poppy asked.

"Not well. Sleeping. Let's go to the kitchen and put a kettle on." They went toward the stairs.

"Amelia, I dreamed all night about Leo. Terrible dreams."

"So did I."

"Do you think he's . . . done himself harm?"

"I hope not, with all my heart. But I think it's possible."

"Yes," Poppy whispered. "I think so too." She heaved a sigh. "Poor Beatrix."

"Why do you say that?"

"She's still so young to have lost so many people . . . Father and Mother, and now perhaps Merripen and Leo."

"We haven't lost Merripen and Leo yet."

"At this point, it would be a miracle if we could keep either of them."

"You're always so cheerful in the morning." Amelia caught her hand and squeezed it. "Don't give up yet, Poppy. We'll hold out hope for as long as we can."

They reached the bottom of the stairs. "Amelia." Poppy sounded vaguely annoyed. "Don't you ever feel like throwing yourself to the floor and crying?"

Yes, Amelia thought. *Right now, as a matter of fact.* "No, of course not. Crying never solves anything."

"Don't you ever want to lean on someone's shoulder?"

"I don't need someone else's shoulder. I've got two perfectly good ones."

"That's silly. You can't lean on your own shoulder."

"Poppy, if you mean to start the day by bickering—" Amelia broke off as she became aware of some noise from outside, the thunder and jangle and gravel-crunching of a carriage and a team of horses. "Good heavens, who would come at this hour?"

"The doctor," Poppy guessed.

"No, I haven't sent for him yet."

"Perhaps Lord Westcliff has returned."

"But there would be no reason for that, especially for him to have come so early—"

A footman knocked at the door, the sound echoing through the entrance hall.

The sisters looked at each other uneasily. "We can't answer it," Amelia said. "We're in our nightgowns."

A maid came into the entrance hall. Setting down a pail of coal, she wiped her hands on her apron and hastened to the door. Unlocking the massive portal, she tugged it open and bobbed a curtsey.

"We'd better go," Amelia muttered, urging Poppy back to the stairs with her. But as she glanced back over her shoulder to see who had come, the sight of a man's tall, dark form struck sparks inside her. She stopped with her foot on the first step.

Cam.

He looked disheveled and disreputable, like an outlaw on the run. A smile came to his lips as his gaze met hers.

Amelia rushed to him without thinking, and threw herself at him.

Cam caught her up with a low laugh. The scent of outdoors clung to him—wet earth, cold night air, leaves. The mist on his coat sank through the thin layer of her robe. Feeling her shiver, Cam opened his coat with a wordless murmur and pulled her into the tough, warm haven of his body.

Amelia was vaguely aware of servants moving through the entrance hall, and her sister's presence nearby. She was making a scene—she should pull away and try to compose herself. But not yet.

"You . . . you must have traveled all night," she heard herself say.

His lips pressed against her head before he replied. "I had to come back early. I left some things unfinished, but I couldn't stop thinking of you. Tell me what's happened."

Amelia opened her mouth to answer, but the only sound she could make was a rough sob. Her self-control dissolved. She shook her head and choked on more sobs, and the more she tried to stop them, the worse they became.

Cam gripped her firmly into his embrace. The appalling storm of tears didn't seem to bother him at all. He took Amelia's hand and flattened it against his heart until she could feel the strong, steady beat. In a world that was disintegrating around her, he was solid and real.

"It's all right," he murmured. "I'm here."

Alarmed by her own lack of self-discipline, Amelia made a wobbly attempt to stand on her own, but he only hugged her more closely. Noticing Poppy's awkward retreat, Cam sent her a reassuring smile. "Don't worry, little sister."

"Amelia never cries," Poppy said.

"She's fine." Cam ran his hand along Amelia's spine in soothing strokes. "She just needs . . ."

As he paused, Poppy said, "A shoulder to lean on."

"Yes." He drew Amelia to the stairs, and gestured for Poppy to sit beside them.

Cradling Amelia on his lap, Cam found a handkerchief in his pocket and wiped her eyes and nose. When it became apparent that no sense could be made from her jumbled words, he hushed her gently and held her while she sobbed and hid her face.

As Amelia hiccupped and quieted in his arms, Cam asked a few questions of Poppy, who told him about Merripen's condition and Leo's disappearance and even about the missing silverware.

Finally getting control of herself, Amelia cleared her aching throat and breathed deeply. She lifted her head from Cam's shoulder.

"Better?" he asked, holding a handkerchief up to her nose.

Amelia nodded and blew obediently. "I'm sorry," she said in a muffled voice. "I shouldn't have turned into a watering pot. I'm finished now."

Cam seemed to look right inside her. His voice was very gentle. "You don't have to be sorry. You don't have to be finished, either."

She realized that no matter what she did or said, no matter how long she wanted to cry, he wouldn't mind at all. Her hand crept to the open neck of his shirt, her fingers curling around the linen placket. "Do you think Leo might be dead?" she whispered.

He offered no false hope, no empty promises, only caressed her damp cheek with the backs of his fingers. "Whatever happens, we'll deal with it together."

Comforted, Amelia closed her eyes as his lips followed the wing of her eyebrow. "Cam . . . would you do something for me?"

"Anything."

"Could you find some of that plant Merripen gave to Win and Leo for the scarlet fever?"

"Deadly nightshade? That wouldn't work for this, sweetheart."

"But it's a fever."

"Caused by a septic wound. You have to treat the source of the fever." His hand went to the back of her neck, caressing the tightly strung muscles. He looked down at her, appearing to think something over. His tangled lashes made shadows over his hazel eyes. "Let's go have a look at him."

"Do you think you could help him?" Poppy asked, springing to her feet.

"Either that, or my efforts will finish him off quickly. Which, at this point, he may not mind." Lifting Amelia from his lap, Cam set her on her feet, and they proceeded up the stairs. His hand remained at the small of her back, a light but steady support she desperately needed.

As they approached Merripen's room, it occurred to Amelia that Win might still be inside. "Wait," she said, hastening forward. "Let me go first."

Cam inclined his head and stayed beside the door.

Entering the room with caution, Amelia saw that Merripen was alone in the bed. She opened the door wider and gestured for Cam and Poppy to enter.

Becoming aware of intruders in the room, Merripen lurched to his side and squinted at them. As soon as he caught sight of Cam, his face contracted in a grimace.

"Bugger off," he croaked.

Cam smiled pleasantly. "Were you this charming with the doctor? I'll bet he was falling all over himself to help you."

"Get away from me."

"This may surprise you," Cam said, "but there's a long list of things I'd prefer to look at other than your rotting carcass. For your family's sake, however, I'm willing. Turn over."

Merripen eased his front to the mattress and said something in Romany that sounded extremely foul.

"You too," Cam said equably. He lifted the shirt from Merripen's back and pried the bandage from the injured shoulder. He viewed the hideous seeping wound without expression. "How often have you been cleaning it?" he asked Amelia.

"Twice a day."

"We'll try four times a day. Along with a poultice." Leaving the bedside, Cam motioned for Amelia to accompany him to the doorway. He lowered his mouth to her ear. "I have to go out to fetch a few things. While I'm gone, give him something to make him sleep. He won't be able to tolerate this otherwise."

"Tolerate what? What are you going to put in the poultice?"

"A mixture of things. Including *Apis mellifica*."

"What is that?"

"Bee venom. Extract from crushed live bees, to be precise. We'll soak them in a water and alcohol base."

Bewildered, Amelia shook her head. "But where are you going to get—" She broke off and stared at him with patent horror. "You're going to the hive at Ramsay house? H-how will you collect the bees?"

His mouth twitched with amusement. "Very carefully."

"Do you . . . do you want me to help?" she offered with difficulty.

Knowing her terror of the insects, Cam slid his hands around her head and pressed a hard kiss to her lips. "Not with the bees, sweetheart. Stay here and dose Merripen with morphine syrup. A lot of it."

"He won't. He hates morphine. He'll want to be stoic."

"Trust me, none of us will want him to be awake while I'm applying the poultice. Especially Merripen. Roma call the treatment 'white lightning' for good reason. It's not something anyone can be stoic about. So do whatever's necessary to put him out, *monisha*. I'll be back soon."

"Do you think the white lightning will work?" she asked anxiously.

"I don't know." Cam cast an unfathomable glance at the suffering figure on the bed. "But I don't think he'll last long without it."

WHILE CAM WAS GONE, AMELIA CONFERRED WITH HER sisters in private. It was decided that Win would be the most likely to succeed in making Merripen take the morphine. And it was Win herself who stated flatly that they would have to deceive him as he would refuse to take it voluntarily no matter how they begged him.

"I'll lie to him, if necessary," Win said, shocking the other three into speechlessness. "He trusts me. He'll believe whatever I say."

To their knowledge, Win had never told a lie in her life, not even as a child.

"Do you really think you could?" Beatrix asked, rather awed by the notion.

"To save his life, yes." Delicate tension appeared between Win's fine brows, and splotches of pale pink appeared high on her cheeks. "I think . . . I think a sin committed for such a purpose may be forgiven."

"I agree," Amelia said swiftly.

"He likes mint tea," Win said. "Let's make a strong batch and add a great deal of sugar. It will help hide the taste of the medicine."

No pot of tea had ever been prepared with such scrupulous care, the Hathaway sisters hovering over the brew like a coven of young witches. Finally, a porcelain teapot was filled with the strained and sugared concoction, and placed on a tray beside a cup and saucer.

Win carried it to Merripen's room, pausing at the threshold as Amelia held the door open.

"Shall I go in with you?" Amelia whispered.

Win shook her head. "No, I can manage. Please close the door. Make certain no one disturbs us." Her slender back was very straight as she entered the room.

MERRIPEN'S EYES OPENED AT THE SOUND OF WIN'S FOOT-steps. The pain of the festering wound was constant, inescapable. He could feel the toxins leaking into his blood, feeding poison into every capillary. It produced, at times, a perplexing dark euphoria, floating him away from his wasting body to the periphery of the room. Until Win came, and then he gladly sank back into the pain just to feel her hands on him, her breath on his face.

Win shimmered like a mirage in front of him. Her skin looked cool and luminous while his own body raged with miasma and heat.

"I've brought something for you."

"Don't . . . want . . ."

"Yes," she insisted, joining him on the bed. "It will help you get better . . . here, move up a bit, and I'll put my arm around you." There was a delicious slide of female limbs against him, beneath him, and Merripen gritted his teeth against a dull burst of agony as he moved to accommodate her. Darkness and light played beneath his closed eyelids, and he fought for consciousness.

When Merripen could open his eyes again, he found his head resting against the gentle pillow of Win's breasts, one of her arms cradling him while her free hand pressed a cup to his lips.

A delicate porcelain rim clicked against his teeth. He recoiled as an acrid taste burned his cracked lips. "No—"

"Yes. Drink." The cup advanced again. Her whisper fell tenderly against his ear. "For me."

He was too sick—he didn't think he could keep it down—

but to please her, he drank a little. The crisp, sour taste made him recoil. "What is it?"

"Mint tea." Win's angel-blue eyes stared into his without blinking, her beautiful face neutral. "You must drink all of this, and then perhaps another cup. It will make you better."

He knew at once Win was lying. Nothing could make him better. And the bitter tang of morphine in the tea was impossible to conceal. But Merripen sensed an intent in her, a strange deliberateness, and the idea came to him that she was giving him an overdose on purpose. His exhausted mind weighed the possibility. It must be that Win wanted to spare him more suffering, knowing the hours and days to come were beyond his endurance. Killing him with morphine was the last act of kindness she could offer him.

Dying in her arms, cradled against her as he relinquished his scarred soul to the darkness . . . Win would be the last thing he would ever feel, see, hear. Had there been any tears in him, he would have wept in gratitude.

He drank slowly, forcing down every swallow. He drank part of the next cup until his throat would no longer work, and he turned his face against her chest and shuddered. His head was spinning, and sparks were drifting all around him like falling stars.

Win set the cup aside and stroked his hair and pressed her wet cheek to his forehead.

And they both waited.

"Sing to me," Merripen whispered as the blinding darkness rolled over him. Win continued to stroke his head as she crooned a lullaby. His fingers touched her throat, seeking the precious vibration of her voice, and the last sparks faded as he lost himself in her, his fate, at last.

AMELIA LOWERED HERSELF TO THE FLOOR AND SAT BESIDE the door, her fingers laced in a loose basket. She heard Win's tender murmurs . . . a few rasping words from Merripen . . . a long silence. And then Win's voice, singing gently, humming, the tones so true and lovely that Amelia felt a fragile peace steal over her. Eventually the angelic sound faded, and there was more quiet.

After an hour had passed, Amelia, whose nerves had been stretched to the limit, stood and stretched her cramped limbs. She opened the door with extreme care.

Win was easing from the bed, tugging the bedclothes over Merripen's prone form.

"Did he take it?" Amelia whispered, approaching her.

Win looked weary and strained. "Most of it."

"Did you have to lie to him?"

A tentative nod. "It was the easiest thing I've ever done. You see? . . . I'm not such a saint after all."

"Yes, you are," Amelia returned and hugged her fiercely. "You are."

EVEN LORD WESTCLIFF'S WELL-TRAINED SERVANTS WERE inclined to complain when Cam returned with two jars of live bees and brought them to the kitchen. The scullery maids ran shrieking to the servants' hall, the housekeeper retreated to her room to compose an indignant letter to the earl and countess, and the butler told the head groomsman that if this was the kind of houseguest Lord Westcliff expected him to attend, he was thinking seriously of retiring.

As the only person in the household who dared to go into the kitchen, Beatrix stayed with Cam, helped in the boiling, straining, and mixing, and later reported to her revolted sisters that it had been great fun crushing bees.

Eventually Cam brought what appeared to be a warlock's brew up to Merripen's room. Amelia waited for him there, having laid out clean knives, scissors, tweezers, fresh water, and a pile of clean white bandages.

Poppy and Beatrix were commanded to leave the room, much to their disgruntlement, while Win closed the door firmly behind them. She took an apron from Amelia, tied it around her narrow waist, and went to the bedside. Placing her fingers at the side of Merripen's throat, Win said tensely, "His pulse is weak and slow. It's the morphine."

"Bee venom stimulates the heart," Cam replied in a matter-of-fact tone, rolling up his shirt sleeves. "Believe me, it will be racing in a minute or two."

"Shall I remove his bandage?" Amelia asked.

Cam nodded. "The shirt too." He went to the washstand and soaped his hands. Amelia almost smiled at the sight, being reminded of Merripen's similar habit.

Win helped her to remove the linen shirt from Merripen's prostrate form. His back was still heavily muscled, but he had lost a great deal of weight. The sides of his ribs jutted beneath the skin.

As Win went to discard the crumpled shirt, Amelia untucked the end of the bandage and began to pry it loose. She paused, however, as she noticed a curious mark on his other shoulder. Leaning over him, she stared more closely at the black ink design. A chill of astonishment ran through her.

"A tattoo," was all she could manage to say.

"Yes, I noticed it a few days ago," Win remarked, coming back to the bed. "It's odd that he never mentioned it, isn't it? No wonder he was always drawing pookas and making up stories about them when he was younger. It must have some significance to—"

"*What did you say?*" Cam's voice was quiet, but it reverberated with such intensity, he might as well have been shouting.

"Merripen has a tattoo of a pooka on his shoulder," Win replied, staring at him questioningly as he reached the bed in three strides. "We've never known about it until now. It's a very unique design—I've never seen anything quite like—" She stopped with a gasp as Cam held his forearm next to Merripen's shoulder.

The black winged horses with yellow eyes were identical.

Amelia lifted her gaze from the astonishing sight to Cam's blank face. "What does it mean?"

Cam couldn't seem to take his gaze from Merripen's tattoo. "I don't know."

"Have you ever known anyone else who—"

"No." Cam stepped back. "Sweet Jesus." Slowly he paced around the foot of the bed, staring at Merripen's motionless form. He picked up a pair of scissors from the tray of supplies.

Instinctively, Win moved closer to the sleeping man's side. Noticing her protectiveness, Cam murmured, "It's all right, little sister. I'm just going to cut the dead skin away."

Leaning over the wound and working intently, Cam didn't resemble a physician so much as a warlock weaving a spell. After a minute of watching him clean and debride the wound, Win went to a nearby chair and sat abruptly as if her knees had been unbuckled.

Amelia stood beside him, feeling a sting of nausea in her throat. Cam, on the other hand, was as detached as if he were repairing the intricate mechanism of a clock rather than treating festering human flesh. At his direction, Amelia fetched the bowl of poultice liquid, which smelled astringent but curiously sweet.

"Don't let it splash into your eyes," Cam said, rinsing the wound with salt solution.

"It smells like fruit."

"That's the venom." Cam cut a square of cloth and pushed it into the bowl. Fishing it out gingerly, he laid the dripping cloth over the wound. Even in the depths of his sleep, Merripen jerked in reaction and tried to move.

"Easy, *chal*." Cam laid a hand on his back, keeping him in place. When he was assured Merripen was still again, he bandaged the poultice firmly in place. "We'll replace it every time we clean the wound," he said. "Don't tip the bowl over—I'd hate to have to go back for more bees."

"How will we know if it's working?" Amelia asked.

"The fever should go down gradually, and by this time tomorrow, we should see a nice leathery scab forming." He felt the side of Merripen's throat and told Win, "His pulse is stronger."

"What about the pain?" Win asked anxiously.

"That should improve quickly." Cam took Amelia's shoulders in his hands. "You're in charge now, hummingbird. I'm leaving for a little while."

"Right now?" she asked in bewilderment. "But . . . where are you going?"

His expression changed. "To find your brother."

Amelia stared at him with mingled gratitude and dread. "Perhaps you should rest first. You traveled all night. It may take a long time to find him."

"No, it won't." With a wry twist of his lips, he added, "Your brother's hardly one to cover his tracks."

Chapter Twenty

A pproximately six hours after his search for Leo had be-gun, Cam knocked at the front door of a prosperous manor farm. A piece of tavern gossip had led to someone who had seen Ramsay with someone else, and they had gone to another place, where their plans had been overheard, and so forth, until finally the trail had led to this place.

The large Tudor house, with the date *1620* inscribed over the door, was located almost ten miles from Stony Cross Park. From the information Cam had gathered, the farm had once belonged to a noble Hampshire family, but had been sold out of necessity to a London merchant. It served as a retreat for the merchant's dissipated sons and their playmates.

Hardly a surprise that Leo had been drawn to such company.

The door was opened, and a trout-faced butler appeared. His lips twisted disdainfully as he saw Cam.

"Your kind isn't welcome here."

"That's fortunate, since I don't intend to stay long. I've come to collect Lord Ramsay."

"There is no Ramsay here." The butler began to close the door, but Cam braced a hand on it.

"Tall. Light eyes. Ruddy-complexioned. Probably reeking of spirits—"

"I have seen no one of that description."

"Then let me speak to your master."

"He is not at home."

"Look," Cam said irritably, "I'm here on behalf of Lord Ramsay's family. They want him back. God knows why. Give him to me, and I'll leave you in peace."

"If they want him," the butler said frostily, "let them send a proper servant."

Cam rubbed the corners of his eyes with his free hand and sighed. "We can do this the easy way or the hard way. Frankly, I'd rather not go through unnecessary exertion. All I ask is that you allow me five minutes to find the bastard and take him off your hands."

"Begone with you!"

After another foiled attempt to close the door, the butler reached for a silver bell on the hall table. A few seconds later, two burly footmen appeared.

"Show this vermin out at once," the butler commanded.

Cam removed his coat and tossed it onto one of the built-in benches lining the entrance hall.

The first footman charged him. In a few practiced movements, Cam landed a right cross on his jaw, flipped him, and sent him to a groaning heap on the floor.

The second footman approached Cam with considerably more caution than the first.

"Which is your dominant arm?" Cam asked calmly.

The footman looked startled. "Why do you want to know?"

"I'd prefer to break the one you don't use as often."

The footman's eyes bulged, and he retreated, giving the butler a pleading glance.

The butler glared at Cam. "You have five minutes. Retrieve your master and go."

"Ramsay isn't my master," Cam muttered. "He's a pain in my arse."

"THEY'VE BEEN IN THE SAME ROOM FOR DAYS," THE FOOT-man, whose name was George, told Cam as they ascended a flight of carpeted stairs. "Food sent in, women coming and going, empty wine bottles everywhere . . . and the stench of opium smoke spreading through the entire upper floor. You'll want to cover your eyes when you enter the room, sir."

"Because of the smoke?"

"That, and . . . well, the goings-on would make the devil blush."

"I'm from London," Cam said. "I don't blush."

Even if George hadn't been willing to lead Cam to the room of iniquity, he could have easily found it from the smell.

The door was ajar. Cam nudged it open and stepped into the hazy atmosphere. There were four men and two women, all young, all in various stages of undress. Although only one opium pipe was in evidence, it could have been argued that the entire room served as a huge pipe, so thick was the sweet smoke.

Cam's arrival was greeted with remarkable unconcern, the men listlessly draped across upholstered furniture, one coiled on cushions in the corner. Their complexions were cadaverous, their eyes filmy with narcotic dullness. A side table was littered with spoons and pins and a dish filled with what looked like black treacle.

One of the women, who was entirely naked, paused in the act of lifting a pipe to a man's slack mouth.

"Look," she said to the other woman, "here's a new one."

A drowsy giggle. "Good, we need him. They're all at half-mast. The only stiff thing left is the pipe." She twisted to look at Cam. "Gor', what a pretty man."

"Oh, let me have him first," the other one said. She petted herself invitingly. "C'mere, love."

"No, thank you." Cam was beginning to feel slightly dizzy from the smoke. He went to the nearest window, opened it, and let a cold breeze into the room. A few curses and protests greeted his actions.

Identifying the one in the corner as Leo, Cam went to the quiescent figure, lifted the head by the hair, and stared into his future brother-in-law's puffy face. "Haven't you inhaled enough smoke lately?" he asked.

Leo scowled. "Sod off."

"You sound like Merripen," Cam said. "Who, in case you're interested, may be dead by the time we return to Stony Cross Manor."

"Good riddance to him."

"I'd agree with you, except that probably means I'm on the wrong side of the argument." Cam began to tug Leo upward, and the other man struggled. "Stand up, damn you." Cam hoisted him with a grunt of effort. "Or I'll drag you out by the heels."

Leo's bloated bulk swayed against him. "I'm trying to stand," he snapped. "The floor keeps tipping."

Cam fought to steady him. When Leo had finally gotten his bearings, he lurched toward the doorway, where the footman waited.

"May I help you downstairs, my lord?" George asked politely. Leo responded with a surly nod.

"Close the window," one of the women demanded, her naked body shivering as the autumn wind swept through the room.

Cam glanced at her dispassionately. He had seen too many of her kind to feel much pity. There were thousands of them in London—round-faced country wenches, just pretty enough to attract the attention of men who promised, took, and discarded without conscience. "You should try some fresh air," he advised, reaching for a discarded lap blanket beside the settee. "It promotes clear thinking."

"What do I need to do *that* for?" she asked sourly.

Cam grinned. "Good point." He draped the blanket over her shivering white body. "Still, you should take some deep breaths." He bent to pat her pale cheek gently. "And leave this place as soon as you're able. Don't waste yourself on these bastards."

The woman lifted her bloodshot eyes, staring in wonder at the black-haired man with the glittering diamond in his ear.

Her plaintive voice followed him as he left. "Come back!"

IT TOOK THE COMBINED EFFORTS OF CAM AND GEORGE TO load the grumbling, protesting Leo into the carriage. "It's like hauling five sacks of potatoes all at once," the footman said breathlessly, pushing Leo's foot safely inside the vehicle.

"The potatoes would be quieter," Cam said. He tossed the footman a sovereign and climbed into the carriage after Leo. They started back to Stony Cross Manor in silence.

"Do you need to stop?" Cam asked midway through the trip, seeing that Leo's face had turned from white to green.

Leo shook his head morosely.

"I have some questions for you," Cam said.

"Don't want to talk."

"I don't care. You owe me some answers after I've spent the day looking for you."

Those curiously light eyes turned toward him, the color of icicles when blue twilight shone through them. Unusual eyes. Cam had seen someone with eyes like that before, but he couldn't remember whom or when. A distant memory hovered just beyond reach.

"What do you want to know?" Leo asked.

"Why do you bear Merripen such ill will? Is it his charming disposition, or the fact that he's a Rom? Or is it because he was taken in by your parents and raised as one of you?"

"None of that. I despise Merripen because he refused the one thing I ever asked of him."

"Which was?"

"To let me die."

Cam pondered that. "You must mean when he nursed you through the scarlet fever."

"Yes."

"You blame him for saving your life."

"*Yes*."

"If it makes you feel any better," Cam said, settling back in his seat, "I'm sure he's had second thoughts about it."

They were silent after that. Cam relaxed and let his mind wander. As darkness fell and Leo was cast in shadow, the unnerving eyes flickered silver-blue—

—and Cam remembered.

It was in childhood, when Cam had still been with the tribe. There had been a man with a haggard face and brilliant colorless eyes, his soul ravaged by grief over his daughter's death. Cam's grandmother had warned him to stay away from the man. "He's *muladi*," she had said.

"What does that mean, *Mami*?" Cam had asked, clinging anxiously to her warm hand, which was comfortingly gnarled and tough like the buttressing roots of ancient trees.

"Haunted by a dead person. He loved his daughter too much."

Feeling pity for the man, and worry for his own sake, Cam had asked, "Will I be *muladi* when you die, *Mami*?" He had been certain that he loved his grandmother too much, but he couldn't stop feeling that way.

A smile had appeared in his grandmother's wise black eyes. "No, Cam. A *muladi* traps his beloved's spirit in the in-between because he won't let her go. You wouldn't do that to me, would you, little fox?"

"No, *Mamì.*"

The man had died not long after that, by his own hand.

Now, as Cam looked back on it with the understanding of an adult rather than a small boy, he felt a chill of apprehension, followed by searing pity. How impossible it would be to relinquish a woman you loved. How could you stop yourself from wanting her? The seams of your heart would rip open with grief. Of course, you would want to keep her with you.

Or follow her.

As Cam entered the manor with the unrepentant prodigal at his side, Amelia and Beatrix hurried toward them, the former frowning, the latter smiling.

Amelia opened her mouth to say something to Leo, but Cam caught her gaze and shook his head, warning her to be silent. She swallowed back the sharp words and reached out for Leo's coat. "I'll take that," she said in a subdued tone.

"Thank you." Both avoided looking at each other.

"We've just finished supper," Amelia muttered. "The stew is still hot. Will you have some?"

Leo shook his head.

Beatrix, missing the seething undercurrents in the air, launched herself at Leo and wrapped her arms around his thick waist. "You were gone so long! So many things have happened—Merripen is ill, and I helped make a potion for him, and—" She stopped, making a face. "You smell bad. What—"

"Tell me how you made the potion," Leo said gruffly, making his way to the stairs. Beatrix chattered without stopping as she accompanied him.

Cam looked over Amelia carefully, not missing a detail. She was disheveled, her hair cascading down her back, her eyes tired. She needed to rest.

"Thank you for finding him," she said. "Where was he?"

"At a private home with some friends."

She drew closer to him, sniffing gingerly. "That smell . . . it's on both of you . . ."

"Opium smoke. Your brother's taken up an expensive new habit."

"We couldn't afford the old ones." Amelia scowled, her foot beginning a restless staccato beneath her skirts. "The only reason I didn't murder him just now is because he looked too numb to feel it. But when he sobers—"

"How is Merripen?" Cam interrupted, running a gentle hand from her shoulder to her elbow.

The tapping stopped. "Still feverish, but better. Win's with him. We changed his poultice. The wound looks slightly less disgusting than before. Is that a good sign?"

"It's a good sign."

Her concerned gaze chased over him. "Shall I get you something to eat?"

Smiling, Cam shook his head. "Not before I have a good, thorough wash." There were many things they needed to discuss, but it could all wait. "Go to bed, *monisha*—you look weary."

"So do you," Amelia said, standing on her toes. Cam held very still as she pressed her lips to his cheek. "Will you come to me tonight?"

"No." He took her into his arms. "You need to sleep."

She leaned harder against him. "Come to me," she insisted. "Hold me while we sleep."

"Hummingbird," he returned, his lips brushing her brow, "If I hold you, I don't trust myself not to make love to you.

So we'll sleep in separate beds." He looked down at her with a smile. "Just for tonight."

IT TOOK THREE SOAPINGS AND RINSINGS FOR CAM TO REMOVE the taint of opium from his skin and hair. After toweling his hair dry, he donned a black silk robe and walked through the darkened hallway to his room. It was storming outside, the rain and thunder sweeping in on an easterly, battering the windows and roof.

The hearth in his room had been replenished, the blaze shedding warmth and light. Cam's eyes narrowed in curiosity as he saw a small shape beneath the covers.

Amelia's head lifted from the pillow. "I'm cold," she said, as if that were a perfectly reasonable explanation for her presence.

"My bed is no warmer than yours." Cam approached her slowly. His body had gone hard beneath the black silk, all his muscles tight with anticipation.

"It would be if you were in it," she said.

Her hair fell over her shoulders in dark ripples down to her hips. Sitting close beside her, Cam touched one of the shining locks, following it over her chest, the tip of her breast, and down to the end. Amelia drew in a quick breath. He wondered if the blush on her face had spread to the skin he couldn't see.

Restraining his urgent need, Cam held still as she reached out to him, stroking the black silk that covered his shoulders. She rose to her knees and impulsively kissed his ear, the one with the diamond stud, and touched the damp, slightly curling locks of his hair.

"You're not like any man I've ever known," she said. "You're not even someone I could have dreamed. You're like someone from a fairy tale."

"The prince?"

"No, you're the dragon, a beautiful wicked dragon." Her voice turned wistful. "How could anyone have an ordinary everyday life with you?"

Cam took her in a safe, firm grip and lowered her to the mattress. "Maybe you'll be a civilizing influence on me." He bent over the slope of her breast, kissing it through the muslin veil of her gown. "Or maybe you'll acquire a taste for the dragon." He found the bud of her nipple, wet the cotton with his tongue until the tender flesh pricked up against the teasing friction.

"I th-think I already have."

"Then lie still," he whispered, "while I breathe fire on you."

The women he had slept with in the past had never worn this kind of prim white nightgown, which struck Cam as the most erotic garment he had ever seen. It had intricate folds and tucks and lace trimmings, and it went from the neck to the ankles. The way it lay over her like a layer of pale, crisp icing made his heart pound with primal force. He followed her shape, searching for her scent, her heat through the cotton, lingering whenever she arched or twitched. The front was held closed by a long row of covered buttons. He worked at them while her hands slid restlessly over his silk-covered back.

He kissed her, his tongue searching the sweetness of her mouth. The top of the gown slipped open, revealing the gleaming rise of her breasts, the tempting shadow between. He pulled the garment lower, lower, until her arms were delicately trapped and her chest was exposed. His head lowered and he took what he wanted, licking a taut nipple, prodding with his tongue, making it wet and deep pink. Amelia sighed deeply, her eyes half-closed, her body lifting helplessly as he bent to her other breast.

Cam's breathing turned ragged as he pulled the gown

lower, freeing her arms, exposing the curves of her hips and stomach. He spread his hands over her body, his fingers and palms translating heat into sensation. He kissed her navel, the ticklish skin around it, the place where the crisp curly hair started.

Her legs tautened against him, caught beneath his weight. Moving upward, he straddled her body. He took the signet ring off, the one she had refused before, and held it out to her.

"You can have what you want," he said. "But first put this on. You can take it off after we're finished."

"You're being absurd."

"You're being stubborn." Cam leaned over her, bracing his forearms on either side of her. "Just for tonight," he whispered. "Wear my ring, Amelia, and I'll give you as much pleasure as you can bear." He kissed her throat, his hips shunting gently against her. She gasped at the feel of him, hard and swollen behind the black silk. His mouth traveled slowly up to her ear. "I'll enter you, fill you, and then I'll hold you still and quiet in my arms. I won't move. I won't let you move, either. I'll wait until I feel you throbbing around me . . . I'll follow that rhythm deep in your body, that sweet pulse . . . I won't stop until you weep and shiver and cry out for more. And I'll give it to you, as long and deep and hard as you want. Take my ring, love." His mouth descended to hers in a smoldering kiss. "Take me."

Fitting himself against her soft cleft, he felt her heat seep through the robe, wetness and silk stretched tightly between them. Her small hand touched his, fingers unfolding, and she let him slide the ring back on.

Cam stripped her naked and laid her back into his discarded robe, her skin pale against the glimmering pool of black. He kissed her everywhere—the crooks of her elbows, the backs of her knees, every curve and hollow. His mouth slid between her thighs, teasing lightly until she groaned with every breath and begged him to take her.

Fighting for self-control, Cam moved over her. He aligned himself and entered her in a strong, deep thrust. She moved and arched and nearly drove him insane. "Sweetheart, wait," he said shakily, trying to calm her. "Don't move. Please. Don't . . ." A laugh rustled in his throat as she hitched up against him desperately. "Be still," he whispered, brushing kisses across her parted lips. "Hold me inside you. Be still, still . . ."

Breathing hard, Amelia tried to obey. Her flesh pulsed helplessly around the invading hardness, wringing sensation from him, making it almost impossible to hold back. He began to move carefully, using himself to pleasure her, stroking her inside and out.

She enclosed him in softness and strength, letting him feast on kisses while he rode the swift hot pulse of her. Tenderly he bracketed her small, beautiful face in his hands, whispering in Romany *I am yours*. He watched her eyes close in the sweet temporary blindness of rapture and felt it echoing in himself, stronger and stronger until the world caught fire.

Afterward they lay tumbled together like the survivors of a shipwreck, stunned in the wake of a storm. When Cam could gather the strength to move—which was not soon—he rolled to his side and nuzzled Amelia's throat, loving the fragrant damp warmth of her.

Amelia groped for the ring and began tugging and twisting it. "It's stuck again." She sounded disgruntled.

Cam pinned her wrist and bent his head, taking her finger into his mouth. His tongue swirled around the base, leaving it wet. Gently, he used his teeth to draw the gold band off. Taking the ring from between his lips, he slid it back onto his own finger. Her hand, now bare, flexed a little as if bereft, and she looked at him uncertainly.

"You'll get used to wearing it." Cam smoothed his hand along the plane of her midriff and stomach. "We'll try it on you a few minutes at a time. Like breaking a horse to harness." He grinned at her expression.

Pulling the covers over them both, Cam continued to stroke her. Amelia sighed, nestling against his shoulder and biceps.

"By the way," he murmured, "the flatware's back in the silver cabinet."

"It is?" she asked drowsily. "How . . . what . . ."

"I had a talk with Beatrix while we were crushing bees. She explained her problem. We agreed to find some new hobbies to keep her busy. To start with, I'm going to teach her to ride. She said she barely knows how."

"There hasn't really been time, with all the other—" Amelia began defensively.

"Shhh . . . I know that, hummingbird. You've done more than enough, keeping all of them together and safe. Now you have some help." He kissed her gently.

"But I don't want you to feel as if you have to—"

"Go to sleep," Cam whispered. "We'll start arguing again in the morning. For now, love, dream of something sweet."

AMELIA SLEPT DEEPLY, DREAMING OF RESTING IN A DRAGON'S nest, tucked beneath his warm leathery wing while he breathed fire on anyone that dared approach. She was woozily aware of Cam leaving the bed in the middle of the night, pulling on his clothes. "Where are you going?" she mumbled.

"To check on Merripen."

She knew she should go with him—she was concerned about Merripen—but as she tried to sit up, she was reeling with exhaustion, stupefied with it.

Cam coaxed her back down into the welcoming depth of the bedclothes. She fell asleep again, stirring only when he returned to stretch out beside her and gather her in his arms. "Is he better?" she whispered.

"Not yet. But he's no worse. That's good. Now close your eyes . . ." And he soothed her back to sleep.

MERRIPEN AWAKENED IN A DARK BEDROOM, THE ONLY GLIMmer of light coming from the quarter-inch space between the closed draperies. That one sliver was brilliant with the whiteness of midday.

His head ached viciously. His tongue seemed twice its normal size, dry and swollen in his mouth. His bones were sore, and so was his skin. Even his eyelashes hurt. In fact, he'd undergone some strange reversal in which everything hurt *except* his wounded shoulder, which glowed with an almost pleasant warmth.

He tried to move. Instantly someone came to him.

Win. Cool, frail, sweet-smelling, a lovely spirit in the darkness. Without speaking, she sat beside him and lifted his head, and gave him sips of water until his mouth was moist enough to allow speech.

So he hadn't died. And if he hadn't by now, he probably wasn't going to. He wasn't certain how he felt about that. His usual appetite for life had been replaced by shattering melancholy. Probably the aftereffects of the morphine.

Still cradling Merripen's head, Win stroked her fingers through his matted, unwashed hair. The light scratch of her fingernails on his scalp sent chills of pleasure through his aching body. But he was so mortified by his uncleanliness, not to mention his helplessness, that he shoved irritably at the gentle hand.

"I must be in hell," he muttered.

Win smiled down at him with a tenderness he found unbearable. "You wouldn't see me in hell, would you?"

"In my version . . . yes."

Her smile turned quizzical and faded, and she laid his head carefully back on the bed.

Win would be featured prominently in Merripen's hell. The most profound, gut-wrenching pain he had ever experienced was because of her—the agony of wanting and never having, of loving and never knowing love. And now it appeared he was going to endure more of it. Which would have made him hate her, if he didn't worship her so.

Bending over him, Win touched the bandage on his shoulder, beginning to untuck the end.

"No," Merripen said harshly, moving away from her.

If she continued touching him, tending him, his defenses would be smashed, and God knew what he would say or do. He needed her to go as far away from him as possible.

"Kev," she said, her too-careful tone maddening him further, "I want to see the wound. It's almost time to change the poultice. If you'll just lie flat and let me—"

"No." Had he been a prayerful man, he would have begged the pitiless heavens never to let Win know what he wanted or how he felt.

A long moment passed before Win asked in a perfectly normal tone, "Who do you want to change the poultice, then?"

"Anyone." Merripen kept his eyes closed. "Anyone but you."

He had no idea what Win's thoughts were as the silence became heavy and prolonged. His ears pricked at the sound of her skirts swishing. The thought of fabric moving and swirling around her slender legs caused every hair on his body to rise.

"All right, then," she said in a matter-of-fact tone as she reached the door. "I'll send someone else as soon as possible."

Merripen moved his hand to the place on the mattress where she had sat, his fingers splayed wide. And he fought to close his heart, which contained too many secrets and therefore could never be shut all the way.

DESCENDING THE GRAND STAIRCASE CAREFULLY, WIN SAW Cam Rohan coming up. She felt a spasm of nerves in her stomach. Win had always felt nervous around unfamiliar men, and she wasn't certain what to make of this one. Rohan had assumed a position of influence over her family with astonishing speed. He'd stolen her older sister's heart with such adroitness that she didn't even seem to know it yet.

For all Rohan's charm, he seemed slightly dangerous to Win. At the very least, he was acquainted with a side of life the sheltered Hathaways had never been exposed to. He was a man who harbored secrets . . . like Merripen. Those identical tattoos had caused Win to wonder at the connection between them. And she thought she might know what it was, even if neither of them were sure.

She stopped with a timid smile as they met on the stairs. "Mr. Rohan."

"Miss Winnifred." Rohan's unnerving golden gaze moved across her white face. She was still upset from her encounter with Merripen, and she knew Rohan could feel the color burning across the crests of her cheeks.

"He's awake, I take it," Rohan said.

"He's cross with me for tricking him into drinking the tea with morphine."

"I suspect he would forgive you for anything," Rohan replied.

Win rested her hand on the balcony railing and looked over the edge absently. She had the curious feeling of wanting, needing, to communicate to this friendly stranger, but she had no idea what she wanted to say.

Rohan waited in companionable silence, in no apparent hurry to go anywhere.

"You saved Merripen's life," she ventured. "He's going to get well."

Rohan watched her intently. "You care for him."

"Oh yes, we all do," Win said too quickly, and paused. Words gathered and flew inside her as if they had wings. The effort to hold them back was exhausting. She was suddenly glassy-eyed with frustration and desolation, thinking of the man upstairs and the untraversable distance that was always, always between them. "I want to get well, too," she burst out. "I want . . . I want . . ." She closed her mouth and thought *Good Lord, how must I sound to him?* Feeing chagrin at her loss of self-control, she passed a hand over her face and rubbed her temples.

But Rohan seemed to understand. And mercifully, there was no pity in his gaze. The honesty in his voice comforted her immeasurably. "I think you will, little sister."

She shook her head as she confessed, "I want it so much, I'm afraid to hope."

He smiled at her. "Never be afraid to hope. It's the only way to begin."

Chapter Twenty-One

Amelia was at a loss to understand how she could have slept until after luncheon, as if she were an upper-class lady from London. She could only attribute it to Cam, whose mere presence in the house caused her to relax. It was as if her mind automatically handed over all worries and cares to him, allowing her to sleep like an infant.

She didn't want to depend on him, and yet she couldn't seem to stop it from happening.

After dressing in a chocolate-colored gown with pink trim, she went to visit Merripen, whose surliness didn't dampen her joy in his recovery.

Upon going downstairs, she was told by the housekeeper that a pair of gentlemen had just arrived from London, and Cam was meeting with them in the library. Amelia guessed one of them must be the architect Cam had sent for. Curious about the visitors, she went to the library and paused at the doorway.

The masculine voices stopped. There were men grouped around the library table, two seated, two leaning casually against it, and another—Leo—lurking in the corner. The men all rose, except for Leo, who merely shifted in his chair as if the courtesy were too much effort to be bothered with.

Cam was dressed in well-tailored clothes, but no shirt collar or cravat. Approaching Amelia, he took one of her hands and raised it to his lips.

"Miss Hathaway." Cam's tone was polite, but there was a warm, teasing glint in his eyes. "Your timing is perfect. These gentlemen have arrived to discuss the restoration of Ramsay House. Allow me to introduce them."

Amelia exchanged bows with the men: a master builder named John Dashiell, and his assistant, Mr. Francis Barksby.

John Dashiell was a large-framed, beefy man with a neatly trimmed beard, warm brown eyes, and a ready smile. "A pleasure, Miss Hathaway. I was sorry to learn of the fire, but very glad everyone escaped alive. Many families are not so fortunate."

She nodded. "Thank you, sir. I'm most anxious to learn what can be made of our house now."

"I'll do my best," he promised. "You and Lord Ramsay are more than welcome to accompany us on our visit to the estate this afternoon. We'll be making some sketches and taking preliminary survey adjustments."

"I'm afraid Lord Ramsay will have to stay here with me," Cam said. "We're going to meet with the estate manager, Mr. Pym."

"Why?" Leo asked, disgruntled.

"To discuss how we can keep the few tenants you have left from fleeing."

"I don't give a damn whether they stay or go," Leo muttered.

The comment was roundly ignored.

After a few more minutes of conversation, Cam took Amelia aside. "I shouldn't let you go with them," he murmured with a frown. "You'll be the only woman there. I don't like it."

"It's not your place to *let* me do anything," she retorted. "Besides, it's all very circumspect. They're both gentlemen, and I'm—"

"Spoken for," Cam said curtly. "By me."

Amelia looked up into his eyes, the hint of a smile tugging at the corners of her lips. "I know," she said softly. She could almost feel the pleasure radiating from him at the small concession.

"Tonight," he murmured, and she felt the word down to the marrow of her bones.

"I'M GRATEFUL YOU'VE COME TO HELP US," AMELIA SAID AS she walked around the remains of Ramsay House with Mr. Dashiell. "Lord Ramsay also appreciates your efforts on our behalf."

"Does he?"

"Oh, yes. I'm sure he would have said so, except he's understandably distracted by all that's happened."

"I met him once, actually," Dashiell said. "Two years ago, when he was still articled to Rowland Temple. I was very much impressed with him at the time—he was a pleasant fellow, full of plans." He paused. "Now he seems a different man altogether."

"He hasn't yet recovered from his fiancée's death. He loved her very dearly."

"He must have," Dashiell said gravely, "to have been so altered by her loss."

Amelia's gaze traveled along the uneven roofline of Ramsay House. It looked so weary, the windows like wounds in its side. The windows . . . she saw movement in one of them, a shimmer, a tangle of moonbeams and shadows.

A face.

She must have made a sound, for Mr. Dashiell looked at her closely. "What is it?"

"I thought . . ." She found herself clutching a fold of his sleeve like a frightened child. Her thoughts were in chaos. "I thought I saw someone at the window."

"Perhaps it was Barksby."

But Mr. Barksby was coming around the corner of the house, and the face had been at a second-floor window.

"Shall I go in to have a look?" Dashiell asked quietly, his eyes narrowed with concern.

"No," she said at once, managing a shallow smile. She let go of his sleeve. "It must have been a curtain moving in the breeze. I'm sure no one is there."

AFTER RETURNING FROM RAMSAY ESTATE, AMELIA WENT to find Win.

Her sister was in a private family parlor upstairs, curled in the corner of a settee with a book in her lap.

Win looked up with evident relief as Amelia came to her. "Tell me how the visit to Ramsay House went." She moved her feet to make room for Amelia. "I've nearly withered away from boredom."

Amelia found it difficult to speak casually about the event. She swallowed hard. "Win, I feel like a lunatic saying this. But when I was walking with Mr. Dashiell and looking at the house, I saw a face in one of the upstairs windows."

"Someone was inside?" Win reached out and took Amelia's chilled fingers in hers.

"Not a person. It was . . . it was Laura."

"Oh." The word was a mere wisp of sound.

"I know it's difficult to believe—"

"No, it isn't. Remember, I saw her face on the magic lantern slide the night of the fire. And—" Win hesitated, her slim white fingers moving over the back of Amelia's hand. "Having been close to death once, I find it easy to believe such apparitions could be real."

Amelia struggled to be rational, to make sense of impossible things. She spoke with difficulty. "Then you think Laura is haunting Leo?"

"If she is," Win whispered, "it would be out of love."

"I think he's going mad from it." At Win's silence, Amelia continued desperately, "How can we stop it from happening?"

"We can't. Leo's the only one who can."

"Pardon me if I can't be fatalistic," Amelia said, annoyed. "Something has to be done."

"If you don't stop trying to control everyone around you at every given moment," Win said, "you're going to push Leo over the edge."

Amelia scowled. She was tired of everything, all of it, tired of thinking and worrying and fearing, and getting nothing for it but the singular ingratitude of her siblings. "Damn this family," she said and left before harsher words could be exchanged.

Foregoing supper, Amelia went to her room and lay on the bed fully clothed. She stared up at the ceiling until the room grew dark, the sun extinguished, and the air grew still and cool. She closed her eyes and when she opened them again, the room was filled with impenetrable blackness. There was movement around her, beside her, and she started and put her hand out. She encountered warm human flesh, an arm lightly covered with hair, a strong wrist. "Cam," she whispered. Relaxing, she felt the smooth gold band at the base of his thumb.

Cam undressed her slowly, one garment at a time, and she accepted his ministrations in a dreamlike silence. The troubled feeling in her chest eased as sensations rose and blossomed.

He found her mouth and licked it open, kissing her fully. She lifted her arms to the dark, gorgeous creature over her, the powerful flowing strength of him covering her. With every breath he took, his chest slid against the stiff tips of her breasts, the light friction eliciting muted cries from her throat.

His mouth broke from hers, exploring her shoulders and chest with hot open kisses, as if he were intent on tasting every part of her. He caressed her stomach with the backs of his fingers, teased his thumb around the rim of her navel, his hands clever and sublimely gentle. He had not entered her yet, but she already felt him at the center of her, the pulse, the heat.

She reached for him blindly, but he resisted with a silken laugh, spreading her wide beneath him. His mouth dragged over her, sucking and teasing, and between her thighs, she went utterly wet. He touched her with his tongue, delving with the tip until he found the sensitive place that throbbed so exquisitely. The muscles in his arms bulged as he slid them beneath her legs, making a cradle of her hips. She struggled a little, not in protest but supplication, shivering with each swirl and glide of his tongue.

Dazed and aching, she felt herself lifted in the darkness, his hands arranging her, closing on her legs. He made her kneel over him, pulling her hips down, pushing them back and forth in a gentle rhythm. His mouth was on her again, and she groaned helplessly as she was rubbed repeatedly across the heat and wetness and the tender flicking tongue. His teasing fingers slid inside her, and she began to pant with ecstasy, sensation wrapping around on itself—

A knock at the door startled her.

"Oh God," Amelia whispered, freezing.

The knock repeated, more urgent this time, along with Poppy's muffled voice.

"Poppy," Amelia called out weakly, "can't it wait?"

"No."

Amelia clambered off Cam, her nerves throbbing viciously at the abrupt halt to their lovemaking. Cam rolled to his stomach and uttered a soft curse, his fingers digging into the bedclothes.

Lurching around the room as if she were on the deck of a tossing ship, Amelia managed to find her robe. She pulled it on and fastened a few random buttons down the front.

She went to the door and opened it a mere two inches. "What is it, Poppy? It's the middle of the night."

"I know," Poppy said anxiously, finding it difficult to meet her gaze. "I wouldn't have—it's just—I didn't know what to do. I had a bad dream. A terrible nightmare about Leo, and it seemed so real. I couldn't go back to sleep until I made certain he was all right. So I went to his room, and . . . he's gone."

Amelia shook her head in exasperation. "Bother Leo. We'll look for him in the morning. I don't think any of us should go chasing after him tonight in the dark and cold. He probably went to the village tavern, in which case—"

"I found this in his room." Poppy held out a slip of paper to her.

Frowning, Amelia read the note.

I'm sorry. I don't expect you to understand. You'll be better off this way.

There were another few words, scratched out . . .

I hope someday

And at the bottom, once again:

I'm sorry.

There was no signature. No need for one. Amelia was surprised by how calm her own voice sounded. "Go to bed, Poppy."

"But his note—I think it means—"

"I know what it means. Go to bed, dear. Everything will be all right."

"Are you going to find him?"

"Yes, I'll find him."

Amelia's artificial composure vanished the moment the door closed. Cam was already yanking on his clothes, tugging his boots on, while Amelia lit the bedside lamp. She gave the note to him with trembling fingers. "It's not an empty gesture." She found it hard to breathe. "He means to do it. He may have already—"

"Where is he most likely to go?" Cam interrupted. "Somewhere on the estate?"

Amelia thought of Laura's face in the window. "He's at Ramsay House," she said through chattering teeth. "Take me there. Please."

"Of course. But first, you may want to put on some clothes." Cam gave her a reassuring smile, stroking the side of her face with his hand. "I'll help you."

"Any man," she muttered, "who wanted to marry into the Hathaway family after *this* should be shut away in an institution."

"Marriage is an institution," he said reasonably, retrieving her gown from the floor.

THEY RODE TO RAMSAY HOUSE ON CAM'S HORSE, POOKA, whose long-stretching canter covered ground at near-frightening speed. It all seemed part of another nightmare, the rushing darkness and gnawing cold, the feeling of hurtling forward beyond her control. But there was Cam's hard, steadfast form at her back, one arm locking her securely in place. She feared what they would find at Ramsay House. If the worst had already happened, she would have to accept it. But she was not alone. She was with a man who seemed to understand the very warp and weft of her soul.

As they approached the house, they saw Leo's horse grazing disconsolately over patches of grass and gorse. It was a welcome sight. Leo was here, and they wouldn't have to go scouring through Hampshire to find him.

Helping Amelia to the ground, Cam took her hand in his. She held back, however, as he tried to pull her toward the front door. "Perhaps," she said tentatively, "you should wait here while I—"

"Not a chance in hell."

"He may be more responsive if I approach him by myself, just at first—"

"He's not in his right mind. You're not going to face him without me."

"He's my brother."

"And you're my *romni*."

"What is that?"

"I'll explain later." Cam stole a quick kiss and slid his arm around her, guiding her into the house. It was as still as a mausoleum, the chilled air scented of smoke and dust. Exploring the first floor silently, they found no sign of Leo. It was difficult to see in the darkness, but Cam made his way from room to room with the sureness of a cat.

There came a sound from overhead, the squeak of shifting floorboards. Amelia felt a quake of nervousness, and at the same time, relief. She hastened toward the stairs. Cam checked her, his hand tightening on her arm. Understanding that he wanted her to go slowly, she forced herself to relax.

They went to the staircase, Cam leading the way, testing each step before allowing Amelia to follow him. Grit scraped beneath their quiet feet. As they ascended, the air turned colder and colder still, driving needles into her bones. It was an unholy chill, too bitter and ghastly to have come from a natural source. The bitter coldness dried her lips and made her teeth ache. Her hand tightened inside Cam's, and she kept as close to him as possible without tripping him.

A feeble frosted glow came from a room near the end of an upstairs hallway. Amelia made a sound of distress as she realized where the lamplight was coming from.

"The bee room," she said.

"Bees don't fly at night," Cam murmured, his hand coming to the back of her neck, sliding across her nape. The warmth of his palm brought her frozen nerves to life. "Love, if you'd rather wait here—"

"No." Summoning her courage, Amelia squared her shoulders and went down the hall with him. How like Leo, perverse wretch that he was, to hole up in a place that scared her witless.

They paused at the open doorway, Cam partially blocking Amelia from view.

Peering around his shoulder, she gasped.

It was not Leo, but Christopher Frost, his lean form gilded in lamplight as he stood before an open panel in the wall that contained the bee colony. The bees were subdued but far from quiet, millions of wings beating in a thick, ominous hum. The stench of exposed wood decay and fermented honey hung thick in the air. Shadows pooled on the floor like spilled ink while the lamplight twisted and writhed at Christopher's feet.

At the swift intake of Amelia's breath, he swiveled and pulled something from his pocket. A pistol.

The three of them froze in a dark tableau, while a sting of shock ran over Amelia's skin.

"Christopher," she said in bewilderment. "What are you doing here?"

"Get back," Cam said harshly, trying to shove her behind him. But since she was no more eager to have Cam in front of the pistol than herself, she ducked beneath his arm and came up beside him.

"You've come for it, too, I see." Christopher sounded astonishingly calm, his gaze flicking to Cam's face and then Amelia's. The pistol was steady in his hand.

"Come for what?" Amelia stared at the gaping hole in the wall, a rectangular space at least five feet tall. "Why have you made that opening in the wall?"

"It's a sliding panel," Cam said tersely, not taking his gaze from Christopher. "Made to conceal a hiding place."

Wondering why they both seemed to know something about Ramsay House that she didn't, Amelia asked blankly, "A hiding place for what?"

"It was designed long ago," Christopher replied, "as a place for persecuted priests to conceal themselves."

Her bewildered mind tried to make sense of things. She had read about such places. Long ago, Roman Catholics had been hunted and executed by law in England. Some of them had escaped by hiding in the homes of Catholic sympathizers. She had never suspected, however, that such a place had been incorporated in Ramsay House.

"How did you know about . . ." Finding it difficult to speak, she gestured stiffly to the cavity in the wall.

"It was referenced in the private journals of the architect William Bissel. The notes are now in the possession of Rowland Temple."

And now, Amelia thought, after two centuries, this hiding place had been revealed . . . with a colony of bees in residence. "Why did Mr. Temple tell you about it? What are you hoping to find?"

Christopher glanced at her with amused contempt. "Are you pretending ignorance, or do you really have no idea?"

"I can guess," Cam said. "It probably has something to do with a bit of local lore concerning hidden treasure at Ramsay House." He shrugged at their curious glances. "Westcliff mentioned it once in passing."

"Treasure? Here?" Amelia scowled in disgruntlement. "Why has no one mentioned it to me before?"

"It's nothing but unfounded rumor. And the origins of the supposed treasure aren't usually mentioned in polite company." Cam sent Christopher a cold glance. "Put the gun away. We've no intention of interfering."

"Yes, we do!" Amelia said irritably. "If there is some kind of treasure at Ramsay House, it belongs to Leo. And why are the origins of it so unmentionable?"

Frost answered, the gun still trained on Cam. "Because it consists of tokens and jewels given by King James to his lover back in the sixteenth century. Someone in the Ramsay family."

"The king had an affair with Lady Ramsay?"

"With Lord Ramsay, actually."

Amelia's jaw slackened. "Oh." She frowned and rubbed her frozen arms through her sleeves in a futile effort to warm them. "So you think this treasure is here in one of Bissel's hiding places. And all this time, you've been trying to find it. Your offer of friendship—your regret for having abandoned me—that was all a sham! For the sake of some wild-goose chase."

"It wasn't all a sham." Christopher gave her a scornful, vaguely pitying glance. "My interest in renewing our relationship was genuine, until I realized you had taken up with a Gypsy. I don't accept soiled goods."

Infuriated, Amelia started for him with her fingers curled

into claws. "You aren't fit to lick his boots!" she cried, struggling as Cam hauled her backward.

"Don't," Cam muttered, his hands like iron clamps on her body. "It's not worth it. Calm yourself."

Amelia subsided, glaring at Christopher, while increasing cold chills rippled through the air. "Even if the treasure were here, you wouldn't be able to retrieve it," she snapped. "The wall is filled with a hive containing at least two hundred thousand bees."

"That's where your arrival turns fortuitous." The pistol was trained directly at her chest. He spoke to Cam. "You're going to fetch it for me, or I'll put a bullet in her."

"Don't you dare," Amelia said to Cam, gripping one of his arms in both of hers. "He's bluffing."

"Are you going to risk her life on the possibility, Rohan?" Christopher asked.

Amelia struggled to hold on to Cam as he disengaged his arm from her grasp. "Don't do it, don't—"

"Hush, *monisha*." Cam gripped her shoulders and gave her a little shake. "You're not helping." He looked at Christopher. "Let her leave," he said evenly. "I'll do whatever you ask."

Christopher shook his head. "Her presence provides excellent incentive for you to cooperate." He gestured with the pistol. "Get over there and start looking."

"You've gone mad," Amelia said. "Hidden treasure and pistols and skulking about at midn—" She stopped as she saw a shimmer of movement, of silvery whiteness, in the air. A rush of biting cold swept through the room while the shadows congealed around them.

Christopher seemed not to notice the abrupt drop in temperature, or the dance of translucent paleness between them. "Now, Rohan."

"Cam—"

"Hush." He touched the side of Amelia's face and gave her an unfathomable glance.

"But the bees—"

"It's all right." Cam went to pick up the lamp from the floor. Carrying it to the open panel, he held it inside the hollow space and leaned in. Bees began to settle and crawl over his arm, shoulders, and head. Staring at him fixedly, Amelia saw his arm twitch, and she realized he'd been stung. Panic tightened around her lungs, making her breathing quick and shallow.

Cam's voice was muffled. "There's nothing except bees and honeycomb."

"There has to be," Christopher snapped. "Go in there and find it."

"He can't," Amelia cried in outrage. "He'll be stung to death."

He aimed the pistol directly at her. "Go," Christopher commanded Cam.

Bees were showering onto Cam, crawling over his shining black hair and face and the back of his neck. Watching him, Amelia felt as if she were trapped in a waking nightmare.

"Nothing's here," Cam said, sounding astonishingly calm.

Now Christopher seemed to take a vicious satisfaction in the situation. "You've hardly looked. Go inside and don't come out without it."

Tears sprang to Amelia's eyes. "You're a monster," she cried furiously. "There's nothing in there, and you know it."

"Look at you," he said, sneering, "weeping over your Gypsy lover. How low you've fallen."

Before she could respond, a blue-white burst of light filled the room in a noiseless strike. The lamp flame was extinguished in a freezing blast. Amelia blinked and rubbed the moisture from her eyes, and turned in a bewildered circle as she tried to find the source of the light. Something shimmered all around them, coldness and brilliance and raw energy. She stumbled toward Cam with her arms outstretched. The bees lifted in a mass and flew back to the hive, the blue light causing their wings to glitter like a rain of sparks.

Amelia reached Cam, and he caught her in a warm, hard grip. "Are you hurt?" she asked, her hands frantically searching him.

"No, just a sting or two. I—" He broke off with a sharp inhalation.

Twisting in his arms, Amelia followed his gaze. Two hazy forms, distorted in the broken light, struggled for possession of the gun. Who was it? Who else had come into the room? Not a heartbeat had passed before Cam had shoved her to the floor. "Stay down." Without pausing, he launched himself toward the combatants.

But they had already broken apart, one man tumbling to the floor with the pistol in his grip, the other running for the door. Cam went for the fallen man, while the air crackled as if the room were filled with burning Catherine wheels. The other man fled. And the door slammed shut behind him, although no one had touched it.

Dazed, Amelia sat up, while the fractured light dissolved into a faint blue radiance that clung to the outlines of the men nearby. "Cam?" she asked uncertainly.

His voice was low and shaken. "It's all right, hummingbird. Come here."

She reached them and gasped as she saw the intruder's face. "Leo. What are you—how did you—" Her voice faltered at the sight of the pistol in his hand. He held it loosely against his thigh. His face was calm, his mouth curved with a faint, wry smile.

"I was going to ask you the same thing," Leo said mildly. "What the devil are you doing here?"

Amelia sank to the floor beside Cam, her gaze remaining on her brother. "Poppy found your note," she said breathlessly. "We came here because we thought you were going to . . . to do yourself in."

"That was the general idea," Leo said. "But I went to the tavern for a drink on the way. And when I finally got here, it was a bit too crowded for my taste. Suicide is something a fellow likes a bit of privacy for."

Amelia was unnerved by his tranquil manner. Her gaze fell to the pistol in his hand, then returned to his face. Her hand crept to Cam's tense thigh. The ghost was with them, she thought. The air had turned her face numb, making it difficult to move her lips. "Mr. Frost was treasure hunting," she told her brother.

Leo gave her a skeptical glance. "A treasure, in this rubbish pile?"

"Well, you see, Mr. Frost thought—"

"No, don't bother. I'm afraid I can't summon any interest in what Frost thought. The idiot." He looked down at the pistol, his thumb gently grazing the barrel.

Amelia wouldn't have expected a man contemplating suicide to appear so relaxed. A ruined man in a ruined house. Every line of his body spoke of weary resignation. He looked at Cam. "You need to take her out of here," he said quietly.

"Leo—" Amelia had begun to tremble, knowing that if they left him here, he would kill himself. She could think of nothing to say, at least nothing that wouldn't sound theatrical, unconvincing, absurd.

Her brother's mouth quirked as if he were too exhausted to smile. "I know, darling," he said gently. "I know what you want and what you don't want. I know you wish I could be better than this. But I'm not."

He blurred before her. Amelia felt tears sliding from her

eyes, the wetness turning icy by the time they reached her chin. "I don't want to lose you."

Leo bent both his knees and braced an arm across them, his fingers remaining curled around the gun handle. "I'm not your brother, Amelia. Not anymore. I changed when Laura died."

"I still want you."

"No one gets what they want," Leo muttered. "Not now."

Cam watched her brother intently. A long silence unfolded in pained degrees as a burning cold breeze fanned over the three of them. "I could try to persuade you to set the gun aside and go home with us," he said eventually. "To hold off one more day. But even if I stopped you this time, one can't keep a man alive when he doesn't want to be."

"True," Leo said.

Amelia opened her mouth with a shuddering protest, but Cam stopped her, his fingers pressing gently over her lips. Cam continued to stare at Leo, not with concern but a sort of detached contemplation, as if he were focusing on some mathematical equation. "No one can be haunted," he said quietly, "without having willed it. You know that, don't you?"

The room grew even colder, if that were possible, the windows rattling, the lamplight flickering. Alarmed by the taut vibrations in the air, the sense that an unseen presence was circling them, Amelia huddled against Cam's back.

"Of course, I do," Leo said. "I should have died when she did. I never wanted to be left behind. You don't know what that's like. The thought of finally ending this is a bloody relief."

"But that's not what she wants," Cam said.

Amelia knew that Cam wasn't referring to her, but to Laura.

Hostility flared in Leo's eyes. "How the hell would you know?"

"If your situations were reversed, would you choose this for her?" Cam gestured to the gun in his hand. "I wouldn't ask that sacrifice of someone I love."

"You have no bloody idea what you're talking about."

"I do," Cam said. "I understand. You grieve too much, *phral*. You've forced her to stay and comfort you. You have to let her go. Not for your sake, but hers."

"I can't." But emotion had begun to spread across Leo's face like cracks in an eggshell. Blue light danced through the room, while a frigid wind lifted a few locks of Leo's hair like invisible fingers.

"Let her be at peace," Cam said, more quietly now. "If you take your own life, you'll end up condemning her as well as yourself to an eternity of wandering."

Leo gave a wordless shake of his bent head, cradling his folded knees in a posture that reminded Amelia of the boy he'd once been. And she understood his grief with a thoroughness that had been impossible for her before.

What if Cam were taken from her without warning? She could never again know the feel of his hair in her hands or the feel of his heartbeat. No consummation of all she had begun to feel, the promises, smiles, tears, hopes, all ripped from her grasp. Forever. How much she would miss. How much could never be replaced by anyone else.

Aching with compassion, she watched as Cam moved to her brother. Leo hid his face and jerked a hand up, fingers spread, palm facing out in a broken, helpless gesture. "I can't let her go," he choked.

The lamp blew out, and a pane of glass shattered, while a freezing blast of air swept around them. Energy crackled through the room, tiny snaps of light appearing around them.

"You can do it for her," Cam said, putting his arms around

her brother in the way he might have comforted a lost child. "You can."

Leo began to cry harder, each breath a burst of angry despair. Amelia was afraid for him—she had never seen him at the mercy of his own emotions, not even when Laura had died. But as he wept, the atmosphere seemed to settle, glacier cold and calm, and the blue light, like the afterglow of a distant dying star, began to fade. There was a quiet drone of wings—a few bees venturing from the hive, then flying back to settle for the night.

Cam was murmuring something now, holding Leo in a firm protective grasp. A promise, a compact, offered to a fading, formless spirit.

Until the room was warm again, and all that was left were three people sitting among shattered glass in the darkness, and a discarded weapon on the floor.

"She's gone," Cam said softly.

Leo nodded, his face hidden. He was damaged but still alive. Broken, but not beyond the hope of repair.

And reconciled to life, at last.

Chapter Twenty-Two

After they had taken Leo back to Stony Cross Manor and put him to bed, Amelia stood outside his room with Cam. She couldn't quite look at him. Her emotions were brimming so high and strong, it took all her strength to contain them. "I'm going to Poppy's room to tell her he's all right," she whispered.

Cam nodded, silent and distracted. Their fingers tangled briefly.

They parted company, and Amelia went to find her sister.

Poppy was in bed, lying on her side, her eyes fully open. "You found Leo," she murmured as Amelia came to her.

"Yes, dear."

"Is he . . ."

"He's fine. I think . . ." Amelia sat on the edge of the mattress and smiled down at her. "I think he'll be better from now on."

"Like the old Leo?"

"None of us are exactly like our old selves."

Poppy yawned. "Amelia . . . will it make you grumpy if I ask a question?"

"I'm too tired to be grumpy. Ask away."

"Are you going to marry Mr. Rohan?"

The question filled Amelia with dizzying delight. "Should I?"

"Yes, you've been compromised, you know. Besides, he's a good influence on you. You're not nearly so much of a hedgehog when he's around."

"Delightful child," Amelia observed to the room in general and grinned at her sister. "I'll tell you in the morning, dear. Go to sleep."

She walked through the somber stillness of the hallway, feeling as nervous as a bride as she went to find Cam. It was time to be open, honest, trusting as she had never been before, not even in their most intimate moments. She went to Cam's room, where lamplight seeped through the fissure of the partially opened door.

Cam was sitting on the bed, still clothed. His head was lowered, hands braced on his knees in the posture of a man who was deep in thought. He glanced up as she came into the room and closed the door.

"What's the matter, love?"

"I . . ." Amelia approached him hesitantly. "I'm afraid you won't let me have what I want."

His slow smile robbed her of breath. "I have yet to refuse you anything. I'm not likely to start now."

Amelia stopped before him, her skirts crowded between his parted knees. The clean, salty, evergreen scent of him drifted to her nostrils. "I have a proposition for you," she said, trying for a businesslike tone. "A very sensible one. You see . . ." She paused to clear her throat. "I've been thinking about your problem."

"What problem?" Cam played lightly with the folds of her skirts, watching her face alertly.

"Your good luck curse. I know how to get rid of it. You should marry into a family with very, *very* bad luck. A family with expensive problems. And then you won't have to be embarrassed about having so much money, because it will flow out nearly as fast as it comes in."

"Very sensible." Cam took her shaking hand in his, pressed it between his warm palms, and touched his foot to her rapidly tapping one. "Hummingbird," he whispered, "you don't have to be nervous with me."

Gathering her courage, she blurted out, "I want your ring. I want never to take it off again. I want to be your *romni* forever"—she paused with a quick, abashed smile— "whatever that is."

"My bride. My wife."

Amelia froze in a moment of throat-clenching delight as she felt him slide the gold ring onto her finger, easing it to the base. "When we were with Leo tonight," she said scratchily, "I finally, truly understood how he felt about losing Laura. He told me once that I couldn't understand unless I had loved someone that way. He was right. And tonight, as I watched you with him . . . I knew what I would think at the very last moment of my life."

His thumb smoothed over the tender surface of her knuckle. "Yes, love?"

"I would think," she continued unsteadily, "'Oh, if I could have just one more day with Cam, I would fit a lifetime in those few hours.'"

"Not necessary," he assured her gently. "Statistically speaking, we'll have at least ten, fifteen thousand days to spend together."

"I don't want to be apart from you for even one of them."

Cam cupped her small, serious face in his hands, his thumbs skimming the trace of tears beneath her eyes. His gaze caressed her. "Are we to live in sin, love, or will you finally agree to marry me?"

"Yes, yes, I'll marry you. Although . . . I won't promise to obey you."

Cam laughed quietly. "Just promise to love me."

Amelia gripped his wrists, his pulse steady and strong beneath her fingertips. "Oh, I do love you, you're—"

"I love you too."

"—my fate. You're everything I—" She would have said more if he had not pulled her head to his, kissing her with hard, thrilling pressure.

They undressed with haste, tugging at each other's clothes with a clumsiness wrought of desire and fervor. When at last their skin was laid bare, Cam's urgency eased. His hands smoothed over her with deliberate slowness, every caress bringing tremors of pleasure to the surface. His features were austerely beautiful as he rolled her to her back. His mouth lowered to her breasts, his hands cupping and lifting the rounded flesh, tongue and teeth gently navigating the tips.

Amelia moaned his name as he rose to kneel between her legs. She reached for him, needing his weight on her, unable to pull him down. All she could do was whimper and arch as he caressed her, his thumb making light, wicked swirls, his thighs solid beneath her straining hips. Her breath hissed between her teeth, while her hands clenched around handfuls of the bed linens.

His fingers slid away from her, leaving her shuddering as her body closed in vain around the emptiness. But then he was pushing into her, filling her completely.

Her hand crept blindly from his shoulder to his face, where she felt the shape of his smile. "Don't tease," she muttered, trembling with need. "I can't bear it."

"Sweetheart . . ." His silky whisper caressed her cheek. "I'm afraid you'll have to."

"Wh-why?" She caught her breath as he withdrew slowly.

"Because there's nothing I love more than teasing you." And he took an eternity to enter her again, so lazy and slow and delicious and merciless that, by the time he was fully inside her, she'd already climaxed. Twice.

"Stay inside me," she begged hoarsely as he began a steady rhythm, the heat building again. "Stay, stay—" The words flattened into a long moan.

Cam bent over her, driving ruthlessly hard, his breath coming in hot puffs against her face and throat. He stared into her dazed eyes, taking fierce satisfaction in the sight of her pleasure. His hands slipped beneath her head, cradling her as he kissed her. He buried a vehement groan into the sweet depths of her mouth, and let his release spin out inside her.

Cuddling her afterward, Cam traced lazy patterns on her back and shoulders. "After the wedding," he murmured, "I may take you away with me for a little while."

"Where?" she asked readily, turning to press her lips against his chest.

"To look for my tribe."

"You've already found your tribe." She hitched a leg over his hips.

A chuckle vibrated in his chest. "My Romany tribe, then. It's been too many years. I'd like to find out if my grandmother is still alive." He paused. "And I want to ask some questions."

"About what?"

Drawing her hand to his forearm, Cam pressed it to his tattoo. "This."

Thinking of Merripen's identical tattoo and the strange coincidence of it, Amelia frowned. "What kind of connection might there be between you and Merripen?"

"I have no idea." Cam smiled ruefully. "God help me, I'm afraid to find out."

"Whatever it is," she said, "we'll trust in fate."

Cam's smile widened. "So you believe in fate now?"

"And luck," Amelia said, her hand tightening on his arm. "Because of you."

"That reminds me . . ." He raised himself on one elbow and looked down at her, dark lashes sweeping over glowing amber. "I have something to show you. Don't move—I'll bring it here."

"Can't it wait?" she protested.

"No. I'll be back in a few minutes. Don't fall asleep."

He left the bed and drew on his clothes while Amelia took possessive pleasure in the sight of him.

To keep from falling asleep while he was gone, she went to the washstand and used a cold cloth to freshen herself. Hurrying back to the bed, she sat and tucked the covers beneath her arms.

Cam returned, carrying an object that was approximately the shape and size of a slipper box. Amelia regarded it quizzically as he set it beside her. The heavy box was made of wood and heavily tarnished and pitted silver, the whole of it giving off an acid-sweet reek. As Amelia ran her fingers experimentally over the surface, she discovered the surface was slightly tacky.

"Fortunately, it was wrapped in oilcloth," Cam said. "Otherwise it would have been soaked in fermented honey."

Amelia blinked in astonishment. "Don't say this is the treasure that Christopher Frost was looking for!"

"I found it when I was getting the crushed bees for Merripen's poultice. I brought it back for you." He looked vaguely apologetic. "I meant to tell you about it earlier, but it slipped my mind."

Amelia stifled a laugh. "Only you," she said, "could go looking for bee venom and find hidden treasure." Lifting the box, she shook it gently, feeling the movement of weighty objects within. "Blast, it's locked."

Cam reached into the wild disarray of Amelia's coiffure, combing with his fingers until he found a hairpin. Gently he pulled the pin out, bent it with deft fingers, and inserted it into the ancient lock.

"Why didn't you tell Mr. Frost you'd already found the treasure?" Amelia asked as he worked to find the catch. "Then you might have been spared being swarmed by all those bees."

"I wanted to save this for your family. Frost had no right to it." Before another minute passed, the lock clicked, and the box was open.

Amelia's heart pounded with excitement as she lifted the lid. She found a sheaf of letters, perhaps a half-dozen, tied with a thin, braided lock of hair. Gingerly, she picked up the bundle, pulled the top letter out, and unfolded the ancient yellowed parchment.

It was indeed a love letter from a king, signed simply, "James." Scandalous, ardent, and sweetly written, it seemed far too intimate for her to read. It had never been meant for her eyes. She closed the brittle folds and set it aside.

Cam, meanwhile, had begun to pull objects from the box and lay them in her lap: a loose ruby at least an inch in diameter, pairs of diamond bracelets, ropes of massive black pearls, a brooch made of an oval-shaped sapphire easily the size of a sovereign, with a teardrop diamond hanging beneath, and an assortment of jeweled rings.

"I don't believe it," Amelia said, jostling the glittering heap. "This must be enough to rebuild Ramsay House twice over."

"Not quite," Cam said, casting an experienced glance over the lot, "but close."

She frowned as she sorted through the trove of priceless jewels. "Cam?" she asked after a long moment.

"Hmm?" He seemed to have lost interest in the treasure, absorbed in playing with a loose lock of her hair.

"Would you mind if we kept this from Leo until he's . . . well, a bit more rational? Otherwise, I'm afraid he'll go out and do something irresponsible."

"I'd say that's a valid concern." He picked up the jewelry in careless handfuls, dumping it into the box and closing it. "Yes, let's wait until he's ready."

The covers slipped between them. Amelia shivered as the cool air wafted over her naked back and shoulders. "Come back to bed," she whispered. "I need you to warm me."

Cam stripped away his shirt and laughed quietly as he felt her hands plucking at the buttons of his trousers. "What happened to my prudish *gadji*?"

"I'm afraid"—she reached into his open falls and stroked his aroused flesh—"continued association with you has made me shameless."

"Good, I was hoping for that." His lashes lowered, and his voice turned slightly breathless at her touch. "Amelia, if we have children, will you mind that they're part Rom?"

"Not if you don't mind that they're part Hathaway."

He made a sound of amusement and finished undressing. "You know, it would terrify a lesser man, trying to manage your family."

"You're right. I can't imagine why you're willing to take us on."

He gave her naked body a frankly lustful glance as he joined her beneath the covers. "The compensations are well worth it."

"What about your freedom?" Amelia asked, snuggling close as he lay beside her. "Are you sorry to have lost it?"

"No, love." Cam reached to turn down the lamp, enfolding them in velvet darkness. "I've finally found it. Right here, with you."

And he lowered himself into the clasp of her waiting arms.